THE ROOSTER
AND THE
FADED ROSE

A SMITHSON EVERMORE NOVEL BOOK 2
2ND EDITION

THE ROOSTER AND THE FADED ROSE

A SMITHSON EVERMORE NOVEL BOOK 2
2ND EDITION

By

Vance Arnett

ARNETT PUBLISHING
2025 Greenville, SC

Paperback Edition
ISBN 978-0-9966600-9-9
Published by Arnett Publishing
224 Glenbrooke Way
Greenville, South Carolina 29615

Cover and interior design by Meaghan Scalise
and Shawn Scalise
Tada Traditional and Digital Arts
www.traditionalanddigitalarts.com

The proceeds of this book after costs will be donated to support non-profit organizations that serve the needs of the survivors of human trafficking. Your support for the author's rights is greatly appreciated.

Dedicated

This book is dedicated to my amazing wife and life companion Jane who I lost the past spring to breast cancer. She was tireless and dignified to the end. It is also dedicated to the men and women in law enforcement that work tirelessly to stop human trafficking, as well as the courageous survivors of sexual exploitation and human trafficking.

PREFACE

This is the second edition of the second book in a series dealing with human trafficking. The Smithson Evermore group is, unfortunately, a figment of my imagination. Such a well-funded private entity does not exist to assist law enforcement in the anti-trafficking mission. What does exist is a network of non-governmental agencies that do support and work with the survivors of all forms of human trafficking. They exist in all communities and are there to support these people as they make their transition from trafficking victim to trafficking survivor. The proceeds of all these books, after the costs, will be donated to those entities that take on the challenge of helping these people put their lives back together. It is a daunting task. This problem is too easily swept under the rug in a hail of statistics and national debates and political judgements that have little to do with the dignity these people deserve.

Each book centers on a different aspect of human trafficking. I have not had the courage to tackle child trafficking as yet but perhaps by the third book I will. But any entity that indulges in this type of enterprise works from the premise that people are mere commodities. That is not a premise that any of us can afford to tolerate or turn away from.

If I have a request other than that you buy this book, enjoy it and learn something, it is to not turn your face or your attention away from this crime. It exists on local, national, and international levels. The research is no longer anecdotal. It is substantive and it is persuasive. Unfortunately for just those reasons it is altogether too easy to avoid.

Every race, every demographic level, every ethnic group, every cultural entity had their own hideous version of this type of slavery. We'd like to think it doesn't exist in the United States, or in our state or our town. It does and it has to be constantly addressed. It affects all of us not just the least of us as some would like to think.

Please take a moment to explore your community. Teach your children how to stay safe and how to say something if they see something.

I began this writing journey in Tampa, Florida in 2017 with the publication of Tampa Traffick. This second book was produced during the global pandemic as we shelter in Tampa. Post pandemic I moved with my amazing wife Jane to Greenville, South Carolina in August of 2021 and began writing the third book.

In the spring of 2025, I lost my sweet life companion to cancer. I vowed to keep writing and to keep this project going as long as I can. This second edition of Rooster and the Faded Rose is being released at the same time as the third book to celebrate the life of Jane Arnett. I hope you learn and become vigilant and engaged with the anti-trafficking efforts in your community.

Vance Arnett

Greenville, SC September 2025

ACKNOWLEDGEMENT

As in all human endeavors that get this far out of someone's head and onto paper, this book is a cumulative effort. The bulk of this work was done during the Covid-19 pandemic. The first person I need to thank is the amazing woman with whom I was quarantined, my wife Jane. Having the time to talk through story lines and character development was a new endeavor as was being so close to this work all the time. We've been together for over thirty years now and it was just such a fresh experience to have the time to work together.

My characters are created from the people I know and love in my life. They are compilations of imagination but the stimulus comes from the people I interact with on a daily basis. To recognize all of them would be impossible but I must mention the artistic contribution of Meaghan and Shawn Scalise of Tada Traditional and Digital Arts. I gave them a concept and within days, not weeks or months, but within days I had a great cover design that reflects the content of the book and makes such a contribution to the overall work. I cannot thank them enough.

I received a great deal of special information from a private pilot friend of mine, Alain Corbeil. His assistance was incredibly helpful. I have always been fascinated by airplanes but never enough to trust myself to fly one.

Lastly, Tampa Florida, has become one of those flash points of this corona virus. I have traded my tie rack for a mask rack. I have become an expert at Facetime and Zoom. Even with, what some would call isolation, I have never had a day that someone didn't check on us and make sure we were well. Leading the way was my good friend and muse, Jen Ripple of DUN Magazine. To them, my comrades in confinement, I give my thanks. Without that human contact, a writer who depends on living intentionally would not have had a chance.

Other Works

Works by Vance Arnett

Fiction:

Tampa Traffick:
A Smithson Evermore Novel Book 1
Second Edition

Non-Fiction:

Not Done Yet: Retirement as an Encore Not and Ending

CHAPTER 1

The Start of Everything

*Even when the evening is peaceful and happy, unexpected
things can happen.*

Hank emerged from the restaurant in Puerto Vallarta, Mexico. He and
Kip Patterson had chosen one of their favorites to have their final dinner and
drinks together before they would both fly back to the States to satisfy their
citizenship requirements. Kip was inside paying while Hank was watching all
the beautiful people having a good time on the street. One young man caught
his eye in particular but Kip emerged and interrupted his thought.

"That was a great way to finish. I will see you when we both return in a
month."

Hank looked around as he spoke. "I'm not looking forward to the trip.
Now that I no longer own my businesses, I'm not sure why I go back. I just love
this place and the friends I have made here."

Kip smiled at him as he gave him a hug. "You have to go back every six
months just like the rest of the expatriate population. You will be back in three
weeks on the same schedule as the rest of us. Now travel safely. Have you called
your ride yet?"

Hank looked at him surprised. "I thought we could share. I will be happy
to walk the half-mile from your place to mine once we are up the hill."

Kip shook his head. "Always trying to save that small buck while the big
ones fly out of your wallet. Of course, you can share. Angelina is on her way."

They waited about five minutes before the dark sedan that belonged to
their favorite ride-share driver pulled up. They both waved at the doorman and
said good night and jumped in the back of the sedan. Kip spoke. "Thank you,
Angelina, Hank will be getting out at my place." The woman in front nodded

and pulled from the curb and headed north up the hill to the residential section where they both lived. About a half block from Kip's house the car slowed and then stopped as if there was something wrong. Kip leaned forward. "Angelina, is there something wrong? Why are we stopping? Are you alright?"

The woman turned in her seat, held up the aerosol can and sprayed them both. "No, Señor, there is nothing wrong except that I am not Angelina."

They were both slumped on the seat within seconds. The woman stopped the car completely as two men emerged from a van parked on the curb next to the car. One of them opened the rear door. "Who is this other guy?"

The woman responded. "His rich friend. We will deal with him later but for now take them both. We need to get moving to stay on schedule. I will dump the car and meet you in Chihuahua."

With that they all disappeared into the night.

CHAPTER 2

*Even if we plan to get away from our responsibilities, it
never quite happens all the way.*

Aggie and Slade had just walked out on the deck when Aggie's phone rang. She answered on the second ring. "Good morning, Lola. Sweetheart, please calm down. I can't understand you when you are so excited and my Spanish is not good enough to fill in the blanks when you speak so rapidly." The woman on the other end of the line took a deep breath and spoke slowly. As Aggie listened, Slade watched her expression suddenly cloud over and become concerned. "How long has it been since you saw him last?" Aggie listened and looked intently at Slade as she gave her final instructions. "Lola, I want you to get Jorge to talk to the local people and call me back as soon as he has. He will know what to do and, Lola, tell him everything you just told me." Aggie hung up the phone.

They went back inside and Slade sat down at his desk and opened his computer. "That didn't sound good. What have we got?"

Aggie thought about her answer before she responded. "Lola is concerned that Hank Kessler has apparently been missing for a couple of days. Lola had just returned from visiting her sister in Acapulco when she discovered that he hadn't been seen and his room hadn't been slept in. She questioned the gardener, and he said he had not seen Hank since he had gone down to the city center to meet Kip Patterson on Saturday night. There is no sign he returned and Lola is concerned because Hank is very good at letting her know his whereabouts. In addition, no one has seen Kip Patterson since that night either."

Slade began typing as he spoke. "Do you think she has cause to be concerned?"

"Lola doesn't panic without cause and she is in a panic. That tells me she has talked to someone who thinks it is serious. Hank has never done this before and Kip is experienced enough not to want to worry anyone, so my gut tells me we need to get more information. Who do you want to activate?"

Slade was going over in his mind what he had just heard. Hank Kessler was a long-time friend and also served on the Board of Directors for Smithson Evermore. Like many board members he often used their properties for vacation. Their facility in Puerto Vallarta was his favorite and now served as his home base. He would return to the United States periodically to maintain his travel status, but lived the life of an expatriate with the other Americans who made Mexico their home. Hank listened to the beat of his own drum even when it was hitting him over the head. He was considered eccentric by many and charming and engaging by all. He would not just disappear, at least without announcing he was disappearing. His closest friend was Dr. Kendrick Patterson better known in the community as Kip. He was a retired professor of international studies and the ex-husband of Senator Henrietta Patterson of New York. They had maintained a very close relationship with each other after the divorce and shared the love of three grown children. Senator Patterson was considered a rogue by her party and was constantly in the news. The conservatives in the party were ruffled because she put the people who elected her before party interests. The party wanted to win; she wanted to represent her district. There was no question she represented her constituency and not necessarily the interests of those who had contributed to her first election bid or who happened to be in the White House at the time. That quality had made her unbeatable in three subsequent elections. The two had met in the Washington D.C area while he was completing his PhD and Henrietta was finishing her masters in political science. Kip was well known as a specialist on immigration policies and even though he was retired, he often was asked to lecture on the subject and on occasion testify before Congress. Dr. Patterson was not the kind of individual to just vanish without letting someone know where he was. Slade finally looked up. "I think we should wait to hear from Jorge, then at least brief the command team."

Aggie nodded. "L and Oscar are in Tampa dealing with the on-going operation along the northern border. SiSi is on vacation in the northeast but has her communications pack with her. Claymore Jenkins is filling in for her in Tampa. Marcus is visiting friends in San Diego, and Rufus is on the north end of the island, checking our airplane. Lily and Alex are on their way here from Seattle and should land down at the seaplane base in about thirty minutes."

They were speaking in the Smithson Evermore property on Orcas Island, Washington. The compound sat on a hill above Cascades Bay in East Sound and almost every window in the three buildings looked out over Rosario Channel. Aggie, Slade, and Rufus Songbird, their chief pilot had been taking some time to regroup and do some fishing and whale watching. Rufus had also been giving Aggie flying lessons in their Cessna 208 seaplane that was moored at the seaplane base just below them. He was at the Orcas Island Airfield checking one of their other planes, a King Air. The Smithson Evermore jet was at the private air terminal in Seattle.

Slade picked up his phone and dialed Marcus Moreno, their logistics coordinator in San Diego. The phone rang once before Marcus picked up. "Good Afternoon, Slade. How are things going up in the San Juans?"

Slade laughed. "Apparently, they are going better here than they are at the house in Mexico. It appears that Hank Kessler has not been seen for several days and neither has his friend Dr. Patterson. Lola has become concerned and we are waiting on Jorge to give us an update. He is checking to see if we need to be concerned. I'm sure his street contacts will be able to give us some information as to how serious this situation might be. Just in case, who do you have nearby and what assets do we have that could coordinate from Puerto Vallarta if we need to go further?"

Marcus was quick to respond. "Of course, we have Jorge and his team. They have great contacts with both the local police and the cartel members we trust. If we need to broaden the search, I believe SiSi had outfitted Hank with a GPS chip but I am not certain. If they are together, that could help us find both. We have one of our MH65E helicopters currently assisting U.S. Border Patrol near Tucson, Arizona. We have been testing the new navigation and communication link with them, ICE and the FBI. Two of our best pilots, Pierce Martin and Fred Holcomb, are there with it. Our southwest recovery team has been working with them but they have been up for three nights. If we need to deploy to search, my file shows that Lily Michaels is about to arrive at your location with Alex Pellegrino. Alex is about the best 'boots-on-the-ground' forward intelligence operative we have. If we could get them headed that way, we could have a search capability with air support within four hours using some of the team in Arizona."

Slade thought then responded. "Let's get the information first. If we do have to move, we will fly Lily and Alex to Seattle and have Paul fly them down in the King Air. I will talk it over with them. We are about done here anyway. We are all well rested and ready to get back to work. I will have L check from Tampa with the Senator to see if she has heard from her ex-husband. For right now, just let everybody know we may be moving soon and when we do, it will need to be swiftly. How much will this deplete our resources from our responsibilities with the agencies along the northern border?"

"The resources we have in the southwest should be able to handle it. We are getting spread a bit thin in the northeast sector. I will let the southwest team and the pilots know to fuel up and be ready to move. I will put everyone in Tampa on alert and you can make your decision when you hear from Jorge and L. Anything else?"

Slade smiled. "As usual, you are right on the mark. I will call you as soon as we know something." Slade hung up and dialed L at the Smithson headquarters in Tampa. She was just getting ready to head out with Oscar to Ybor City for an early dinner.

The phone rang once and L picked up. "Hello. Do you miss us?"

Slade laughed. "Of course, we miss you. How is everything going there?"

"We are great. But I just saw the master communications board light up between you and Marcus and I also noticed that Lola called Aggie from Puerto Vallarta. Is something happening that I should patch Oscar in on the call?"

"That is not a bad idea. We don't know how serious to take the situation but let's have the conversation only once."

Oscar Dorian's voice joined the conversation. "Slade, what have we got?"

Oscar rarely beat around the bush about anything with Slade.

Slade related the information he had received since Lola had called. Oscar got on another line and ordered dinner in. He thought they would probably be activated soon. He had great instincts. The conversation was over in ten minutes.

Just as Slade hung up, Aggie and Slade heard the hum of an approaching seaplane. They looked down to Cascades Bay and could see the plane gliding in for a landing that would bring it right to the Seaplane base at Rosario. They had just enough time to get in the car and head down the hill to meet Lily and Alex. They pulled up just as the two were stepping onto the floating dock. Aggie was always amazed at how small and muscular Alex was. She did not look like a woman that could carry a 250-pound man very far but she could and she had many times. She and Lily had been participating in Emergency Rescue Training at Joint Base Lewis-McChord south of Tacoma, Washington. They had been testing new intelligence and communication technology with several of the armed forces stationed there. Lily Michaels had been promoted to the central command team of Project Recovery when Oscar Dorian had been promoted to fill in for a retiring Earl Tippit. She was a seasoned operator and a great field coordinator. Alex had taken a much different path to the Project Recovery Team. She had finished nursing school and entered the Navy. She had served two tours before she left. After a stint as a smoke jumper in Colorado and as an air rescue paramedic/nurse with the Forest Service she was considering re-enlisting when she was contacted by Oscar Dorian to consider a career with Smithson Evermore. She spoke fluent Spanish, Mandarin and Vietnamese. In addition, she had an uncanny amount of strength for a woman with her build. She was tiny to say the least. This allowed her a great advantage as a forward observer and intelligence gatherer. She had many talents that lent themselves well to the Project Recovery mission of rescuing kidnapped and trafficked victims. She had many rescues to her credit.

Lily and Alex looked up and saw Aggie and Slade and smiled. Lily spoke first. "It is good to see you both. I hope we are going back to work soon. We are both bored and tired of training exercises."

Slade replied as he hugged them both. "It is good to see you as well. I trust the new gear worked as the lab had planned."

Alex responded. "We found a couple of things but the lab worked it out online and reprogramed both the new helmet design and the satellite-based communication module and pack. With the new communications gear, Lily and I could hear each other breathing. I would say they will all be ready for release to the military soon. The guys we trained with seemed to be ready for the new technology. The new drones are amazing. Claymore can brief you on the geeky stuff. But I'm with Lily. I need some real activity."

Aggie laughed. "The two of you are nuts. One of these days we will have to send you to training to teach you how to relax. But we have a situation that may have you headed back out on assignment very shortly. Is that quick enough for you?"

The two women looked at each other and high-fived. Slade spoke. "Put your gear in the car and we'll head up to the house for a video conference. Alex, you will be joining your old buddies on Recovery Team One in the southwest. They are in Tucson resting at the moment. Lily, you will work with Marcus from the Tucson office to follow-up on another issue. I will let you all catch up at the video conference rather than go through it all more than once."

They got into the car and headed the short distance up to the house where they ran into Rufus. "Ladies, it is good to see you. Slade, the King Air is ready to go. Just let me know the schedule and I have alerted Frank at SeaTac to get the jet ready. We are good to go in any direction when you give the word."

CHAPTER 3

*By definition surprises are unexpected. That can be good or
disastrous.*

SiSi Holmes stood on the dock and watched Brad circle the Cessna
182 as he prepared to land on the south end of Moosehead Lake in Maine.
When he touched down, he hardly made a ripple in the surface as he turned
the seaplane toward the floating dock. He had been on assignment to the U.S.
Border Patrol and the Canadian Border Services Agency and was returning
from a task force meeting in Calais, Maine. Their mission was to stem the
flow of people being trafficked through Canada into the United States. SiSi
Holmes was the chief communications and technology specialist for Smithson
Evermore. She was one of several team members assigned to the Smithson
Evermore central command team for the private non-profit that supported
international law enforcement to recover the survivors of kidnaping and
human trafficking. Brad Freeport was the team leader for the operations team
in northeastern America. He was not only an accomplished pilot, but was also
well-trained in all forms of electronic surveillance and counter terrorism, and
supervised over twenty operational team members who were on standby to
help law enforcement agencies in cases of kidnapping and human trafficking.
Slade Smithson had guided their effort, internationally known as Project
Recovery, for many years as part of the overall company mission to assist all
governments in the recovery of as many victims and survivors as possible. Both
SiSi and Brad were well known to law enforcement agencies and enjoyed a
high level of cooperation with them as they supported efforts to curb this form
of modern-day human slavery. What was not well known even to their team
members, was that SiSi and Brad's relationship had become intimate. While
their personal relationship did not violate any policy for Smithson Evermore,
they were both very private people.

SiSi had never had much time for romance in her life. She had graduated
from MIT at nineteen and had immediately begun work on a PhD which

she earned two years later with cutting edge research. SiSi, who normally was awkward and aloof in a social setting was completely the opposite when it was just she and Brad. Their relationship had begun at the wedding of Earl and Sasha Tippit four years earlier. Earl was one of the founding members of the operational arm of Smithson Evermore's recovery program and had retired. The command team, of which SiSi was a member, was still adjusting to his departure. SiSi and Brad had worked hard to keep their personal relationship quiet. SiSi walked down to the mooring just as Brad stepped onto the dock. She encircled him in her arms and kissed him so hard that her glasses almost fell off her head. Those glasses were not only essential for her vision correction but in the lower left lens was a constantly streaming computer feed that kept her aware of everything that was going on in the company. As she straightened them, she noticed that there were three notifications all coming from the retreat where Slade Smithson and his bodyguard Aggie Rothberg were vacationing. The first notification was a call from the house in Puerto Vallarta, the second was between Slade and Marcus Moreno, the chief of Smithson Evermore Logistics, and the third was between Slade and their command center in the Channel District of Tampa, Florida. One call would have been routine. Three was anything but. SiSi grabbed Brad by the arm as he hefted his pack onto his shoulder. "We need to get back to the house. I have a feeling that are about to be interrupted for work." She reached up and kissed him again.

By the time the two had entered the compound they shared with Brad's brother Chuck and his family, both of their phones alerted to be on standby status. They would soon learn that Chuck's phone had alerted as well. Chuck Freeport was the head of the Project Recovery's canine program. His wife Celeste was a veterinarian who took care of the canine members of the Smithson Evermore K-9 search team while operating a successful local practice in central Maine.

Their twenty-three-year-old daughter, Cari, was well known as one of the best local nature guides, a consultant to Maine Forestry, and was an award-winning musher with enough national wins with her sled dogs that she was currently training for the Iditarod race.

Smithson Evermore also was home to a major research and development enterprise that created and perfected communications and surveillance hardware and software for the military and law enforcement. The Evermore component had been founded by Slade's parents and was dedicated to providing support for abandoned infant children. The children were paired with loving and vetted parents, officially adopted and supported with generous trusts created by the Evermore Foundation. Like SiSi, Brad Freeport had been a Smithson Evermore abandoned infant who had been adopted by the senior Freeports and raised with Chuck in rural Maine. They were closer than real brothers and it was Chuck who suggested Brad to Slade Smithson when he had finished his military service as a Marine helicopter pilot. The Project Recovery K-9 team was composed of twelve dogs, all saved at local shelters, that were trained in various forms of search and rescue as well as security. Seven of the twelve were always ready for deployment and the others remained on training status. Each was trained to be transported long distances by any means possible. They were incredible and had a record of finding people in difficult circumstances.

SiSi opened her computer and called the central desk in Tampa. It rang once before L Street, another Smithson Evermore rescued infant and head of Research and Intelligence answered. "SiSi, how is your vacation going?"

SiSi laughed. "It has been great but it is about to be interrupted, isn't it?"

"At this point we are all on standby. It appears that our favorite millionaire is missing from the Puerto Vallarta house. He has been unaccounted for since last Saturday night when he and Kip Patterson went to dinner. I am checking on Dr. Patterson's status now and Jorge is checking in Puerto Vallarta to see what we can find out there. Please tell Brad that we will be contacting him within the hour for an update on the Canadian joint operation."

SiSi was busted. "So, you know that Brad and I are in the same location. Of course, you know. You are looking at our transponder signals which are in close proximity."

L was gentle. "SiSi, your business is your business and Brad's is his. If they happen to be the same business, then it is none of my business until you make it so. He is an amazing guy. Speaking of transponders, were you ever able to get Hank to allow you to give him one?"

SiSi almost laughed out loud and she never laughed out loud. "He was way more than adamant that I not put one of those privacy-invading thingamajigs on him, in him, or around him. He almost climbed a lamp to get away from me when I showed him his options.

"That totally sounds like Hank. How about his phone?"

SiSi responded quickly. "I do have a track on both his phones. He uses one as his personal phone stateside and one as his 'Mexican' phone. He has no idea they are location enabled. I just checked and it looks like both were switched off on Saturday night. This is interesting. It looks like the Mexican phone was turned off halfway between Puerto Vallarta and Chihuahua on Mexico 45 just north of Torreón at about 02:00 on Sunday morning. From what I remember of Hank, at two in the morning he would be fast asleep or wide-awake watching CNN. He would not be on the road.

L responded almost instantly. "That absolutely doesn't sound like our Hank."

SiSi paused a moment. "Chuck has been alerted to get two of the canine team ready. Is that from Slade or from Oscar on the Canadian operation?"

Oscar Dorian, the chief of operations for Smithson Evermore broke in on the call. "Hi, SiSi. It was me. About ten minutes after Brad left the meeting, we got a call from the Canadian Border Service that their intelligence group had received information that the group out of Moncton was going to attempt to cross with an unknown number of people. They suspect human trafficking rather than just smuggling. I'm afraid Brad is going to be heading right back out again. Sorry."

SiSi was ruffled. "Does everyone on the team know about my relationship with Brad?"

Oscar laughed. "Of course. We are all delighted. It's one of the hazards of working with a team like ours, SiSi. But, don't feel bad, I would guess you will be very busy within the next few hours. If Hank is really missing, and the Canadian operation kicks into high gear, we will need our Technology Chief at her console. Slade has scheduled a briefing in one hour. I would pack if I were you."

SiSi answered. "I have already started. Claymore will hold everything together in Tampa until I get there. It looks like he is on top of it."

Oscar was quick to reply. "He was a good choice for a fill in for you to get some time away but we are spread thin and are going to need everyone.

"Be safe, Oscar. I will see everyone in a few hours, I'm sure."

Back in Mexico, Hank was just coming out of his drug-induced stupor. It took him awhile to focus. His arms were bound behind him. He was alone in the room and was lying on his side on a bed. He struggled to his feet and managed to stand up only to fall right back down again. It took him another few minutes to be able to get his balance back. Whatever they had given him was potent. He had enjoyed some great dreams about the old days. But he was awake now and having his hands bound behind him didn't seem like a sign that things were going well. He remembered jumping in the ride-share with Kip and then being sprayed. He managed to get to his feet and take a few steps toward the window that was located at about eye level on the far wall across from the door. He stretched up and looked out. It was light out and he could see the backyards of at least three other houses around him. They were hovels with dogs rolling around in the dust and running amongst the litter of old tires and car parts. The trash had been tipped over and redistributed by the dogs. This wasn't Puerto Vallarta or at least the part he lived in. He had no idea where he was.

He could hear voices outside the room. Hank felt there was no time like the present to take charge of the situation. He marched over to the door and kicked it as he screamed. "You people better get in here and release my hands pronto, comprende?"

The people in the room on the other side of the door grew quiet. Hank took this as a sign that he was getting through to them and decided to up the stakes. "You don't have any idea who you are fucking with here. I warn you. Get in here and take these things off my hands and tell me what is going on. I have friends who could chop you up and spit you out so you better pay attention. I'm counting to five and someone better open this door and release me."

From the other side of the door the woman with dark hair responded. "We're sorry. If you step away from the door and go sit on the edge of the bed, we will be in and release you. We had no idea who you were or how important you are."

Hank seemed pleased with this answer. "You're damn straight you will. And, you better get my friend in here. He has a plane to catch so if you have him in some other room, you need to release him too. You wait until Slade hears about all of this."

The man and the two women on the other side of the door suddenly all looked at each other. The dark-haired woman who had kidnapped him went over and picked up one of the phones they had taken from him. She turned it on and quickly went to the contact list. She typed in an S and there it was, bigger than life, 'Smithson Evermore-Slade Smithson'. She looked at the man. "Fuck. That is the last thing we need. I'll shut him up. We need to think of something fast."

The man nodded. "Sir, we are really sorry. Please go over and sit on the bed and we will come in and release you." They heard Hank move across the bed and the springs give as he sat down. The dark-haired woman put her mask on, adjusted the eyeholes, and unlocked the door. She pushed it open, walked across the room to where Hank was eyeing her with contempt and promptly sprayed Hank again with the sleep agent they had originally used. Hank fell over to his left and the woman called the man to readjust him on the bed so he wouldn't aspirate. They closed the door, locked it and looked across the room at the blond woman. She spoke. "What in the hell are we going to do with him? I seriously don't want Smithson people breathing down our necks. Shit, did you turn his phone off?" She rushed across the room and punched the phone off.

She was too late. The phone had registered on the Smithson tracking map the minute it was turned on. It offered just enough time for them to lock in on the signal that recorded the location of the phone on the Smithson map before it was switched off. It alerted on L's console in their headquarters.

The blond woman who was in charge looked at the others and spoke. "We are going to have to alter the plans. I am sure Smithson saw the signal and will know that phone is here. Who the hell is that guy? He does not look like anyone who works for Smithson."

The man who up to now had been silent, spoke. "It doesn't matter who he is. If he has Slade Smithson's direct number, they will know soon enough he is not where he is supposed to be. They take that stuff seriously. I think you are going to have to get your primary out of here and as far away from that guy as possible or you are going to have more company than you ever signed on for. I suggest I take this guy one direction and you move your primary in the other. They will follow me if they follow anyone. You have to leave right now. You can't stay here. They are probably already on their way. I suggest we stuff all his crap back in his pockets and let me take him. They will be busy trying to recover him while the rest of you can deliver the other guy. We are about to have federal agents from two different countries after us not to mention the Smithson Evermore team."

The woman who had kidnapped them now put down the spray can and removed her mask. "Where will you take him?"

The man next to her responded. "It is really best you don't know that."

The other woman in the room asked, "Will you kill him?"

"That is likewise something you don't need to know. Where is all the crap we got out of his pockets?"

The woman in charge nodded. "I have his stuff right here. I think your idea is a good one." She turned to the other two. "Get Patterson ready to transport and check to make sure he is not awake yet. We don't need him alert and observant until we hand him off to our clients. I will get another pilot.

Remove any trace we have been here. We will leave in ten minutes." She turned to the man who would take Hank. "Use your best judgment on where and in what condition you drop him. We don't need to be connected with that at all."

They all nodded and went about packing. The man who would be transporting Hank went in and re-stuffed his pockets with his belongings. He put a copy of Hank's passport that he always carried into his back pocket. He put one of his phones in his right pocket along with a handkerchief that had contained at least a half dozen small pills. In his left pocket the man stuffed a small plastic baggie that contained several different types of gummy candies, which he suspected were laced with THC, and the other phone. When he was ready, he checked the flex cuffs and then picked Hank up and threw him over his shoulder. He took him out to the pick-up truck in the back yard and put him in the passenger seat and belted him in and then waited by the truck. The woman who was the leader came out with his travel bag and put it in the back of the truck. "You be careful. Follow the plan and I will see you in three days. Lead them away from us. Once the nut jobs behind this pay us, you and I are off to Belize. He can't be found for three days so make sure you hide him well." She reached up and gave him a long lingering kiss. "Be well and I will see you soon."

She turned, joined the others, and drove off with Kip Patterson towards the airport. The man watched until their lights were out of sight and then waited a few minutes more. He went back in the house and checked it one more time. When he was sure there was nothing there, he splashed a gallon of gasoline in the two rooms that had held their captives and the main room where they had stayed. He placed a small packet on the table with a wire and a cell phone attached. He walked out and got in the truck and headed for Highway 16 West toward Hermosillo in the Sonora Province. It would take him about nine hours to get there. He drove until he got to the edge of town. He pulled out his cell phone and dialed the number of the phone on the table wired to the package. It rang once; he heard a roar and the line went dead. As he headed west the fire department was just arriving to a chorus of barking dogs. The houses around the one they had used were abandoned so no one would be there to testify to who they were. Hank was next to him in the truck and would be no problem for the time being. He settled down for the drive.

The other three headed to the private airside of the Roberto Fierro Villalobos airport. They drove right to the waiting plane that was already fueled. The Mexican pilot, who had been arranged at the last minute, was on board with all the necessary paperwork they needed as an air ambulance evacuation. They strapped Kip Patterson onto the medical gurney and all of them climbed on board. They were airborne thirty minutes after they had left the house in the barrio. They would soon be back in the U.S.A. This plane would stop in Houston to clear customs because of the medical emergency. The Mexican pilot would return while they boarded a second plane. That plane would be piloted by people friendly to the cause that had hired them. From Houston, it was on to Demopolis, Alabama, for refueling and a second stop at Mountain Empire Airport near Marion, Virginia. They would finish their air journey at Sullivan County Airport near White Lake, New York. Upon their arrival they would travel by car to Liberty, New York, where they would turn their package over to their employer and get paid. Other than the second guy who no one had expected, the job had gone without a hitch, but a guy connected to Smithson Evermore could be a giant hitch. They should have asked for more background on Patterson. The dipshits they worked for had no clue what they were in for. By the time they figured it out, this group would be long gone with the money.

The man driving toward the west coast of Mexico with Hank sedated next to him was a former employee of Kenderson Park Insurance. His name was Forrest Mack and up until three years ago had been a kidnap recovery specialist with that company. His main job had been to recover kidnap victims and return them for the insurance company. Two of the three people he was working with on this job were ex-employees of that company who likewise had been laid off. The fourth was the husband of the woman who had carried out the kidnapping. Mack had once worked closely with the Smithson Evermore Team so he knew their capabilities and was determined to create as much distance as he could between them and him while he thought. The others could look out for themselves. He didn't like being on this end of the business but he needed the money. He made his living flying helicopter whale watching trips for cruise companies in the Gulf of California. He has also ferried hunters to a remote island off the coast near Punta Chueca known as Tiburon. The Seri Tribe owned the island and managed everything that went on there. Since Tiburon translates to 'shark' in English, it was easy to imagine what was cruising the coast off the island. It was all rocks, mountain, and scrub. He was well respected and accepted by the Seri. He knew Tiburon Island well. It would be a perfect place to hide his sleeping companion. One can reach the island from land by boat but it was his intention to fly from Hermosillo, where his chopper was waiting, to the island. He had no intention of killing Hank but it was necessary that the others felt he was capable of that. He wasn't sure what they were capable of. He had never taken the life of someone who could not defend themselves when he worked on the recovery side. He wasn't about to do it now he had been forced to the other side. Desperation had been a driving force but he drew the line at wanton murder. He had a plan to make sure that this man would be found. He resolved that Hank would be alive when that happened. He drove on into the night as Hank snored loudly beside him.

He thought about Serena, the woman leader who had recruited him. There was no question that she wanted a more lasting commitment than he did. He had never agreed to meet her in Belize. She had just assumed that. He felt sorry for her. It had been difficult for her since her husband had died. He actually didn't believe the plan was going to play out the way she thought it would. They were not professional criminals. They were easily duped because most people didn't understand the complicated process of taking people against their will. Since the victim was living in Mexico, Serena needed someone familiar with the country who was a pilot. Mack had maintained a house in Mexico for twenty years. He knew and understood the people.

Serena had never had much contact with anyone except at work. After the loss of her job and the loss of her husband and income, she had been easy pickings for the nut jobs that were part of the organization that had hired them. Forrest Mack didn't trust any of them including their millionaire-loaded

Board of Directors. He believed that everyone who had done all their dirty work, including himself, was expendable. He hoped Serena would be safe but his experience told him otherwise. Either way, he had no intention of meeting anyone, anywhere. His focus had to be the safety of the man sitting next to him whose testimony could almost assuredly send him to jail in the United States or worse, get him sentenced to life in a Mexican prison.

Hank interrupted his thoughts with a loud shriek. He was dreaming. Forrest thought, "Dream on and enjoy. I will figure this out."

CHAPTER 4

*Help doesn't always come from where it is expected. Once it
arrives, it doesn't matter.*

In Puerto Vallarta, Jorge Pascal, the Smithson Evermore team leader, had been on the phone with his contacts in the municipal and federal police as well as with the local cartel that was very reliable with information about its most prized residents. The cartel had been responsible for the safety and security of the expatriate community since the boom of the sixties in Puerto Vallarta. It was in their best interest, economically, that the city remains safe for its wealthy visitors. They were very good at keeping the peace and protecting the public. They were able to handle violence swiftly in a way that anyone contemplating a crime would have a lasting and unpleasant example of what happens to people that hurt the cartel's economy. It was big business at its finest and Smithson Evermore had a good relationship with the cartel bosses and their workers. It was a mutually beneficial arrangement with a higher level of trust than working with local officials. It was almost sad to see the local police officers with their low pay and old equipment next to the better-equipped cartel members. The police were dependent upon whatever funding the government could provide. That support was tied to political control and the politics of Mexico at the local level were driven by chaos. The cartel was driven by a much more substantial motive, money. The cartel had unlimited funding opportunities and played by a much different set of rules. It was not uncommon to see thieves paraded through the streets as an example to other thieves. Sometimes they would have the same body parts they had when they committed the theft. Many times, they did not, and looked much the worse for wear for their crime. It was deterrence written with a capital D.

It took Jorge about thirty minutes to determine the sequence of what had happened to Hank and Kip. The very high-quality closed-circuit video, courtesy of a grant to the city from Smithson Intelligence Labs supplemented by the cartel funds, had revealed the kidnapping. They could clearly see both

Hank and Kip get into a sedan outside the restaurant. They were able to track the sedan to a point within a block of Kip's house where they could see the sedan pull over. They would have to enhance the video feed to determine what happened but it appeared a van pulled away shortly after the sedan pulled over and headed straight to the main highway headed north out of the city. The sedan had traveled to the airport where they had found the car and the sedated ride-share driver. They would need the additional video to see how the kidnap driver escaped.

As Jorge was reviewing the video on his phone, he received a call from Manuel Guzman, a main cartel official and a trusted source of information for Smithson Evermore. "Manuel, it is good to hear from you."

Manuel answered. "Likewise, it is a shame that we only seem to have a discussion when there is an issue."

Jorge was quick to reply. "We think we have some friends missing and the video you sent me confirms that. Do we have an issue?"

The answer was immediate. "We both do. Our sources tell us that both Dr. Patterson and Mr. Kessler were taken last Saturday early evening. Their favorite ride-share driver, Angelina, was found drugged and tied up in the trunk of the sedan that you can see in the video. She is one of our people. The sedan was left at the airport. One of our people got a text to go look for the car. Apparently, the kidnappers did not want to encourage our wrath so they made sure Angelina was found."

Jorge jumped in. "I know Angelina. Is she OK?"

"She is a bit shaken but she is fine. I will tell her you inquired about her. She will appreciate that. She is very concerned about our two friends. Her story provides more details. She was waiting down the street from the restaurant for Dr. Patterson to call. A woman walked up and asked for directions to the airport. As Angelina was starting to give her directions, the woman sprayed her with an aerosol that completely sedated her. That is all she remembers except one thing that is the most interesting. The woman was an American. She was definitely not one of our normal operators who cause problems. The van you see in the video was stolen from a rental lot near the airport earlier in the evening. The quick look we were able to get of the plates indicates they were switched. It is our belief that Dr. Patterson and Mr. Kessler were immobilized with the same type of aerosol spray and transferred to the van. We have contacted our associates, or at least the ones we are on good terms with, to the north. We did get a confirmation that the same van purchased fuel early Sunday morning in the town of Jose Mariano Jimenez. Their information is that there were two men in the van. At least one was American."

Jorge was quiet for a moment then asked. "Do you know of any organizations operating in Chihuahua province that include kidnapping in their portfolio of services? Not all of the cartel organizations are as above board as yours."

There was a quick answer. "There may be a few politically motivated groups but there is much more of a return moving drugs, weapons, and people wanting to migrate than there are those that take Americans for money. That behavior has a distinctly Central or South American flavor to it. But, because of the new U.S. policies on immigration, I can assure you that none of the Mexican groups would be utilizing Anglo-American kidnappers. There is simply a great deal of mistrust in that area of anyone from north of the border."

Jorge had heard enough. "Thank you for the information you have provided. We will begin checking at our end. Do not be alarmed if you see an enhanced presence at our villa. Both of these men are important to us. I am going to speak to Mr. Smithson in a few minutes and update him. As always, I will keep you informed of any actions we will take in your area and make sure we are working together. Will you keep me informed on anything else you might find out? The direction they are heading can lead to a variety of different outcomes. Without divulging anything that will put your operations at risk, if they were going to try to move these people out of Mexico, how would they do that?"

Manuel thought for a moment. "The closest secret crossing is near Presidio. There are several options there. There is always the small aircraft possibility. But, we like hanging on to our rich friends from the north. They are worth more to us out spending in our area than they are locked up and held for whatever ransom might be available. I will keep checking our sources but for right now, that is the best I can think of. I will call you when we get more information."

"Thank you, Manuel. We appreciate the assistance. You have always been great to work with. I will keep you updated as well."

Jorge hung up and decided to activate his entire team before he updated Slade. The villa would immediately be locked down and he would place a surveillance team at Dr. Patterson's villa as well. Jorge was in the command room of their Puerto Vallarta villa just downstairs from where Hank Kessler should have been staying. The monitor in front of him lit up with a conference call alert. Within seconds the screen filled up with four contact points. Slade had instructed Claymore Jenkins to activate a four-point conference from their main command center in Tampa. In the upper left-hand corner of his screen, Jorge could see Slade and Aggie with Lily and Alex standing in the background. The upper right-hand corner of the screen contained a view of SiSi, which was connected through her mobile command module in Maine. The lower right-hand side of the screen contained the view from the command center in Tampa with Oscar Dorian and L seated in the main conference room. Jorge's picture was in the lower left-hand side.

Slade began the conference. "Before I ask Jorge to update us on what he has been able to find out in Mexico, I am going to ask L to update us on information she has just received in Tampa from the FBI. L go ahead."

L began slowly. "Hello everyone. I contacted Senator Patterson's office to see if they had heard from Dr. Patterson. Special Agent Bill Paisley of the Washington field office answered the phone. He was not very forthcoming about why an FBI agent was answering the private phone of a U.S. Senator but he agreed he would check through his chain of command and get back to me. Within five minutes, I received a call from Special Agent in Charge Terry Fry who is the head of their congressional affairs division. She asked why we were calling. I advised that we were concerned that Dr. Patterson was missing from his villa in Puerto Vallarta along with one of our close associates and hadn't been seen since Saturday evening. She thanked me for the information and asked us to keep our information confidential and to keep her informed directly of anything else we discovered. She seemed to know about our organization but I can't find she ever has worked with us before. SiSi, I hope it was OK but I had Claymore generate a secure line and contact number for her here. That is a couple of steps ahead of our protocol but this seems to be developing rapidly and I wanted her to know we had secure capability. If I were to guess, I would say that they know Dr. Patterson has been kidnapped and may even have been contacted already. That is about the size of what has transpired here."

Slade directed the next request to SiSi. "SiSi, have we got any idea where these two men might be from any signal, we might be able to connect to Hank?"

SiSi answered quickly. "We got a preliminary ping on the system from the transmitter located in Hank's Mexican phone. That phone was shut off in the early hours of Sunday morning on one of the main highways leading north toward Chihuahua province. That is all I have so far. He rarely turns his personal phone on in Mexico."

Slade then turned the conference over to Jorge who briefed them all on what he had learned from the information provided by Manuel Guzman of the Vallarta cartel. When he had finished, Slade spoke. "So, if I can summarize, it appears both men were abducted using a sleep agent on Saturday evening and the last known location, at least for Hank, is on a highway several hours later headed north. From what L has said, it would appear Dr. Patterson was the main target. The fact that the FBI is now answering Senator Patterson's phone is confirmation of that. The kidnappers have to know that Kip and the Senator were once married and still have a good relationship. They also have to know that the risk of going up against the FBI operating on behalf of the Senator is high. The big question is why Hank. I don't think anyone would want to take us on any more than they would the FBI unless they are totally clueless. They obviously knew that Dr. Patterson would be having dinner at the restaurant and they knew enough to use the trust he had in his driver to make him careless. Anyone have any idea how Hank got in the middle of this?"

L and SiSi both spoke almost at the same time. "He was saving the ride fare."

Slade looked astonished. "What? You think he was in that car just to save the equivalent of $2.50?"

They both answered as one again. "Definitely."

Slade then continued. "I guess if you're are not expecting bad things to happen you behave normally and both of them had no reason to think they were going to be taken. L do we have any information on kidnap insurance for Hank. I know he asked me once about whether or not I thought it was a good idea for him."

L took a moment to scan her file on Hank. "I'm showing that he did purchase a fairly good policy. I am showing that he was warned once for not sharing his plans to travel with the agency. I am also showing that when they raised his premium, he stopped paying the premium on the policy and it was cancelled. There is a fairly salty note in the file from the company indicating that he called them a bunch of 'opportunistic crooks and vultures.' I have to admit that sounds like Hank."

Slade paused and then continued. "At this stage of the game it would appear to me that without any insurance to be collected, Hank is more of a liability than he is an asset to the kidnappers. Anyone else have an idea about that?"

The conference screen was silent. Oscar broke the silence. "The kidnappers have three options. If they have Hank's phone, they have his sister's number. They may want to contact her to see if they can get some ransom out of their joint accounts. She knows to call us if that happens. The second option would be to try to sell Hank to another group and let them try to collect on his return. Since we know that at least the team that took both of them is Anglo, I doubt they could make the proper connection to make that happen, but it is possible. Third, they could just decide to cut their losses and dump Hank somewhere."

Aggie spoke next sitting next to Slade. "Oscar, you don't think they would keep them together?"

"I don't. I think that just pulling this off with the FBI breathing down their neck will be an issue."

It was L that spoke next. "If they didn't expect that Hank would be with Dr. Patterson, would they necessarily know that we would be involved? It could be that they don't know about our connection to Hank."

Oscar answered. "They could have discovered it when they looked in his phone. Either one of them would have our contact numbers. I get an uneasy feeling that they are going to lower their risk by disposing of Hank."

Slade finished the call with his normal level of organization. "Either way we are going to have to find our friend. Aggie and I are going to fly back east with Rufus tonight. SiSi, I hate to cut your vacation short but I would like you to return to Tampa as soon as possible. Alex arrived in the San Juan Islands a short while ago with Lily. I am going to ask them to pick up Marcus and fly to Tucson and meet the Southwest recovery team there. Alex and the team will mount a search operation in Mexico. If Alex can't find him, then no one can. Lily, you work on finding out as much as we can about Dr. Patterson's trail from Mexico. Someone had to have helped them with the border issues we have with Mexico right now. Oscar, I want you to head to Maine to deal with the Canadian project. You will join Brad and his team there. I am fairly confident that Dr. Patterson is alive because he is worthless to anyone dead. I am as unsure about Hank as Oscar is. Marcus, please stay current with our resources. We will fly to Florida tonight and coordinate from our command center in Tampa for the time being. I will call our liaison at the FBI and try to establish a closer link before we take off. Jorge, your team will provide security for both houses in Puerto Vallarta while Alex is searching and Lily is working on the case. Let's make sure that whatever we learn we share as quickly as possible. If we are going to save our friend, we are going to have to do so quickly and we are already behind. That is all I have. We will talk tomorrow morning after everyone is in place."

L broke in. "Slade, our system just alerted on a signal from Hank's personal phone. It pinged the tower near the southern section of Chihuahua.

It was only on for a few seconds, but the computer has finally given me the location."

Slade responded quickly. "Get the coordinates to Alex, Lily, and Jorge. That is the first break we have had. I hope it is not the last. See you in the morning."

That same phone now sat silent in Hank's pocket as he and Forrest Mack were on their way to Hermosillo on Mexico Highway 16. Hank was still asleep from the last time he was drugged. Mack was running through his options in his mind. He knew he might have to dose him one more time to keep him manageable. He wasn't worried about Hank physically although he was tall and fairly lean. He just didn't want to find out if Hank was capable of causing trouble at the wrong place at the wrong time. Mack did not trust the aerosol agent they were using. Forrest was sure Hank had a sedative with him and he decided that he might be able to get Hank to swallow it just as he was waking up. Mack knew the dose of most of them and he trusted it better than the aerosol. If he caught Hank at just the right time of waking, Hank might just take the pill before he came to full consciousness. Hank had a pocket full of various pills, which Mack believed were probably prescribed in the States but purchased in Mexico. That made it more difficult to identify what they were. Hank wasn't stirring so it wasn't an immediate concern but Mack liked to stay a few steps ahead of the situation. He was making good time and had more than enough fuel to make it to the next stop. He would watch Hank closely until then.

Meanwhile the plane carrying Dr. Patterson had been in the air for about an hour. Serena Moore, the blond woman who was actually in charge of the whole operation, pulled a life-like synthetic mask from its package. It had been made to resemble the picture that was on the passport they would present to the customs authorities when they cleared U.S. Customs in Houston. They had been given special clearance to proceed there directly rather than the closest point of entry because of the medical condition. The authorities expected that the ill person on board would be transferred to Houston Medical directly upon landing and being cleared. With the help of the other woman, Lucy Frost, she slid the mask over Kip Patterson's head and face and snugged it. She laid him back on the pillow of the gurney and pulled out the passport to compare. The mask was perfect. Any agent inspecting a man believed to be dying of cancer would be fooled unless he wanted to try to wake him and their story was that he was heavily sedated and being transported to Houston as a last resort. She doubted that an agent would interfere. After all, the passport looked real.

Their whole group had been employed by an ultra conservative political action committee. She had no idea why they wanted Dr. Patterson but she was fairly sure they would do him no harm. Lucy had worked with Serena for almost twenty years at Kenderson Park insurance company. That is where they had met Forrest Mack. They had all been downsized. Serena had been a regional vice president for claims and Lucy had been her steadfast personal assistant. The fourth member of their group was Aaron Frost, Lucy's husband. Aaron hadn't worked for the insurance company. He hadn't worked for anyone in fifteen years. He had pieced together a living doing construction, lawn maintenance, moving furniture etc. The one thing he was very good at was doing whatever Lucy told him without question. He was big, strong, and not too bright. He was so compliant that many thought he might be suffering from some lack of capacity. The truth was he could think. He just chose to let Lucy do the heavy mental lifting. There was a point in the whole process where they weren't sure the aerosol sedative would work. Aaron listened to the women discuss their concerns for about two minutes then just picked up the can and sprayed himself. That was how the sedative was tested.

None of these people seemed dangerous other than the fact they didn't quite think about the potential consequences of their actions. That is what had made them all vulnerable as their former company began the slow decline towards receivership. Mack was the only one they hadn't known for years but Serena had fallen for him in a big way. He had taken calculated risks. He was no stranger to difficult and dangerous situations. It was that quality that Serena had pursued. He had not been involved in any of the planning. He was just supposed to be the pilot but if things started to go wrong, he would know what to do. Serena was kicking herself for not stopping Lucy from turning on Hank's phone. But they were in the air now and were about to cross into U.S. airspace. They all fully understood there was no going back now. The Mexican pilot who was unaware of all this, advised they should be preparing the patient for transfer as they would be landing in Houston soon. Once on the ground he would taxi to the American ambulance that was waiting for them. Customs would clear them before they made the transfer. They had only the baggage that made them look like they had been vacationing in Mexico. The bags would be checked, the passports would be checked but it was doubtful that customs would conduct any more than a cursory glance at a comatose American man headed home to die. But there was another plane waiting, staffed with individuals 'friendly' to the cause of the PAC. This was the last risky part for the operation. Their 'package' was doing well. He had been hooked up to an IV and was resting comfortably. He didn't even know where he was. The lights dimmed in the cabin as the Mexican pilot made his final descent.

Lucy Frost sat up forward and watched as Serena was preparing Kip Patterson. She smirked inwardly. Lucy had known who Kip Patterson was before she had even started working for the insurance company and Serena. She knew Kip Patterson and she knew his ex-wife Senator Henrietta Patterson. She knew her only too well.

CHAPTER 5

*If you care about someone for the right reason, you will
accept the small personality quirks that are interesting.*

The Smithson Evermore King Air with the team onboard left the north end of Orcas Island and arrived at the private airside at SeaTac south of Seattle within a few minutes. Lily and Alex remained on the King Air while Slade and Aggie moved to their corporate jet. Rufus had the jet headed to Tampa as soon as they taxied and cleared. Alex, Lily and Frank Pierson the second pilot, were all headed in the King Air first to San Diego to pick up Marcus Moreno and then on to Tucson to join the Smithson Evermore Southwest Recovery Team.

In the jet, Slade dialed the contact number he had for their liaison with the FBI. Deep in the headquarters in Washington D.C. the phone rang and was answered in two rings. Slade didn't mince words. "Good evening. This is Slade Smithson. Somehow one of our close friends has become involved in what may be the kidnapping of Dr. Kendrick Patterson. When we tried to contact his ex-wife, Senator Henrietta Patterson, her phone was answered by one of your agents. We received a call back within minutes from your congressional liaison. We will be available to assist in any way we can but you need to know we will be moving forward with the recovery of our friend who appears to have been taken with Dr. Patterson. It has always worked better when we cooperate on such things. I would suggest that we set up a direct liaison. It would appear that the two individuals we have spoken to are unaware of our capabilities. It would be good for you to bring them up-to-speed. We don't have time to educate them. I will be back in Tampa in a few hours." With that said, Slade hung up the phone.

Aggie looked at him. "Well, that was certainly short and not-so-sweet. Is there a bee under that bonnet that I need to know about?"

Slade smiled. "Since the change in administration and the internal changes at the FBI, it is sometimes best to be direct with the feds. They need to know the exact situation. We can't rely on our past experiences with their agents. Many of them have been transferred or are gone. The agency has its own internal struggles but I have confidence they will get through. I'm not about to waste time with their nonsensical 'group think" which has more to do with 'political fall-out' than it does with tactical decision making when Hank's life might be in danger. I'm not so sure that Kip is out of danger either so until we hear from Alex and Lily, we are moving full steam ahead."

Aggie smiled. "Be careful you could end up in a nasty tweet."

Slade looked at her puzzled. "What's a tweet?"

Aggie laughed. "Never mind. While you get your thoughts together, I am going to go over the latest information on the Canadian operation. We may have a chance to put a whole group of traffickers in custody, which would increase our chances of getting to know how they operate. We know FBI agent Bridgett Moss and Agent Steve Wiley of U.S. Border Patrol. We have Maria Montalba with the Border Patrol and Emilio Cortez from ICE so I think we should do all we can to support them. We also have our two favorite Canadian agents, Mattey Borge of the RCMP and Erick Brandhoff from border services assigned to Mattey that have been amazing for us on this and other cases.

Slade nodded. "I have the greatest amount of respect for all of them. They are old timers from many of our operations. Do you think I am getting too distracted with the other problem?"

Aggie laughed again. "I will make a guess and say no. I have never known you to be unable to balance things but our personal relationship with Hank reminds me of three years ago when we didn't know for sure whether Earl Tippit was alive and well. It has the same feel. In my heart I knew Earl was good, and I feel that Hank is. Like you, I don't know what advantage someone would have by kidnapping Dr. Patterson other than possibly trying to influence his wife."

"What do you mean?"

Aggie continued. "I think this may political. Henrietta Patterson will be one of the most important votes on the adoption of the congressional immigration package. As you may guess, she is not going to support some of the more draconian notions implicit in the legislation. That translates to a problem for those supporting the legislation. They base their theories of immigration reduction upon controlling crime and they mention the Sinaloa Cartel every time they speak. Hank's phone last pinged in Chihuahua, which is part of their area of operation. We may be the only people with the information that the kidnappers were possibly American. Until we know more, the fact that the Senator's ex-husband has been taken in Mexico in an area of criminal cartel activity may have an impact on her thinking."

Slade thought. "Do you really think that these people would go that far to influence her vote?"

Aggie looked at him. "Some of the PACs we have been reading about are just short of domestic terrorist mindsets. Groups of nationalist patriot militias are roaming the southern border in tactical gear conducting their own searches and seizing people to turn over to the Border Patrol and National Guard along the border. Do you really think that one of these groups would hesitate for a moment to prove their point?"

Slade was quick to respond. "We have no idea who has taken Kip or why. Perhaps it was Sinaloa using American operators."

"That would be a first and particularly now with tensions what they are. Besides Sinaloa can make more money moving fentanyl and cocaine than they can kidnapping Kip Patterson. I don't think they would even dirty their hands with this. And, don't forget that the only source we have that says these people were American is our contact with the Vallarta Cartel. Even that group, with which we have a good relationship, has been in somewhat of a conflict since their clashes with the national police in 2015. I don't know how the FBI would take to information provided by them. Until we all are operating from the same information base and we know more, let's keep an open mind."

Slade thought and then responded. "You're right, as always. I don't really see the upside for any cartel taking Kip or Hank. I will have L check Dr.

Patterson's latest publication and speech content to see if he has said anything to inflame anybody in Mexico or in the United States. He normally has a very practical approach."

Aggie smiled. "That practical approach may be just the one that can set off some of these more conservative groups." She turned back to her computer to review the reports that Brad had just filed detailing the information from the conference in Calais, Maine. She was surprised by some of the details. The FBI and ICE had been able to make several arrests in a human trafficking operation in Kansas City, Missouri. There they were supplying local cleaning services in hotels and businesses. In Cleveland Ohio, they provided nail salons with people and enhanced the sex trade establishments with girls. What surprised Aggie was that the trafficked women were multi-national, including Asian and South and Central Americans. In addition, they all testified that they had been trafficked through Canada. The women who had been recovered in Kansas City had described their route through Canada. The traffickers who had been arrested confirmed at least that the women in Kansas City had crossed the border somewhere in northern Michigan. All the women indicated that they had started their journey on a ship that had come into Canada through the port at Vancouver, British Columbia. The intelligence indicated that this trafficking group utilized several entry points and some of those were along the border in Maine. The most current information indicated that they were going to make an attempt to cross in the next few days. Months of preparation and hard work could be about to achieve some results. It all depended on the cooperation of several agencies in both countries. The agencies knew it, the investigators knew it, and most of all, the traffickers knew it.

It was almost morning on the third day since Hank and Kip had been taken. Forrest Mack drove on toward the western coast of Mexico. Hank sat next to him awkwardly positioned with his hands still secured behind his back. He was restless in his drug-induced state. Mack hated the position he had put himself in. As he drove, he periodically glanced over at Hank and made note of how uncomfortable he appeared to be. He made a decision and pulled over to the side of the highway. He got out on the pavement and shined his flashlight on the edge of the road. The side of the road seemed clear of danger. He pulled the passenger side door open and carefully reached in and cut the flex cuffs that secured Hank's hands. Hank never even winced and automatically moved into a more comfortable position.

Forrest knew the risk he was taking but he was tired of being someone he wasn't. He got back in the truck and started the drive west again. It took a half hour before Hank began to murmur in his sleep. It was hard for Forrest to make out what he was saying but there was no question that he began to cry. It wasn't loud and it wasn't annoying. It was just a whimper so sorrowful that it pulled at Forrest's heart. He kept repeating a name. This went on for about ten minutes before he settled back into what appeared to be a peaceful sleep. He then began to snore loudly. From experience, Forrest knew that this was a sign that he would be waking soon. He was returning to his normal sleep functions and the drug was beginning to wear off. Forrest had no idea what he was going to do to explain things to Hank but he felt better about the situation with Hank more comfortable. Forrest thought, "Hank, how did you end up here?"

It was getting near 6:00 am when Forrest began to see the signs of the approaching city of Hermosillo, Mexico. His casita was located southwest of the airport. He was glad to be this close with Hank still asleep, but it wouldn't be long until he was awake and Forrest didn't want to have that happen suddenly while he was driving. He made another decision as he saw Hank begin to stir. He took a turn north toward the lake located on the east side of town. He pulled into one of the side roads that led to the lakeshore and parked near a bench. He got out and retrieved a thermos of coffee he had packed in his carryall and two metal mugs. He took the keys and went and sat on the bench. It was still dark but wouldn't be for long this time of year. He sat for about thirty minutes before he heard the door of the truck shut. He turned around and saw Hank trying to hurry up the road. He was still partially under the influence of the drug so it was more a wobble than it was a run. Forrest smiled.

"You're going the wrong way. That leads back where we came from. You're not quite awake yet so you need to come back and sit here and have some coffee. I have a couple of fried pork sandwiches as well. You need something in your stomach to help you regain your senses."

Hank stopped the wobble up the road. "Why should I do that you monster? You kidnapped me and tied my hands behind my back and sprayed me with stuff and God knows what else. Why should I even think you aren't going to kill me, you bastard, you horrible, horrible bastard." He kept shouting but he also stopped wobbling.

Forrest replied in a calm voice. "If I was going to kill you, I would have done so while you were out if for nothing else but to save myself that last rant. I may be a bastard but I'm the one that brought you this far and you are still alive and relatively safe."

Hank turned around and looked at him. "What do you mean I'm relatively safe, you prick?"

Forrest continued to be calm. "Well, if you continue to stay over there it won't be long until a rattlesnake finds you. Most of them have already hunted, but younger ones hang around the lake here to catch frogs and small birds. You are making enough noise to keep the timid ones away. But if you keep up, you may rouse an old bastard like me that will bite you just to shut you up. Now stop ranting like a dumb shit, come over here and get something into your stomach."

Of all the things that Hank disliked in the world, and there were many, snakes had to be near the top of the list. He stopped, looked around and decided to hurry back toward the man on the bench. Forrest almost laughed out loud. When Hank, even sober, attempted to hurry with anything more than a brisk walk, it looked like a bird trying to run. He made good time but it was comical to watch. Hank made it to the bench and sat down, took a sandwich and promptly turned his back on Forrest in a display of rejection that only Hank understood. Forrest reached around him an offered him a cup of coffee and a bottle of water.

He took the coffee but left the water standing there. "I never drink the water in Mexico even if it is in a bottle." He continued to face away from Forrest.

Forrest almost laughed out loud. "That water was bought in San Diego a week ago. The sandwich, however, is from a roadside stand outside Chihuahua. I'd be careful with that. I'm not sure if it is pork or dog, and slow down. When was the last time you ate?"

Hank grumbled a response with his mouth full. "The last time I ate was with my friend Kip. We had a lovely snapper over saffron rice with a great bottle of Spanish white from Rioja and two extremely well-made martinis. Wait, where is my friend Kip? You better not have hurt him or I will make sure you die a thousand horrible deaths. I have friends in low places that I've known for forty years that would make mincemeat of you. Where is Kip?" He was shouting again.

Forrest waited until he turned around. "Why are you shouting. I'm sitting right here. Your friend is probably back in the States right now and the last time I saw him he was resting peacefully. The bobble heads that have him don't have plans to hurt him and if anything happens to him it will be more by accident than by design. I am not happy about the fact that either of you were taken. If you will stop shouting and we can start talking perhaps all your questions will be answered."

Hank turned around to him and faced him square on. "When was the last time you shaved? You look grubby as hell."

Forrest looked at him with amazement. "You are a kidnap victim. I am part of the plot that kidnapped you. You shouldn't even be seeing my face because in most circumstances that would mean certain death for a victim, and all you can think of is to make an asshole comment about my lack of a shave?"

"Well, you need one and I always tell the truth, at least most of the time. Why aren't you set on killing me? I could be the end of you and I will be. You better kill me now because I have friends who will be looking for me and I will testify against you and pull the switch myself."

Forrest laughed. "You were kidnapped in Mexico. They did away with the death penalty in 2005. It doesn't mean much because a life sentence in a Mexican prison doesn't last very long. I know that Slade Smithson has probably launched a full-scale search for you although I can't imagine why with that mouth of yours. I need to get you safe just in case the others or the people they worked for had a back-up plan they didn't share with me. I intend to do that even if I have to spray you again so you settle down. We have to get moving. We are going to stop at my place to get you cleaned up and then we are going somewhere I know you will be safe and we can wait for the Smithson folks to find both of us. I don't know the full plan for what will happen to your friend but I do know more than they do right now which will help you both get home."

Hank thought about that a moment. "Why the hell don't you just give me my phone and let me call Slade?"

Forrest responded as he stood up and threw out the rest of the coffee in his cup. "I'm not sure who else is monitoring that phone or the operation. It was too well financed to not have serious help and the equipment and those sprays you were hit with were very sophisticated. Someone with deep pockets wanted your friend and by now they know you are not with him. They will be looking for you. They may be closer than Smithson so let's be cautious and make sure we are found by the right team of people. Besides, your phones have been in you pocket along with that makeshift drug store you carry during the whole trip."

Hank stood up and with as much bravado as he could muster threw out the rest of his coffee too. "I don't know why I am even listening to you. Where are we going?"

"First, we get cleaned up and if you are going to be so critical, I will shave and you shower. You have peed on yourself twice at least but I'm too much of a gentleman to point that out to you. Then we are going to the beach."

Hank paused. He looked down at the stain on the front of him. He spoke as he followed Forrest to the truck "The beach is my favorite. I didn't bring my lotions or my swimsuit. I hope it's not this fucking muck of a lake. I like swimming in the ocean."

"We are going to an island in the Gulf of California but there will be no swimming."

"Why on earth would we be on a beach on an island and not swim in the ocean? You are a man with a small mind." The last was spoken as an intention to hurt Forrest's feelings.

Forrest ended the conversation as he got in the truck. "I may have a small mind but I don't swim with sharks, at least not the marine variety."

Forrest drove to his casita where they got cleaned up. Forrest gave Hank some new clothes and made sure he got to pick out a swimsuit. Hank explained to him that he had never dressed so shabbily in his life. Forrest began a long-standing tradition of many who knew Hank. He began to ignore every other word. There was something about Hank that he was beginning to like. He reaffirmed to himself that he was going to protect him until his friends found him. First, he needed to get him out of this part of Sinaloa. There were too many people here with the inclination to make a quick buck.

They arrived at the small airfield at the edge of the larger airport and Forrest had them pull his helicopter out of the hangar. Hank began another rant. "If you think for one minute that I am going to get in that fucking thing, you are crazy. They are horrible and noisy and they fall out of the sky. I absolutely refuse, do you hear me?"

"The whole city hears you. That is our way out of here that will stop them long enough to give us and Smithson a chance. Now, you will either get in that seat or I will spray you again."

Hank thought it over for a minute. "How big a dose? It wasn't that bad."

"Jesus, I don't know why anyone would want to save you. This crap is not good for you. How about if you take one of those pills you had in your pocket?"

Hank mulled that one over. "I still have those? I normally only take a half just to take the edge off."

Forrest looked at him with dismay as he pointed at the pocket that contained the folded handkerchief with the stash of pills that Hank had with him when he was taken. "I suggest you take a whole one and get your ass in that seat. We have got to get out of here."

Hank paused a moment and then took out a pill and swallowed it without water while he put the rest of the pills back in his pocket. He climbed in the seat and took the handkerchief and tied it around his eyes like a blindfold and grabbed onto the hand bars in the cockpit.

Forrest got in, put on his communication headset and helped Hank into his. He belted them both in. He left the blindfold in place. Hank fought with him for a brief moment then as the noise began to grow, gave up and helped him adjust the headset. He couldn't help himself. Forrest pulled out his phone and took a picture of his blindfolded companion hanging on for dear life before they had ever left the ground. The rotor began to pick up speed as Forrest quickly went through his preflight check. They lifted off and gained altitude. Forrest looked back over his shoulder as they banked to head due north. He saw three Mexican Police vehicles pull up to the pad they had just taken off from. They were already in the truck and he was sure they would note that he was heading north. He made sure to remain clear of air traffic and as soon as he was out of the range of the airport radar, turned back southwest toward Tiburon Island, which was only a few minutes away off the coast directly west of where they had just taken off. It wouldn't be long before whomever had accepted a bribe would be advising the people who had paid them that they were last seen headed north toward the U.S. He wasn't flying to the States and he knew right where he was going and who he could rely on to help him keep Hank safe. He hoped he had enough of a lead.

Hank removed the blindfold and looked out around him. For a time, he seemed fascinated. He watched as they skimmed across the land. Within a few minutes he could see the vast expanse of the Gulf of California with Baja on the far side. He heard Forrest ask him a question through the headphones. "What was the name you were murmuring in your sleep?"

Hank turned and looked at Forrest with the slightest hint of anger. "Fuck You." He then retied the handkerchief over his eyes for the remaining ten minutes of the flight.

Forrest set the chopper down on the north end of Tiburon Island. Hank felt the gentle touchdown and heard the rotor begin to slow down and took off his makeshift blindfold. "Where the hell are we and who are those people running up to us?"

Forrest was busy shutting down switches. "Be careful when you get out. We landed on a storage skid for the helicopter. They are going to pull it into that Quonset hut over there so no one can see it from the air."

The got out of the helicopter as six local men performed the well-rehearsed exercise of securing the rotor and using a small tractor to pull the helicopter toward the hut. It was completely hidden in five minutes. They left the doors open so the heat and fumes could escape.

Hank looked at Forrest. "Well, who are these people? God, they are the darkest Mexicans I have ever seen."

Forrest looked at Hank and answered. "The are members of the Seri Tribe. They own this island and they are friends. Try to be nice to them. I know you know how to be nice because people I respect are looking for you. But be extra nice to them. They, like you, have been hunted in the past. They were here before the Spanish and when you are criticizing them, please keep in mind, that many believed they were cannibals."

Hank looked at them. "Why are they looking at me that way? I look good but not as a first course."

Forrest countered. "I don't believe they were cannibals. But I do know that part of the myth surrounding them before Columbus is that tall men with blond hair visited them. They very well could think you are one of these ancient gods but only if you keep that nasty yapper of yours shut and don't insult them. Several of them speak enough English that they know when they are being insulted."

Hank looked at them differently. "Well, if they think I am a god, I certainly believe them to be intelligent and I suppose I can be nice for purely cultural reasons. I am a considerate person."

"That's good to know. I hadn't seen much evidence of that."

Hank looked hurt. "You kidnapped me. What did you expect? You drugged me and did things to me and made me wear these clothes. Wait, what things did you do to me?"

Forrest looked at him hard. "I hesitate to guess what you are thinking but I can assure you that you are as chaste as when you went to sleep in the back of the car in Puerto Vallarta. Neither man nor woman has had their way with you."

Hank responded quickly. "Well, that's good because if they did, I would at least like to be awake enough to enjoy it."

Forrest looked pained. "What are you, confused about your sexuality?"

Hank didn't waste a second. "No, I'm an opportunist, and I have had a hell of a lot of fun over the years with that perspective. Now, where is the beach and more importantly, where is the alcohol? I'm dying for a drink.

Forrest turned to the men and ask them in Spanish to get them a bottle of tequila, some water, some food, and meet him at the cabin by the beach. They all smiled and nodded. The leader pointed at Hank and spoke in a very clear voice. "Gallo Espléndido".

Hank looked at him then at Forrest for a translation.

Forrest smiled. "He just called you a 'Splendid Rooster.' Now let's get moving before your ego slows us down.

Hank turned to the men and smiled. They smiled back. He spoke as they walked. "What a nice place with nice people."

CHAPTER 6

Deception is almost always driven by fear, lust, greed.
sometimes all three.

It had been over two months since JinJing Zhao had legally entered Canada. She and her friend Lan Li had traveled together. They were both from mountain villages in the Sichuan Province of China. Jin, as her friends knew her, was twenty-two years old. Her father and mother had died when she was sixteen. Her father's brother and his wife had raised her. Her uncle had accepted this responsibility unwillingly but did not want to suffer disgrace in the eyes of the people who lived in the village. Jin had managed to learn some English from the missionaries who had settled in their area. While she was far from fluent, she was comfortable in her struggle to make herself understood when speaking it. The dialect of Mandarin that was spoken in their province was a unique one but could be understood by anyone who spoke Mandarin. She and Lan had left the village in mid-July on an adventure that JinJing's uncle had arranged. They had received their legal visas to fly to Vancouver and work as office workers or maids in Chinese owned businesses there. The Chinese presence was heavy in Vancouver and it accounted for much of the growth in the area. They had boarded the plane with fifteen other girls from various parts of China. They had a female guide for their trip who, just prior to landing in Canada, gathered their passports under the pretense that they would process through customs as a group. All of the young women who had made the flight willingly handed over their documents to the guide. They were told that representatives of the program that was sponsoring their work assignments would meet them. What they didn't know was that there was another purpose for their journey. All of them had been sold to Chinese businessmen in Canada as brides. Once they cleared customs, two Chinese women greeted them and welcomed them to Canada. These women were dressed in western clothing. They were loaded onto a bus and taken to an apartment house on the northeast side of the city. The bus was driven by a Sikh who was friendly and welcoming and probably the first one any of these girls had ever seen. The bus was modern and fitted with video screens. A western movie was playing in Mandarin. The whole charade was meant to distract these simple girls from noticing that no one had returned their documents to them. It wasn't until several days later after they had been taken around Vancouver to get their bearings and learn the city that it dawned on JinJing that no one had returned her passport. It happened by accident. They were on the wharf when an American ferry docked. All the people getting off the ferry seemed to be putting their documents away after they had cleared the customs booth. Seeing this reminded JinJing that she had not seen her passport since she had handed it over on the plane. Later as the bus was pulling into the apartment house parking lot to drop them all off, she raised her hand and asked when they would be getting their documents back. The guide smiled and told her she would eventually have her documents returned once she reached her final assignment. The companies needed them to help file for the proper paperwork for them to remain in the country for their assignments. That satisfied JinJing's curiosity for the moment. At the end of the second month, several of the girls had left the group ostensibly for their work assignments. The remaining ten were told that their assignments had been transferred to central and eastern Canada and that they would be traveling across Canada by bus. The thought of seeing this much of Canada was sold to them as an additional perk and that their return to their families would be coordinated once they had fulfilled their obligation to the sponsors. Most of the girls were thrilled. JinJing was skeptical for some reason about the new arrangement but after talking to Lan, decided to just wait and see what happened.

They left Vancouver on a smaller bus more suited to the lower number. The female guides were replaced with two men and one woman. That seemed like a large number to JinJing but again she decided to try to enjoy herself. They drove almost eight to nine hours a day. A different Sikh drove aided by an assistant driver. They conducted the trip like a tour pointing out interesting points along the way through the Canadian Rockies and then on to the vast prairie that composes most of the interior of southern Canada. After a stop in Regina, Saskatchewan, all of the girls noticed that one of the girls did not rejoin the tour. They were all told that her work assignment was located there.

They continued on until they got to Winnipeg, Manitoba, where two other girls got off the bus allegedly for their work assignments. By the time they reached Montreal there were only three girls remaining. As the bus pulled into Quebec City, JinJing and Lan were the last girls remaining on the bus. The bus pulled into the parking lot of the train station and the woman and the men got off the bus with the two girls. Waiting for them were two older Chinese men. The girls were told that these two men would be their sponsors and benefactors and that their journey was over. The two girls hugged and promised that they would keep in touch since they were both in the same city. They each climbed into their sponsors' cars.

Once JinJing and her sponsor arrived at the house where she would stay, they went inside and JinJing was introduced to the other people that lived there. The man was single but was joined by a Chinese maid and a young man who was his nephew. JinJing was shown to her room and told to unpack her things. She was told she would be familiarized with her new responsibilities at dinner that evening. Something in the back of JinJing's mind put her on edge. She opened the closet to put away her things and found a full wardrobe of western clothes and shoes. The things she had brought with her were more traditional. She didn't know who these clothes were for, but they were all in her size, even the shoes. She went over to put her modest things in the dresser and discovered once again a full array of women's underwear, some of it very revealing, and other garments such as gloves, sweaters, etc. all in her size. She put her things in beside the ones already there and took out her toilet bag to freshen up. The housekeeper knocked on her door as she was about to go into the bathroom. She opened the door and the older woman came in the room and smiled.

She went to the closet and pulled out a dress and shoes. She then went to the dresser and pulled out underclothes and a pair of stockings and laid them on the bed. She turned to JinJing and spoke in the same dialect that JinJing had grown up with. "Mr. Wu wishes you to dress in these clothes for dinner tonight. Also, please feel free to clean away the grime of the trip before you come down. You have about an hour before you hear the bell for dinner. If you need help just ring the bell on your nightstand and I will come back and help you. Please, if you don't mind my asking, how old are you?"

JinJing was stunned. "I am twenty-two. Why do I need to dress in these clothes? I have my own, thank you."

The maid smiled a friendly but firm smile. "These clothes are gifts to you from Mr. Wu. They are your clothes now and part of your new life here. Forgive me, I thought you would be a bit younger."

JinJing asked her what her name was. She was beginning to feel more uncomfortable. She thought it was very improper for Mr. Wu to take such a liberty with a young woman he didn't know.

"My name is Ti. I am Mr. Wu's housekeeper and I will be happy to help you make the transition to your new role. You are a very lucky girl. Mr. Wu is a very wealthy man and is very generous."

JinJing stopped her short. "What is my new role here, Ti?"

The older woman smiled. "My dear you have been afforded the opportunity and the luck to be Mr. Wu's wife. The arrangements were made with your uncle in China and everything was arranged for you to be transported here. It was not without a great expenditure and much planning. You will be married to Mr. Wu in a traditional Chinese ceremony that will also satisfy the Canadian authorities tomorrow afternoon."

JinJing looked at her in horror. "I don't even know Mr. Wu and I can assure you I don't have any intention of marrying anyone. I came here to work in an office, improve my English and to see this part of the world. I am part of a work program not a marriage program. I want to talk to someone in charge. I am not going to be a part of this."

The woman smiled the sinister smile again. "You are a Chinese girl. You have no one left in China. Your parents are both dead. Your uncle is the one who negotiated the marriage contract and has already been paid. He will not be welcoming you back. You, my dear, have no other choice. Your contract has been bought and paid for. We have control of your passport and documents. You belong to Mr. Wu now. I would be careful what you demand and what you say. You are older than your contract stated. In this world you are a 'faded rose'. Mr. Wu prefers women to be younger and certainly you should feel happy and appreciative that he has accepted you even though you're older than he expected. Now, get dressed in those clothes and come downstairs and act like you are supposed to act for a husband who has purchased you and wants to make you comfortable."

JinJing stood up in defiance but before she could speak, the older woman stepped forward and slapped her so hard she flew back against the closet door. "Don't overstep your bounds my faded little rose. You are our property now and the sooner you know your place, the sooner you will begin to enjoy the benefits. Be downstairs, clean and odor free in fifteen minutes and be sure to dry your hair and put on makeup. I would suggest the same makeup that you wore in your picture in the catalogue. It makes you look younger." She wheeled and left the room.

JinJing was so angry she couldn't cry. She stood up and looked around her. She was weighing her options but decided that there was nothing to be gained by making her stand now. She showered, dried her hair and put on the clothes. She was going to leave off the stockings but decided that it was better to have them on than to appear in bare legs. She looked for her leggings in her suitcase but found they had been removed. She finished by putting on the dress and her makeup. She looked around the room. She thought she could be in a worse prison cell and she wasn't married to the man yet. Perhaps she could reason with him when she was alone with him.

She went downstairs and entered the dining room. The older man and the young nephew were already seated. Mr. Wu motioned without looking at her to the chair closest to his. She sat down and dinner was served. It was some of the most delicious food from her own region she had ever tasted. It looked beautiful, it tasted wonderful, and was served in traditional style. There was very little conversation at the dinner table. Afterward, Mr. Wu motioned for JinJing to follow him into the living room. The nephew disappeared somewhere else in the house. They sat down and Ti brought in sweet rice cakes and tea with a bowl of fresh fruit. She pulled the doors closed behind her and for the first time

JinJing was alone with the man that she was supposed to marry the next day.

He waited until she was settled in the chair across from his. He spoke in a low and measured tone in Mandarin. She could understand every word. "Thank you for changing into the clothes I purchased for you. I understand from Ti that you did not know the conditions under which you were brought here. I am sorry she slapped you and I hope it won't happen again. I do not like bruises or other imperfections. I paid a great deal for you and your travel expenses. That total comes to over $80,000. That is not a great investment for me but one I take seriously. The marriage contract between your uncle and me was drawn up legally in China. Of course, it has no bearing in this part of the world but is fully enforceable there. I could, because of the discrepancy in your age, force him to give the money back. I doubt he would want to do that so I would have to pay for extraordinary means to collect it. That would put what little family you have left back in China in grave danger. I am assuming that the other condition that I requested, that you be a virgin is still the truth. I can overlook the age lie; I could not overlook the fact that you are no longer a virgin."

JinJing looked at him calmly. "I am still a virgin but I don't think that is the point. Why would you want to marry someone you don't know and who does not love you?"

He smiled. "I can see you have had more exposure to the west that I thought. In our culture, particularly for a traditional man such as myself, love comes secondary to more formal arrangements. I don't wish you to be unhappy and I hope you will adjust to the obvious age difference. But, once we are married, I will expect the full range of obedience and service that a wife should perform for a man of my wealth, age, and distinction. Success and money are always greater bonuses than the frivolous nature of young men these days. My nephew is a good example of that. I could have easily purchased you to be his wife, but he is a fool and you would soon tire of his nonsense. I know, I have. I hope you will learn to care for me for the qualities I possess. I am gentle to a fault. I am wealthy beyond your wildest dreams. I own one of the largest trucking and transport companies in Canada. You will never have a day that you will want for anything. The only things I ask in return are respect, loyalty, and on a few occasions, the more physical aspect of a wifely visit. You will have your own room and not the one you are in now. That is a guest room for the sake of appearances. Your quarters will be down the hall adjoining mine. I will expect fidelity until I pass on to my ancestors. That means your sexual attention will be directed only at me. You will be the chief heir of all of this along with my nephew. I won't even expect you to produce an heir for me. I don't even know if I am still capable of getting a woman pregnant but I am certainly eager to find out. But that is not a requirement for you to fulfill your part of the contract."

JinJing thought before she spoke. "First, I appreciate your kindness and your obvious generosity. I have enjoyed my trip until an hour ago. What are my options if I decide that I absolutely cannot marry you?"

The man took a sterner tone. "My dear, I am afraid you have no options. I own your contract and I have your travel documents. You were admitted to this country on a visitor's visa not a work visa. You will be illegal in a month if you don't marry a citizen here. I do have an option. I can sell your contract and documents to others who may be less kind than myself. I am a businessman. I will want to recoup some of my investment so that would limit my possibilities for potential purchasers. I am sure there are people who would find a way to capitalize on your attractiveness and your age. Even though you are a bit older than I prefer, you would still be very attractive to some of the less seemly organizations that are operational here and in the United States."

JinJing took a bit more defiant tone. "I don't have permission to go into the United States. That would be illegal. I am not sure that being treated like a 'slave' is legal in Canada either. I could go to the authorities and tell them that I was brought here under false pretenses and that I am being traded like a piece of meat. Is that what you want me to do?"

He waited before he spoke. "I am sorry that this conversation has taken such a sour tone. Out of respect for you I will give you three days to think it over. I will postpone the wedding for that long. After that, we shall see. You need to know that I do not respond kindly to threats. You don't even speak the language here. I speak Mandarin, French and English fluently. You speak an archaic dialect of Mandarin and from what I can gather, less than enough English to get by. You would have a challenge just to make yourself understood by the authorities. I want you to take the extra time that I am so graciously giving you to consider your true position and come to the conclusion that I have a significant control over your life now. That can either lead to a comfortable life with few restrictions or a very uncomfortable life at the hands of others. As you yourself have said, there is no love that has developed as yet between us. I hope that happens but if it does not, I am the one that will resolve that issue not you. You belong to me." He stood up, bowed slightly and left the room.

JinJing sat there in silence. Ti came into the room and cleared the dishes but didn't say a word. The nephew snuck back into the room like a weasel. He sat across from her sneering at her with a lustful glare that made her feel naked before him. He spoke in halting Mandarin. "You shouldn't piss Uncle off. He is a very powerful man. He owns you." He licked his lips after his last statement.

JinJing rose from her chair and left the room. She went upstairs to the room she had been given. She closed the door and changed into the nightclothes she had brought from China. she put the fancier negligee that Ti had laid out for her back in the drawer. As she lay down, she heard the lock turn in her door. She didn't need to get up to know that she had been locked in her room. It was a fitting end to a day when you learned you were a slave and groomed to be a whore all at once. It took her an hour to get close to sleep and even then, she wasn't deeply asleep. She was awake when she heard all the other doors on the hallway close. She was just dozing off when she realized that the whole house had retired for the night. At least she thought that the whole house had retired.

She had been asleep about an hour when she woke up to find someone on top of her pulling her nightgown up. She struggled but she was held fast to the bed. She couldn't believe that this nightmare of a day was continuing. She fought as hard as she could but soon her legs were pried apart and her panties were literally ripped from her hips. She pushed and turned and was still held fast. She grimaced with pain as she felt him plunge forcefully inside her. Her virginity was no match for his strength and she felt her innocence give way to the same brute force that had been carried out in such acts since the dawn of man to defile and debase women. She kept struggling until she was hit so hard with a fist that it knocked her unconscious. Then it was over almost as fast as it had begun. She wasn't even awake for the final act of disgrace as he distributed his semen all over her belly and breasts. He got up and left just like the animal that had crept into the room moments before. He thought to himself. "Now you won't be accepted. You have broken the final rule."

She woke up a short time later. She hurt all over. She climbed out of bed and walked straight to the shower. She took off her torn nightgown and threw it in the corner. She stood under the hot water and cleaned the blood and his defiance off of her as best she could. She had suffered the ultimate defilement. She was toweling her hair when she walked back near the bed. She turned on the light to pull out a T-shirt to sleep in and retrieve another pair of panties when she saw the blood on the sheets that had now soaked into the mattress pad. There was no way she could hide the fact that this had happened. She changed and left the bed as it was. She tried to sleep sitting up in the easy chair by the closet. She was so exhausted from her struggle that she fell asleep. That is how she was found when Ti unlocked the door and came in.

Ti saw the sheets, the torn underwear and the torn nightgown in the corner. She knew immediately what had happened. She let JinJing sleep. She changed the bed as quietly as she could. The mattress pad was replaced and the bed was made up with new sheets. She took the torn underwear and nightgown along with the mattress pad and left the room. She locked the door once again. She went downstairs to her rooms in the basement and immediately treated the mattress pad with bleach and hydrogen peroxide and put them in the washing machine. She folded the torn clothing neatly and placed them in a plastic bag. The sheets she folded and put in another plastic bag. She then went upstairs and started breakfast. She was relieved that Mr. Wu had decided to postpone the wedding. There were other things he would finally have to confront now. She had no doubt that his worthless nephew was to blame. She had no doubt that Mr. Wu would take the necessary steps to deal with him. She also had no doubt that there would be no wedding now.

JinJing woke up and looked around. The bed was made, her torn clothes were gone and the sheets were missing. She pulled the new sheets back and found that the mattress pad had been replaced as well. There was only one lasting piece of evidence that remained of her rape. It dwelled inside her and could never be repaired. She brushed her hair, and took stock of the rest of her body. She had bruises on the insides of both thighs and on her pudendum. She still felt a slight trickle of blood so she probably was more injured inside than just a torn hymen. She surprised herself that she didn't feel more shame. She knew what had happened had been discovered. But, for now, she needed to keep focused on what was next. She got dressed in her original clothes and went downstairs.

Mr. Wu was sitting in the dining room alone. He motioned for her to take a seat near him at the table. Ti came in and delivered her breakfast and freshened Mr. Wu's tea. He returned to reading his paper quietly. When JinJing was done he seemed to sense she was finished and put the paper down and removed his glasses and looked straight at her. He spoke. "Ti has told me of an unfortunate incident that occurred last night."

JinJing broke into tears and yelled at him in Mandarin. "It was more than an unfortunate incident. You raped me. You stole the one thing that I could not protect. You took my innocence and my dignity in the most violent of ways. You raped me. I thought you were more honorable than that."

Ti came in from the kitchen area and slapped JinJing across the face. "Mr. Wu did no such thing. Keep quiet, you stupid girl. He didn't have to rape you. He had nothing to gain by raping you." Mr. Wu touched JinJing on the shoulder. She stopped crying but moved to the other side of the table. He spoke to JinJing and Ti. "There has been enough violence in this house. There has been more violence since you arrived than there has ever been in this house. I did not rape you JinJing. It was not me."

JinJing gathered herself together. "Then who was it? I wouldn't even have been here but for some archaic remnant of our culture that allows old men to 'buy' young women and hold them against their will. I trusted that you would not violate me. Now, I am violated and spoiled."

Mr. Wu sat quietly and let her regain her composure. He motioned for her to sit back down. JinJing did as he asked. She was already exhausted from the depression that constitutes the first phase of posttraumatic shock. Mr. Wu turned to Ti. "Would you ask the others to come in?" Ti nodded and opened the kitchen door and spoke in English to the people in the next room. Two large Chinese men entered with the nephew held up between them. He had been beaten severely and was bleeding from his ears, nose and mouth.

Mr. Wu spoke. "There is no doubt that this is the 'thing' that betrayed my trust and that violated your body in the most violent way. He will never be able to do that again. He is being cast out of my household and out of our community. He is no longer my heir and is no longer a part of any of my life because of the crime he committed against you. As I believe in the old traditions of our culture, I also believe in our older ideas of justice. I will not bother the Canadian legal system with this little monster. He will receive his punishment as he deserves. JinJing, you are too young to remember the type of justice I speak about. That is a good thing because I don't believe you need any further bad dreams at my hands. Take this 'thing' out of here and do as I asked you to do." The men turned and left the room.

JinJing didn't quite grasp what had just happened. "I don't understand. Why would he do such a thing?"

Mr. Wu answered her. "The answer is greed. He was unhappy when I first announced my plans to have a wife. He was my sole heir. He didn't want to share at all. He was listening last night when he heard me describe the conditions of the contract. He felt that if you were no longer a virgin, it would end the situation. It had everything to do with money and greed. I'm so sorry that happened to you. You were right. I am ultimately to blame for what happened to you and what will happen to him. That is why I am going to have to distance myself from this whole thing. I will decide what to do with you by the end of the day. Please go to your room and wait. I need to evaluate every option I have."

JinJing got up and turned to him as she was about to leave the room. "You could give me my papers and just let me go. I wouldn't say anything."

He looked at her speculatively. "I almost believe that is the case. I will give that some thought."

She went back upstairs and sat in the chair in her room. She was still so tired. She crawled up on the bed and soon was fast asleep. She slept until around 4:00 pm. Ti came in and asked if she would like some tea in the living room. She was tired of being in the room where her virginity was taken from her so she followed Ti back downstairs. She sat looking out into the garden as tea was set next to her. She picked up the mug and felt its warmth. Behind her Mr. Wu came into the room. She turned to him and began to get up out of her seat and he motioned for her to stay seated. He looked at her gently and spoke. "JinJing, I have thought about what I must do. I have trusted younger ways too much and relied on older ways that no longer serve appropriately. I am meant to be alone with no one but Ti to care for my needs. I am at peace with that." JinJing wasn't sure but she was finding it hard to focus on him. He continued. "For that reason, I have sold your contract to another business associate that assures me he will take your current situation into account. I have trusted him before and I have no reason not to trust him now. His people will be here shortly to pick you up."

JinJing would have liked to fire back a response but what ever had been put in the tea had taken hold. All she could do was look up at him and blink. He reached down and took the cup from her before it fell to the floor. He patted her on the cheek. "I'm sorry. This is the way it has to be." He turned and nodded at Ti who opened the door for the men to come in. They were not Chinese but Canadians. They picked up JinJing as if she were as light as a feather. Ti handed them an envelope with her passport and other documents in it. They nodded at Mr. Wu and Ti and took JinJing out the back door to a waiting van. As she was loaded into the van, she was certain that she saw the body of the nephew near the back of the garden. One of the men she had seen holding him earlier was digging a new flowerbed and it was going to be a deep one. She noticed the bright red stain on the nephew's chinos that spread from just at the beltline down the insides of both legs of his pants. The zipper was gaping open but all she thought she could see was a dark deep red and purple void where something else, something sinister to her, used to be. She passed out with that as the last memory she would have of her short engagement to Mr. Wu.

CHAPTER 7

Safety is always relative to the situation at hand.

In the jet, Aggie looked up from the report on the Canadian operation. "Slade, how far have you gotten in this report?"

Slade didn't look up. "I'm nearly finished. It has got some interesting twists to it, doesn't it?"

Aggie continued. "I'm wondering if we are being too quick to move SiSi back to Tampa. She is fluent in both Mandarin and Spanish. The nationalities of the survivors seem like an odd mix for traffickers. What do you think about leaving SiSi in Maine for the time being?"

Slade finished reading the report. "They are reporting they believe that victims have come through both Vancouver and Halifax. That is the first time we have seen that kind of combination in the same trafficking network. Let me see if I can catch SiSi before she gets on the plane." He dialed her number.

It rang once. "Yes Sir."

Slade laughed. "SiSi, where are you in your journey home?"

"Brad is driving me to Bangor so I can catch a plane home. We are halfway there."

Slade thought a moment then spoke. "Aggie and I have just read the latest report from Brad about the information shared at the conference. Have you had a chance to look at it?"

SiSi responded. "Yes. I am going through it for the third time marking sections I would like to code into the intelligence file. I thought it was a unique situation. I can't remember Asians being trafficked right alongside Hispanics before. It makes sense because of the ports. Both are high volume for containerized freight and difficult to monitor totally. Also, some women were certain they entered legally with papers that were never found. It is not unusual that human smugglers would take their papers as collateral but traffickers are sure to keep them for leverage and control."

Slade hadn't made the connection with the ports. He responded. "How is your Mandarin these days?" SiSi answered him in the language also referred to as Standard Chinese. "Sounds like it is totally up-to-speed."

SiSi answered. "You never forget the language you were raised with. Before you ask, my Spanish is doing very well also."

Slade didn't hesitate. "You have your communication pack with you. If you need anything else, we will fly it up to you from Tampa when we arrive and get settled tomorrow. I think Claymore can hold the fort until you return, don't you?"

SiSi began to smile at the thought that she could get off the phone and tell Brad to turn around and head back to the lake house. "Claymore is very good and has been able to keep things moving. I may need my larger laptop. We also may have an excellent chance to test out the new drones. You might want to give that some thought. We will return and wait for your instructions."

Slade finished the call. "That is great. I'm sure you are not too unhappy about getting to spend some additional time with Brad and his family. I will be in touch tomorrow morning unless something breaks loose tonight. Good night to both of you."

SiSi turned to Brad. "I can't believe that every one of the team knows about us. I thought we were being so careful."

Brad reached over and grabbed her hand. "I don't care who knows about us. I am tired of trying to act neutral around everyone outside the house. I am taking it you want me to turn around."

"Yes, yes, crap. I'm sorry I forgot to tell you." She squeezed his hand.

Brad laughed. "SiSi, did you just say the word 'crap'? He kept laughing as he pulled over to turn the car around. SiSi tried to ignore him but she couldn't any longer. She was very glad that everyone knew. She obviously wasn't good at hiding things from her teammates.

Thirty minutes after takeoff from Houston, Serena Moore had leaned over and removed the mask they had placed on Kip Patterson in order to clear customs. It gave her the creeps looking over at a silicone version of her dead husband, but the mask had worked perfectly. The inspecting Customs agent didn't even get close enough to really get a good look. He stood in the aisle and compared the picture on the passport to what appeared to be the dying man on the gurney. That was as close as he wanted to get. That is the funny thing about disease and death. Most of us want to stay as far away as possible until we have to really confront it, then, we want it over quickly. Serena was convinced that they had passed the last potentially dangerous roadblock in their mission. Once the fake ambulance had transferred them to another plane, they had been airborne in no time They had two refueling stops and then they would be in Liberty. She would call her contact, a half hour before their final refueling. Members of the organization known as Patriot Green were standing by to assist the refueling in Demopolis, Alabama, and at Mountain Empire near Marion, Virginia. She wanted the group's representative to meet them at the airport near Liberty, New York, as planned with the money. She and the other two would then head their separate ways. She and Forrest had agreed to meet in Belize. She had developed what she called a 'fondness' for Forrest during the time they had worked together. For this, he had been a reluctant participant. She trusted that Forrest would resolve the issue of the extra victim in a way that would give them enough time to start a new life. She didn't know Forrest that well, but what she did know, she liked. She had always considered herself a good judge of character. But that same judgment told her that their employers were rich, entitled and crazy sons-of-bitches that were way over the line legally in their willingness to do anything to help the PAC, the party and the current resident of the White House. Their representative had first approached her at a political rally. They knew way too much about her dire financial situation. One of their banks even held the mortgage to her house. After she had been laid off by Kenderson Park, she had been unable to find a permanent job. She couldn't figure out how every interview she went on went bust. She was qualified for the jobs. She was confident she had interviewed well but, somehow, she never got a call back. With no income and the medical bills, she and her husband soon burned through their savings. Then her husband was dead in three months. When this 'job' was finished, she was promised she could walk away from the mortgage and with extra money. It would be enough to give her a new start with Forrest and it would be a great start. Lucy and Aaron had joined because of Lucy's undying loyalty to her. Lucy and Aaron had agreed that they would never see Serena again. Continued contact would get them caught. They didn't know her plans about Forrest. In truth, she hadn't even discussed it with Forrest but she was sure she was still attractive enough to lure him into a longer relationship. She had never had much trouble getting men to do anything for her. She expected no trouble this time.

Kip Patterson was resting comfortably in a drug-induced state of cooperation. He was unharmed and as far as Serena was concerned, he would stay that way. Unbeknownst to Lucy and Aaron, she had been contacted by the FBI. The agent who had called her was Peter Crescent and he had explained that the plot had been uncovered and that the FBI was interested in Patriot Green. Crescent had promised her and her friends immunity from prosecution and that the FBI would intervene before anything happened to Dr. Patterson. She had to promise not to tell Lucy and Aaron. Since Lucy had volunteered to be the one to actually spray and kidnap the two, she thought of herself as just 'escorting' this guy back to the United States. Agent Crescent would help sell that story. Aaron and Lucy had been the real kidnappers. She didn't know where or how Aaron found the other man that helped them drive the victims to Chihuahua. She didn't need to. Her job was to make sure this guy got back to the U.S. in one piece. Her thoughts were interrupted when the man on the gurney next to her began to murmur and stir.

Kip Patterson's eyes opened wide and he looked around. "What has happened? Where am I?"

Serena relied on her most soothing voice. "Relax, you passed out just outside the restaurant after dinner with your friend. You are on your way back to the United States to be thoroughly examined. Your friends in Mexico arranged for the airlift. You have been given a sedative to help you sleep until we get to New York."

Patterson looked confused. "I feel woozy. Where are we going?"

Serena had to think quickly. She didn't want him to act out. "We are going to a small clinic that your ex-wife arranged for in New York. They think it might be something neurological. We will be stopping twice to refuel, once in about an hour then again about an hour after that. Would you like some water?"

The mention of his ex-wife seemed to calm Patterson a bit. "Yes, please."

Serena poured him some water. He took a couple of sips then rested his head back on the pillow. She reached down and administered just a touch more medication into his line. He was back asleep in moments. They flew on. The plane landed in Alabama and refueled without a hitch and was back airborne within twenty minutes. No one had even cracked the door of the plane. When they were within thirty minutes of touchdown for the last refueling stop, Serena dialed the number for her contact. He answered immediately. "How is our package? All tidy and uninjured, I hope. What did you do with the other one? I am not happy about that type of intrusion or how you handled it. He should not have been left in Mexico."

Serena answered with confidence. "Our man is resting peacefully and we should be landing in Virginia in about fifteen minutes. My associate has taken the other one in the opposite direction from us. There is no way this will be linked to you or your organization as promised. It was an unfortunate turn of events but it has been dealt with. I would like to finalize the arrangements. Once we land in New York, he will be your responsibility. After that, I don't ever want to hear from any of you again. You will certainly not hear from us. Is that agreeable?"

The man was not used to being dictated to by a woman but he bit his tongue and responded courteously. "That is acceptable. We have no wish to continue with you or your little demimonde. We will see you in Liberty." He hung up.

The plane banked hard and began its descent in five minutes toward Mountain Empire Airport in Marion, Virginia. It landed and taxied toward a remote area near the hangers. As the plane came to a stop, a van pulled up next to the plane where the fuel truck should be. A man got out and approached the pilot side of the plane. The co-pilot emerged from the front cabin and opened the door of the plane. A man stepped into the cabin. The man looked straight at Serena as the other two looked on. He pointed at Serena as he pulled his badge. "I am Agent Peter Crescent with the FBI. You, join me outside now. The rest of you stay seated." He turned and went back out. Serena followed with a frantic look.

"Agent Crescent, what is going on?" He led her away from the other men in the van and the airplane.

Crescent looked at her sternly. "Serena, this is the way it has to be. Somehow the PAC got wind of the plan. You need to get out of here now. These guys work for me so there is no way you will be linked to this. Here are the keys to that blue sedan parked by the fence. There is a briefcase with several thousand dollars in it. That should be enough to get you away from this part of the country. I want you to drive to this address in Atlanta. It is one of our safe houses. Here is my number. Call me tomorrow for further information but you need to disappear now."

She looked at him with confusion. "What about Lucy and Aaron?"

He didn't skip a beat. "They will remain to help us carry on the charade a bit longer but I didn't want you to get that close. This investigation is moving quickly. They will be fine. Someone is going to have to carry this off as if it went as planned. You have done nothing other than keep him safe, but you are the one we need to protect right now. You are the only one that had direct contact with the PAC. We will need you later for that. Now you need to go."

Serena looked at him carefully but decided she didn't have much choice. She saw one of the men carrying her bag to the sedan. "I don't even know where I am or how to get to Atlanta."

Crescent smiled. "The GPS in the car is already programmed. The house is in East Atlanta. It will take you just a little over six hours to get there. You will be fine but you need to leave now."

She looked back at the plane just as the van pulled away. The pilots were out of the plane but she didn't see Lucy or Aaron. She saw a plain sedan pull up next to the plane. It was what she imagined an FBI car would look like. She turned and walked briskly toward the sedan she was to use. She got in, started the engine and left the small airport. Crescent turned and walked back toward the plane.

As he approached the car, two men got out and walked toward the plane as Crescent got on his phone. He dialed the number and spoke just one sentence. "All good here." He hung up and watched as Lucy and Aaron were led from the plane, blindfolded with their hands securely fastened behind their backs with flex cuffs. Aaron was put in the front seat and Lucy right behind him in the back. As the van he had arrived in pulled away, he stepped inside the plane and saw that the gurney had been removed and that the seats had been readjusted. The sedan with Lucy and Aaron pulled away. Crescent left the plane and got in an SUV that pulled up. He looked at his driver. "She bought the whole story. Let's go meet the sedan." He bent down and took the phone he had with him and pulled out the battery and reloadable card. It was a 'burner' and is standard issue for the underworld. He destroyed the card and once they were on the outskirts of the airport, had the driver pull over where he dumped the phone in a sewer.

The sedan with Lucy and Aaron headed west toward Hungry Mother State Park up into the mountains. It turned onto a gravel and dirt road that led along one of the narrow service roads and continued on until it came to a sharp curve in the road with a drop off on the right. There were two other men waiting next to another car that was poised on the cusp of the drop off. The two that were waiting reached in and pulled Aaron out of the sedan. He was dead from an injection that brought on a heart attack. The two took him to the car and placed him in driver's seat. They maneuvered his hands around the steering wheel. The men quickly lifted the trunk lid placed a gas can in the trunk. Crescent showed up and watched as they closed the lid and pushed the car over the drop off. It slid almost forty feet down the side of the embankment that had been built up to support the road and then dropped off another fifty feet landing nose down of a rocky plateau next to a swollen stream that looked more like a river with the extra water.

A man emerged from the far side of the stream. The car had landed almost exactly where he had planned it. He walked all the way around the car to make sure that there was enough of a margin that there would be no damage to the surrounding forest. He raked back some leaf litter until he was satisfied that he had a good margin then waved to the men up top. They got back in their vehicles and headed for their next meeting place. The man below opened the trunk and carefully spread the gasoline where he needed it throughout the front passenger compartment to make it difficult to identify the occupants. He then took a flint and steel fire starter out of his pocket and went to the end of one of the gasoline trails that extended from the rear of the car. He bent down and lit the trail. He immediately crossed back across the water using part of the inflatable boom he had set up to contain any fuel spill should his calculations have been wrong. They weren't. He got to the other side as the car began to burn. There was no explosion just a slow burn. That's what happened when you just used the right amount of fuel and had an empty gas tank. He just needed enough of a burn to cover any trace. The story would hold up. The big guy had a heart attack and drove off the edge. The woman died on impact and the small amount of fuel in the tank burned with a spark created by impact. He pulled the boom to his side of the river and deflated it and folded it. He put it in his backpack, looked one last time at the burning car and disappeared into the forest. He had calculated that it would take about ten minutes before the ranger in the tower to the north spotted the plume of smoke and another thirty before the forestry fire service would arrive. He knew the whole routine. He was an ex-ranger himself. He disappeared back into the world he knew so well.

The fire service arrived just as he had planned. The fire was almost out and posted no problem to the surrounding trees. The firefighters quickly deployed their own boom but there was no need. They would remove any contaminated soil or rocks after the bodies had been removed and the car lifted on a crane to the road above. He watched through his binoculars and imagined the conversation between the sector chief and the rescue team. He had earned his money and had helped the cause. These two fucks were just two-bit nothings. The story wouldn't even make the front page of the local rags.

The sedan with those who had staged the accident met with Crescent and his driver at a house just outside of Atkins, Virginia. Two of them were told they would be driven to Dulles International just outside of Washington and leave for Mexico as soon as possible. The other two were instructed to continue on with the sedan to Atlanta. At the end of both journeys were loose ends that needed to be dealt with. After the four men left, he reached in his pocket and pulled out the badge he had used with Serena Moore. It didn't even look real. He had purchased it at a flea market. His real name was Phillip Tandor, the son of Thomas Tandor, the head of multi-national corporate holding and founder of a conservative PAC. He looked at the remaining people in the group and smiled. "Patterson will soon be on his way to his final stop."

Lucy Frost smiled back.

Serena Moore arrived in Atlanta right on time. It took her longer to get to east Atlanta because of a traffic backup behind an accident. The address was in a neighborhood that looked like it was in the process of gentrification but hadn't quite got there yet. Serena hated Atlanta. She didn't go in the house once she found it. She looked in the bag and found it contained about $25,000 in different denominations. She pulled out five hundred and put it in her purse. She decided she was starving. She had spotted a place she thought would be a good place to eat. She hadn't had a good American burger in three weeks. She was starving since they had been forced to shorten their timeframe. She parked across the street from the bar she had seen and walked across and entered. She was surprised at how crowded it was. There was one seat left at the bar and she pulled out a stool.

The woman tending the bar handed out three cans of beer and approached her placing a cardboard coaster down on the bar. "Hey there. My name is Tess. What can I get for you?"

Serena answered immediately. "What is your signature burger?"

Tess gave a small frown. "Here is a menu. How about I start you out with a water while you decide what you want to eat."

Serena looked at the menu. "I would like the Deluxe Burger with a glass of Chardonnay please. You can hold the fries."

Tess smiled, turned and drew a pint of a Belgian Wheat beer and put it in front of Serena. "Trust me, you don't want the Chardonnay or any other wine we serve here. This will work great with your burger and the fries will be worth it. She then set down two shot glasses in front of Serena and poured a shot of tequila for both of them. "This will go down well. How was your trip to Mexico?"

Serena looked startled and almost spat the words out. "How do you know I have been in Mexico?"

"Whoa, calm down, your jewelry gave you away. I spent a year there working at a west coast resort owned by the Japanese. That type of turquoise and silver only comes from that area. It's not your normal 'squash blossom' stuff you get at the airports or market stalls. Now cheers, we need to take the edge off you."

Serena relaxed as she lifted her glass. "You are very observant. What did you say your name was?"

"My name is Tess. I have always been good at paying attention and noticing things. It comes in handy in this line of work. Want another?"

Serena nodded. They downed another shot. For the first time in a long time Serena felt safe.

CHAPTER 8

There is always a different way of looking at things.

The cabin Forrest had referred to was on a bluff just above a cove on the east side of the island. It was completely hidden from the air as was the path that led from the main building on the north side of the island. Hank's first task anywhere unfamiliar was to quickly assess the value of the décor and share it with his host, most times politely, but not always. He also went through every cupboard and closet to look for anything that might be harmful. His trust wasn't totally cemented with Forrest. But the cabin was well appointed, comfortable and had a view. It also had a refrigerator stuffed with fresh fruit, beautiful vegetables and two large shark steaks. There was a plate of freshly made tortillas on the table wrapped in a warm cloth. It was the first time he noticed that he was famished.

Forrest came up from the beach after taking a look around. He had posted several of his Seri friends along the trails that connected the beach and the meeting house and Quonset hut to the cabin. He didn't want to be surprised when whoever was coming actually got there. The local police didn't venture out here. They were too wary of the Seri. If someone were coming it would be someone else and if they were white, they would stand out. The moment he walked into the cabin Hank was on him.

"When do we eat or are you going to starve me to death rather than feed me to the sharks?"

Forrest laughed. "I'm not sure any self-respecting shark would feed on you but I have already started the grill for the shark steaks so you will soon have an opportunity to reverse the tables. There should be some rice and squash casserole that the local women make in the fridge. It will go nicely with the fish but we need to put it in the oven. Do you think you can make it for thirty more minutes? In the meantime, there are some toasted pumpkin seeds in the canister and I will get you a beer and a shot of tequila."

Hank shrugged his shoulders. "I guess I can wait. Beer bloats me and I get drunk too easily on tequila. Don't you have some vodka in this joint? God, I would kill for a vodka with cranberry juice."

Forrest opened the freezer compartment and handed Hank a bottle of vodka he had stored there and a glass. He pulled out two limes from a basket and cut them. "Here, I have no cranberry juice but you can make yourself a fake gimlet. There is agave syrup on the table."

"Finally, I find a remnant of civilization in this hacienda. Thank you. I shall be on the porch. Let me know when dinner is ready."

Forrest was quick to reply. "Listen Hank, I am not your servant and this is not a guest house. You can pour yourself a drink and get your ass over here and put this casserole in when the oven is heated. You can then set the table while I make a salad." He pulled out the shark steaks, cut another lime and squirted the juice over them. He then added salt and pepper and several dashes of hot sauce and took the steaks out to the grill. He returned with a handful of cherry tomatoes that he had picked from the pot on the porch. He chopped some cilantro and onion and squeezed the other half of the lime onto them with some olive oil and put the bowl in the refrigerator to cool while he pulled a beer out and popped the cap. He looked at Hank standing staring at him from across the room, his arms defiantly folded across his chest. He was about to launch one of his trademark insults but what cut short by Forrest. "Hank, if I were you, I wouldn't say a word." Hank thought for a moment and decided that was good advice. He poured himself a drink and checked the oven.

Dinner was ready right on time and they sat across from each other. There was no question Hank liked his meal. He inhaled his shark steak and over half of the casserole. He poured himself a second drink and finished off a bottle of water. Forrest sat quietly watching him. He then pushed the piece of his shark steak still on his plate across to Hank. Hank gladly accepted it.

Hank finished it, wiped his mouth and spoke. "That was delicious. Thank you so much for not killing me and fixing me dinner."

Forrest laughed out loud. "You are one strange fellow, Hank. Since I didn't kill you can I know what your last name is?"

Hank nodded. "Yes, you can, but only because you didn't kill me. My name is Harold Nathan Kessler. I was born and raised in the Ybor City section of Tampa and founded my business nearby in the Channel District there. I sold it to my partners four years ago. I sold the building at the same time to Smithson Evermore. As part of that deal, I can use in any of their worldwide properties for the rest of my life. They had one in Mexico and I started coming to Puerto Vallarta to relax at the invitation of my friend Dr. Kendrick Patterson who I hope your friends haven't killed. If they have, I shall have my friends kill you, but thank you for dinner."

Forrest nodded. "You're welcome and I wouldn't call them my friends. They were more like associates although I would guess that one of them would like more than that. She thinks I will be joining her later. I will not be and if those idiots do hurt your friend, your friends will have catch up to me, because I will be hunting the ones that took you both. That is what I did for a living before I was laid off. I hunted people down and brought them home safely. But we have a more pressing problem. There are people on the way here for bad purposes. We need to take care of that first."

Hank looked confused. "That sounds like the company I sold my building to, Smithson Evermore. They do the same kind of work. So, you think your associates are coming here to kill me so I won't be a witness to Kip's kidnapping?"

Forrest replied. "I don't think the ones that took you could put that together. But the people they work for could. They would need to clean up loose ends. What could you say about what happened? Could you identify any of them other than me?"

"I could identify the dark-haired bitch that sprayed the Good Night Hank cloud of gas. Is that why they want to kill me?"

Forrest looked square at Hank. "They aren't coming for just you. I'm the one that can cause a bigger problem. They are coming to kill both of us and I don't want you to become collateral damage. Now, help me with the dishes and tell me who you keep talking about in your sleep."

Hank got up but did not answer. He began to wash the dishes but remained silent. Forrest let it go for the time being. He left Hank in the kitchen and walked back up the trail. He found one of his friends watching the boat landing near the main building. "Any sign of any visitors?" The man smiled and shook his head. Forrest continued up the trail to the main building. He checked to make sure the lock was on the hanger where his helicopter was stored. He ran into a second watchman. The watchmen would alert him if anyone came near the island or flew over it.

Forrest returned to the cabin. Hank was sitting on the porch. He looked up and spoke in a quiet voice. "The name belonged to my partner for almost thirty-five years. We traveled the world together. He was a successful businessman but was kind and supportive to me as I built my business. He has been dead for over fifteen years now. I still miss him. When I called out his name, I was probably dreaming of better times. I really do appreciate that you are trying to keep me safe. I'm just confused about how you got involved in all of this."

Forrest smiled. "You are no more confused about it than I am. I was supposed to fly your friend back to the states. That was it. I wasn't there in Puerto Vallarta. My plane that we were supposed to use is still sitting in Chihuahua. Once we found out about your connection to Smithson Evermore the whole procedure had to change. My guess is that started a chain reaction. If she was smart, the woman that was running the show didn't mention your connection to the people who hired her. In reality, I would bet that we are all expendable. I doubt very seriously if they are still alive. If they are, it is just a matter of time."

Hank thought a moment. "Who told you about my connection to Slade Smithson?"

Forrest laughed. "You did. You threatened us through the door. That is why you got sprayed. And for the record, I didn't spray you. The woman who kidnapped you did but I would have. I was afraid you were going to make it worse. Are you aware you have a tiny anger management issue?"

"What the hell is that supposed to mean? I had been kidnapped and I want to remind you, I was under the influence of drugs. I cannot be held accountable for my actions at the time. Speaking of them, when do you want me to contact my friends at Smithson?"

Forrest thought a moment. "If half of what I know about them is true, we will only need to turn your phone on and they will come. We have friends watching tonight but I don't want them to come in harm's way. I suggest that we turn your phone on for five minutes and then turn it off. That will get Smithson headed this way."

Hank looked perplexed again. "I wouldn't let them put any tracking device on me. I do have my right to privacy and I don't need my comings and goings to be monitored."

Forrest answered quickly. "The moment you dial that number, there is a better than even chance that the bad guys will be monitoring the call and I bet they are closer than the Smithson people. Did Smithson Evermore supply you with your phone?"

Hank nodded. "Yes, but I was adamant about the tracking device. They gave me both the phones."

Forrest laughed. "Slade Smithson would not take on the responsibility of offering you access to his home without having that girl genius of his install passive tracking on your phones and you were dumb to not let them inject you with a tracking pellet. Which phone was the one tied to the States?"

Hank pulled the phone out of his left pocket and handed it over. Forrest pushed the power button and as soon as the screen lit up, looked down at his watch. In five minutes, he turned the phone off and handed it back to Hank. "Give me the phone you use most of the time in Mexico."

Hank pulled the phone out of his right pocket and handed it to Forrest. Forrest put it in his pocket. "I have to go out for a bit. I want you to stay here in the cabin. There are books on the shelf. I will be back in an hour." With that he left just as the sun was setting over the mountain behind the cabin.

Hank called after him. "Can you get me a pack of cigarettes? I dying for a smoke."

L was on the phone to all parties within five minutes of seeing Hank's phone activate. She passed on the information that it had activated for five minutes on an island off the west coast of Mexico. Aggie was awake on the plane and acknowledged the reception and made sure that Alex and Lily had seen it. She then went back to sleep. She knew in a short time Hank would be rescued. She also knew it would be long days ahead until Kip Patterson was safe. She looked down at Slade who had roused but went back to sleep. She leaned down and kissed him on the cheek.

Forrest walked down to the dock below the cabin. He pulled the inflatable hard bottomed boat out of the boathouse and started the outboard on the back. It took him about fifteen minutes to cross the inlet to the pier at Punta Chueca, the Seri village on the mainland. He walked up the hill to the house where the headman, a shaman for the tribe, lived. The man opened the door smiling. They sat at the table in the center of their dwelling and each drank a shot of his homemade liquor. It was a tradition they had carried on for some time. Forrest explained his predicament to him. He listened intently then agreed to help Forrest keep the tall white man safe. Forrest asked him his thought on how just to do that. The Seri had been defending that island against all enemies since before the Spanish arrived in the Americas. The headman laid out a plan to Forrest and asked how he would know when the unfriendly people arrived. Forrest looked at him directly. "Because you are a wise man, you will know." Forrest handed the man Hank's Mexican phone and told him what he needed him to do with it. They said goodbye.

Forrest left, bought a pack of cigarettes for Hank and went back down to the harbor. He didn't smoke but figured that if it helped keep Hank calm, it was worth the effort. He launched the inflatable and headed back across the bay. The current in the pass was legendary and it took him a bit longer to return. He stowed the boat back in the shed and walked to the cabin. He didn't see the eyes watching him but he felt them. The Seri were skilled hunters and fishermen. He had worked hard to gain their trust and he had never valued it more than he did now. He got back to the cabin and Hank was fast asleep with a book open on his chest to the first chapter. Forrest took the book and covered Hank with the blanket on the couch. It was the first time Hank had slept in days without being drugged. Forrest turned out the lights and went into the bedroom and collapsed on the bed himself. He didn't think anyone would arrive for at least twenty-four hours. He decided to sleep while he could and within minutes, he was having his own dream.

In the morning, the Seri headman waited until almost 9:00 am and then turned on the Mexican phone. The two men that had been sent from southwest Virginia received a call in five minutes directing them to the small town of Punta Chueca.

Alex and Lily met Marcus at the small airfield just outside of San Diego. Alex spoke first. "The phone was activated on Tiburon Island in the Gulf of California across from Baja. I think we are closer here. I suggest you let me wait here and you send the chopper my way. I need to get on the island to get a better handle on what is going on."

Marcus and Lily agreed. Marcus got on the phone to Pierce Martin in Tucson. "I need the chopper to pick Alex up here in San Diego. I will get the clearance for you to make the flight into Mexico after you pick her up, head for the coordinates that Alex gives you and insert her on the island then set up a safe staging zone nearby probably on the Baja side of the water. Jorge will be arranging additional support if you need it."

Pierce responded that he understood and grabbed his gear along with several members of the southwest response team. They were in the air in fifteen minutes.

Lily and Marcus were headed to Tucson. They would try to pick up Kip Patterson's trail from there. They hoped Slade would have additional information by morning. As they were getting ready to take off, Marcus's phone rang. It was Jorge from Puerto Vallarta.

"Marcus, we have learned that an air ambulance left the airport near Chihuahua within an hour of Hank's phone activating. There were four people on board plus the Mexican pilot. The pilot says he was hired at the last minute to transport a man and his wife with two friends to Houston, Texas. He says he came back once they had transferred the man to an ambulance. He had all the proper paperwork and they had medical exception to clear customs in Houston. The only odd thing was the short notice. He just figured it was an emergency."

Marcus listened and then responded. "I need a four-person team to be ready to go to Baja as support for Pierce and Alex if necessary. They are headed to Tiburon Island. Lily and I are headed to Tucson and will arrive shortly. Is there any way you can get more information from Chihuahua? We need as much information as possible about that flight and any others. I would bet it was Kip Patterson in the air ambulance. That is the way we would do it."

Jorge laughed. "I'm on my way when I get off the phone. I will use our Cessna. The team will be standing by in our old Bell Jet Ranger. We Mexicans don't get the fancy tools you guys do but I love that chopper. Of course, it can't land on water like those new ones but it gets us around."

Marcus laughed. "Hey, mi amigo, you are speaking to another Mexican. Thanks. We will be in touch and I am sure Slade will want to hear everything you have to say. They are flying back to Tampa as we speak. Let me know what you find out. We have both decided to just catch naps until we have Hank back."

Jorge responded. "Sounds like a plan. I will be in touch in about two hours. I will have to wake someone up in Chihuahua. That is tricky business. Talk soon."

By the time Marcus hung up with Jorge, Pierce Martin was almost half way to San Diego, He contacted Alex on her phone. "I will let you know when I am twenty minutes out. I have an insertion pack ready for you here. Do you have your headset with you?"

Alex laughed. "I have it hanging around my neck with the new operational headgear we tested. I am waiting outside the back door of the hangar. Don't even turn the engine off. I'm so glad to be operational again I could cry."

Pierce laughed. "You're insane as always. Just remember to duck as you get near the door."

It was Alex's turn to laugh. "I would have to jump up for the rotor to reach me. See you soon." She placed the earpiece in her left ear and fitted the headset around the back of her head. She plugged the lead end into her communication pack that was located on the front cross strap of her backpack and pulled the other connecter out ready to plug into the console next to the rear seat of the chopper where she would sit. She then pulled on her helmet that was custom made to fit over the communications ear piece and started scanning the sky to the northeast where she knew Pierce would approach. She didn't have to wait long.

She ran toward the helicopter as Fred Holcomb, the technician on board slid the service door forward and offered her a hand. She was in her seat plugged in before Fred pulled the door shut and Pierce had the helicopter up and on their heading before Fred got back to his seat. Alex greeted the other team members. Alex could hear Pierce through her headset. "Welcome aboard. We are headed to the Baja. The map will show on your display in two seconds."

Alex pulled her face shield down and the map popped up on the left side. She spoke. "If possible, I need you to do a silent drop at the north end of Tiburon Island. That is where the target's phone went off. I will make my way from there. Thanks for the pack. I can do a wet entry, just put me in close. I may be little but this island got its name from our friends in the water and they may be in the mood for a snack. I will track you once you leave." Pierce affirmed his reception of the message and they settled in for the flight, which would not be a long one.

Pierce crossed the border and received the authorization to enter Mexican airspace in less than two minutes. They flew south and just as they were reaching the northern coast of the island, he engaged their stealth feature. It reduced the noise and vibration they made by half. He came in low and hovered about ten feet above the surf approximately twenty yards from the beach. Alex dropped into the water as soon as she saw the green light. She used her fins to paddle toward the shore and was on the rocky beach in record time. She said out loud to herself. "Pierce you are a wizard. No Alex for dinner tonight little razor toothed friends."

Pierce was up and away from the island in seconds headed west toward the Baja. The Seri guard near the Quonset hut thought he heard something but when he got to the top of the hill all he saw were the blinking lights of a helicopter headed away from them. He made note of the time reported to the headman on the mainland and repositioned himself so he could watch in that direction just in case.

Alex stashed her fins and wet suit. She activated her night vision and moved according to the map projected on her face shield. Smithson had developed this technology for the Navy. The equipment Alex wore was even more advanced. She could see that the track of the helicopter and the location where Hank's phone had pinged were marked on her map. She moved with the quiet grace she had become famous for. She found the trail to the main house. She went north to approach from the other side. She was sure that if a sentry were posted, he would be looking in the direction of any noise made by the chopper. She was right. It took her a while to find him. She knew that whoever he was, he was not alone and he was a hunter like her. She kept moving down the eastern side of the island. She used the rocks and brush as cover. She decided to go higher to get a better vantage point. She found a place where she could see the main building and the Quonset hut. She could also see a small beach and a floating pier next to a small boathouse. She decided to wait. She never assumed that the people she was tracking weren't tracking her as well. Sometimes just sitting still and taking stock was the best solution. She set up forward and rear scanners that would alert her if she was not alone by triggering the vibration in her watch and her tactical vest. She settled in to see what type of activity she could identify.

She didn't have to wait long. She saw a small boat approaching with four men in it. It pulled up to the floating dock and the men got out. She decided they were locals most probably from the village. They were familiar with their surroundings. What didn't compute was they were armed. She saw them walk straight up to the main building. She saw a fifth man emerge from the undergrowth near the beach and walk up to join them. She turned slightly to her left and saw the man she had identified earlier move toward the main house. The six men met in front of the building. The two that had been hidden on the island walked back down toward the beach past the path that led into the trees and kept moving further down the island. Two of the new men moved toward the north end of the island and the other two moved west. Alex had seen this before. They were widening their perimeter and enforcing their watch. She tapped a message into her satellite transmitter that immediately popped up on several screens in Tampa, Tucson, and the Baja. "I have company. Unsure as to friendliness. Stand by. They are here to guard someone."

Alex decided to move higher and further toward the center of the island. She found a new location. From that vantage point she noticed a structure just up from the boat ramp. It registered more from a heat signature than it did from a visual. She loved her new equipment. She moved further down to her left. She could just make out the front of what looked like a cabin. There was a faint light coming from a window and it looked like someone was smoking on the porch. She amplified her night vision and focused closer in. She stopped. She raised her shield and pulled out her binoculars. She looked again. There was no question. There on the porch, smoking a cigarette was Hank Kessler.

CHAPTER 9

Violence sends a clear message. Brutality sends the same
message more clearly.

JinJing woke with a jerk. She was lying on a mattress on the floor in a room with other mattresses all filled with girls. Not all of the women were Asian. She could hear male voices outside the door speaking in a language other than English. She heard a woman cry out from another room. The woman had cried out in Mandarin and she was sure it was her friend Lan Li. Then she heard the unmistakable sound of a woman being slapped. It had its own cross-cultural tone and needed no translation. It was the same slap felt by thousands of other women held in bondage or paralyzed in abusive relationships. It had a sound all its own and once you heard it or felt it you never forgot it. JinJing had felt it. She winced when she moved from the residual pain from her rape. Even a simple girl from the mountains of Sichuan Province could recognize when she was a prisoner. She looked around. The girls that were awake were sitting silently staring out into space. The girls that were asleep were tucked into the same fetal position they had retreated to when they had been thrown on the mattresses. They were all prisoners. JinJing had no idea where she was, or who her captives were. She had heard the language before but was having trouble recalling it. She knew she was still under the effects of whatever it was that Ti had put in her tea. Hours earlier she felt that there was nothing that could make her feel more violated or vulnerable than the rape she had endured. It was plain now as she realized she was a prisoner; true helplessness can only be felt as a captive.

The door flew open, a man with a mattress came in and kicked one of the girls that was asleep to move her to the side. His shoe had landed squarely in the middle of her lower back. She cried out in pain. He threw the mattress down as another man came in and threw a crying bleeding girl down on it. They left the room.

The girl that had been kicked began the rhythmic contractions that signify either a massive spasm or a convulsion as she grabbed at her back crying and writhing. JinJing slid across the room and wrapped her arms around her and pulled her as straight as she could. The spasm subsided but the girl continued to shudder with the aftershocks of a thousand tiny earthquakes up and down her back. Plate tectonics are alive all up and down the human spinal column and just as the earth convulses when the plates collide, bone on bone injury with the nerves running in and around those fragile peaks and valleys can be unbearable. JinJing had seen this before in her village. She did not know if the pain would subside but she could not sit on her filthy mattress and not give this girl comfort.

The girl finally began to settle and got her breathing under control. Either JinJing had pulled her spine back in alignment when she grabbed her or it was just the pain of a nerve being so traumatized had begun to subside, but the girl's breathing finally began to return to normal.

The other girls in the room kept to their mattresses. They had seen this before and they knew what consequences lay ahead for any girl that offered another comfort. The idea was to demonstrate the wrath that awaited disobedience. Each woman in the room experienced her own pain at hearing and watching the torture that the one girl went through. Getting caught helping would mean that you would be the one used as the example next time. JinJing didn't care. She had to risk it and the girl had quieted. But, JinJing wasn't stupid either. She scrambled back to her own mattress just at the door swung open and a blast of light filled the room.

There, suspended between the two men, was Lan Li. Her head was wedged between two bamboo rods that were crossed under her chin holding her upright in a vice. The front bar came across her throat and the back bar held the back of her head forward. She was literally being strangled as she was carried into the room. They took her to the middle of the room and raised the bar high over their heads. Lan Li was gagging trying to get a fragment of air. The men separated the rods and she fell to floor banging her head. The larger of the two men leaned over and spat on her as they both left the room. The second man stopped in front of JinJing as he was about to leave and backhanded her hard across the face. All in the room heard him say in broken English, "Stay on your mattress bitch. That is your safe zone."

The room went dark again. JinJing wiped the blood from her upper lip and nose and crawled over to Lan Li. She could hear her gasping for breath. JinJing patted her on the back gently to help her regain a rhythm to her breathing. The gasping soon became replaced with a more measured form of labored breathing. Lan Li was bleeding where the bamboo had cut into her neck. She was also bleeding from the nose and it looked like one of her fingers was broken.

JinJing heard a voice in Mandarin from the dark in the corner. "She must have fought them getting out of the van. I have the same injury where they slammed the door on my hand. Please help her back to where they dropped her. They will be back in a moment with a mattress for her."

JinJing helped Lan Li, then scrambled back to her mattress and, just as predicted, the men came in. One lifted Lan Li up while the other threw down a filthy mattress. The man then dropped Lan Li on it. She landed hard and the two men laughed. They left the room.

JinJing spoke to the voice in the corner. "Do you know what is going on?"

The voice was low and confident. "I do. The best thing to do, for now, is go along with their demands. Those two will be in trouble for the injuries they have caused. We are not worth as much to them crippled and scarred. Your friend will be alright as soon as she gets her breath back and her hand will heal. Mine has. When we are passed on someone will bandage it. What was that you did to ease the pain for the girl that was kicked?"

JinJing began to calm down. "It is something I saw my father do to a man who had fallen off the roof in my village. When he did it, he told me that it would either help the man or kill him. It helped him I think, by putting the bones back in line. My father was a farmer but he was wise and people came to him to heal."

"Where is your father now?"

"He died of something he couldn't heal and we did not have the money for the medicines and healing he needed. He has been gone for years."

The woman in the corner continued. "And where is your mother that you should end up here?"

JinJing became somewhat defensive. "She died not long after my father. I think of grief. We lost the farm to the government. When she died, I lived with my uncle and his family. I thought I was coming to Canada to work in an office. They then told me my uncle had sold me to a man to be his wife. His nephew raped me and the man sold me as damaged goods."

The woman continued the conversation. "At least that part is over for you. My name is Han Tu. I was born in Dong Hoi. I am bui doi, the result of a black American soldier and a Vietnamese mother. After the Americans left, my mother fled to the north and married a Chinese businessman. That is how I know your language. Besides Vietnamese and English, I also speak French which is what those two fools were speaking when not murdering English."

The two women fell silent as the door opened again. The lights were turned on. For the first time JinJing could see the room. She kept her head down following the advice of Han. There were two other men with the first two. They were speaking English. They looked at each girl. The taller of the new men spoke. "Get these women cleaned up and into other clothes. They stink. I will decide who needs to see a doctor but there better be no more injuries. It will come out of your share." He then bent down and looked at the girl who had been kicked. "This one is first on the doctor's list and you better hope that her back is not broken." He then walked over to Lan Li. He bent down and looked at her hand and the cuts on her neck. "She goes next for the hand and the neck. Where are the sticks?" The two men looked at each other and then one left and came back with the two bamboo rods that had been used to carry Lan Li into the room. The tall man took one of the sticks and beat them both until they were whimpering on the ground. Neither of them resisted and when it was done, they just lay there bleeding. "You will not use these on the merchandise again, do you understand better now?" He broke the unused stick on them both with a second beating that was worse than the first.

Both men struggled to cover their heads. As a result, their hands were torn and cut. Knuckles and fingers were probably broken and at least one nose was sacrificed for sure.

The tall man looked around the room. Every woman in the room that could move her head was starring at the ground. "You have all learned well. I hope you learned from this. If you follow our instructions, everything will be work out and you will be safe. It is in our best interest to keep you in good condition. If you make trouble, no matter who you are, you now see what will happen to you." He looked at the other man who had come in with him. "Get these two out of my sight for now and the rest in here to help these women get cleaned up. I will get the doctor." With that they both turned the light out as they drug the two beaten men from the room. The women were once again left in darkness.

Han spoke from the corner. "I was expecting that. I told you. The important thing now is to listen and comply. If we are to live through this, we must be vigilant. There will be an opportunity later to run."

JinJing was still shaken by the beatings. "Where would I run to? They have my papers. I have no money. I have no one. I don't know where I am and I don't understand anyone but you and Lan Li. I'm not sure she will ever be able to speak again. It's hopeless."

Han was quick to reply. "It is only hopeless if you decide it is hopeless. Do you speak any other languages?"

JinJing almost whimpered. "I speak a little bit of English."

Han inquired further. "Did you understand everything he said? He was speaking English."

JinJing whimpered. "I understood 'doctor' and 'clothes. But then he started shouting and beating those men and I just stopped listening."

Han spoke in a soothing voice. "That is what I mean by being vigilant. You have to train yourself to never stop listening. Here is what I heard. They are getting us cleaned up and they are treating the girls who have injuries. They are grooming us and preparing us to be transported somewhere. My guess is into the United States. This border is easier to cross than the one with Mexico now, but it will still be difficult for them. He was going to beat those two brutes anyway. He just did it in front of us to continue the control he gains by fear. You now see how complete his wrath is. The other ones will be just as bad but more careful with the 'merchandise."

"Merchandise?"

"That is what we are now. What is your name and where are you from?"

"I am JinJing and I am from Sichuan Province. Where are these other girls from?"

Han took a moment. She was imagining the room as she had seen it when the lights were on. "The girl that was kicked is from a Spanish speaking country. I don't know her name. She was beaten for speaking to the five girls in the corner. They have to be from central or south America. They only speak Spanish but different dialects. Part of how they work is to keep us isolated by language. The two fools that were beaten didn't have enough sense to do that. They don't know I speak Mandarin so they may allow us to be together. This will probably be the last time you see your friend once they take her to the doctor. I doubt we will see the injured girl again. She may be too injured. The first beating had to have broken her ribs and she is probably bleeding internally. She will be left along the way."

"I don't think I could bear to see that."

Han continued. "They will make sure we all see it as well when they unburden themselves with the two brutes. It will be another example of total control."

JinJing had been doing some math in her head. Talking to this woman was beginning to start her thought processes again. When humans become afraid or under stress their brains redirect energy to survival rather that the cognitive processes. Her cognitive process was beginning to function as normal. "If you were born after the war with Americans, how old are you?"

Han laughed. "Finally, you have begun to pay attention. I am almost fifty-seven but my friends tell me I look thirty. There is a market for older, wiser, and more experienced Asian women in America."

JinJing thought and then spoke. "How do you know all of this, Han?"

The voice from the corner was clear and direct. "It is not my first time. I am looking for someone."

JinJing was astonished. "You mean you have been through this before? Why would you do whatever it was you did to expose yourself to this again? Who are you looking for?"

The answer was immediate. "I am looking for the man who killed my daughter."

The door flew open, the lights were turned on, and a completely new group of men and women came in. First, they picked up the injured woman and laid her on a gurney and took her out. Then they picked up Lan Li and carried her out. The Hispanic girls in the corner were ushered out together. Then, Han, JinJing, and the others were taken to a large shower area. JinJing believed this was some kind of abandoned school because they had been kept in what appeared to be a classroom and they were taken to shower room. The two women never looked up and they followed instructions.

Once they had showered, they were all taken to a room with racks of clothes where three women looked them over and then handed them clothes to wear. JinJing received new underwear, socks, hiking boots, a pair of jeans, a T-shirt, a flannel shirt, and a jacket. She did the best she could to keep her head down but still take in as much as she could see. She was following Han's instructions and being as vigilant as possible. No one was allowed to speak so it was impossible to hear any languages but she did hear English. She concentrated on several words she knew. Among them were, size, here, try, go, and you. She was about to leave when she noticed Han was across the room. She did look much younger than her age and she was beautiful. JinJing thought Han was beautiful enough that most men wouldn't think twice about wanting to spend time with her. JinJing laughed to herself. Mr. Wu had thought she was a 'faded rose' and she was only twenty-two. Would he have said the same to Han? She watched as Han picked up an extra shoelace from the floor and rolled it up in the bottom of her jeans. No one saw. JinJing began to understand the concept of vigilant. She had missed an opportunity. She wouldn't miss another one.

All of the women were then shown to separate rooms. JinJing was sure they had once been classrooms. There was a bed that was made up rather than a filthy mattress on the floor. It was meager but at least it was off the floor. There were sheets and a pillow and blankets. For the first time JinJing noticed she was chilled. Her thoughts ran to the time of year. Once again, her mind was returning to normal processing rather than being trapped in the cycle of fear. She counted to herself. She believed it was sometime in mid-September. She hadn't even thought to check before now. She had been that distracted. One of the women came in and pointed to the bed. JinJing nodded that she understood. She was instructed to take off her new clothes and put them on the chair. She looked at the flannel shirt she had just removed. The label read, 'made in China'. It was one of the few English phrases she knew. She thought 'just like me'.

She lay there for a bit then the door swung open again. A man walked in with the woman. JinJing got up and responded to their order to stand up. The woman stripped her naked. The man began to examine her. He had her lay back down on the bed and then the woman forced her legs apart while the man gave her a more thorough exam of her privates. In her mind, JinJing felt a pang of fear. He was surely a doctor and he would surely determine she was no longer a virgin and probably that she had been raped. He examined her gently and quietly.

When he was done, he smiled at her and told her in English to get dressed. She understood enough from his hand movements and the words to put her underwear back on and the T-Shirt. He said something to the woman. He then examined her eyes and ears and checked her scalp closely with a flashlight and a comb. She had seen this may times before in her village when the government doctors had come. She had never been infested with lice but some in the village had. The woman returned with a small cup with four pills in it. The doctor handed her the first one and patted her stomach just above her pubic area. JinJing had heard about the pill that would stop a baby but never thought she would be given one. He then gave her a cream to use. The woman then mimicked how and where she should use it. Again, it had to do with her private area. The woman then gave her the rest of the pills. She didn't want to be drugged again but took them anyway. Once they were sure she had swallowed them, the two got up, turned out the light and she heard the door lock as they left.

She lay there quietly expecting to have the effects of the pills she had been given but nothing happened except that she realized how exhausted she was. She soon drifted off to sleep and slept all the way through until morning.

She woke up to sounds in the hallway. She could see light around the boarded-up windows. She got up and put her clothes on and sat in the chair thinking. I have to stay alert. I have to pay attention. The door opened and the woman from the night before came in with another man. He took her by the arm and led her down the hallway and a flight of stairs to what appeared to be a loading dock on the back of the building. There were other women there being loaded into passenger vans. She was put in the far back of one with two of the Hispanic women and other Asians. She kept her head down but tried to get an idea of what was happening. She saw Lan Li out of the corner of her eye loaded into another van. She had a bandage on her hand and was moving under her own power. She sat there for a long time. She estimated it to be about an hour. She decided that it was early in the morning by the position of the sun in the sky. The trees had already begun to shed their leaves. There were seven vans in all and they were filling up fast. She saw Han escorted in a group of five women. JinJing was relieved when Han was loaded into one of the seats further forward in the same van. When they were done loading, the vans were started and they all pulled out and headed in different directions. As they were departing, she saw that the bed sheets and blankets were piled in back and had been set ablaze. It was being tended and controlled. Han had been right. JinJing would remain vigilant from now on.

Their van drove for hours before it turned off the main highway. It drove several hours more before it turned off the road onto a gravel and dirt road. She had seen this type of road before. She was sure they were headed to a farm. They drove on until they pulled up in front of a massive barn. It was the largest JinJing had ever seen. There were two other vans there. The women were led inside where a table was set with food. It was basic but filling. They were served some sort of stew, bread, canned fruit, and water. It was the only food she had been given since she had drunk that cup of tea and lost her senses. There was a large bathroom in back. Each group of women was given the opportunity to use it. There were bales of some sort of grass all around the inside of the building. They were instructed to rest on the bales. There must have been thirty women and they all did as they were told. JinJing looked around to find Han. When she did their eyes locked but Han shook her head to discourage any contact. She was being more vigilant than JinJing.

They could see that darkness was falling. It seemed that it was coming early to JinJing the man who seemed to be in charge called them all together. They were herded outside. The tall man who had delivered the beatings was there with several other men. He ordered them all to look up. The two brutes were there bound from behind. It was obvious their wounds hadn't been treated. Once everyone was outside, and the tall man was sure he had everyone's attention, he walked over behind the two men who were forced to their knees. They were crying and mumbling as they looked up at the women that just a day earlier, they had kicked and beaten. Someone handed the tall man something and with one mighty sweep of his arms, the man kneeling on the right lost his head. It tumbled forward toward the girls. There was a collective gasp as he walked around, stood in front of the other man who was screaming, looked right into his eyes and with another giant swipe lopped off his head. It dropped like a stone with the last scream still frozen on his lifeless face. His dead eyes were starring back at his body, which was held upright.

The tall man then took what was clear to everyone by now was a machete and cut off both sets of hands. While the horrified women watched, the parts were gathered up in separate plastic bags and loaded in four separate panel trucks. After the vans had departed, the women were loaded back into their passenger vans but this time they were grouped differently. Han was loaded in another van. They drove out as soon as they were loaded.

If one of the women started to whimper the driver would pull over and slap her on the breasts. JinJing could only imagine how painful that was. She forced herself not to whimper and they hadn't traveled very far before there was no more whimpering. They drove all night and all day. JinJing fell asleep. She woke up as she was being pulled from the van. They were led into what appeared to be a large hotel in a remote area. The roof was falling in in some places. They were herded into a large room that looked like it had once been a dinning room. There were just chairs. Each woman was given a bottle of water and a sandwich. JinJing couldn't recognize what it was but she ate it and nursed her water. There was another bathroom break. The people who had driven and tended them during the day were replaced with another group. She fell asleep again. She had no idea what the next day would bring but just before she closed her eyes, she saw Han across the room. She then looked around. All of the women in the room were Asian. The Hispanics had been taken somewhere else. What would tomorrow bring?

CHAPTER 10

*Help is always nearby. We just look carefully and be ready to
be helped.*

In Atlanta, Serena had drunk too much tequila with Tess the bartender. She had given Tess the directions to where she was staying so Tess knew they could walk. The car Serena had been given was left in the lot across the street from the bar in East Atlanta Village. Serena woke up and it took her a while to get her bearings. This house wasn't much but she guessed that the FBI didn't spring for mansions and she knew that since their activities had been compromised, this was a better place for her to wait it out. She smiled thinking that the man they had snatched would be safe and the people really responsible were probably already in handcuffs. She got up, went to bathroom to take a shower when it dawned on her that her suitcase with the rest of the money and her clothes was still in the car. She hated it when she drank too much. She showered anyway, rinsed her mouth out, tried to brush her hair with her fingers and dressed in the clothes she had traveled in. It wasn't that far of a walk to the village. While she was walking, she decided that she would call Agent Crescent to get further instructions. She dialed the number. She got the message that the phone was no longer in service. She dialed it again and got the same message. That didn't seem right. She continued the half-mile walk back into the village. She crossed the street to check the car when it dawned on her she didn't have her purse. She began to panic. She didn't know what to do. She looked across the street and saw that the restaurant, where she had spent the evening with Tess, was just opening up. She tried the number for Crescent one more time and got the same message. She crossed back to the restaurant to see if they had a way to contact Tess to see if she had left her keys and purse there. When she walked in Tess was sitting at the end of the bar talking to the bartender and waitress.

Tess looked at her and immediately realized her panic. "Serena, are you OK?"

"No, I can't find my keys and purse and my suitcase isn't in the car. I must have left the keys and purse here on the bar and somebody decided to rob me. Every cent I have in the world is in that suitcase."

Tess stood up and immediately went over and touched her on the arm. "You don't need to be broadcasting that in Atlanta, sweetheart. Calm down, I have your keys, your purse and your suitcase. I took them last night as a community service to the rest of east Atlanta. You can't handle tequila very well. I brought your suitcase upstairs to my place. It is fine. It is just as intact as you left it and I haven't opened it. You're fine."

Serena collapsed into her arms and began to cry. "I am in so much trouble. I don't know what to do."

Tess pulled back and looked at her. "I don't work until four this afternoon. Let's get two coffees to go and a couple of breakfast sandwiches and go upstairs to my place where we can have a conversation half of east Atlanta isn't party to." She looked down the bar at the five old regulars that were already in their spots at the bar. "These gentlemen will do you no harm but the normal mix in here has a high percentage of opportunists that no one trusts. Becky, can you have Jeeps bring the food upstairs when its ready?"

The bartender handed her two coffees in to-go cups and looked around at the oldest of the five men. "Jeeps you up to making a delivery fee?"

The old man smiled. "Sure, for Tess I will give a discount."

Becky laughed. "Simmer down there, it's just up the stairs."

The old man laughed. "I been looking for a reason to go upstairs with Tess for six years now."

Tess responded from the hallway as she was leading Serena to the internal staircase. "Keep looking, Jeeps. It's just a food delivery this time."

They climbed the steep staircase to Tess's apartment. They opened the door and were greeted by Tess's two cats, Merlin and Nose Trouble. Tess pointed to the suitcase next to the sofa. Serena walked over, lifted it onto its side and opened it. She gave out a loud sign of relief. "Thank you so much for doing that. I'm sorry about the scene downstairs. This really is all I have in the world at this point. I'm sort of in a holding pattern and I'm having trouble contacting the person that can help me."

Tess handed her the coffee and sat down on the sofa. "That is a wad of cash. What is going on, Serena? It's none of my business but you look really worried about something. I don't know you at all but I have a pretty good nose for when someone is in trouble. You can't settle down. You spent half of your time last night looking at the door to the bar every time someone came in. You don't have to tell me anything but if you need help, I'm a good listener. You have to be to have been a bartender as long as I have."

Serena bit her lower lip. "I have gotten myself involved in a crime, a bad one. I don't think anyone has been hurt but I'm not sure. I lost everything when I lost my job and then my husband died. I was so desperate. Then I met a man at a meeting who listened to me and said he and his friends could help. I trusted him. And, now I have been involved in what amounts to a kidnapping."

Tess jumped up off the couch. "What the fuck are you talking about Serena? You kidnapped someone? Who? Why? I'd say if that is the kind of trouble you're in, I'm not going to be much help to you. That is about the worst crime you can commit next to murder or beating animals. I may not want to know any more." She walked across the room and opened the door to take the food from Jeeps.

Serena became to sob and started to speak. Tess stopped her and nodded toward the door she had just closed. She opened it up again and caught Jeeps with his ear against it. "Jeeps, do you want to lose your bar privileges?

The old man began shaking his head side to side and his eyes moistened in fear and embarrassment.

"Good, then get your nosey ass downstairs and back at the bar." He nodded and left. "He's harmless but too curious."

Serena continued to sob. "Jesus Tess. I'm a forty-year-old woman that is out of work and on the run for a serious federal offense. I have a little over $25,000 in cash in that suitcase and nothing else. I don't know where my friends are or even if they are still alive. I have become entangled in this weird political group in Virginia with a man that is horrible. The man I was starting to care about is missing with the other one we kidnapped in an attempt to save him and now the FBI guy that I was working with is not taking my calls."

Tess sat there with her mouth hanging open. All she could think to say came out. "I need to think. Eat your sandwich before it gets cold."

Tess's phone rang. She answered and listened. "Are they still there?" She listened some more then hung up.

She turned to Serena. "That was Becky downstairs. She said two men just came in and showed her a picture of you and asked if she had seen you.?"

Serena got up and walked toward the window. She pulled the curtains open and saw two men looking around her car. "I don't recognize either one of them. Oh Jesus, Tess, they could be cops or sent by the FBI. What do I do? I can't think straight."

Tess looked over her shoulder. "Those aren't cops, Serena. They are muscle for someone and the worst kind, redneck muscle."

Serena stepped away from the window. "Why would the FBI send thugs to look for me?"

Tess pulled her back to the couch. "Tell me more about this FBI guy. How did you hook up with him?"

Serena thought before she spoke. "He called me out of the blue and told me they had placed the group I was working for and its leaders under surveillance. They had surmised that we had been hired to kidnap the man because we had no criminal records and because these guys never wanted to do their own dirty work. He advised me, even encouraged me, to go forward with the plan and keep him informed. He assured me that when we got caught, he would intercede and none of us would be charged if we cooperated with the FBI. He made me promise not to tell the others involved."

Tess looked at her. "Did you think to check him out with the FBI?"

"For Christ's sake, Tess. I was planning on kidnapping a person for money. Do you think I could just dial up the number and explain it all to them and make sure that Agent Crescent was a real agent?"

"Sorry you're right. When did you meet him in person?

Serena thought. "I told you; he called me."

Tess kept her cool. "No sweetheart, when was the first time you actually laid eyes on this guy? Did you look closely at his identification?"

Serena thought. "I had talked to him on the phone twice. The first time I saw him was at a small airport in Virginia when the plane landed and all the plans changed. He showed me a badge and told me we had been discovered. He gave me the keys to the car and the money and told me to call him when I got to the Atlanta address he gave me. That is where you took me last night."

Tess sat down. "I don't think he was a real agent and I definitely don't think those guys are with the FBI. I think you and your friends have been set up. Have you talked to the others that were involved with this?"

Serena was just holding off her hysteria as she realized the validity of what her new best friend had just said. She walked over and pulled her phone from her purse. She dialed Lucy's number. It went straight to voicemail. She began to shake as she dialed it again with the same results. She looked at Tess, "It's going to voicemail. Maybe they are out of range or something."

Tess looked at her calmly. "Think, Serena, where should they have been by now?"

Serena began to shake even more. "They should have landed hours ago and be on their way to our meeting point near Newark. We were all going to fly out in different directions. The tickets had been pre-purchased."

"Did you have a physical pre-purchased ticket?"

Serena understood what Tess was asking. She dialed the number of the airline booking. She was told that the purchase and confirmation number had been cancelled. Serena began to understand what was happening.

Tess continued. "What about the other man, the one you liked that took the other kidnap victim. Have you contacted him?"

Serena dialed the number for Forrest Mack's phone. It rang in the cabin almost two thousand miles away. He answered. "Serena, where are you?"

Alex was watching Hank walk down to the dock. He didn't seem to be under any duress at all. He had a cup of coffee in his hand and was looking out toward the mainland. Another man came out of the cabin and walked toward him. They talked for a brief second then both of them hurried back toward the cabin.

Alex checked her watch. She had put out her sensors and was confident she was alone. She pulled out a small square object that looked like a camping headlamp but much smaller. Across from her she affixed it to a tree with its Velcro strap. She then adjusted the strap on the front of her communications pack on her chest and unfolded a small computer screen with its own small keyboard. She waited.

Back in Tampa, L, Aggie, and Slade had assembled in the main control room. L was going to coordinate the conference. The screen began to fill. In one corner you could see SiSi and Brad broadcasting through SiSi's communication pack from Maine. In the opposite corner the image included Lily and Marcus in Tucson. The lower left-hand corner contained the image of Slade and Aggie who were soon joined by Oscar Dorian. The final corner contained Jorge Pascal using his tablet. In the center of the screen was the broadcast image of Alex from her hidden location on Tiburon Island.

Slade began the conference. "Alex we will hear from you first then I want you to stow the video and just listen through your earpiece. It is important that you concentrate on your surroundings. Pierce, are you online? We do not have video but I need to know if you are hearing all of this."

Pierce's voice came through the speakers. "I'm copying loud and clear. We have established a base of operations on Baja. We are alone and monitoring. We have aerial visual of where we feel Alex is and we have her location pinpointed. Alex if you need help, we are about ten minutes away so you will have to buy us that much time to get to you."

Alex acknowledged his information then started her report. "I have had several visuals of Hank which I have sent to L just now. He seems to be in good shape and not distressed. He actually appears to be friendly with the man I have seen with him. I have sent a visual of him as well that I just captured. Someone in the cabin received a phone call. My mike picked up the ring but not the conversation. There are armed locals on this island that have surrounded the cabin in all directions. My gut tells me that they are not there to guard Hank from escape, but to guard both of them from the outside. I have seen no indication that they have discovered me and that surprises me because they are good at blending into the surroundings. If I had to guess I would say that the man with Hank is convinced that someone is coming and they don't expect it to be a friendly visit."

Slade continued. "Thanks Alex. Now switch off and pay attention to your mission. Jorge, tell us what you know."

Jorge began his report. "The locals here including the cartel contacts say the house where they suspect these people held Dr. Patterson was burned two nights ago. Around the time the fire department was dispatched a local contract pilot flew an air ambulance mission to Houston. He was totally legitimate and cooperative with me. He had all the necessary paperwork from this side of the border and returned from Houston according to his flight plan. They had been approved to clear customs in Houston because of the medical nature of the flight. He said there were two women and one man plus the man on the stretcher. He did not see the exchange between customs and his passengers. He was outside on the tarmac dealing with his part of the clearance but he said an officer entered the plane and came out without raising any alarm. Sinaloa sources believe that this would be an effective way to smuggle Dr. Patterson back into the United States. The only tricky part would be getting past customs but the people here feel that would not have been difficult because the plane was full of U.S. citizens. I am glad Alex has seen Hank because no one here had any idea where he might be. That is all I have here. With your permission, I am going to take some of my team and provide support for Pierce and Alex from Baja. There has been no additional action in Puerto Vallarta and I have both our villa and Dr. Patterson's home secured."

Slade then turned the conference over to Aggie for her thoughts. Aggie began, as usual, right on the point. "We need to find Kip Patterson now that we have a good idea of where Hank is. It also occurs to me that this whole thing in Mexico was amateurish in its execution. They left a trail that anyone could follow. Professionals would have killed along the way. The driver would have been killed in Puerto Vallarta, Hank would have been killed in Chihuahua and left in the burned house, and they would have left no trail on how they were moving Dr. Patterson. Something made them change their plans."

L interrupted. "I think that something was Hank. I think he wasn't supposed to be in the car with Dr. Patterson. I think they made the connection between Hank and us. I don't know how."

Slade then spoke. "If Hank thought he was being held, he would not have been shy about throwing our name around. That would have been all that was necessary if someone with Hank had prior knowledge of our work. Anybody got any ideas on who that could have been?"

Aggie continued. "They would know how serious we take a threat to our organization and our friends. That could be why they got sloppy but I still think it looks like we are looking for people with little experience in kidnapping and no experience in killing. I think the people are guarding Hank, are doing so against an outside threat. Since he wasn't part of the original plan or we would have known by now, he is a 'loose end' that needs to be dealt with. The person who Alex saw him with could easily have done that by now. Someone turned on Hank's phone. If Hank was in control, he would have just called us. I think the man who is with him, regardless of what his motivation was before, is now doing everything he can to protect Hank. I think he activated that phone to let us know where they are."

L broke into the conversation. "Slade, Claymore tells me that Senator Patterson is on the secure line for you. I think you better take it."

Slade stood up, "Excuse me everyone. Oscar, please take over and bring everybody up to speed on the Canadian operation. Alex, you drop off and keep in touch and no crazy risk taking. Your help is ten minutes away and that is an eternity and we need you on the ground with eyes on the target to help guide us when we do decide to move." Everyone heard Alex click her mike key indicating that she had heard the instructions.

Oscar stepped into full view taking Slade's place next to Aggie. "The Canadian intelligence and the Border Patrol sensors have picked up some unusual activity in the locations I have just indicated on the map. The first is near the border adjacent to Lake Penobscot. The sensors near the Passamaquoddy Indian land have picked up sensor activity that does not collate with legitimate operations in the area. The second target point under consideration is north of Ravignan and south of St. Aurélie. The third area of interest is just north of La Frontière close to Presley Lake on the American side. They expect that they will be moving people at one of these spots over the next three days. Brad, are we set for deploying with Border Patrol and ICE?"

Brad leaned forward. "We are. Maria Montalba is standing by in Saint Francis, Maine. Inspector Brandhoff is stationed in Saint-Pamphile, Quebec. Both have tactical rotary wing support. Each agency has at least a half dozen agents within close response to each of these locations. I am going to relocate to our wilderness facility on Lake Umsaskis with Chuck and the two dogs in case we need to track. With your permission we are going to take Cari with us. She can help with the dogs and knows all of that area like the back of her hand. She has been guiding a national forest service team on moose research. We think she will be a valuable asset."

Oscar thought a moment. "Confirmed but she stays clear of any action.

SiSi we are shipping three of the new drones along with your command laptop. Where are you going to be?"

SiSi didn't hesitate. "I am going to relocate to Wallagrass, Maine. We have a tower there for the new communications system that supports our new drones. I will be able to keep track of everyone from there. I have given Brad several of the new communications devices that Aggie had delivered up here to both the ICE and Canadian teams. Everyone should know what is going on. Agent Cortez will be picking me up within the hour."

Oscar was about to close the conference. "Lily, I want you to stand by for a call from Slade once he has finished with the Senator. Everyone else, be careful. This whole deal has a lot of moving parts we are not sure of."

It was fifteen minutes before Lily and Marcus received a message. It would set their part of the operation into motion.

Back in Atlanta, Serena hung up the phone. She looked at Tess. "He thinks all of us that participated in this crazy thing are in danger from our former employers. The man he took is safe. What do you think I should do?"

Tess had been watching the two men who had split up. One had gotten in a car and headed south. The other walked across the street to a bench and sat down watching the car. "Well, I know what you are not going to do. You won't be going near that car and you won't be going back to that house. Do you have all your stuff with you?"

Serena shook her head yes. "Everything that I traveled with is right here thanks to you."

Tess took a moment. "I don't know jack shit about anything related to kidnapping or any other criminal crap. But I used to work with someone here who does. I don't know if she can help us but I am gong to text her to see if she will give me a call back." Serena nodded and Tess sent the text.

In five minutes, the phone rang and Tess answered it. The voice on the other end was calm and familiar. "Tess, it's Lydia. What's up?"

Tess told her the whole story. There was a moment of silence and then Tess hung up.

Serena looked at her. "What did she say?"

Tess smiled. "It was pure Lydia, she told me to stay by the phone that she would have someone call me as soon as possible."

"Why did you call her, is she with the police?"

Tess smiled. "Even better. Four years ago, she was kidnapped and trafficked to Florida. She was rescued by a guy named Earl Tippit. He worked for a company that has taken care of Lydia and helped her ever since. That company is better than just the police."

Serena looked at her. "Does the guy calling back here have anything to do with a company called Smithson Evermore?"

Tess smiled. "We are to sit tight and wait for the call. Oscar Dorian has everything to do with Smithson Evermore."

CHAPTER 11

Unexpected results are not always bad results.

There were ten Asian girls in the van with JinJing and Han. They drove for hours seemingly in circles on back roads. There were three male guards. They finally stopped at the end of a road where an empty van was waiting. The girls were pulled out of their vehicle and forced to line up. They split the ten girls up into two sets of five each with three escorts. Somehow Han and JinJing ended up in the same van once again. Each van pulled out and at the first intersection, went in different directions. No one said a word including the escorts. The women had no idea where they were and they had reversed and turned so many times it would be impossible to remember the route they had taken. They had been driving since they had witnessed the butchering of the men who had mistreated them. The fear hung in their minds constantly and the vision of blood and brutality was impossible to forget. JinJing had never expected to see such a thing. In her village even when animals were slaughtered, they were treated in a more humane way. Han had stayed focused. She didn't try to remember the turns or the routes but she knew they were driving in a circuit from the signs and other features of the landscape. She had studied maps and remembered things from the last time she had been through this when she had been gripped by fear not just for herself but for her daughter. This time she was just gripped by hate, driven by it to the point that she was hyperaware of her surroundings. After she had survived the last time and had returned to Vietnam, she had studied the geography of southern Canada and the northern part of the United States. They had come further east than the last time. The first time, she had ended up in a town called Cleveland, in a place called Ohio. She had been moved with a larger number of women using trucks instead of vans, and boats at the end. Nearing the end of the journey while on the water, she had seen her daughter dumped over the side of the boat into a lake. She would later find out it was called Huron, a lake as big as an ocean and as impossible to find a lost Chinese girl as the Pacific. She was killed to prove a point. A tall man killed her. He had held her over the side by her hair and then just dropped her into the dark water. He was the same man that had butchered the men that morning, just to make a point. If he showed up again and she knew he would, Han knew someone was going to die. She would do what she could to make sure it was him. She would do it just to make a different kind of point. Along the way she had picked up several things to help. In the cuff of her rolled up jeans was a shoestring. Up her left sleeve was a coat hanger that she had taken from the clothes rack. They were getting sloppy and trusting fear too much. They weren't paying enough attention. She was going to do it differently this time. That first time, she and many of the other girls had been rescued. They had cooperated with the police who had helped save them but as soon as they had given all the information they could remember, others came and deported them back to their home countries. Obviously, nothing had happened on either side of this border to the monsters that terrorized and enslaved them. The only person she felt was going to be punished was the stupid Korean woman in Cleveland who kept them in a trailer and forced them to work in her nail salon. It was obvious that none of them were ever going to make enough money to buy their documents back. Her daughter thought she was coming to study at a university. She thought that she was coming to support her daughter. They had been in the country a week when it dawned on Han that there was not going to be any education. Now there wasn't any student either. It had been easy enough to get taken back into the system. She knew the brokers and she was still pretty enough that they were tricked into signing her up. But, this time the government of Vietnam knew who she was. They were going to assist her once she escaped to bring these people to justice. She had paid very close attention to each face of those who had been involved in moving her from Vietnam through Vancouver to Montreal. Every ounce of her attention was directed at remembering, and remaining vigilant, just as she had instructed JinJing. She had a very good idea that they were driving a circuit along the western border of Maine. They went up the interior and then turned back down the edge of the border as close as they could get. She surmised that there would be sleeping in the van or in the woods tonight. Then tomorrow there would be one more big show of 'control' by the tall man before they would attempt to cross the border. Someone would die to keep them distracted and terrified. That would be her opportunity. She had become a survivor and would never be a victim again. She would die first.

Bac k on Tiburon Island, Alex saw two more changes of the guard but the last one had brought more armed local men to the island. She was sure that if something was going to happen, it was going to happen soon. She decided to move closer to the action. She packed up her gear, pulled in her sensors and texted Pierce that she was on the move. She was able to pull up the latest satellite image taken during the last flyover. The heat signature showed ten men forming a perimeter around the main building, the Quonset hut and the cabin. There were two sentries very well hidden by the floating dock. She closed her communications console by folding it into her chest pack and began to move. It was like a cat creeping through the grass. Anyone filming it would not see a leaf move or hear a twig snap. It would take her a long time but she had time. If something began to happen, she would stop and let it happen around her. Her job was to observe and report. She would only act if she determined that Hank was in critical danger. She carried her Glock Model 30.

She moved down the side of the mountain. Pierce was watching her progress and would signal her with a vibration if danger was near. She was within twenty-five yards of the rear of the cabin totally hidden when she felt the vibration and stopped. She withdrew into the underbrush. They would have to step on her to discover her, but she knew these men were experienced hunters and hunters can sense things that shouldn't be there, especially things that don't belong. She almost burrowed her way into the ground. Her legs were beneath the surface, her hood was pulled up and over her tactical helmet. They would have to see the whites of her eyes.

She could hear them approaching and talking in a strange language that was interlaced with Spanish. It didn't sound like Maya or Nahuatl. The Seri language is an isolate and didn't share much with the other pre-Columbian cultures. But she could tell from the inflection that there was a mixture of determination and concern. They stopped about twelve feet away as if they were listening for a sound. Alex hoped it wasn't her because she still had no idea which side, they were on and she was not in a good defensive position. There was no question that they were listening. Then she heard it too.

She focused her attention to the vibrating rhythmic sound of the rattle. She was about six feet from Alex looking right at her. Her tongue darting out scouting the air for any sign of movement that would trigger the strike. Alex returned the stare. Alex had to admit she was beautiful. Almost six inches in girth and at least six feet long if Alex was counting the number of coils correctly. Alex remained still. The only exposure was her face. She had not thought it a good idea to lower her shield because that was a sure way to get noticed by an experienced hunter. A face could blend in. A face shield, even though made of non-glare bullet-proof polymer, was not anything that looked like vegetation. The snake seemed to notice the sound of the men behind her as well. She pulled her head back from a striking position and repositioned her coils to escape should she need to. But her focus was still on Alex and the repositioning had put her less than four feet from Alex's face. She was definitely within striking range.

Alex was hoping upon hope that Pierce would not signal her. The vibration would be silent to humans twelve feet away, but totally aggressive and recognizable to the Western Mexican Rattlesnake tracking her every movement. She and Alex locked gazes again. Then an experienced hand came out of nowhere and snatched the snake just behind the head. His boot ended up an inch in front of Alex's nose. The other men applauded and the man held up the snake. Alex lay perfectly still but she could still see that the snake was at least six feet long. He put the snake carefully in a sack that another man gave him. They moved on down the trail toward the cabin. Alex remained motionless until she got another vibration that meant that group was no further danger.

Once they were far enough down the trail, she felt she could continue, Alex changed direction to come up behind the cabin. She began to dig quietly under the cabin making sure that she wasn't disturbing any other snakes.

It would be a natural place for them to make their den but she supposed it normally had too much activity around it. It took her an hour to burrow a tunnel under the shed and also an escape burrow back to the north side of it. She set a sensor behind her, and a video feed to the north side of the cabin a quarter of the way up a small tree. There was no sound coming from the cabin. She was able to get a message to Pierce about her situation and finished it just as she heard voices approaching. One of the voices was Hank's.

"Why are we hurrying back to the cabin? I was enjoying myself with the village folks who brought us all the food and then you have a hissy fit and hurry us back here. What is that all about?"

Forrest looked at him. "Don't let their attention go to your head. You don't have any idea what they are saying. The headman has warned me there are strangers in Punta Chueca asking about us. They were also trying to get someone to bring them over to the island. We may need to move to a safer location."

Hank looked indignant. "What are the villagers saying? I see the adoration in their eyes. They aren't speaking any kind of Spanish that I ever heard and I was raised in Ybor City and my mother was a cigar roller."

Forrest laughed. "They speak their own ancient language as well as Spanish. I told you; your height and your blond hair are significant to them. One version of their mythology and ancient belief system includes a visit from tall white men with blond or red hair. You remind them of those stories. Besides, if you believe another myth about them, they may be talking about what vegetables to cook you with, so simmer down. Sorry about the pun. They have been mysterious for centuries. But I trust them. They trust me and they will do what they can to protect us. Right now, they are talking about just two Americans doing the looking. I don't think those people are from Smithson coming to rescue you although I hope the Smithson people are not too far away. These two are coming for us."

Hank looked perplexed. "That is ridiculous. I am the one that you kidnapped. I demand to speak to them as soon as they get here."

"They are coming for me because you are supposed to be dead, remember? Whether you are dead or not, I am a loose end. Once they find you that will be another loose end that needs to be cleaned up. And as far as you 'speaking' to anyone, I still have a can of the spray and I will use it to keep you alive if that is what it takes to keep you quiet."

Hank blinked. "Don't spray me again."

Forrest glared back. "Then don't demand an audience with your executioners."

This whole conversation happened on the porch where Alex could plainly hear it. They went inside. Alex thought that his hope about the "Smithson people" was going to be realized sooner rather than later. It also meant she hadn't been discovered yet. She had to make a decision. If they were going to move, she would have to change location with them. Since she knew they would be escorted she would have to either get ahead of them or risk being discovered following them. She flipped down her communication screen and sent a message to Pierce to give her some options from his vantage point. It may be time to bring in some help once she saw which way they were going.

Across the bay, Pierce saw the message at the same time L did in Tampa. L immediately sent Pierce the latest topographic data she had on Tiburon Island. There was a multitude of potential hiding places. Pierce got on the satellite phone with L. "What do you think. I feel if we move Alex halfway up the hill, we can put her in a position to at least advise which way they went. I am fairly sure the local group can keep Hank safe. From Alex's last transmission I don't think they are hostile but I don't want to find that out too late. I hate hurting people who appear to be helping but I don't want us to be mistaken as the ones trying to kill whoever that man is."

L sent him a cleaned-up version of the picture Alex had been able to send both of them. "I think that man's name is Forrest Mack. We worked with him several years ago on a straight up kidnapping. He led an insurance recovery team that brought a kidnapped oil engineer back from Brazil. We have had no contact with him since. We found information that he has been working in the Gulf of California area as a pilot. That would fit with the other part of the scenario that is developing. I think Alex needs to shift her mission to gather information on whoever it is that may be coming. I have discussed it with Oscar and he agrees."

Pierce listened then spoke. "I have found a trail junction not too far up the hill from Alex's first observation post. I suggest that she set a listening device on the cabin, and a video on the trail. I am also going to step up our readiness to move out. Who do you want us to evacuate when the time comes?"

Oscar Dorian came on the line. "Take them both, Pierce. We need to get Hank safe and off the operational load here and I would prefer to do that in a way that minimizes ground contact and we don't want any of the locals injured." All of them signed off.

Pierce texted the instructions to Alex. She waited until she saw a group of the Seri guards coming up the porch and several coming down the trail behind the porch. It took them about five minutes to gather Hank and Forrest and head out up the mountain along the same trail that Alex had used to come down. Once they were gone, Alex set another video feed on the front of the house and a listening device in the house. She didn't want to venture to the dock. She then turned and worked her way once again in the underbrush up the side of the hill to the location Pierce had identified for her. She stopped half way up the hill. She took cover and activated the video feed on her helmet. She documented two white men and a native man operating the boat. He dropped them off but refused to get out of the boat. They walked up the path toward the cabin and then began a tactical but clumsy approach. They were not professionals. When the man in the boat saw them pull their weapons, he backed the boat out and headed back to the mainland. They didn't even see him leave.

Alex thought that if they were 'hit' men they were novices. You never go into a situation without having a plan to retreat. Now they were trapped on the island. They had no idea what they were up against. Alex sent the information to the Tampa headquarters and to Pierce at the same time. Just as she transmitted, the microphone on the house indicated they had discovered that Hank and the other man were gone. She heard them make plans to follow the trail. She reported that and waited for any instruction. She received a response immediately. It was simply stated and it was from Oscar to both her and Pierce. "Execute recovery and evacuation."

The choppers blades began to turn just as Alex began to move swiftly. To this point she had not pulled her weapon but she now had two armed individuals behind her. Just as she reached the junction her communicator vibrated with a new message. It was as simple as the first. "Team ETA six minutes. Secure the rear."

Alex stopped. She walked back down the trail and set a sensor. Ten feet up the trail from that location she stretched a trip wire across the trail. She attached the wire to a device known as a slam-bang grenade. It was intended to startle not kill so she set it far enough behind and off the trail that the men coming up would be stunned but not killed. She found a defensive position and opened her communication console. She typed one word. "Secured."

She set the countdown clock visible on her face shield which was now lowered to four minutes and watched it begin to tick off the seconds.

Just off the coast, Pierce engaged the stealth mode of the helicopter. He was watching the heat signature of the group escorting Hank and Forrest as they made their way up the mountain. He advised the crew they would do a rappel entry. Once they had control of the situation, he would pick them up in the parking lot of the main building. They too were equipped with stun grenades. They did not want anyone to be injured.

Alex could hear the two men coming up the trail. They made enough noise that she could have heard them on the mainland. They were complaining about having to do this. They had their guns drawn but were rushing up the hill so fast that they weren't paying attention to the trail ahead. She recognized the southern drawl of Tennessee or Virginia.

Alex reached up and closed the helmet earpiece as she had done with the helicopter. She knew it was going to be loud. It was. The blast was so loud and the concussion so directed that they both fell dazed onto the trail face down. Alex was on them in a heartbeat. The first one was cuffed before his ears stopped ringing. The second one had time to look at Alex in amazement as she rolled him over and fixed his hands with the flex cuffs on her vest. She hit the transmitted for her microphone and said in a loud clear voice, "Pursuit secured and contained."

The group with Hank and Forrest heard the concussion grenade go off. Forrest stopped everyone in their tracks. He turned to the Seri men and asked them to put their weapons down. It was going to be OK. Hank looked at him in astonishment. "What the hell was that and why are we stopping."

Forrest looked at him in earnest. "I want you, for once, to say in a loud clear voice, this is Hank. It's OK."

Hank looked at him. "I am not about to scream anything. First, we are running up a hill because you tell me killers are behind us and then I hear and explosion and they you want me to tell them where I am. Fuck that, Forrest. I'm not doing anything of the sort. This whole episode is just a horror!"

Forrest pulled out the spray can. "Hank unless you want to become a friendly casualty, scream out that it is OK"

Hank paused looking at the can. He thought for a moment.

Forrest raised the can. "Unless you want all your new followers to see you completely immobilized and pissing yourself, you will scream now. You have two seconds."

Hank didn't hesitate. "It's OK".

"Louder and what I told you."

"THIS IS HANK. IT'S OK."

Six heavily armed men in Smithson Evermore tactical gear stepped out of the surrounding bushes and rocks. The Seri people applauded and smiled. Hank looked around in amazement.

Coming up the trail behind them was Alex and four more Seri men who had been following the two 'assassins' up the hill. They had the two by their arms. Alex raised her shield and smiled. "Hello Hank. It is good to see you are still as stubborn as you have always been."

Pierce got on his radio and relayed the results of the mission to the Smithson Team. He then asked everyone there to head toward the main building on the north end of the island. Two of the Seri men guided them on the quickest route. One of the team members stepped forward toward Forrest with a zip tie. Alex interceded. "I think this man is how we got here. You don't need to secure him."

Forrest looked at Alex and held out his hand. "My name is Forrest Mack. I am very glad to see you finally. You are very good at what you do."

Alex smiled. "I know who you are Mr. Mack. What I don't know is what role you played in all of this. We are going to have to have a talk. Do we need to cuff you?"

Hank stepped forward. "You will not cuff him. He kidnapped me then had a change of heart and saved me."

Alex smiled. "Hank, you and Dr. Patterson were kidnapped by a woman. We are glad you are safe. We are not securing Mr. Mack because we know that we can count on him to use his spray if you get too uncontrollable."

Hank looked indignant. "Young lady, I have never been out of control." Hank then thought better of what he was going to say next as Forrest raised the can.

CHAPTER 12

*In all things, movement means change whether it is in the
woods or on the streets of a city.*

Slade's conversation with the Senator had revealed a great deal. The most important thing was that he now had direct contact with her as well as Special Agent Walt Haskell of the FBI. They had worked with Agent Haskell on rescues before. He learned that the Senator had received a series of emails containing photos of her ex-husband bound and gagged. The messages and images had all arrived from different re-routed servers all over the world. They were impossible to trace but there was no question that the person in the pictures was Kip Patterson. He looked unharmed but tired. No one had made any demands as yet. Both the FBI and the Senator felt that the kidnapping was tied to an upcoming vote on legislation related to immigration. The Senator had been a vocal critic of the legislation and was a key vote for the bill to either fail or continue on its path. Many of her constituents depended on legally documented foreign workers to be successful. She was equally concerned about the human rights issues that had arisen with the current processing of individuals seeking work visas and asylum. She was also worried about the impact of people who had been here for years and under the previous administration been granted extensions. She was convinced that Kip's hostage situation was about that and not money.

Slade had relayed this information to Lily and Marcus in Tucson. He and Aggie were discussing the next when Slade's phone rang. It was Walt Haskell.

"Agent Haskell, this is Slade. We are on a scrambled line."

The agent spoke quickly. "Slade, it's good to be working with you again although the circumstances that bring us together are always bad. One of these days, promise me we will go fishing together. I have some spots in Connecticut and Vermont that I would love to fish with you."

"That sounds like a great idea once we get this thing cleared up. We have an update on a development at this end. We have recovered Hank Kessler in Mexico. He is the man that was kidnapped with Dr. Patterson. As part of that rescue, we have also come in contact with a man called Forrest Mack. He may very well have information we need. He is providing information to our people in Mexico. It appears he knows details but was not involved in that actual kidnapping. We also believe that he secured Mr. Kessler's safety. As soon as we know more, we will share it. In addition, there were two Americans that were neutralized before they could get to Mr. Kessler. They were both armed with Glock 40 caliber hand guns with three magazines apiece. They refused to give us their names. They were turned over to the provincial police captain in Hermosillo. He charged them with possession of unregistered weapons, being armed on tribal land and refusing to cooperate. You might want to have the embassy check on them. They were sent by someone and I doubt the Mexican authorities will take kindly to their actions, particularly the not cooperating part. They have different rules for seeking cooperation. You may need to send someone to get them before they disappear. There is not much love in Sinaloa for armed Americans of the 'redneck' variety right now.

Haskell thought a moment. "I am going to trust that if this Mack fellow was involved in the kidnapping, you will make arrangements to turn him over to us as well as soon as possible. We need to know who is behind this."

Slade hesitated then spoke. "We are doing a quick debriefing in Mexico and then I will advise you further. We have very little yet to give us an idea of how Dr. Patterson was brought into this country or even if he was. As soon as we know something, as always, we will share. I think we both want to move forward to identify who is involved and who orchestrated the entire charade. I promise that he will answer for his part, but until then I would like you to bear with us until we get some additional information. Neither one of us would benefit from him disappearing into the federal system. Until we know more, we need to proceed carefully. I also want to remind you that what we do know is that both men were kidnapped in Mexico not the United States. Let's be cautious until we know more."

"Slade if it was anybody but you, we would already be down there and there are people in my organization that will want part of the headline that goes with this thing. The political nature of this whole deal needs to be handled carefully if we are going to get Dr. Patterson back safely. You do know that I only have control over my little empire here and right now, because of the Senator, I am holding onto that control. Call me when you get more information, please. The newest development at this end is that another email has arrived. This one had a message with the picture. The picture was one of Dr. Patterson tied to a chair upright with a masked man and a hunting knife. Behind him was an American Flag and this morning's New York Times. These guys have been watching too much Middle Eastern television. The message was pretty clear. The newspaper refers to an upcoming senate committee hearing on immigration. Obviously, Senator Patterson is on the committee and all eyes will be on what she says and the questions she asks. The message was two words. They were 'skip meeting'."

Slade responded. "Is the Senator going to skip the meeting?"

Haskell laughed. "Of course not. Her statement to me was her ex-husband would never speak to her again if she did. I can't get my ex-wife to stop speaking to me. That is one very different relationship but you have to admire it. From what I know of Kip Patterson, that is exactly what he would say. By the way, he was scheduled to speak before this same committee soon. Now you know what I know."

Slade's message was concise. "We will be in touch."

Aggie had been in the control room with L speaking with Marcus, Lily, and Alex. She turned to Slade as he walked in. "They are transporting Hank and Mack back to Puerto Vallarta. Jorge will secure both of them in our villa. What do you think about sending Lily to Mexico to gather additional information with Alex from Forrest Mack?

Slade remained silent.

Aggie continued. "I think we need to move Marcus back here. We are balancing too many balls in the air at one time for my comfort zone. At least Hank is off the recovery calendar. He hasn't stopped talking about how they treated him like a 'god' on the island. About the only thing that has quieted him down is Lola. Forrest Mack seems eager to speak with us but is worried about what is going to happen to him with the authorities. He says he is ok getting what he deserves but he wants a chance to keep Dr. Patterson safe. I think we should give him that opportunity. He had a stellar career doing the same thing we do for several insurance agencies."

Slade thought a moment. "I agree with you, but I would like to fly Lily back here with Marcus. Let's get together with Oscar an hour after he gets back to go over our full resources. Send Rufus and the jet to pick up Marcus and Lily. Alex can handle the debriefing of Hank and Mr. Mack."

SiSi heard her phone ring and answered it immediately. "Brad, did you all arrive safely with the dogs?"

Brad smiled. "We did. Thanks for asking. What happened to the matter-of-fact SiSi that I communicated with so many times before?"

That made SiSi smile. "She still exists and you will hear her soon when we get rolling but if it's just you, sorry you get this SiSi."

"That works but I long for that authoritative 'affirmative' you always bark out over the airways. I have news for you so you can bring our people up to date. We are going to go visit the three potential entry points. Agents Montalba and Cortez are flying up here to join us. Cari is going because she has just been up to the same area a few weeks ago on an Outward-Bound trip. She knows two of the three entry points. We will have Ruca and Slick Willy with us. Both are trained to human scent. We are going to survey where we have had reports of unusual activity. One of our handlers is here and another is standing by in Greenville, Maine, if we need to bring in more dogs. As of tonight, we are cooperating with ICE and Border Patrol to pre-position one of our teams and two of their teams at each potential entry point. If we are wrong, at least we haven't wasted the entire field unit on a wild goose chase."

SiSi was typing his report into the messenger program as he was speaking and the people in Tampa were watching it in real time. "I have just updated everyone. Please let us know as soon as you can about any activity. By the way, Alex and Pierce were able to recover Hank in Mexico. He had someone with him that we want to talk to for possible additional leads to Dr. Patterson but nothing solid yet. Oh, and for your information mister, I don't 'bark'. Do we need to send you anything?"

Brad thought a moment. "I think we are good unless Oscar thinks of something else. We are sort of playing a waiting game right now. I hear the chopper landing. I will advise when we know more about the sites. Take care."

SiSi caught herself just before she sounded too involved knowing that the moment Oscar's name was mentioned he was alerted. She reverted back to the matter-of-fact SiSi. Her reply was as expected. "Affirmative."

Oscar had heard the exchange and decided that Brad had the situation well in hand. He wanted to concentrate with Slade and Aggie on finding Kip Patterson. He was about to head down to the conference room when his phone rang with a number that made him smile.

"Bailey, how is my favorite bartender?"

Bailey O'Connell who was a close associate of Smithson in Tampa, was considered by many as a street heroine of the less fortunate man, woman or beast and was all business. "Lydia just got a call from an old friend in Atlanta that she bartended with. Her name is Tess Atkins. I have texted you, her number. Has Hank Kessler been in any difficulty lately?"

Oscar was quick to reply. "How do you know about Hank Kessler's difficulties?"

She responded as quickly. "I don't, but Tess is trying to help a woman who claims she was involved somehow in his kidnapping. Apparently, this woman is freaking out. Will you call Tess and give her some advice? Lydia says she is the one person in Atlanta that she misses and the only one she would trust."

Oscar replied. "Of course, I will and, if this turns out to be what I think it is, we will do more than help Tess and this woman. Thanks Bailey. Give Lydia a kiss from me and as usual, no discussion on this one till we get back with you, please."

Bailey laughed. "Oscar as far as you are concerned, I think Lydia has much more in mind with you than just a kiss, but I will tell her and of course we will keep still. Just let us know that Tess is OK." She hung up.

Oscar immediately called the number. A woman's voice answered. "Hello."

"Is this Tess Atkins, a friend of Lydia Pierce?"

The woman's voice answered. "Is this Oscar Dorian?"

"It is. Tell me what's going on up there. We will help in any way we can."

Tess answered. "I want to hand the phone over to the woman I called Lydia about. Her name is Serena. Please be as gentle as you were described to be. She is very afraid and we have at least two goons downstairs that I am convinced are looking for her." She handed the phone to Serena.

Serena got on the phone and gave him a quick synopsis of what she had been through since she drove to Atlanta. She then started to go into the details of what had led up to her trip and Oscar stopped her. "Serena, don't say another word over the phone. We will speak in person. I am going to send some people to pick you up. I want you to stay with Tess and don't open the door to anyone except my associate. His name will by Tyler. I am texting Tess his picture. Stay away from the windows as well. If they knew you were there, they would already be trying to get to you. I want you to follow Tyler's instructions completely, no matter what he asks. We are going to get you to a safe place and I promise you can trust us. Tyler will give you his number and my number. I promise I will answer the phone. Can you put Tess back on the line?"

Tess took the phone. "Oscar what can I do?"

"Is your apartment secure enough to allow us the time we need to get to you?"

Tess looked at the three locks and the two chains on the door. "Oscar, I am a woman living alone in Atlanta above a bar. I have more lock hardware on my door than paint."

Oscar laughed. "I am texting you a picture of one of my people. His name is Tyler Glass. He has a red beard and is rarely without a baseball cap. He won't look like a knight in shining armor but he is one of mine and I can assure you he and the rest of my team will be happy to deal with these guys. I am going to leave them in place until this is over to watch over you. I promise you won't even know they are there but you have helped Serena and if these guys or any others are looking for her, I don't want you to be caught up in whatever this turns out to be. Is that OK?"

Tess thought a moment. "I get to keep working right?"

"Of course, you carry on as usual. You will just have a few more customers than normal and I will need you to let Tyler know when he returns if you are planning any trips."

Tess laughed. "I'm always up for more customers. Tell them to tip big. I'm planning a trip to Florida to see my girl Lydia as soon as I have saved enough. I will keep Serena here safe until they get here." She hung up.

Oscar got on the phone to Marcus, Slade, and Aggie. "I just got what I think is a good lead on additional information on Dr. Patterson's abduction from a friend of Lydia Pierce in Atlanta. There is a woman named Serena in Atlanta claiming she is in danger and was involved in the abduction. She has voluntarily agreed to meet with us. I'm sending Tyler's team to pick her up and provide security for Lydia's friend Tess Atkins. How quickly can we get Serena on a plane headed our way? I don't know how big the crew is that is looking for her. I think she would be safer here until we find out the extent of her involvement."

Marcus spoke up. "We have a small jet at Fulton County Air Field about 30 minutes away. I can have them ready to go by the time Tyler arrives."

Oscar continued. "Slade does this sound like it will work better than trying to talk to her there?"

Slade didn't hesitate. "This could be one of the people that Forrest Mack is worried about. I think, since she has agreed to come, voluntarily, that we need her here. Go for it."

Oscar hung up and contacted Tyler Glass. He gave him his instructions. Tyler and his team were on the way five minutes after Oscar hung up.

Tess stood back from the window and looked out. She could still see the car but the man who had crossed the street to the bench was nowhere to be seen. She called Becky downstairs. She answered. As soon as she answered Becky spoke. "Before you ask, the answer is yes. One is nursing a beer at the bar and the other is sitting at a table outside. That one had disappeared for a short time. They keep going back and forth to the bathroom like they are trying to check the place out." I would use the back door. I don't think they even know it is there."

Tess listened. "Becky, there is a guy with a red beard and a baseball cap that is on his way to help us out. Make sure he gets to the stairwell and see if you can distract those two when he arrives."

Becky laughed, "That won't be any problem at all. I will use Jeeps and the boys."

In fifteen minutes, Tyler arrived. Becky gave him the nod toward the back room. No one noticed him move through. She also nodded to Jeeps, Winslow, and Hector who got up and moved toward the table where the inside goon sat. Jeeps spoke up as they all sat down. "Hey how about you buy the locals a beer, buddy?" It had the same effect every time they used it. The man stood up told them to fuck off and went outside with his friend. The boys laughed and went back to the bar where there were new beers waiting for them and a shot next to each pint. They toasted each other on their crowd control capabilities.

Tyler knocked on the door and entered. He introduced himself to Tess and Serena. He gave them both instructions. Tess was first. "Tess, I want you to carry on as usual. You will always have four of my people with you until we tell you the threat has passed. You won't even know we are there unless someone poses a threat to you. There will be no disruption in the bar. Some of my team are outside. They will give me a signal when we have distracted the men we see. Is there another way out of here?"

Tess told him the way.

Tyler turned to Serena. "I want you to stay close to me. An SUV will pull up to the back door on the street behind. We will get in. We are going to the Fulton County Airport about 30 minutes northwest of here. You will get on a jet with some of my team and be taken to a safe place where we will sort out this problem. Are you good with that? You have to agree or we have to get the police involved now."

Serena didn't even think. "Yes, I will go anywhere as long as you get me out of here alive. I haven't heard from the others that were involved. Have you heard from a man in Mexico?"

Tyler smiled. "You will get all of these questions answered as soon as we know you are safe but right now, I don't know what we are up against here. Are you willing to trust us?"

Serena looked at Tess who was quick to respond. "Jesus, Serena, you're kind of running out of options here. We can always call the Atlanta Police. I'm sure there will be down here in a couple of days or, they might even surprise us and send the SWAT team which would put all of us in jeopardy. Give the man an answer."

Serena nodded and answered. "Yes, let's go."

Tyler took off his hat and jacket and put it on Serena. He went over to a rack on Tess's wall where several hats were hanging. He picked the pink one, adjusted the size, and put it on. Tess laughed. "Sure, you can borrow it. Do you want the matching pink skinny jeans that go with it? I want that back." She laughed so hard she snorted.

Tyler smiled. "I will bring it back to you myself. You stay put for a bit. Call the woman downstairs to get an all clear in about fifteen minutes."

Tess nodded and thought, "He's confident and he has an amazing smile. Not a bad ass either. They turned and were headed to the back landing to the stairwell that led to the back exit.

Tyler was speaking into an unseen microphone. "We are on our way. Front team, execute threat resolution."

Two women arrived at the bar instantaneously and sat at the outside table next to the two men who had been watching Serena. Upon hearing the command one woman stood up and approached the man sitting next to her and screamed, "What did you just say to me motherfucker?"

Both men looked shocked and the one she was screaming at stood up. She immediately kneed him in the groin and he went down like a stone. The other man moved to catch him just as the woman reached past him and hit him with a small Taser. He dropped like a stone. Both women, started yelling "he's got a gun" that drew a group of people to hold the men. The women dropped two twenties on the table they had been sitting at. The second woman called 911. In a breathy voice she reported her location and she thought she saw two men with guns about to walk into the bar at her location.

At the same time this was happening, the SUV was pulling up to the back door and Tyler and Serena jumped into the back. A second SUV pulled up to the corner behind them and the two women that had dealt with the rednecks got in. Three other members got out and located themselves inside and outside of the bar. The second SUV followed the first all the way to the airfield. They pulled out onto the private airside tarmac. The two women and one of the men in the rear car got into the jet with Serena. They were wheels up and headed to Tampa less than forty-five minutes after Tess had made her call to Lydia.

Tyler got back in his SUV and instructed the driver to return to the bar. "I have a hat to return and I want to make sure Atlanta PD has our two friends in custody."

CHAPTER 13

Sometimes progress is made by standing still.

Kip Patterson was awake but groggy. He was chained to an eyebolt located under the bed with just enough length for him to get to a bathroom and to an easy chair next to the bed. The chain was not long enough to get to the door. By the high location of the lone window which was completely covered, he surmised he was in a basement. He had no idea how big or where the house was. He had only been out of the room once. They had tied him to a chair and put a gag in his mouth. He was posed for photographs that reminded him of the terrorist videos. No one had spoken to him. He hadn't spoken to them. Each person he was around wore a balaclava. He had no misgivings about the fact he was a captive. He was being treated OK except for the chain and he was given meals on a regular basis. The food was actually above standard as if it were prepared by a professional chef. He was allowed to shower once a day and was given clean underwear and a T-shirt and sweat pants. He had looked at the labels. There were high quality and expensive. Whoever his captors were, they didn't shop at discount stores. All of this was useful information for him. He figured at some point in time he was going to be asked to make a statement or a video plea. He wanted to incorporate as many clues as he could so his wife and the law enforcement world would have as much information as he could provide.

He had been served breakfast and lunch. He figured it was about an hour before they brought him the evening meal. The room was furnished with good quality furniture. Whoever had set the room up had planned it well. His eyes, pulse, and blood pressure were checked on a regular basis. He was given his blood pressure medication more regularly than he took it himself. It was a very odd form of imprisonment.

The more Kip thought about the situation, the more he concluded this entire episode was about politics and influence. His money was tied up in trusts for his daughters and bequests to academic programs. He felt that surely his kidnappers would have discovered that it would be almost impossible to liquidate much of it for cash. He lived a comfortable but frugal existence in Mexico. He didn't own his villa, he rented it. He didn't own a car. If he needed one it was well within his means to just use the rideshare or hire a driver for the day. He just couldn't connect the dots for the motivation to kidnap if the purpose was to extort money. He was much more inclined to believe that the purpose was to influence his wife. That was the only thing that made sense to him. Boy, had they gotten that wrong. Kip laughed to himself. Henrietta was her own woman when it came to being a Senator. She would know that he would stay strong and not want her to bend to such a cheap underhanded ploy. While he didn't think he was in danger, he was quite aware that the situation itself was dangerous.

The thought occurred to him that he should concentrate on who might be at the root of his kidnapping. Who out there would want to influence her decision-making or maybe just hurt her in some way? There had been many attempts to taint Henrietta's reputation already, usually from right wing blogs and periodicals. They had all failed because she was more firmly on the high and moral ground than anyone he had ever met. He began to go over in his mind the groups and individuals he thought capable and motivated enough to stoop to such a level. They also had to be naïve enough to believe they were somehow above the law. Narrowing that field would take some mental effort since almost everyone believed that the laws didn't apply to them anymore. The current climate was based on 'winning' not representing any specific ideology. Kip had to admit that enough people out there had grasped enough of the extreme positions that it had altered the face of the political system forever. But kidnapping was hard to fathom given any ideological position in the American landscape. Kip shuddered at that thought that things may have progressed that far. It wouldn't have been the first-time home-grown violence had been connected to political or radical American based groups. Almost every month, horribly violent acts that dominated the headlines were carried out in the name of one organization or another. Each movement had their fringe members that were capable of anything. He would listen, and think, and figure out how to communicate clues about his captors. He might be wrong but at least it would give the people looking for him some direction.

A little under a thousand miles away on the southern outskirts of Moncton, New Brunswick Canada, three men sat around a table in a farmhouse. The first man was the tall violent man in charge of the women that were about to be transported across the border into Maine in one of the largest attempts to move trafficked individuals that had ever been attempted. His name was Maurice Taurant. He was a veteran of international trafficking and an expert in controlling people with panic and fear. He was ruthless and had already killed two of his own crew on this trip to induce a sense of hopelessness in the minds of his captives. They had not been the first and would not be the last.

The other two men were his counterparts on the American side of the border. The first was Horace Morton. He was an ex-con at the federal level with a long record of violence. He had narrowly escaped the collapse of their trafficking network in Cleveland and Kansas City. His job was to help re-distribute trafficked and smuggled individuals into major metropolitan areas in the northeastern corridor of the United States. He had customers waiting in several sweatshops in the back streets of New York who needed people to sew fake designer clothing and work in sweatshop laundries. There was a contractor who needed workers in his soft goods warehouse in Boston. Baltimore needed sex workers, the younger the better but that was tricky with its current crack down on that industry. They had plenty of slots to fill since the stream of legitimate migrants had been cut so drastically with the new policies on immigration. His business was booming.

The other American was Patrick Detweiler. He was nothing more than a transporter of illegal human cargo. He owned a fleet of modified trucks that could hide up to twenty people at a time. His job would be to have those transports ready as soon as the women were across the border. The only member of the American side of the enterprise that wasn't present at the meeting was Bobby Martel. Martel was as ruthless at dealing with humans as Maurice Taurant was. He had no value of human life other than his own. Just like Taurant he was born without one ounce of empathy. They both fit well within the psychotic spectrum and both were very intelligent. Martel had brokered many trafficking victims for labor but specialized in special-order women for the sex trade.

Taurant spoke first. "We have been moving the cargo back and forth along the border for a day. If we don't go within the next 48 hours, I am going to have to re-warehouse them. That will double the price and will double the wear. I may already have lost two girls due to the two headless assholes. Their best use turned out to be as an example. The cargo has been quiet ever since. We have to make a decision on when to move."

Detweiler spoke next. "All four locations have been checked daily. Each one has a short access route to the pick-up point in case their working sensors alert border patrol personnel and they are spread so thin that there is no way they will be able to cover all our intended crossing points. We should be loaded and gone before your team gets back across. We have picked up nothing from our snitches about Canada and the United States cooperating on anything. There will be a dark moon for the next three nights. All of the locations will work. Morton's people will be waiting to move them to me to get them out of the area quickly. The longer we wait the more of a risk we take with that many people and someone discovering them and starting to pay attention."

Taurant sat listening. "Where is Martel anyway?"

Morton answered. "We don't travel together or meet face-to-face. He will do his job don't worry. You just take care of your end."

Detweiler interjected. "My task is done. I have purchased three busses from the same company that Greyhound uses. They are decorated to look like Northeast Tour buses. They will attract no extraordinary attention. In Maine those buses load and unload at various shopping centers and gas stations. There are no bus stations. As long as we do the transfers during low activity times, no one will notice. We have already been stopping and picking up and discharging our own people just to get the locals used to seeing the busses."

Taurant nodded and smiled. "I say we go in the next two days just before midnight. Any civilian traffic on either side of the border will be in bed by then and we should have no problem. My men will deliver them to your collection team on time and without a hitch. Any problem will be killed and taken out of the area. I will be leading one of the groups myself. We will get them to you at the transfer spots, but give us time to withdraw. We don't need all of us in one place at one time. None of those girls will be going anywhere for the ten minutes it will take us to get back across the border."

Morton caught him. "Martel wants to be assured that the special package for him is ready. I will take her myself."

Taurant nodded.

The three men all agreed. They each left in separate directions. A lone pair of eyes watched them and keyed his radio. "Their meeting is over. If we have aerial support to track them, center on the man in the Green SUV. He is the tall one in charge of the girls now and he might lead us right to them."

A firm female voice came back over the airways. "Affirmative."

The Atlanta-based Smithson Evermore jet landed in Tampa. It rolled to a stop on the tarmac just as the larger Smithson Evermore jet landed from Tucson. Lily and Marcus stepped out of the second jet as it rolled up next to the SUV that had just arrived. They got in and the driver moved over to the aircraft containing Serena Moore and her escorts. Serena got in the SUV and it pulled away just as the main aircraft was being moved to its hangar and the Atlanta jet was being refueled. It was soon on its way back to Atlanta and would touch down in less than an hour.

The SUV that had picked up Serena, Lily, and Marcus was soon joined outside the airfield fence by another vehicle that followed it all the way to the Channel District headquarters of Smithson Evermore. The first SUV pulled right into the rear of the building in the protected garage. As they exited the vehicle, Oscar Dorian and Aggie were standing there in the secure entrance. Aggie spoke first. "Hello, Serena, welcome. My name is Aggie Rothberg. This is Oscar Dorian who you have already met on the phone. I see you have also met Lily Michaels and Marcus Moreno. Let's get you upstairs and settled then we will have a bite to eat while we talk. Do you have your luggage?"

Serena turned toward Lily who held the suitcase up.

"It will be safe. No one here will even open it up."

Serena shook her head. "I got on a plane with total strangers. There is no question I have trust issues but I am good with you looking in that case anytime you want to. There may be things in there that will help you. Here is my phone. It is the only one I have ever had. There is no second one related to this stupid thing I got myself mixed up in. There are numbers and a record of calls that you will want to examine sooner rather than later. I want to do all I can to try to help the man that I helped kidnap." She looked at Lily as Lily lowered the suitcase and began to carry it inside. It was headed straight to L for a thorough analysis.

They all went upstairs where Ella, the Cuban head of the household staff for their facility, had arranged lunch. For the next thirty minutes they all sat down and ate together. Slade was not with them. He was upstairs in the command center speaking with Senator Patterson and Special Agent Haskell on a secure conference call.

Slade was finishing up his briefing. "We have just welcomed a person here that we believe is a very strong lead that will help us locate Dr. Patterson. That will give us some idea of the plan they used. I assure you Walt, you will know what we know, but we have the resources to keep her safe while we determine if she is even involved. Have you made any headway on trying to determine who might have the means and motivation to try this stunt?"

Walt Haskell turned his notebook back and began. "We are convinced that this is a group rather than an individual. There are just too many moving parts. We have focused on an analysis of groups or entities that have been staunchly against any position the Senator has taken. We have come up with five. First, we have a right-wing periodical and blog run by someone that goes by the name of Homer Doom. He produces Doom's Report. He has a ton of backers and is staunchly nationalistic and conservative. He stops most of his rhetoric just short of violence and outright rebellion. We believe it wouldn't take much for his followers to take it the rest of the way. Second, a group called Patriot Green makes the list. They have organized as a PAC and have several millionaire supporters. They have not been known to exhibit any radical discourse but they do have views that are exactly opposite those of the Senator on immigration policy. They also have over a hundred individual businesses and several hundred donors and followers. They will take some time to decipher. Third, there is a group called Final Days. It is a neo-Nazi group of supremacists who don't like anything the Senator or half of the rest of government represents or stands for. They are well organized but busy down at the southern border with their own militias. It is doubtful they could have pulled anything off in Mexico without turning up as floaters in the Rio Grande River courtesy of at least half a dozen cartels. The militias have cost the normal coyotes money and opportunity. Coming in at fourth is a right wing think tank/political action committee that goes by the name Tomorrow's Freedom. They have the funds and the means but have recently been more accepting of the Senator's centrist position at least on the immigration issue. Finally, there is a religious-based organization that calls itself 'One True Good'. They go by OTG and came of age during the abortion debate. In prior years they were believed to have financed several attacks on doctors, some ending in the deaths of those physicians outside of the clinics they believed were performing the procedures. More recently, they have become more involved in lobbying and legal activism but they made the list because the Senator was at the head of their 'hate' list and has remained there. They don't flinch at all when asked about their willingness to move forward violently if necessary. They are listed at five because they are actually being more successful the less radically they act. Their leadership has assured us that the 'old days' are behind them. Our threat assessors aren't so sure."

Senator Patterson interrupted him. "Slade, as the agent read those names, I was reviewing my interactions with each one of them. I concur with all but the last one. I think they will avoid any situation that will link them to their violent past. They had to almost completely rebuild their support base and have people that I don't believe would condone the kidnapping of Kip. Of all of the names Agent Haskell read off, I would concentrate on the first two. They have consistently had followers showing up at my speaking engagements and hearings openly demonstrating outside the meetings and disrupting inside. Each time, law enforcement has had to remove them. The second one is very well financed. They put millions into the campaigns of those that have run against me and Patriot Green spent a significant amount on the most recent smear campaigns. They have a heavy presence on social media and a broad base of finance and followers. The first one, Doom, has a large following that shows up almost everywhere I go. They are younger and many are disenfranchised having lost their jobs in the auto and coal industry. Recently there has been a negative series running on the blog about Kendrick and his most recent presentations on a more collaborative immigration process. I am not going to go so far as to say these are the groups, but their rhetoric certainly has been consistent and threatening."

Slade listened, then spoke. "Walt, we will look for more current information on all of these but will center on ones the Senator has mentioned. I will have L send you the intelligence report once she has it together. Have you picked up any indication that anyone in Mexico might have an axe to grind or participated in any way?"

Walt Haskell was quick to respond. "We have not and just as you pointed out in your last written update, we don't think this group was particularly professional in how they pulled this off. They certainly had a ton of money with all the aircraft and stuff but it doesn't look like they were willing to pay 'real' bad guys to do it. I still don't trust that these people aren't dangerous because of that."

Slade was quick to agree just as a message popped up on the console in front of him. "Walt, I just had a notice from my people downstairs working on this. Do you have an agent by the name of Peter Crescent working for you?"

"I will have to check. We have a lot more agents that I can keep in my head. I will get back to you quickly on that."

Slade shifted the question. "Senator, does that name ring a bell with you?"

"I'm sorry Slade, it does not. If I have contact with the FBI, it is either in a committee meeting or through our congressional liaison."

Slade paused then continued. "Senator, there is the possibility that this has nothing to do with politics and that it is personal for either you or your ex-husband. Is there anything in your history or Kip's background outside the political arena that might be linked to this?"

Walt started to reject the question but, the Senator interrupted. him. "I understand what you're asking. There could be. Kip and I were together for twenty plus years and knew each other from college when we started dating. I will think about it and have my assistant provide you any information that seems relevant. I would like to ask that you discuss what you suspect with me before you act on it."

Slade finished the call. "Of course, Senator. We will be discreet and discuss anything we find with you. Thank you both. I want to get downstairs and find out more from our sources. Walt, do you have someone here in Tampa that the FBI could assign to work with us?"

"I do. I will arrange it through our command. His name is Phelps Wheeler. We worked together in DC and at Quantico. I will clear it and have him get in touch with you. I have to tell you that Phelps is a very different type of agent. He is a former Rhodes Scholar with an IQ somewhere around the genius level. He could be making five times as much in the private sector. He could have been promoted some time ago but wanted to remain in the field. He is another breed of cat from what we normally have. I think he will fit in nicely with your team."

Slade thanked them both again and then ended the call. He walked downstairs and headed for the dining room. He found it empty except for Ella. "Where is everyone?"

Ella smiled. "That sweet lady was anxious to get to work with the team. They have all moved to the conference room. I have put your lunch in the control room. You can eat it in there and just listen. I think Lily and Oscar are going to debrief her. Marcus is up in his office getting ready to brief you on all the things you have going." She turned and headed to the service area. Slade headed to the control room adjacent to the conference room where Lily and Oscar were talking with Serena. Just as he sat down with his Spanish bean soup and Cuban bread, his phone vibrated with a text. It was from Walt Haskell. It was a short and a sweet message. "No one at the FBI has ever heard of anyone named Peter Crescent." He transferred the information to Oscar's phone. Aggie joined him just as he began to eat. She wanted to watch as well. Too many people trying to deal with someone like Serena could be overwhelming. Since Lily and Oscar were the two that would act on her information, it was better to have fewer people deal with her in the emotional state she was in.

They had been driving around all day. The van JinJing and Han were in finally came to a stop at a gas station. Each woman was escorted to the ladies' room individually. Han pushed JinJing in ahead of her. Han would be the last escorted. The men didn't follow them into the toilet but they didn't allow them to lock the door either. They used a bungee cord wrapped around the inside door knob and pulled tight to keep the door from shutting all the way. Once Han was inside, she used the bathroom. She turned on the water and reached over and lifted the toilet tank lid off. She set it quietly down on the seat of the commode and reached in and unscrewed the rod that connected the flusher to the chain. She shoved the metal rod up her sleeve. She replaced the lid of the tank just as the man pulled the door open. She raised her wet hands just as he yanked her out of the bathroom. He stepped inside. He didn't see anything amiss so he shoved her toward the van.

They drove for another hour. Han was paying attention to all the signs and landmarks she could. They pulled off the road and headed up a gravel driveway for about an hour. They came to an old lodge that was closed. The girls from the van were all herded into one of the rooms on the first floor. There were at least thirty other girls in the same room. Some they had seen before and some they had not. They were told to rest.

Once she was sure the guard was outside the room, JinJing crawled over to Han and spoke quietly. "What is going to happen? You have been through this before. What are they going to do with us?"

Han looked directly into her eyes. "I want you to stay as close to me as you can. My guess is they are going to cross the border with us in the next couple of days and those of us that survive will be taken on to U.S. cities. You need to stay calm and be aware of what is going on around you. Do not draw attention to yourself and do not try to run unless I tell you to. Promise me?"

JinJing whimpered. "I promise. What did you mean by those of us that survive?"

Han was quick to answer. "The tall man will want to scare us into submission one more time. He won't kill any of his own this time. You see how careful our guards are being with us. We are worth nothing to him if we are damaged. But there are damaged ones we haven't seen. He may use one of them. You must steel yourself JinJing. It will not be pretty but you must not react with anything but the appearance of fear. I promise you we will get through this if you just keep your head. Now, please go back over there. Do not draw attention to me by obviously being with me. Just stay close."

JinJing crawled across the room and pushed herself up against the wall. She tried to get in a comfortable position but the floor was hard and the room was chilly. She finally closed her eyes and fell asleep. She had mixed emotions about what would happen in the morning. Han's words had influenced her greatly. It was the first step in her transformation from victim to becoming a survivor.

CHAPTER 14

Honesty really does take less time than a lie.

Alex and Pierce were sitting in the living room of the Smithson Evermore Puerto Vallarta villa with Hank and Forrest. Both of them had been given time to rest and get cleaned up. Hank was anxious to go down the hill to the Romantica section of Puerto Vallarta to get a drink and catch up with friends. He was shocked when he was told that it would be better if he stayed in until they were sure that the threat to him was over. He pitched his normal fit about how he was being treated more like a prisoner than Forrest had treated him and how much more 'appreciative' of his persona his new native friends were on Tiburon, which he continued to mispronounce as 'Tibbyton' Island. He could stand up to anyone but Alex.

He had always had a special place in his heart for Alex. No one really understood it and Alex had asked everyone not to ask him to elaborate. She had learned long ago to just accept some things because the explanation would probably ruin the feeling. She didn't abuse her special place in Hank's heart but she would use it if she had to. He tried to use every enticement to get his way. He started out with the argument that Alex would be with him. He then suggested they follow him from a distance. Finally, he even offered to pay for everyone, which was something Hank never offered to do. He might do it; he would just never offer to do it. But Alex was tough and she finally got up, walked across the room, kissed Hank lightly on the lips and told him he was staying in and after their conversation with Forrest, they would watch old movies together with popcorn and cheap wine. That was the clincher and Hank got up, sulked up to his room and left the three others alone.

Forrest watched him go. "He is a unique man, isn't he?"

Alex nodded. "He is indeed and we all love him for it. I want you to start at the beginning and not the one you think we want to hear but the one where you first got involved."

Forrest settled back with his iced tea. "After I got laid off from the insurance company, I started flying for the cruise ships and an outdoor adventure company that arranged for hunting trips to Tiburon for the big horn sheep that the Seri control on the island. Some of the cabins and huts you saw were built for the hunters and the tribe charged a significant amount for the licenses. I would fly the people in from Hermosillo. After each trip I flew them back. It was a good living but I was getting to the point where I was going to have to invest in the aircraft. I had the old helicopter and I had the Cessna but one needed an overhaul and the other needed replacing. Not many finance institutions want to invest in a small operation like mine. The rates the cartel was asking were ridiculous and not paying them had only one very painful consequence. I was trying to figure all of this out when I got a call from Serena Moore."

Alex interrupted him. "How long ago was that?"

Forrest didn't even hesitate. "It was three months ago. She said she and her friends had a business deal in the works and she wanted me to fly them from Chihuahua to Houston. She offered me a ton of money up front and a significant amount of money when the job was done. I got suspicious. She explained that it was a private mercy flight for a man who had been sick for six months and needed to be returned to the States."

Alex interrupted again. "He was sick for six months?"

Forrest laughed. "I told you I was suspicious. She said he had crossed legally and was being treated at a clinic for a rare form of cancer. The treatment was not available in the states because the FDA had not approved the treatment and insurers wouldn't pay for it. It sort of made sense but I was still leery. It got even more strange when I found out her partners were her former secretary Lucy Frost and Lucy's husband Aaron. I had remembered Lucy from the company. I didn't think she was very talented but what she lacked in skill she made up for in devotion to Serena. It was almost sick to watch. Lucy was also much smarter than anyone gave her credit for. Lucy's husband Aaron, who was unemployed most of the time I knew the two, operated at reduced mental capacity. I don't know what he suffers from but he has a hard time holding the simplest of things together. He is a whiz at mechanics so my guess is he is somewhere on the spectrum for special needs but having said that, he is functional and would do everything Lucy or Serena asked of him. I agreed and met them all in Chihuahua six days ago. Serena had rented a rundown house in an abandoned area near the airport. I began to ask questions and Serena admitted that the man was reluctant to return and his family was paying for him to be returned even if it was against his will. I became furious that she had involved me in this. She asked that I at least stay and help them transport the man safely. Serena and the other two left to go pick up the man and when they returned, they were in a panic because they had two men with them. Both had obviously been drugged. She showed me the aerosol spray they had used. At first, I thought Serena was the one who had actually taken the two but Aaron blurted out that it had been Lucy that had actually kidnapped them along with Aaron and some other guy. Serena had picked up Lucy at the airport in Puerto Vallarta and driven her to Chihuahua."

Alex held up her hand so she could capture what he had just said. She handed her notepad across for Forrest to look at. "Is that the way they spelled their name?"

Forrest nodded. "I never saw it spelled but that is what I would guess. There was really nothing exotic about them. I'm sorry. I have to ask. Have you been able to determine whether Serena Moore is OK? When she called me on the phone she was in a panic."

Alex took back her notebook and jotted down what she had just heard. As she was writing she asked. "When was the last time you spoke to her?"

Forrest didn't hesitate. It was yesterday mid-morning. You can find the call in the call log on my phone. She was worried that the Frosts weren't answering their phone. She got worried about me. She told me the plan had been completely changed and somehow, she had been in touch with an FBI agent. That whole thing sounded fishy to me. That is why I increased the security around Hank. I figured the change she told me about was the beginning of a process to cover their tracks. Hank, Serena, the Frosts and I were large leftovers. I think you will find that the two you turned over to the police in Sinaloa were sent by whoever is behind the whole thing.

Alex paused again. "When was the absolute last time you saw all of them together?'

Forrest thought then answered. It would have been Sunday evening in Chihuahua. Once Hank yelled out Slade Smithson's name both Serena and I knew we had to change the plan. The original plan was for me to fly them to Houston, clear customs, and then refuel in Alabama and one more time in Virginia before we finished up in an airport in New York. Hank's information changed all that. Serena and I agreed it was best to separate. I would take Hank west and 'dispose' of him somehow and she and the other two would take Patterson and continue the flight to the States. Serena made arrangements for another pilot while we all packed. My plane is still sitting at the airport in Chihuahua. They left about fifteen minutes before I did. The plan was always to burn the house. We didn't need any evidence of any of us being there and we had taken precautions. I set it up and triggered the device from the western outskirts of the town on my way out with Hank."

Alex looked right at Forrest. "Did you intend to abandon Hank in the desert or kill him some other way and dispose of the body?"

Forrest didn't hesitate. "You know what I did for a living. You know that I have killed people before but never an innocent bystander who, through his own blunder, ended up in that type of nightmare. I took Hank to keep him safe. I turned the phone on from the cabin. I had one of my Seri friends trigger his Mexican phone to lead the two who showed up into town so I would know when they were coming. Hank was never in any danger. I'm not sure about Dr. Patterson. I don't think the people I have described would have hurt him. I am not so sure once he is turned over to the people who hired Serena. I hope she is not already dead and if she is, I hope I live long enough to make sure they pay for that. She is not a bad person or, for that matter, a criminal. She is just a misguided desperate woman that was running out of options and felt terribly alone. She was a prime target for the people who recruited her."

Alex spoke softly. "We will do everything we can to get more information about her. We are about finished for now. I just have one more question. Do you know who hired you?"

Forrest laughed. "Serena hired me. As far as who hired her, I can't say. But from what she said, I would guess it was a group of political sideliners. If it were me, I would start looking at Dr. Patterson, his family, and who might be able to leverage his capture for gain."

Alex smiled. "OK, I lied, I have one more question. "Did you know anything about Kendrick Patterson?"

Forrest paused. "I heard him speak once in southern California. But I never had contact with him before they brought him in with Hank."

Alex finished the interview and she and Pierce left Forrest in the living room gazing out toward the Pacific to finish his tea.

Pierce looked at Alex once they were back in their operations center. "Why didn't you tell him we have Serena safe in Atlanta?"

Alex smiled. "It's the first rule of interrogation. Separate your sources and hear their independent stories. You can then compare them. The truth is probably somewhere in between."

Pierce nodded. "What do you think of these guys?"

Jorge joined them with one of his men as she answered to all of them. "From what I saw on the island, Forrest was trying to do everything we would have done to protect Hank. Right now, I believe him. We need to see what the team in Tampa uncovers from the woman, Serena. I do think he is right about one thing. All of them involved in that kidnapping have now become expendable. The two we took on the island were sent by someone. They won't last long under Mexican interrogation. She looked at Jorge and asked. "Any news from the locals in Sinaloa about our two clumsy 'hit' men?"

Jorge answered. "We asked that they be turned over to the FBI at the Nogales crossing. The Mexicans have not agreed to do that yet. The men are still not cooperating. They are not helping their cause. I'm not sure they will make it out with their attitudes. They have only mentioned one name. They say they were sent by an FBI agent."

Alex thought. "Let me guess, his name was Peter Crescent whom we have just discovered doesn't exist at least as an FBI agent."

Jorge nodded in the affirmative. "That would be the one. We did get confirmation that the plane Forrest describes did clear customs without a hitch in Houston. All of the passengers were cleared and the incapacitated man was transferred to an ambulance for continuation. The Mexican pilot returned just as was described. A plane did depart along the route Mack described. It landed once in Alabama and then again at Mountain Empire Airport near Marion, Virginia. The FAA has no indication it left there, at least not with the identification it arrived with."

Alex responded. "Then the plane must still be there. Have we checked?"

Pierce interjected. "That is not necessarily the case. Depending on the type of plane and the ownership they may not have any idea at all."

Alex looked confused. "Wouldn't the FAA check the numbers and know that?"

Pierce smiled. "Not if they changed the tail numbers or didn't file the report."

Alex was perplexed. "How would you do that and not have somebody notice?"

Pierce laughed. "We have done it a hundred times on clandestine missions. You pull the plane into a hangar and either apply new numbers over the top of the originals or pull off fake ones that were installed before. My guess is those numbers the FAA has were put on the plane when it registered its flight plan in Houston. There are so many private pilots and planes out there that it is impossible to check each step. The numbers first show up in Texas and are noted in Alabama at the fuel stop. There is no record they arrived in Virginia. I would look there. We also need to look at any planes that left within 24 hours after that plane arrived at Mountain Empire. It could be they let everything settle down and then flew the plane out under a different registration. They also could have driven away."

"Alex smiled. "We may have just figured out where Dr. Patterson ended his flight. I need to get on the phone with Oscar. If the plane is there, we can check flights going out with different airplanes. Either way, what Mack told us when compared to what Serena is telling us, seems to indicate that the plan is constantly changing."

Jorge stopped Alex to show her a picture on his phone. It was the picture of a Seri man standing with a large rattlesnake. The man was smiling and waving. Jorge continued. "Does this mean anything to you. The Seri headman wanted me to show it to you. He said you would understand."

Alex looked at the picture and laughed out loud. "I have been served. I was eye to eye with that little sweetheart of a snake when someone, with quite a bit of expertise, snatched it up before it could strike. I was hiding from the men who took it. They knew I was there all along. I knew they were good but that will teach me to never underestimate the people I'm watching." They both laughed.

Hank sulked his way back into the room and plopped himself down across from Alex. She looked at him tenderly. "Hank, why don't you tell me about the night you were kidnapped?"

Hank loved telling a story. "Well, it was just a wonderful evening up until the point that bitch sprayed me. We had enjoyed a lovely dinner, healthy of course, and I was enjoying the view outside the restaurant while I waited for Kip."

Alex smiled. "The view of the ocean is beautiful from there."

Hank snorted. "Sweetie, the ocean had nothing on the gorgeous young man across the street. But I digress. We got in the car which we thought Angelina was driving and just before we reached Kip's house, the hag driving stops the car, turns and sprays us. That is all I remember until I woke up in an absolute hovel. I didn't know where I was or what was happening. I'm afraid

I can't tell you anymore about that place since I got sprayed again. They were deathly afraid of me."

Alex smiled. "I'm sure they were. I'm glad you're safe."

In Tampa, Lily's phone rang just as she was sitting down with Serena again. It was Alex who relayed the information she had just discovered concerning the people involved and the information about the plane. Lily listened intently then turned to Serena.

"Serena, who approached you and hired you in the first place?"

Serena smiled. "He told me his name was Patrick Henry but I knew that was bullshit. We met at a rally to support stricter immigration policy put on by that crazy group called Patriot Green. I went with Lucy just for something to do. It was odd because this man seemed to know exactly what questions to ask to keep me interested. He said he represented a group of investors who had common political goals. He asked what type of work I had done. I told him I had worked for an insurance company that specialized in kidnap insurance. I also told him I had never been involved in any recovery operations but had overseen several from my desk. He told me that these men were looking to start a new venture that might be a lucrative opportunity for me. I told him I would need more information. He asked for my card and then asked if he could call me to discuss it further. I said yes. I didn't hear from him for several days and then he invited me to lunch."

Lily interrupted her. "I'm sorry Serena, where was all of this taking place?"

"Sorry, I was living in Reston, Virginia. Our home office had been located in Arlington. When I got laid off, I had to stay there because my husband's condition deteriorated just a week or so after. The last thing I needed to do was move him from the doctors and clinics where he was being treated. His cancer moved quicker than my ability to support us with the temp jobs I was getting. He died and I was in the process of putting the house on the market when I went to this luncheon. It was at a country club near Middleburg, Virginia. I had been a major executive with an elite specialized insurance firm. I dressed in my executive best thinking this might be a way to attract an opportunity. When I was ushered into the dining room, I realized that even in my best, I was underdressed for the occasion. There were four men and two women. The two women were dressed way beyond my normal means and the jewelry each had on would pay for the jet I flew here in. I was awestruck. They described a position for me as what they called a 'facilitator'. I would work directly for the group and answer to the man who had identified himself as Patrick Henry. They told me I could work from a home office they would set up. They offered more than my mortgage, insurance, and taxes together. They said they would pay me a salary of $12,000 per month. That was more than I had made with the insurance company. They wanted me to hire an assistant and they suggested, not me, that I contact my old one. I didn't think anything of it until later but they had already researched all of that. Of course, Lucy jumped at the chance. Since she had been laid off, they were barely getting by. She lived nearby. We could work from my house. New things started showing up at the front door. New office furniture was delivered. The second bedroom that had been the one we had converted to my husband's sick room, was completely redecorated and independent phone, fax, and computer links were installed, all at their expense. I was given a healthy travel budget for both Lucy and myself. We mostly traveled to explore places that they would use to stage rallies and political conferences. We were never asked to attend but were involved in setting them up and working with specific event coordinators to host them. That went on for several months."

Lily had her pause. "How much contact did you have with the man who recruited you?"

Serena thought. "I actually never saw him again after the luncheon at the country club. I never saw any of those people again. My instructions were always via email or phone call. The number I used for all the contact is the one on my phone that has been disconnected."

Lily nodded. "When did they approach you about Dr. Patterson's abduction."

Serena heaved one of those sighs that signals a crying spell. She struggled and regained control. "They approached me with the instructions three months before we left for Mexico. The entire plan was laid out. I was supposed to arrange for a pilot. Of course, I refused. I told them that wasn't what I had been hired for. My phone rang almost the minute after I had pushed send on that email. It was the man who had recruited me. He shouted into the phone that I had been hired to do what I was told. The day after that a van pulled up and disconnected all of the electronics and packed up all the office equipment and other things they had supplied and took them away. Later that day, I received a message from the bank that held my mortgage. They indicated that someone had purchased the mortgage and was foreclosing on it. I showed them that I had been making the payments and they showed me a copy of the mortgage that had a clause I had never seen before that contained my signature indicating that I understood that the mortgage had an on-demand clause. I figure that one of the many things I signed when I was being hired was that mortgage amendment."

Lily interrupted. "You never questioned or reviewed those things you signed?"

Serena heaved again. "I thought I had hit pay dirt. Of course, I reviewed things but it would have been easy to slip a signature block in on something else. I was so vulnerable and they seemed to be 'answering my prayers' with every move they made. The day after, Lucy called me. Her mortgage company had sold her mortgage. The new terms for keeping her home required a cash payment they didn't have. That evening I got another call from Patrick Henry. He said he would give me one more chance. I could either agree to do this for them for a very hefty payout and an agreement to release me from obligations with both houses fully paid off or I could wait and see all of us tossed out on the street with nothing."

Lily interrupted once again. "So, you agreed to carry out the plan to kidnap someone."

Serena blanched. "When you say it like that it sounds much worse that it was. Both Lucy and I were assured nothing would happen with Dr. Patterson and that he would be released. We had tested the spray. We were promised that we would have help along the way. A doctor contacted us and showed both Lucy and me how to administer the drugs that would keep Dr. Patterson sleeping comfortably. They kept telling us that he would not be harmed. The purpose of taking him was to prove a point related to their political agenda. He was always going to be returned unharmed."

Lily stopped her. "And you believed them after what they had threatened you with?'

Serena nodded. "Ruthless and deadly are two very different things. I thought they were vile for the pressure they put on us, but I never would expect them to do anything violent or dangerous. We rehearsed the whole thing having Aaron stand in for Dr. Patterson. He got to enjoy the spray and the drugs too much so once we knew we could do that part, it was all about operating in a way that no one got hurt."

"What about the ride-share driver in Puerto Vallarta?"

Serena responded. "Lucy sprayed her and checked her vital signs. She was fine. I picked Lucy up at the airport where we left her to drive her to Chihuahua. I checked the woman myself. When we left the car, we left the trunk ajar so she could breathe and wouldn't be trapped. We went out of our way to make sure no one got hurt."

Lily looked at her. "Do you want to take a break?"

Serena shook her head. "I need to know what happened to the Frosts and I need to know if Forrest is OK. I know those men were sent to kill me. There would be no other reason for them to follow me. I had a car and I had money and I had the story. That was too much to leave out there. When I talked to Forrest, he agreed with me. Please tell me he is OK."

Lily smiled. "I can tell you that he is OK. We don't know anything about the Frosts. Where and when was the last time you saw them?"

"It was at the airport in Virginia. They were still on the plane when the FBI agent pulled me off and gave me the money, the car, and the instructions to drive to the house in Atlanta."

"Do you have any pictures of the Frosts or Crescent or this Patrick Henry person?"

Serena thought. I have pictures of Lucy and Aaron on my phone. I didn't get any pictures of Henry. There may be one on PAC website. But I don't think that was his real name. I don't have any pictures of Crescent.

Lily responded. "Now I need to take a break to see what we can find out about the Frosts. You need to know that an FBI agent, a real one, is here and will want to go through all of this with you again. You will have to tell him everything you have told me. The men in Atlanta are in FBI hands. The house you were sent to in East Atlanta was burned to the ground yesterday just before we picked you up. It was arson. It is not uncommon in that neighborhood for houses in that condition but we believe you were supposed to be in it. You did the right thing seeking help. I will let the FBI agent tell you about Peter Crescent. Before he comes in, tell me. When and how did you first have contact with Peter?"

Serena thought carefully like she was replaying things. "He first contacted me by phone as we were getting ready to board the plane to fly to Mexico. He said the FBI was onto us but they wanted us to go through with it. They needed us to get Dr. Patterson back in the country. He promised that we would be relieved of any criminal responsibility. He said they understood that we had been pressured into the whole thing and that we would be fine."

Lily nodded her head. "This agent's name is Phelps Wheeler. He is the real deal. He will explain your options to you. It will be up to my boss and his whether or not you stay here or leave with the FBI. For what it's worth Serena, I believe you and I am a tough one to convince. We need all the help we can get to find Dr. Patterson. That will be my job along with Agent Wheeler's. Please speak up if you think of anything you think will help us. We are here to find Dr. Patterson and give you all the help we can legally give you. Having said that, you do understand that you took another human being against his will and transported him across international borders under false pretenses. You will have to be responsible for that."

Serena shook her head. "I knew that before I let Tess make the call and I got in the plane to come here. I'm as worried as you are about Dr. Patterson. But I also want to know what happened to Lucy and Aaron. I got them into this and I am almost certain something has happened to them. Please do what you can to find them and keep them from these people. If you say Forrest is OK, then I believe you. I hope you catch these people and I hope you find and save Dr. Patterson from any harm. I will take full responsibilities for my actions but I am sure I am not the only one these people have manipulated."

Lily got up, shook her hand and turned to leave. She stopped and turned back to face Serena. "Serena, what you did in Atlanta took a great deal of courage. That will count for a lot. Don't lock yourself up with fear or remorse. Keep open and cooperating.

CHAPTER 15

Evil cannot be subtle for an endless amount of time.

In northern Maine, Brad, Chuck, and Cari were on ATVs exploring the northern most site they expected the traffickers to use. They had checked out the other sites earlier and had flown to the most northern one along the border. They had started their tours at the locations of the sensors set approximately a half-mile back from the border. They were working their way back toward any clearing large enough to provide easy access for larger vehicles. It was Cari who noticed it first.

She pulled over and motioned for the other two to join her. They pulled up and cut their engines. She pointed back toward the trail they had just come down. "That is the third time I have seen evidence that someone has widened the trail slightly."

Brad looked back. "How do you mean they have widened it slightly?"

Chuck nodded his head that he understood. "She means that it is barely noticeable to the normal person. But to someone that goes out of her way this time of year to inspect trails like these and make them just a bit bigger so that they can be used for sled dog training and mushing it is obvious. Were the others like this?"

Cari nodded. "Each one of them had been trimmed back at ground level to give a bit more clearance. Just a tad, and it looks like some of the areas where animal activity or motorized vehicles have compromised the under layer, the trail has been built up with gravel and a layer of dirt. There is no vegetation growing. You can see one of those patches over there."

Brad got off his ATV and walked over to the spot. He bent down and inspected it. "You're right. This has had at least two layers added to it for about three feet. How long have you been noticing it, Cari?"

Cari looked back as she answered. "It didn't really hit me someone was doing it. It is the kind of thing my musher's club would do getting ready for snow and training. We inspect and then reinspect during the season. ATVs and snowmobiles are hell on the trails. But that won't start for another two months and we would do the whole trail. What I noticed is that it stops."

Brad looked at her. "What does that mean?"

Chuck continued for Cari because she was off her ATV and walking back up the trail. "She means that a musher would carry it all the way to the next cross-country trail. These weren't done by mushers. These were done by people creating a bit wider path for some vehicle to drive down it. If I had to guess, they stop at places where a larger vehicle like a van or a small truck could operate. If you are coming down these paths and you get to a larger path, you don't need to go farther if you have a larger vehicle waiting."

Brad nodded. "In other words, they are clearing just enough to get to these wider spots." Chuck nodded as Cari came back.

She looked at both of them. "We need to have the other places checked but I would bet that this work is the same between the border and the first clearing. It skirts the area of the sensor and then picks up just after. The signals the authorities have picked up over the last weeks were probably accidental triggers made by the people doing the work getting too close. Someone has widened the trails between the border and the sensors and the sensors and these clearings. This one leads straight down to Irving Road, which leads to several intersections along the way, all the way to central Maine and I-95. It is slick and hardly noticeable. For sure, the average agent or citizen wouldn't see the difference."

Brad got on the phone to his counterparts with U.S. Border Patrol. Maria Montalba said she was going to check the other sites. She would contact Emilio Cortez to do the same. She was about to hang up when Brad stopped her. "What if we put smaller sensors up close to the border to give us a heads up?"

Maria laughed. We can do that. But the animals interfere with them all the time. Fisher cats are the worst. They seem to be attracted to the high pitch of the sensor and they like to play with them. We have lost several to their sharp teeth. But, since we suspect this, we will risk some."

Brad laughed. "I think we might catch a different type of weasel if we do. How often is the fence at these locations and the sensors checked?"

"Not often enough. We set the sensors, check the areas once, then sort of forget it. And let's not forget that we haven't had the resources to perform regular checks. All our attention and much of our resources have been refocused on the Mexican border. We probably haven't checked these areas in a while and there are areas where there is no fence at all."

Brad thought then answered. "I would bet they are watching those sites as much as we are for additional activity. How much of a risk do you want to take? If Cari is right, these three areas have all been altered on both sides. My guess is they have had some adjustment that is barely noticeable on the Canadian side as well. Also, sensors have to be powered. How many different transformers would you have to mess with to shut the fence down for say five minutes?"

Maria answered quickly. "I don't know but I know our friends in Canada do. Let's see what I can find out from them and we will check the camera feeds mounted on the top of the border poles. The vegetation blocks a good bit of the view. I will be in touch." She hung up.

Brad looked at his two family members. "I think this is going to happen sooner rather than later. How many dogs would it take to assist at each entry point?"

Chuck thought a moment. "If Border Patrol brings their dogs and we add six, we could have all three locations covered. We would be ready for whichever location they used."

Cari broke in. "Why would they do this to all three spots if they weren't going to use all three spots?"

Both men looked at her. Brad spoke. "Cari that is brilliant. They could be planning to come across at all three locations the same night. That is why they have cleared all three. We need to get moving just in case they are watching." They left the area and headed back to the trailer and truck they had driven all over the western side of Maine that day.

Royal Canadian Mounted Police Inspector Mattey Paige was sitting with her partner Inspector Erick Brandhoff of the Canadian Border Authority reading the latest report from Smithson Evermore and ICE when their partners in the United States called them. FBI Special Agents Bridgett Moss and Steve Wiley of the Border Patrol had been assigned to track three individuals of interest related to the case. Patrick Detweiler and Horace Morton had both been spotted in Canada. Bobby Martel had been seen in Boston. They believed that was too close to the action in Maine to be a coincidence. They also had received an interesting report from the Transportation Department that an unregistered new bus service might be operating in Maine. A local officer in Augusta had seen a bus picking up and dropping off passengers at a local all-night convenience store. He had checked Maine records and it didn't appear to be registered to do business in the state. The name stenciled on the side of the bus was "Hoover Nature Tours." He didn't think anything of it until all six of the passengers that had been left at the convenience store were picked up by the same van. The officer didn't have legal probable cause to stop them so he just passed the information on and waited for an official instruction to intervene with the bus. He also put the information out over the joint law enforcement network and did a notation of interest in the national information database. There had been nothing further but the FBI agents were going to follow up.

Bridgett delivered this information to the Canadian inspectors. Steve came on the line and asked a question.

"How is the surveillance going on Taurant?" We need to figure out how to get him this time. He is the common denominator from the Midwest case. All the women described a ruthless tall man who spoke French and English."

Mattey answered. "Erick picked him up at a meeting outside of Moncton. Aerial recognizance followed him as far as they could but he pulled into a hotel parking garage and we lost contact on the flyover. SiSi over at Smithson has the video and has their satellite system set to pick up and try to find him. We think they are going to make their move soon."

Steve continued. "Brad Freeport and the rest of the Smithson team believe they are going to try to move at all three sites at the same time. I think that only makes sense if they think we are understaffed and not talking. What do you think?"

Mattey conferred with Erick then responded. "We don't believe they know we are working together. We know they have been poking their noses around all three potential spots. We have done nothing to broadcast our resources or give us away that we can think of. We tracked the last bus that left Vancouver and the one that left Halifax. The Halifax bus kept going west dropping off girls and the bus from Vancouver made their last delivery in Quebec City. If I were a betting girl, I would think that they have stockpiled a large number of women somewhere and they need to move them soon. It is totally possible that they would try a three-pronged approach. Taurant is that arrogant."

Steve spoke next. "Maria at Border Patrol and Emilio at ICE are checking the third site on the American side. We have asked U.S. Border Patrol to give us twelve additional officers. That request is still pending. Did I ever tell any of you how much I hate politics?"

Mattey responded. "No, but we get it, believe me. If they are going to do something this big, they would need a distraction somewhere. It would have to be something that would force all of us to shift resources at least in the air to the distraction. Anyone got any ideas?"

Bridgett thought a moment and answered the question with a question. "What has been the most frequent smuggling MO, planes, boats, trucks? When you answer that, what have they been smuggling. We know down south it is semi-tractor trailers full of people. What is it up here?

Both Canadians answered almost simultaneously. "Pharmaceuticals by mid-sized transit vans."

Bridgett was curious. "Do you think they will attempt to use a distraction?"

Mattey responded almost immediately. "I don't know but I think we have to be ready for almost anything that can happen. There is just too much evidence that they have been planning something big for some time. Both border services have produced intelligence that the main event is going to be smuggling humans but if they have the resources to pull this off as long as it has been building, then they may want to hedge their bets with at least some payoff and a distraction might be a calculated risk they would take if they think we are significantly under-resourced. They proved that in the Midwest deal. I just think we should be ready for anything."

Steve interrupted the call. "Can we call you back in a few? We just got a page to set up a briefing from L at Smithson?"

Eric responded. "No problem. We will see you online. We just got the same page."

From her control room in Tampa, L had Claymore set up the teleconference. It would be a one-way transmission to give both the Canadian and U.S. agencies a briefing. They would then each respond after they had digested the information and performed any updates or inquiries they needed to do. It was a new and very unusual set up. Every agent from each agency would be able to use a unique identifier to sign onto the briefing. It accommodated any secure system and would work on any device that was authorized. The agents from Canada and the agencies in the United States working on the operation including ICE, the FBI and select units of the Border Patrol assigned to the sector would all get the message. It would be the second time this technology was used.

Claymore activated the briefing and screens all over the northeast corner of North America lit up. L began the briefing.

"Hello everyone. We wanted to let you know that we have a situation report that will be issued at the end of this briefing. It lays out new information that we have gathered in northern Maine with comparisons made with the Midwest operation. It is also incorporating information from Maine Department of Transportation, Maine Forestry Service and the Ontario New Brunswick stations for the Canadian Forest Service. We have processed the information with our analysis technology and have isolated three potential scenarios that are supported by information from each of these agencies. They are as follows:

Scenario 1: Trafficking Entity crosses one of three potential sites with at least 10-30 individuals by foot enhanced at some point by motorized trail vehicles with secondary transfer to larger disguised vehicles capable of carrying up to 35 to 40 passengers. The larger vehicles which are likely to be semi-tractor trailers, larger transport vans, or larger transportation vehicles such as buses will then redistribute trafficked individuals to major urban areas.

Scenario 2: Same as scenario 1 with the addition of a distraction designed to draw attention to one of the three sites that has been verified and located as the most likely places to transect the border.

Scenario 3: Same as scenarios 1 and 2 except that the distraction happens at an as-yet-unidentified location and draws attention away from all three smaller locations.

We have applied a probability of success analysis and Scenario 2 or 3 have a high probability because of the paucity of resources to cover such a large event. The event's success grows exponentially if they use all three sites.

The vulnerability assessment indicates the weakest transfer element is the time and distance between the actual point of border crossing and the collection point for the larger vehicles. Smithson Evermore has already activated and has at your disposal for each agency two additional tactical helicopters with infra-red tracking capability and night and stealth operational modes, our new targeted drone surveillance if authorized by all agencies, our satellite surveillance system, and two fully operational ground teams to supplement your resources.

Command personnel available from Smithson for your liaison will be Dr. SiSi Holmes, Senior Technical and Communications Specialist, Oscar Dorian, Chief of Operations, Brad Freeport, Chief of Northeast Operations and Chuck Freeport Chief of Canine Operations. In addition, we stand ready to support your canine efforts with six canines all trained in human tracking. All relevant contact information for all of the above will be coming over your secure network.

Smithson Evermore has already secured the necessary authorizations from your governments and agencies. We are on ready alert meaning all resources are already in place. Any questions can be transferred here. Slade Smithson himself will be coordinating inter-agency cooperation. Oscar Dorian, Chief of Field Operations is on his way to Bangor.

In anticipation of the recovery of trafficking victims, shelters have been established to provide safe haven for debriefing and survivor services. Language capability has been established for all five suspected Asian language groups plus Hispanic and Portuguese capabilities as well. It is projected that said victims have representatives of these cultures.

This ends this briefing. Official notices of this briefing have been forwarded to your respective agencies and all inter-agency agreements have been filed between Smithson Evermore and your respective governments. For the next forty-eight hours we have our aerial resources either on standby or already deployed and our ground support stands at request-on-demand status. This includes our new A4100 small high-definition recognizance drones as well as enhanced refocused satellite flyovers."

The briefing was over. L turned to Claymore who sent out internal orders to each of the Smithson Evermore commanders. If someone was going to be so stupid or so bold as to attempt to smuggle these people across the border in the next 48 hours, a lack of resources or interagency coordination was not going to enhance their potential success.

In a large farmhouse near Saint-Paul-de-Montmini, Dr. Terrance Concorde phoned Maurice Taurant who was sitting in a transport van ten miles from where they had the girls hidden in an abandoned lodge. "We have to move within 48 hours. How soon can you have your people ready?"

Taurant answered arrogantly, "We have been waiting on you. We are ready to go. I am assuming we are going to do the full operation we planned."

Concorde answered quickly. "We will do our full plan. When your people are in position, I will let the other side know to move into position. As soon as they are in position, you will have thirty minutes."

Taurant didn't even give him the courtesy of an affirmation. He didn't like being given orders and even if Concorde was the big money bullshit artist, he was very careful not to get his hands dirty in a job that had a lot of dirty work involved. Taurant made a phone call which set off a chain of phone calls. The girls were at the lodge, which was equidistant to all three sites. He would not have time to give them one more lesson in fear like he had always done. He would figure out how to squeeze in some form of terror before they were loaded into their transport vans and taken to the crossing locations. He would just have to improvise but he hated delivering less than the full number of girls. They were money in the bank. It would have to be something else.

Concorde looked at the phone realizing that Taurant had just hung up. He hated the cocksucker but he had to have someone like that in the organization to help manage the cargo. When they had last met, he sensed a growing unease amongst some of the people Taurant employed. Beheading two of them was probably not the best human resources move but the man was an animal in a business manned by animals. He was big and he was mean and that served a purpose. If this operation was successful, they would have set a standard that would be hard to beat. He looked around the room at his diplomas and his awards for his work in medical research. He was a respected plastic surgeon and medical researcher. None of his colleagues had any idea of the source of the funds that had fueled his research. They would have a hard time linking Dr. Terrance Concorde with Taurant. He had thought many times about getting out of this sideline but the money was just too much to ignore and he was free from the competitive nature of searching for funds to support his research institute. And there were the side benefits. One of them was resting comfortably in the next room.

He had removed Anna Lopez from the school the night she was injured so badly by one of the headless wonders that Taurant had made an example of, along with a young Chinese girl. A third woman was at his clinic. She was a special project for a friend. Anna was from Honduras according to her papers. She had been kicked in the back so hard that it had broken three of her ribs and the X-ray showed that it had chipped one of her vertebrae. She was on just enough painkillers to be 'affectionate'. Her papers told one of the thousands of sad tales about leaving her home country because of gang violence and being turned away at the border crossing near Brownsville, Texas. She, her three kids, her sister and brother-in-law had lived in the wretched tent city at the border before they decided to return to Honduras. Anna and her sister had been kidnapped in Matamoros and loaded into a shipping container aboard a coastal freighter that was bound for several stops along the east coast of the United States and Canada. He sister had not survived the sea journey. The organization had shipped fifty individuals each in two containers. While at sea Anna and her sister were pulled out and chained in service compartments in the lower deck. The crew would stop in and satisfy themselves. Anna had been raped so many times she lost count. There were four refueling stops and two cargo delivery stops. At each stop a portion of the human cargo was off loaded and transferred to shore. Within an hour of arrival, the transferred container would be dropped onto a tractor bed and would be leaving the port as the ship cleared its berth. Anna had made it all the way to Halifax largely because she had been the captain's favorite form of entertainment. By the time Dr. Terrance Concorde had purchased her papers, she was worn out, abused, and quite possibly drug addicted.

After she had been injured, he had taken her back to his clinic and treated her for the broken ribs and medicated her for the spine injury. All of that was healing nicely. She would recover. He had greatly reduced the medication used to keep her compliant. It did not mix well with the painkillers and he had been pleased that she had responded well to his care. Her beauty was an unusual mix of native Mesoamerican and Spanish. He would hate to see her go but she was an investment.

The special project was a young Salvadorian client. Her name was Bettina Ocasio. She was a favor for one of his rich American friends. His services had already been paid for. He had done an amazing job of giving her a new appearance. The Chinese girl, Lan Li, was a different story. She had a badly bruised larynx, a broken septum and two broken fingers. All would heal. She was a hellcat from the first moment she discovered she was under ownership. They would be glad to get rid of her if she made it through the crossing. Taurant had already singled her out as 'too much trouble' but she was young and still a virgin. That was too much of a potential profit for even Taurant to mess with. He would be glad when all of this was over. All three would leave within 48 hours. He didn't like keeping these girls even if it did have its advantages sometimes.

In the next room Anna was carefully going through the trash in the bathroom. An hour before he left to make the phone call, he had satisfied himself with her. She was used to it now but she had turned it into a weapon. She was busy collecting things from his bathroom trash, hair from his hairbrush, and the head he had recently changed on his electric toothbrush. They were neatly tucked in a plastic bag that had contained a sterile dressing. She would do everything she could to please him hoping to gather evidence within herself to testify to his connection. She had watched enough American TV to know that this might be important whether or not she survived. Wherever she was headed, a little bit of this asshole who had feigned his affection would be going with her.

In the other room, Dr. Concorde dialed the number. It rang in Virginia. "Good evening. I hope things are going well in horse country. Your order is ready to be shipped within the next two days. It should arrive within the week."

The voice on the other end laughed. "Special delivery as usual?"

Concorde responded. "You will receive your text with delivery time and location."

CHAPTER 16

If something bad happens it always leaves its calling card.

Alex was getting ready to return to the United States with Pierce. But before she left, she needed to talk with Hank about anything else he could add. She knew the best time to catch him was early in the morning. Alex only slept about four hours per night. She would catch naps during the day when she felt tired and it was possible, but most of the time her 4-hour sleep dose was enough. They were scheduled to leave the following day at noon. Alex decided to be on Hank's veranda at 5:00 am which was his normal wake up time. She wasn't wrong.

"Alex, my God, you scared the life out of me. What on earth are you doing here so early?"

Alex smiled. "I thought it would be a good time for us to have some alone time before I leave today. How are you feeling?"

Hank smiled. "Sweet Alex. I'm fine. I guess I have come to grips with the fact that I was lucky and should be thankful. Forrest is not that bad a guy and I hope nothing horrible happens to him because of what he did. He seems genuine in his desire to help."

Alex took his hand. "Hank, is there anything you can think of that would help us to determine where Kip is?"

Well Alex, as you know I was drugged the entire time. I guess they needed to keep me knocked out to handle me. I still close my eyes and am horrified."

Alex pressed his hand. "That is what I want to talk to you about. What do you see when you close those eyes?"

"Oh, that horrid bitch, with her hand on a spray can! If I ever find that slut, I will make sure she never sprays anyone again. I hope she hasn't hurt Kip. I will never forgive myself."

"Hank, you know that none of this was your fault. Can you remember anything before you encountered the woman?"

Hank thought a moment. "I stepped out of the restaurant ahead of Kip. He is always so long-winded when saying good bye. You'd think he was never coming back." At that moment Hank began to tear up. "Oh my God, I don't believe I just said that."

Alex put her arm around Hank as he struggled to gain control of a sob. "Sweetheart, listen, we are doing everything we can to bring Kip back safely. Is there anything else you remember?"

Hank regained his composure. "Nothing stands out except the street was littered with beautiful people, one in particular. But then that section of the city is always full of young beautiful men and women. Nothing stands out."

Alex felt she had pushed him enough. She slipped onto his lounge chair with him and held him for a bit. He began to doze and she slipped quietly upstairs to finish packing.

Jorge would continue to watch over Hank and Forrest Mack in Puerto Vallarta and for the time being at least, the authorities from both the United States and Mexico were willing to go along with that. Technically the crime Forrest had committed under Mexican law was not much more than conspiracy to kidnap. In Mexico, many saw that almost as a misdemeanor. He had not participated in the kidnap, and if anything in their eyes, had performed a rescue of one of their more effusive foreign inhabitants. The United States was more pissed off. They were going to be seeking something more from Mack but they hadn't quite figured out how to use him. He had given everything he knew both to Smithson and the FBI agent that had come to interview him. Alex, Pierce, and that agent were flown to Tucson in the Smithson Jet. Alex and Pierce had been activated to relocate to the Smithson building in Maine. She would be on the ground in a matter of hours and Pierce would be flying one of Smithson's Bell 525 helicopters in the operation along with his crew from the Southwest.

Lily was finishing up with Serena in Tampa. Between Serena, her phone, and the information supplied by Forrest Mack, Lily concentrated on the flight of the aircraft to Mountain Empire airport near Marion, Virginia. Rufus had tapped his connections at the FAA and was convinced that the plane never went further than that airport. Lily felt she needed to go look. Special Agent Phelps Wheeler had been working with her for two days. They decided that they would go together and try to trace where Kip Patterson might have been taken from there. One question that Serena kept asking that really seemed important was where Lucy and Aaron Frost were. They had not been seen since Serena had been pulled out of the plane and sent on her way. She had asked L to copy and distribute the pictures of them to all agencies.

Smithson resources were stretched thin with the Maine mission as everyone was starting to call it. It was tricky because they were moving resources into place in a way that wouldn't attract the scrutiny of the traffickers. They assigned Frank Pierson to fly Lily and Phelps in the Atlanta-based Smithson Jet to Virginia to pick up the trail and attempt to find out what happened to the Frosts. Serena remained in Tampa in the custody of a female FBI agent at one of their safe houses. Once she knew that Forrest was OK, she had continued her cooperation but she was reaching the limit of her knowledge and fully expected to be transported to the local jail on a federal hold at any time.

Lily and Agent Wheeler touched down in Mountain View and were met by two local FBI agents from the Roanoke office. Those agents had received a report from local first responders that they thought would be useful about a vehicle accident and fire that had occurred off a mountain road between Tannersville and Wytheville, Virginia. They all took a moment to review the reports from the volunteer fire department, the forestry station that had reported the fire, and the Sheriff's department that had responded to the scene. There was also a supplemental report from the Virginia State Police providing support to the Wyeth County Sheriff's Office. The conclusion was that the car had run off the road, caught fire and burned at the bottom of a 100-foot drop to a streambed. Lily got on the phone to L. "We need you to pull a coroner's report for a rural vehicular accident that occurred three days after Dr.

Patterson was kidnapped. It is close enough to the airport where we suspect the plane carrying him landed. I'm looking at both the fire and accident report that indicates there were two people in the car when it burned."

L was typing as she was listening. "I have sent a request to the Virginia Medical Examiner's Office. My guess is that the office in Roanoke will have the record and will probably have done the actual autopsies. I will get back to you. Is there any information about the vehicle in the report? I can track that as well and I will have Claymore check the aerial for the time listed when the fire was reported. We may get lucky and get an aerial view but that depends on the location, the tree cover, and if you can, find out where the wreckage went."

Lily laughed. "How about if I have Phelps make the request for this entire report to be sent to you ASAP? I think that will be quicker than me trying to pour through this report."

L laughed as well. "That will work. Phelps is cute."

"Is he? I hadn't noticed."

L laughed hard. "Lily, you notice everything."

Lily replied. "You're right about that. The first thing I noticed was the ring on his finger. He is cute and so are his kids. His wife is amazing and a physician in Tampa. He's also smart and by that, I mean scary smart. Now stop the silliness and get the information and reply please. Are there any further instructions from Slade or Aggie?"

L went back to her business tone. "Aggie is going to be your primary. Slade is coordinating things in Maine. You will be lucky if you don't end up in Maine. Frank is going to stay with you in Virginia so you have mobility. All the photos of the frosts have been distributed. I have also pulled photos from the Patriot Green website of their events to see if that rings any bells with people. We really do need to find Dr. Patterson sooner rather than later. Good luck."

Lily was walking back toward the FBI agents when she saw a Wyeth County sheriff's office vehicle pull up. The deputy got out and walked over to the agents. Phelps then dispatched the agents to go with the airport director to look at the planes that were stored there. Phelps waited with the deputy for Lily to reach them. "This is Deputy Conner. He is going to drive us out to the site where they found the vehicle. The Virginia State Trooper that was there that afternoon will meet us there along with one of the forest rangers." Lily shook the deputy's hand and they got in his heavy-duty four-wheel drive extended cab.

Lily spoke to the deputy. "This is one serious off-road vehicle."

Conner nodded. "Yes Ma'am. We have to respond to all sorts of things in our county and a good bit of it is off road. I think it is best if we approach the site from below the place the car went off. There is an old farm road that will take us fairly close but it is rough so hang on. Once you look at the fire scene, we can then walk back and drive around to the place above where the car left the road."

Lily laughed. She leaned forward and spoke to Phelps. "Good thing you left your dress shoes back in Tampa and went tactical for this." Lily was the type of woman that owned one pair of high heels but had six different pairs of hiking boots.

Phelps turned around and smiled as the deputy chuckled. "I have them in my bag along with my suit, just in case."

They parked the truck and began the hike. Lily was watching the trail as they went. As part of a team and that had just finished training in Washington State with the military, she was looking for the signs she had learned to look for from recon and rapid response military team members during the training. She was seeing plenty of it. She asked the deputy. "How often would someone be coming this way?"

The deputy paused to think. "Maybe a forest volunteer or ranger once a month. The land is all owned by the federal government at the bottom here. There may have been some hikers but we don't get much of that. It isn't that interesting. Most of the hiking traffic is on the Appalachian Trail, which runs south and east of here near Mount Rogers National Recreation Area. This access road is only known to a few old timers. Most of them are volunteers for the forest service. You are about to meet the ranger that can give you more details."

Lily kept thinking as she was walking. "How much of the fire response and rescue happened from this approach?"

Deputy Conner stopped, turned around and looked at Lily. "None of it. It all happened from the road above that you will see later. The fire group came in from the north approach along a different fire road. If you don't mind, Ma'am, why are you asking?"

Lily looked straight at him. She walked over to the side of the trail and pointed out the broken and hacked limbs on the side of the trail. "Someone has been this way recently. Animals don't make this kind of sign. I have seen bear scat but no bear I know would waste their time breaking off this type of branch. We are higher on their food chain than this weed. Someone has been through here and recently. We have been walking all over boot prints cutting back and forth across this trail. Someone was leaving a trial trying not to."

Both of the men looked at her. The deputy responded as he turned to lead on. "I will have someone come and mark this. You don't think we are dealing with an accident, do you?"

Lily smiled as she spoke. "I don't know. At this point I am just curious."

They got to the site and surveyed it. The deputy sat looking at it until he finally turned to Lily and Phelps. "There should be a larger burn ring."

Phelps looked at him. "What do you mean?"

Conner continued to walk around the outside of the charred area. "This looks more like a site of a controlled burn than a case where a car caught fire. That area should look more random following the path that gasoline would leak from the tank. That would follow the rules of gravity. This looks like it was designed to contain a fire until it burned out. I would expect more damage. There must not have been much fuel in the vehicle. Which leads me to a second question now that I think of it. The report said that the major area of the burn was in the front passenger compartment and the trunk. The front of the car was resting in the creek and the rear on gravel and sand. It rested flat. How did the fuel leap over the backseat area? Also, some of that fuel would have leaked into the creek. We found no evidence of that and the rangers are really clear about that type of thing. These waters are the livelihood of the tourist area. Three states contribute funds to keep them clean. Farmers can get fined to the point they are put out of business for dumping stuff. I am going to request more sampling. They report said that the fire was contained by a quick response. It had to have taken thirty or forty minutes to get here. It has taken us twenty just to hike in without equipment. The fire access road comes in from the north and it is ten miles from the turn off. It may have been a quick response but not quick enough to contain the fuel leak and random spread. I think this fire was contained by limited fuel and directed containment."

Lily was first to speak. "There wasn't any mention of this in the report. You are the deputy for this district. Did you not respond?"

The deputy shook his head. "No Ma'am. It was my National Guard duty week. This is the first time I have seen this scene." He got on his radio and requested a patch through to the Sheriff himself. He requested a crime scene team be dispatched and indicated that he would coordinate with the Virginia State Police once they met up top. He turned to Lily and Phelps. "We have an option here. We can climb up this way. It can be tough but you both look capable. The others are up top. Once we get up there, I will have someone drive us back to my truck and you will get an idea of the distance I am talking about."

There was no hesitation. All three began to climb the hillside. On the way up, Lily asked the question. "How would you limit the leakage if that was what you wanted to do?"

The deputy answered. "You can check this with the ranger when we get up top. I was a volunteer firefighter before I went to the academy and joined the sheriff's office. But you can do it two ways that jump into my mind. First, you can limit the fuel drastically so it burns in place. That would mean that the tank was almost empty and the accelerant was splashed strategically. You could also put out a portable boom in the creek and a small trench around the land spill. The boom soaks up most of what would leak from a burn and the trench could easily be covered over. They do it all the time during controlled conditions. It is a small area. It wouldn't take a large boom. What I'm trying to figure is why?"

Phelps was first to answer. "Because someone loved these woods and that stream more than they loved the two poor bastards that were in the car."

They reached the top of the hill and were given a hand by the trooper and the ranger who were waiting up top. The deputy advised the state trooper as to his conclusions and the conversation with the Sheriff. The trooper immediately leaned his head over and began speaking into the microphone mounted on his left epaulet. Lily, Phelps and the ranger walked around the scene. The ranger detailed the discovery of the smoke plume and the fire response. It was a textbook response which took forty-five minutes once the smoke was reported. Nobody that arrived on the scene suspected anything other than the fact the people had run off the road crashed over the side, landed nose down and the vehicle caught fire. He noted that the vehicle was not in flames upon their arrival. It was just smoldering. It looked like an accident to everyone at the time.

Lily walked back and looked over the side. She stood above the area that they had just surveyed below. She could see one scuffmark on a rocky outcrop halfway down the hill. She could also now clearly see an indentation in the creek bed where the nose of the car had landed before it slammed back to the ground. What she did not see is any evidence that fuel had spilled on the way down the hill. She made a mental note but decided to wait until she heard from L to bring it up to Phelps. She was convinced that this was not an accident. She believed that the two people in the car burned beyond immediate recognition were probably the Frosts. The time frame fit. She was also convinced that they needed to speed things up. If this were the Frosts, the kidnapping now involved murder.

Deputy Conner had arranged for a ride and they all got in the departmental SUV that had been dispatched to return them to his truck. The ranger had decided to meet one of his team on the main road below so he was in the vehicle with them. Lily waited until they were underway. She turned to the ranger and asked him so everyone could hear. "If I wanted to control the burn of that car so that it did minimal damage to the creek and area nearby, who would have that knowledge?"

The ranger looked shocked but answered. "You'd have to talk to one of us or one of our volunteers. That would take a containment boom and a knowledge of how to conduct a controlled burn."

Lily didn't bat an eye. "Who in that category lives close to here."

That made the ranger uneasy enough that he looked at the deputy. Phelps caught the look and with his best FBI voice responded. "This appears to have been something more than an accident and I think what my colleague is suggesting is that if it was not an accident it was intentional. You know I am an FBI agent so you and the deputy both know I have a jurisdictional reason for being here. There is a possibility that the accident may be connected to an on-going kidnap investigation with international implications. Now is not the time to worry about not throwing someone under the bus. Deputy Conner wasn't here; he was off serving his military obligation. You were. You assumed you were just looking at some fool that drove off the mountain into the creek and set his car on fire. Your job was to put the fire out. Our job now may be to determine who caused the fire in the first place. If I were you, I would answer the lady's question before I turn the lady loose on you and the deputy and I take a calculated walk."

The ranger looked at Lily and then looked back at Phelps. "That doesn't sound legal to me."

Lily reached around behind him so that her arm was resting on the seat behind him. "So, you're not just a ranger, you are a lawyer too."

The ranger looked at the deputy who continued to look straight ahead. There was no question he understood the situation much better than the ranger. The ranger looked at Phelps and spoke quietly. "We have a retired ranger who now works as a volunteer. He lives on the other side of the road where we will turn in to get to the deputy's truck. But he is not there. He left to go fishing in Patagonia, the one in South America, last week."

The deputy looked in the rearview mirror at the ranger. "He is talking about Tim Sampson. Tim would have the knowledge and he would have the desire to save the area. He also would have the equipment. I'll get the Sheriff's department here to get a warrant for his place and have them search it. If he has gone to South America and he is involved, he will have been paid for his help. That is an expensive trip. He lives what you could call a 'Spartan' existence. Since his wife divorced him, he hasn't got a pot to piss in. He gives what money he has, about half his pension, to some ultra-conservative group. He's always spouting off about what's wrong with the government. If he is involved in this and has gone south, he won't be back."

They arrived back at the deputy's truck. The ranger started to walk over to the forest service truck that was waiting for him. The deputy called to him. "Don't go anywhere but home or back to work, Leon. I want to continue this discussion after I get more information and when I ask you a question you better well not freeze up like you did with this federal agent or I will be pulling a warrant for your sorry ass. Do we understand each other?" The ranger nodded and got in the truck.

They returned to the airport. As Conner pulled up, he handed Phelps a card. "Here is my number. This airport is in a different county but if you need help let me know. These are good people that live in this part of Virginia. But they are also very conservative thinkers. They would just as soon shut up as say anything if they think it will get a neighbor in trouble with any government agency. You may run into some of that with these airport people. The Sheriff here is the same as my boss. I know him well and he will help. If someone has died or someone has been carried off against their will through his county, he won't care what party you are with, you are going to pay."

Phelps thanked the deputy as he and Lily got out of the car. Deputy Conner looked at Lily and spoke one more time. "Miss, I have three crazy little kids I'm trying to raise to respect the outdoors and other people. I haven't ever seen anyone read a trail like that and I have been hunting these woods and hills all my life. If my kids ever disappear, I want someone like you to help me find them. I will get that entire trail covered and whatever we find we will forward to the FBI. My guess is that it is going to lead straight across to that farmhouse over there." He pointed to the one across the road where Tim Sampson had lived until just days ago.

Lily smiled and nodded her head yes. "If that ever happens, and I hope it doesn't, just let us know. I will be here in hours and we will find your kids. Until then, watch over them. I spend my life finding and helping people that let their guard down just for a second. I hope we never see each other again and thank you." She got out of the truck and headed toward Phelps and the other two FBI agents.

They reported that they believed the plane that had landed with Kendrick Patterson on board was in the hangar. They had called a tech team in to go over it. The agents were going to have the surface of the fuselage tested because they felt they detected an adhesive around the original numbers that would indicate that a second set of numbers had been applied over the first. This plane was registered to a leasing program. It had taken off from the airport the same morning that it was believed that Kip Patterson had cleared customs. It had landed in Houston with two refueling stops, one each way, both at the same airport in Demopolis, Alabama. There was no question in their minds, this was the plane. Phelps and Lily decided not to even wait for lab confirmation. They were on their phones to their respective agencies. It was time to go to work with all their resources to find out which direction and by what means Kip Patterson had left this airport and where were they taking. him. One obvious thought was the area of northern Virginia just west of Washington DC. That is where Serena had been recruited and that was a good starting point unless Smithson and the FBI came up with additional information. Serena had also given them the New York destination.

But Lily was bothered by an intuitive notion that was creeping around in the back of her mind that they were being spoon fed. She looked at the countryside surrounding the airport. It was mostly farmland surrounded by the low hills that was typical of this area of Virginia. It was the perfect peaceful setting to be anonymous. Interstate 81 was roaring by just to the northwest of them. It was the perfect place to create several different diversions with lots of different options. She turned to Phelps. "I think we should stay put and nose around here until we get a better ID on the people who were in the burned car. I also think, before we go launching off to any other location, we make sure we find out about any other aircraft that left here that day and where they were headed. I also think we need to check as many traffic cameras as we can along the way to determine if we can identify any vehicles that might have been large enough to carry Dr. Patterson. Between our resources and your agency's, we need to begin at the last point where we suspect he was and that is at this airport."

Phelps thought a moment. "I think you are right. The best way to send us on a wild goose chase is to have us skip a step. Let's get really basic. There are only two ways they could have moved Dr. Patterson in another plane, or by vehicle. Serena says there was another vehicle, a transport van that pulled up to the plane. So, we can at least believe they had that capability. They had to have had support to bring that vehicle and the one that Serena was given to drive to Atlanta. Someone here must have seen what happened that day. I think we need to get a bit more information and I think we need to take Deputy Conner up on his offer to get local law enforcement to help us."

Lily smiled. "You are remembering what he said about the people."

Phelps nodded. "I am. I would be willing to bet that someone who was here that day is here right now and that they are watching to report what we do. We have to at least narrow our search. I think we also need to make them believe that we have taken the bait."

Lily laughed. "How about this. I am going to get Frank to fly me to the nearest airport that can accommodate the Lear. I suggest that you take the car the Roanoke FBI Office has provided you and drive north. I think Wytheville will be a good place to meet. You can have the local sheriff arrange to bring these people in for conversations. The deputies can take the lead and we can supply the questions. They will think we have gone and we will most likely get a better idea of what happened here on the ground."

Phelps looked skeptical. "If someone is watching right now it is most likely someone who will know we are on to them the minute the deputies bring them in. Don't you think that will stir them up and alert them anyway?"

Lily laughed again. "I most certainly do. But that is what we are going to be doing with a little help from Deputy Conner and the local sheriff. We are going to flush out the folks here that cooperated with the kidnap and transfer."

Phelps shook his head. "That is one hell of a long-shot but I think it's a good idea."

Lily smiled. "I have a sixth sense about this thing. It is no more of a long-shot than the two of us driving without a destination north to urban northern Virginia or New York. If your people can find us a place to stay, we can at least develop a better understanding of what went on here. By that time, we should have more information from the medical examiner and more information on flights that may have departed from here or a nearby general aviation field like this. If they are going to use Dr. Patterson and possibly release him, then they are going to want to be close enough to leave in a variety of directions. If they don't intend to release him alive, then at least we will have concentrated this part of the investigation on the body of facts we know."

She got out of the car and was followed by Phelps to the Smithson plane. She boarded and the plane cranked its engines. It would land in a very short time in Blacksburg, Virginia, near Virginia Tech. Lily would wait to hear where she was to meet Phelps. Phelps had returned to the car and pulled out a map. He went inside to the desk and asked them to give him the quickest directions to western New York. Several of the people in the lounge gathered around the desk and gave their directions. He thanked them and headed for the car.

Even before he opened the door, Horace Allen was on the phone. "They took the bait. The dumb bastards are headed to New York."

CHAPTER 17

Blending in means being still while observing. Otherwise,
you are just being quiet for no reason.

The lights in the dilapidated lodge blazed on and woke up the sleeping women. Han and JinJing discovered that during the night more guards and women had arrived. Han estimated that there were between sixty and eighty women all gathered just on the first floor. They could hear people above on the second floor as well. Some of the guards were now women. JinJing's eyes swept the room for Han but when their eyes met, Han shook her head slightly from side-to-side unsure of whether some of the new women were actually guards as well. Many of them were Hispanic mixed among the Asian women and she noticed that the woman who had been kicked so hard in the back had arrived during the night. She looked like she was in a drug stupor but at least she was alive. JinJing was busy looking through the room for Lan Li. She hadn't seen her since she had caught the glimpse of her two days earlier. She was beginning to worry that she had been sacrificed in some way.

Each of the guards was armed with a long baton to maintain control. One of female guards came around and directed JinJing and the women around her to move toward the bathrooms. They were taking five to ten girls at a time. Each woman was forced to undress completely before she entered the bathroom. They were given the opportunity to use the toilet but the doors were propped open. Then they were lined up in a shower and hosed off like animals in a zoo. The water was freezing. Bars of soap were thrown to them. The naked women instinctively picked up the soap quickly and cleaned themselves. Once again, they were hosed off with freezing water. They were each given a towel and underwear and herded back into the room. As they entered the room, they were given another set of clothes and moved to a different spot. JinJing could see the male guards searching where they had slept.

Han was in the last group to go. When she returned, she was directed to a spot closer to JinJing. Just as she arrived, she doubled over and cried out in pain. The female guard closest to her grabbed her and took her back into the bathroom. She raced to the stall acting as if she was going to burst. The woman backed away in disgust and didn't bother to hold the door open. Inside, Han lifted the commode and removed a much firmer flush rod and chain. She secreted both inside her socks and pant legs. With her prior experience she had anticipated they would be stripped, searched and supplied with new clothes.

While she was gone, one of the men found the first discarded rod Han had stolen earlier but thought it was just trash from the lodge that was falling down around them. It didn't look like a weapon that a terrified woman could use to make anything happen. He had kicked it to the corner of the room. Han was brought back into the room and patted down in a cursory search. The female guard had been so disgusted by her obvious problem that she wanted nothing to do with a more extensive search. Han was directed to yet a third spot. She still had tools.

After all the women had redressed, they were given energy bars to eat and bottled water to drink. As the first groups had finished, some were gathered together in groups of ten and herded out to a waiting small semi-tractor trailer truck where they were loaded into the back. They loaded forty women who had been in the lower level of the lodge. Han realized that she had underestimated the number. More had come from the second floor. She now believed there must be over a hundred. The group she and JinJing were in remained at the lodge as the truck left.

JinJing was watching closely and listening to what was being said. Most of the women with which she was grouped were non-Asians. She had noticed Han and determined that she was picking things up and hiding them. JinJing decided that was a good idea and would adjust her vigilance and become more aware of things that might be useful in an escape. She did not know if she could hurt anyone let alone try to kill them but the brutal killing of the men had affected her a great deal. She was getting tired of being ordered and pushed around but was undecided about how to resist. She had been watching Han closely. She felt that Han's experience would show her the way but she decided that she had spent enough time being so passive. She began to think about how she could improve her chances if given the opportunity to escape. Her fear began to transform into an opportunistic vigilance that increased her confidence that she would survive. She had noticed that Han would pay close attention to who was watching her and stayed near the middle of a group. JinJing had already seen her position herself to be the last one into a group and by so doing, take control of where she was. JinJing decided she was working from a strategy and decided that she would pay attention more closely to everything that was going on. She also felt there were more women than she had seen before. Even with some having been loaded in a truck, the lodge still seemed full. She didn't see many of the women she had been kept with earlier other than Han. She did notice that the woman who had been kicked so badly was back. She too seemed to be watching everything with something in her eyes more than fear or helplessness. The woman had nodded to her from across the room when their eyes had met but JinJing didn't know if she was doing it on purpose or it was because she was possibly under the influence of a drug. From this point on JinJing was determined that whatever happened she would look at everything as an opportunity for escape rather than a confirmation of slavery.

After the truck had departed, they were once again shuffled into different locations within the room. Most of the women were fearful and completely confused. Han was watching closely for any signs that any of these poor creatures had even the slightest glimmer of courage. So far, she knew JinJing had spirit and she suspected that the Hispanic woman who had just rejoined them was also capable of resistance. Enslaving human beings must be done with vigilance and violence. The threat must be renewed and random for the element of fear to take over from the spirit of survival. Han had learned this the first time and at the highest of cost. There had been no reason to kill her daughter in front of her. No one had made any trouble. The first time during a risky part of the trip on the lake, there was a point with a high probably of discovery. If any of the women had made a sound they would have been caught. Nothing directs attention more than the needless taking of a life to prove a point. Seeing her daughter dropped into the icy waters of Lake Huron with her hands and feet bound was enough to take the fight out of the entire group of

15 women that were on board to witness it. Her daughter had just been seated in the wrong place at the wrong time. When it happened, it had paralyzed her and the other women in the group even though a U.S. Patrol Boat passed them moments later. All of them bent down and laid on the deck as they were told. The man had put his foot on her throat to keep her sobs muffled and she almost died from the crushing pressure of his boot. That same scene would return time and time again to Han. It would transform her and drive her to once again come face to face with this man and make sure he did not survive the meeting. She had lost her fear about her own longevity. If she died it would bring an end to the horrible vision of her daughter's death. If she lived at least, she would have the satisfaction of knowing she had carried out her personal mission of revenge. She looked across the room and the young Chinese girl she had been communicating with. She sensed in the girl's eyes that she had also reached the point of subtle resistance. To them, slavery was not going to be an option. They would both prefer death but it had to be one with meaning not just part of their captor's plan. Han had been through this before and she was astounded at how much she was able to predict their movements. She was particularly observant of the oversized bastard in charge. She had watched him behead his own men. That told her that to sacrifice one of these women was not 'cost effective'. Her daughter had been a virgin and he had known that because they had all been brutally checked. Virgins brought more money to their business than 'experienced' women. He had grabbed the nearest girl and made a costly mistake. There would be a time during the next few hours that he would consider the same tactic with a less valuable girl just to make the same point. It would be a time when he needed them to be paralyzed with fear. She would wait and use that to her advantage. Her mission was not to escape their control but use that control to kill this animal. She was surprised he had not recognized her. She had to assume that they all looked more like dollar signs to him than human beings. She had made it a point to be in the middle of the group and in a group she chose. She was not without tools and had selected them and discarded and resupplied herself based upon her experience from the last time. She would be ready when the time came and she was confident that it was approaching sooner rather than later.

JinJing was forced into another location with yet again another group of girls. She realized that she was always the first one to be pushed. She immediately recognized that her youth and her appearance were being used as a marker for the guards. They would search her out and use her to reorganize them into different groupings. At first, she thought that this was a bad idea. but once her alarm buzzers stopped going off, she believed that she would use their silly system of using her to reposition herself closer to Han. She decided she would test it. She sat down and waited for the next shift with her eyes on the two female guards closest to her. They had always been the ones to initiate the regrouping. Each time they looked away she scooted closer to the far end of the group. She would wait to see if they noticed her movement or if they just sought her face out in the crowd and regrouped other women around her.

This dance continued for almost three hours. JinJing had confirmed her suspicions when the guards looked around and sought out her features to determine the next regrouping. She was moved twice and each time closer to Han. It would be another hour before they were in the same group for the first time with little or no distance between them. The tedium had taken its toll on the captive women but it had also taken its toll on the people guarding them. After this last move, the two female guards were rotated outside and a male and female were put in their place. The past three movements had brought both Han and JinJing into the same group as the injured woman. They sat on the floor next to each other with Han in the middle. When the guards turned away to watch the other women, Han grasped both their hands and squeezed. Both of them squeezed back. Thus, was born the triumvirate dedicated to survival and revenge that would become a problem for Maurice Taurant and his fellow traffickers. He wasn't even in that province when it happened and if he had been, he would have underestimated the strength and potential for victory of three women who had been kicked, raped, and mistreated for too long.

Alex arrived in Maine and was met by Oscar Dorian. She jumped on a floatplane in Greenville, Maine, and was flown to a remote lake a few miles from the border called Presley Lake. She hiked toward the border until she could see thought the area where the two countries met. She established an observation base and set out her warning sensors. Then she moved toward her target, which was one of the trails that Brad had reported finding. Alex found it with the help of her heads-up display while L in Tampa and SiSi in Maine were watching. SiSi would relay instructions to Alex and they had a drone positioned above her to help alert her if she had company. Alex loved this part of her job. To see and not be seen had been cast in her DNA from an early time and she blended into the lush forest almost seamlessly. Only a small portion of Maine's population can be found in the largest and most remote part of the State. It is the perfect place for hunters, hikers, campers, and all other forms of outdoor enthusiasts. If her helpers in the sky and monitors elsewhere detected other human activity, she would know and investigate it. She moved to a point where she had a clear view of the ravine where the trail was. She stopped and quietly waited. She had heard nothing for an hour except the abundant wildlife that most people never see or hear in the wild. A family of beavers was busy at work on a stream off to her left. She had seen a flock of wild turkeys go by with three hens and two younger male birds, one of which strutted like a jake, that would soon turn into a gobbler. Alex also had to remain perfectly still as a skunk and her litter of four crossed in front of her with one of the kits coming toward her to investigate her shoe. Other than this, she was free to watch the area from her vantage point. After thirty minutes she decided to shift position to investigate the lower edge of the ravine. That would put her right on the trail currently projected on her visor. Alex looked like a 22nd century soldier. She was a tiny gladiator with a full helmet that hid her facial features while providing her digital data including audio, video and mapping displays. It had taken her several weeks to learn how to direct her attention to the displays at the same time that she maintained visual and audio awareness of what was going on ahead and around her. She had learned not to walk down trails, but move slowly parallel to them like military scouts and forward intelligence agents had done for centuries. Alex just had the benefit of scientific enhancements that made her safe and her job more comprehensive. She found a small gravel area just east of the trail with a small spur that had been cleared to widen the area. She turned northeast and followed the spur for five hundred yards when she saw them.

Standing no more than forty feet away were a moose cow and her two babies. This is one of the most dangerous situations in the northern states where moose live and breed. The cow raised her head and sniffed. She had horrible eyesight like all moose but she had detected a possible threat, either a smell that she recognized, or more probably one she didn't. She was huge, healthy, and showing signs of taking an aggressive position toward Alex. Alex retreated back slowly until she had put more distance between them. Fifteen hundred pounds of concerned moose continued to look in her direction and even did a small charge and bellow, but stopped short. The calves continued to graze aimlessly without showing any notice until she turned her head and made that universal sound mothers make when they are directing their young. They didn't even look at her, they just trotted off in the opposite direction. Alex watched as the cow slowly turned and walked back about twenty feet then turned and bellowed again just to make sure. Alex believed her and stayed put. The cow then turned and trotted off in the same direction that her calves had gone. Alex took a moment to gather her thoughts. She hadn't ever felt in danger but she had felt awe toward this huge mother and her protective behavior. This is what Alex loved about her job. She had been ready to climb a tree if necessary. She had picked a good stout one that would have been tough for the mother moose to push over. She decided to climb it anyway just to get a better look down the trail. She was about halfway up when she saw it.

Alex climbed down the tree and made her way slowly toward what she believed was a building she had seen from the tree. She pushed her microphone key. "I have spotted what I think is a structure of some kind and am proceeding toward it. Do you have any visual of it from your overhead?"

SiSi was the first to speak. "I am searching ahead of you and from the drone, all I detect is tree cover."

L was next. "I have checked the maps and plots and have found nothing that would indicate a building, but that area of wilderness is often disputed between private concerns and land trust folks. Not everything gets reported."

Alex keyed the mike again. "It is completely covered with a camouflaged netting. I only saw it because of a small vent that is protruding near the roof. If I had been further up the tree, I would have missed it. Can you see my track?"

SiSi was quick to respond. "I have you on the map. There is supposed to be nothing there."

Alex responded. "OK, standby for further. I am going to get a closer look. Do you see any signs of other life around? I don't like surprises."

SiSi answered. "Nothing is showing on infrared except a large blip and two smaller ones moving off just northeast of you."

Alex laughed. "That would be mama and the twins. Standby for a report."

SiSi was confused and keyed her microphone for L. "Do you know who mama and the twins are?"

L laughed. "If I had to guess I would say it is one of Alex's close encounters with local fauna. Remember, she sat quietly while a large rattlesnake was coiling to strike her in Mexico."

Now it was SiSi's turn to laugh. "Alex isn't afraid of any animal out there, is she?"

"I don't think she likes kidnappers or human traffickers, child or women abusers, or bullies. A human is the only thing that puts Alex in the defensive mode and that normally doesn't work out so well for the object of her attention."

Alex keyed her microphone. "You two stop exchanging gossip and tell me if there is another road that comes into the back of this property."

They both checked their resources but SiSi was the first to speak. "Nothing is registered on a map."

Alex was quick to respond. "Well drop a pin there because there is a larger trail that looks like heavy traffic has been here lately. Nothing as big as a truck but certainly something powered and on tires not snowmobile skids."

SiSi responded. "I dropped the pin and entered the description. None of that shows from above or is included on any map."

Alex keyed her mike to respond and moved cautiously toward the structure. It was secured by large barn doors on either end. She took out her video console and attached the snake head extender to it. She pried a loose piece of wood away from the frame of the door and inserted the extended tube containing its own light source. She looked down at the small screen and hit the transmit button to send the video feed to both SiSi and L.

SiSi was the first to respond. "What are those things?"

L answered the question partly. "SiSi those are large 6x6 all-terrain vehicles but I don't know what the other things are attached."

Alex answered. "They are trailers, large custom-made trailers."

SiSi was the first to make the point. "Those are the largest ATV's I have ever seen and I didn't know you could pull a trailer with them. What do you think they are there for?"

Alex didn't hesitate. "Several years ago, I would have said logging because these are large and have six wheels. The trailers have off road suspension and tires or at least they look like that from here. We may have just figured out how a smuggler could get people from the border to the trailhead. I'm going to pull back in case they have this place monitored. Let the others know to look for this type of installation at the other suspect points."

L responded. "I'm telling them everything as we speak. Be careful."

CHAPTER 18

*It is easy to hide parts but very difficult to hide the whole
truth of something.*

Kip Patterson was pretending to be asleep when he heard voices near the door to his room. He had no idea what time it was. It was classic kidnapper behavior designed to disorient and isolate. He was not particularly concerned at this point about his safety. He was being treated with care and even a hint of kindness. The food was good and he was given enough leeway with his chain to get to the bathroom without hindrance. But there was no question he was a prisoner and being isolated and confined even without harsh treatment, was frightening. As he concentrated on the voices, he was sure he heard and recognized at least one of the three. The voice sounded female. Only one person ever entered the room at a time and that person was male and always wore a hood. The only time that Kip had been moved from the room, a second person had placed a hood over his head at the door. He got up from the bed and moved as close to the door as his chain would allow. He was sure there was a woman's voice and he was sure that he had heard it before. He was positive that it was the same voice that had turned around in the front seat of a car in Puerto Vallarta and sprayed him with a tranquilizer. But it seemed even more familiar. He couldn't quite recall where he had heard the voice before.

He just made it back to the bed when he heard the lock on the door click. The man walked in rolled him over and handcuffed him from behind. He then unhooked his chain from the floor and yanked him upright. The man moved him toward the door but stopped short of exiting the room so a second individual could cover Kip's head with a hood. He was pulled roughly along a hallway. The floor was solid, highly polished oak with a different colored inlay along the baseboards. It was custom made and it was very well done.

They continued to herd him down the hall and then they turned him sharply to his right through another doorway. His bare feet detected plush carpet as he was slammed into a chair. His cuffs were removed and a waistband was placed around his chest that secured him to the back of the chair. His legs were each bound to a chair leg. The hood was yanked off just as a flood light was turned on blinding him until his eyes adjusted. It took a moment to focus. There were several hooded figures in front of him and at least one behind. One of the figures in front handed him a statement with instructions to read it when he saw the red light come on. He glanced at the prepared script and nodded. He squinted as he looked up and began to read when he saw the red light of a video camera begin to blink.

"By know you should know that my captors mean business, Henrietta. Up to now, I have not been hurt in anyway. But, if you insist on appearing at the hearing, you can expect that kind treatment will end. Just in case you mistake my luxurious imprisonment and excellent care to be the acts of people less seriously committed, you should continue to watch."

There was nothing else on the paper. He looked up and saw the red light still blinking and steadied himself for what he felt was about to happen. Two individuals approached him and grabbed his hands. His right hand was bent back and held firmly while his left arm and hand were placed on the table next to where he was sitting. He felt them secure his hand with a strap that had been threaded through the table. A third individual approached with a pair of bolt cutters and he only had time to take in a breath when he felt them cut off part of his little finger just as he passed out.

Kip didn't know how long he had been out. He woke up with his left hand elevated on a pillow. His hand was bandaged and while he was aware of the pain, he was sure he was drugged enough to make it tolerable. Someone was sitting next to him. He was sure it was a woman but she wore a hood. She leaned over, placed her hand behind his head and tilted a glass with a straw toward his mouth. He took a sip of water and she laid his head carefully back down on the pillow. He saw her move toward an IV line that was established in his right arm and inject something that made him drift back into a state of semi consciousness. Even in the haze he thought they had not noticed the word he had inserted into the text.

A Capital police officer found the video tape in a plain cushioned envelope exactly where the email had directed them to look. He brought it to the Senator's office and handed it to the FBI agent posted just inside the door who immediately took it through the waiting room to the Senator's private office where Henrietta Patterson and Agent Walt Haskell were waiting. An FBI tech carefully gloved up and removed the disc. The tech sealed the envelope in an evidence bag and examined the disc. They took pictures of it from all sides. The technician then placed the disc in a machine that scanned it for any malware or tracking software that would damage their computer while they watched it. It also made a copy of the entire disc. When all was ready, they inserted the disc into the player and hit the play button. As the video appeared, a program was transcribing the audio feed and matching the voice with a recording of Kip Patterson making a speech at the United Nations. There was no question that the voice on the video was Dr. Kip Patterson.

The image showed a very calm Kip Patterson reading a prepared statement and then having his left arm secured to a table next to him and almost all of his left pinky finger being severed with a bolt cutter. Kip had made no sound when it happened but his head could be seen slumping forward as he passed out. The video focused in on the finger so that there would be no question that it was not a fake. A gloved hand came into view and placed the severed finger in a small wooden box and placed a towel over the hand as you could see blood begin to flow into the towel. A voice came on with a simple message. "Do not appear at the hearing or the next time it will be worse." The screen went black and the technician pushed the eject button just as the file began to dissolve. The technician checked the copy they had made and smiled as he gave a thumbs up to Walt that saving the recording had been successful including any elements that could be traced.

The Senator stood there silently as she and Walt watched the video again. She was the first to speak. "Even having his finger cut off didn't stop Kip from giving us a clue."

It took Walt Haskell a moment to process her calm statement. Once he got past her calm demeanor, he almost whispered the question. "What clue did

Kip give us?"

"Luxurious" was all the Senator said.

Walt blinked and looked at her questioningly. She looked at him calmly and continued. "It is horrible that Kip lost his finger and I am agonizing over it internally but he plainly indicated that where he was being held was luxurious. That means it's not in a warehouse or a shed or some backstreet building. The way he said it was a code for the way we used to laugh about what people thought was lavish or fancy. It was not a word his kidnappers put in the statement he was reading. He put that in there. We need to re-evaluate the groups we have been looking at and determine which one of them seems the most likely to have a place that is well appointed, remote, and luxurious. My money is on Patriot Green and their wealthy leader Thomas Tandor. He made his money in importing luxury wood from Africa and South America and Asia without any regard for the environmental damage it was causing. He sold that company for millions and lives in the center of Virginia in Buckingham County on a lavish farm. He founded Patriot Green."

Walt Haskell couldn't have looked more dumbfounded. "You got all that from one word?"

The Senator shrugged. "You would have to know Kip and me better but I think it will turn out that I am right. We will just have to wait until the finger arrives."

It was now Haskell's turn to shrug. "You seem sure they are going to send you the finger."

"Of course, they are going to send us the finger and my guess is that it will arrive by some strange method within the next fifteen minutes. There is no point in taking the finger if you are not going to send it to support their claim. The finger will turn out to be Kip's and the intent will be to reassure me that they will hurt him even further if I go to the meeting. Also, I looked at the pictures that Smithson sent over. There is a woman in one of them that I seem to remember but I can't quite place her. I definitely have seen her before."

Walt nodded. "Please show me this woman you think you recognize."

The Senator's assistant brought up the pictures on the computer and printed them out. There were two. One was of Lucy Frost and Serena Moore. The second was of Lucy and another individual. The Senator pointed at the image of Lucy. "I have seen this woman before but at this point I can't remember where or when."

Walt's phone rang. He answered, listened, and turned toward the door motioning to the technician as he crossed the room. He opened the door. A uniformed Capital police officer was standing with a 12-year old boy in the outer office. The young boy looked up as Walt smiled at him and held out his hand. The boy put a small wooden box in Walt's hand. The boy turned to the officer that had his hand on his shoulder. "Dad, did I do the right thing?"

The officer looked down and smiled. "You did." The officer looked at Walt and began to explain. "This is my son, Jared. He is shadowing me today for a school project. He took a bathroom break and when he came out a man handed him the box and asked him to give it to his dad to take to Senator Patterson's Office. I took it to our X Ray screening station and we got a look at what was inside. We brought it straight up here. I hope that was the right thing to do, Sir."

Walt looked at both of them and nodded. "Does he know what is in the box?"

The office shook his head from side-to-side. "No, he doesn't."

Walt looked down at the boy. "Could you describe the person who gave you the box?"

The young boy smiled and pulled out his phone. He opened his photo application and brought up the latest pictures. He had captured three pictures of the man, a profile, a rear shot, and a partial frontal shot. The boy had been taught to be observant by his father in public places and he had noticed the man watching him as he made his way to the men's room. He took the photos before he emerged from the men's room just in case something strange happened. The guard looked at his son. "I never knew you were paying any attention to my suggestions."

His son replied, "I always pay attention. You have always said, see something, say something. It's just not cool to let you know that I do. What's next? This has been awesome."

The Senator smiled. "What's your name again, young man?"

The boy smiled back as he stepped up and stuck out his hand. "I'm Jared Lincoln, Senator Patterson. I am pleased to meet you." He turned to his dad again. "See, I told you I pay attention."

The Senator shook his hand and looked at his father. "I don't think Jared quite understands the benefit of his actions. He may just have given us our first clue in a very dangerous situation." She then turned to the boy. "Jared, I will be in touch. Thank you for your quick thinking."

The officer smiled and then shook the Senator's hand and left with his son. Walt Haskell had already sent the photos from Jared's phone to two locations. The first was the FBI technology support division and the second was to L. Street at Smithson Evermore. Between the two of them they would have an identification quickly. He also sent the message that the Senator had recognized the picture of Lucy Frost but couldn't quite remember where she had seen her. The technician had bagged the box and the first two thirds of Kip Patterson's left pinky finger and it was on its way to the FBI lab for thorough examination. Walt Haskell turned to the Senator. "I would strongly urge you to not go to the hearing. There is a possibility that there were two related fatalities in Virginia near where Dr. Patterson was last seen. I am convinced that these people will not hesitate to kill Dr. Patterson if their demands are not met."

The Senator sat down behind her desk and folded her hands on her desk. "Please sit down, Walt. I appreciate everything you have done and the opinion you have just shared. But, quite frankly, Kip would kill me if he thought I would bend to this type of pressure. There is no way I am going to willingly go along with this threat unless it puts my colleagues or innocent people in jeopardy. What I would like to do is wait until we confirm the identity of the man who delivered the box, and you and I have a personal discussion with Slade Smithson. I would like to have that in person rather than over the airways sooner rather than later. Can you make that happen?

Walt nodded and pulled out his phone. He hit the code for scramble on his phone and then hit a speed dial. Slade answered on the first ring. "Slade, we need to sit down in person with the Senator as soon as possible. Is there any way you can make that happen?"

Slade answered quickly. "This morning Aggie and I relocated to our northern Virginia office. I assume you want our involvement to remain as low key as possible so I suggest that you arrange something at one of your safe houses. We can be downtown in an hour. Just tell me which one. Aggie will be with me because she is running the operation to locate Dr. Patterson. Will that work?"

"That works. I will text you the location coordinates via the secure line and the exact time." Walt hung up the phone. "Slade Smithson is already in the area. He can be downtown with Aggie in an hour. What is a good time for you, Senator?"

She looked up and smiled. "I should have known he would already be in the area and have Aggie with him. Give him the location as soon as you have it and let's do it within the next two hours. I am beginning to narrow down where I know the woman from but I'm not quite there yet."

Walt was on the phone before she finished the sentence and the secure unit was already preparing the location before he hung up. He texted the six-digit coordinates to Slade via the secure line and a security team from Smithson Evermore was already moving in to provide additional security for the meeting. Walt scrambled an FBI cover team but they would be the second group to arrive. Oscar already had someone on each of the twelve safe houses in the downtown area.

L, with a significant amount of help from Claymore, had already identified the man in the photos as Horace Allen. He was on several files first as a member of the ultra-conservative group, Final Days. That had been one of the groups that the FBI had originally listed as having possible involvement with Dr. Patterson's abduction. He was also listed as an active participant in a recent rally of Patriot Green, a second identified group. What was the most important piece of intelligence was that he showed up in a series of pictures that Lily had sent back from the airport in southwest Virginia where Dr. Patterson had last been seen. He was listed as the agent for a small company that leased airplanes to civilian pilots. He had an office at the airport. Lily had been notified and she and Agent Wheeler were already in contact with Deputy Conner. They were waiting for a call from him. SiSi was busy working with her counterpart at the Capital Police to review all the CCTV footage that captured images of those people in the area of the bathroom that Jared had used. They found Jared and his father on the tapes and backtracked their movements. Horace Allen had emerged from the Metro Station near the Capital Building. They determined he had been in the building for an hour. His movements indicated he could have delivered the video disc but not with any certainty. He then appears again watching the officer and his son move about the officer's rounds. Allen clearly hands Jared the box. You can then see the officer confer with colleagues and then head directly for Senator Patterson's Office. Switching back to other video feeds you can clearly see Allen exit the capital and head back to the Metro station. Claymore contacted the Metro police to see if they could determine from their video surveillance where and when Allen boarded and disembarked from the subway stationed.

In Wytheville, Virginia, Phelps Wheeler received a call from Deputy Conner. The deputy had the results of interviews with the people from Mountain View Airport. "The most significant fact we learned is that a man named Horace Allen made a call shortly after you and Ms. Michaels left the airport. He is a leasing agent for Craft Wing Aircraft Leasing. He processed the plane we suspect landed with Dr. Patterson. We pushed the ground crew here and they told us that a van pulled up next to the airplane. They remember a fancy SUV pulling up behind the van and a man greeting a woman who had disembarked from the plane. He walked her to a sedan that had been parked for a couple of days inside the fence at the airport. None of the crew saw anyone else get off the plane nor did they see Dr. Patterson transferred from the plane to the van but that would have been easy to conceal once the crew was released to wait for the pilot to give them orders on the plane. Since there was no refueling, they weren't near that plane for over an hour. That would have been plenty of time to move him without anyone noticing. When the crew did return to the plane, the SUV and everyone but the pilot was gone. The pilot gave them instructions to store the plane in the hangar where we found it. When they checked the tail numbers to record it for insurance purposes because it was being stored, the numbers were the ones we found on the plane, not the ones that left Houston. That flight documentation is nowhere to be found. This whole thing looks sloppy all the way around. There is no passenger manifest anywhere. It has been removed or it never existed. After he made the call the day you two were here, Allen disappeared. No one has seen him since. When we checked the office, the phone's been disconnected and the only thing in there is a desk and two chairs. It has been cleaned out. There is nothing left of his company or Allen at this airport. What else do you need me to look for?"

Phelps was quick to reply. "Does this Allen guy live in the area?"

Deputy Conner responded. "He does. We have checked the house. His car is gone and there is no sign of life. I have a deputy sitting on the house to bring him in for questioning. The neighbors say they haven't seen him for at least three days and he doesn't socialize with anyone we have been able to find. He has been in the area for six months."

Phelps thanked the deputy and hung up. He went down the hall to Lily's room and knocked on the door. She opened it in her robe fresh from the shower and ushered him in as she was towel drying her hair. It was the first time he had seen her with her hair down. It was amazing. He caught himself and began to speak. "I just got off the phone with Deputy Conner. He says there is a guy named Horace Allen that made a call just after we left and hasn't been seen since. He is definitely connected to the plane we believe delivered Dr. Patterson to Mountain Empire. The crew remembers a woman being escorted to a sedan and leaving the airport just as Serena described. They did not see anyone else get off that plane and they were instructed to store the aircraft. The was some craziness with the numbers which we suspected."

Lily listened intently as her phone buzzed on the desk She went over and read the message. She looked at Phelps. "A man identified through facial recognition as Horace Allen delivered the severed finger of Dr. Patterson to the Senator's office an hour ago. L and Claymore are waiting for more video from the transit system. L has forwarded a copy of the full autopsy report from the medical examiner's office for the bodies found in the burnt-out car. The male body in the driver's seat has been confirmed as Aaron Frost.

The female has been confirmed as Loretta Sampson, the ex-wife of Tim Sampson the ex-volunteer ranger that took off for Patagonia the day after the accident. The report also confirms that both of them were dead before they went over the cliff since they found no evidence of smoke in their lungs. Mrs. Sampson's remains indicate she died of blunt force trauma with a broken neck. Aaron's death looks like a massive dose of Ketamine."

Phelps thought a moment. "If the woman is the former Mrs. Sampson, where is Lucy Frost?"

Lily shrugged her shoulders. "I don't know but I bet we will find out the closer we get to the location of Dr. Patterson. Aggie is suggesting that we relocate to the Smithson Evermore office in Burke, Virginia. She wants us to wait until we get a report from Rufus Songbird, our chief pilot. He hasn't given up on a second plane being used. We should have that report in an hour. I am going to finish getting dressed and packed and we should have the report by then."

Phelps nodded his head but looked down at his phone as he remained in the chair he had taken. Lily laughed. "Phelps, a little privacy please."

He stood up immediately. "Sorry, got lost in thought. I'll just let myself out."

Lily nodded and turned toward the bathroom door as she finished toweling her hair. She poked her head back out just to make sure Phelps had left her room. She smiled to herself as she pulled out her brush and started the hair dryer.

CHAPTER 19

Borders and boundaries are just lines in the mind.

In Maine, Oscar was going over the most recent intelligence reports from the sources in both Canada and the United States. He was looking for anything that could help identify a strategic response for any attempt to smuggle humans at any or all of the three points. Smithson computers were busy recording every piece of information that anyone had detected. In the past twenty-four hours they had been able to move resources into place from both countries as well as their own private reserve. It was Oscar's nature to remain skeptical in the event their data and their plans had nothing to do with what was about to happen. Their objective had been to move personnel into locations that could intercept the effort quietly and without drawing undue attention. The area they were working in is so thinly populated that any new influx of people or activity could easily be seen by the trafficking organization. Oscar had no doubt they were watching and there was no question that the magnitude they were expecting required a large orchestrated and sophisticated trafficking organization.

His computer alerted and Slade appeared on his screen. "It's just about time for our conference. Anything new show up in your review?"

Oscar, without looking up, spoke. "Looking at our resources on the map gives me the feeling that we are too spread out. The border is porous at best and non-existent at worst. Some places don't have a fence. It is designed for law abiding people not the people we are dealing with. Even with the pooled resources from both countries and our teams, it just seems like such a huge area to cover. We will need a great deal of luck to come up with any positive outcome. We are talking hundreds of miles. The bad guys have unlimited resources and have had time to plan and we have multiple jurisdictions with cost cutting measures. Sorry to sound so pessimistic. But if they are as sophisticated as we think they are, I think we have to refocus our assets and maybe revise our approach."

Slade sat and thought a moment. "We only need to save one victim for me to feel we did our job. Remember, we are not shooting blind. We have some good intelligence at least for the three locations and Alex's reports help narrow it down. I think we will find other facilities just like the one in Alex's report. I think they are going to bring these people across quickly and transport them to waiting larger vehicles that will then move them out of state. Larger vehicles make it cost effective. Fortunately, larger trucks have to negotiate the same roads as everyone else. This time of year, some of those primary and secondary roads are under construction to take advantage of the decent weather before the winter sets in. Let's have L get with Maine transportation and see which of these roads are under construction right now. A traffic blockage would affect their transport. If these people plan as we expect they do, they will have checked and chosen routes that will not require stops or delays. Identifying those roads and how they connect to the locations we have identified would give us an idea where to concentrate our resources."

Oscar nodded as he sent L the request to check with Maine DOT. "There is the other piece of information about the Canadian agent shadowing Maurice Taurant. This Taurant guy keeps popping up all along the whole border with Maine and Canada. He has been seen in at least ten different locations. He is constantly on the move. That means he is looking for his best opportunity. Canada has been unable to arrest him. That makes me mistrust some of the information. Either he has someone alerting him they are close or he is lucky."

Slade thought a moment. "It could be there is another explanation. It could be some of those sightings are not Taurant. If he is getting ready to move as many people across the border as we think he is, he is going to have to be in a position to support the operation. He can't just keep moving along the border."

Oscar agreed but seemed to be concentrating on another thought. Slade noticed it. "What are you concentrating on so hard? Have we missed something?"

"Maybe. Maybe we are working in the wrong direction. I just put the facts in reverse order by starting at the end and working backwards. Did Alex's report give the number of the all-terrain vehicles and off-road trailers she found?"

Slade scrolled down on the screen to Alex's report. "She indicated that she found eight ATVs and twelve trailers."

Oscar thought. "We need to think about why there are four more trailers than there are ATV's to pull them. We need to figure out how many people could be hauled approximately two to five miles to a larger vehicle from any site where we find those trailers. Let's be conservative. Let's assume there are eight ATVs pulling eight trailers. They are large ATV so with two escorts you could fit two trafficking victims on each ATV and at least four on each trailer, that would be forty-eight victims at that site minimum. If there is some way to hitch those four extra trailers to another trailer, that could be an additional sixteen victims bringing the grand total to sixty-four victims at each crossing. If they use all three in the same way that is one hundred and ninety-two victims coming across at one time. Even if you go with the minimum, it would still be a record. That is a large group of victims and they are being kept someplace right now if they are getting ready to move them across the border. Unless they have a huge payroll, which would be difficult to manage personnel wise, it seems likely they have them all in one or two places. Where do you hide that many people? It has to be somewhere near the three points and it has to be large enough and remote enough to allow for storage and staging. These victims aren't going to be marched to these points. They will have to be transported in bunches. We need to concentrate our attention on possibly trying to find where they might be keeping this large a number of people."

Slade was typing as he was listening. L was already sending out requests and updates to all parties. He paused. "How would you be able to maintain order with that many victims?"

Oscar paused a moment. "What if all of them are not victims? What if some vof those people are there willingly and have paid money to be moved across the border? Think about it. It's a brilliant idea. Take the folks that have the desire to come to the United States and use them to help control the ones that have been kidnapped and are being trafficked. You get paid at both ends of the delivery system and it's not like those being smuggled have a choice about having to help control the others as part of a transport cost. The traffickers, smugglers, whatever, are in total control. The traffickers have combined human smuggling with trafficking."

Slade sat motionless for a moment. "So, you use some of the willing cargo to watch and control the unwilling cargo. There are people in desperate enough situations to go that far particularly from the south. Has there been any evidence from the Midwest case that would suggest that?"

Oscar answered. "I don't think we've looked. Given all of this, what we know is that at least at that one site, they have the capability to move a larger than average group of people illegally across the border. Whether they are transporting willing illegal entrants or unwilling trafficking victims, both are against the laws of both countries. We need to get with ICE and Border Patrol to get more information on the Midwest operation and in particular, more about who was recovered.

Slade glanced down at his screen and motioned for the local technician to project his version onto the large display. It was split into three views. In the extreme left-hand panel was Alex, obviously broadcasting from the field via her helmet cam. In the middle was Inspector Mattey Borge of the Royal Canadian Mounted Police, and in the right-hand panel was Agent Emilio Cortez of Immigration and Customs Enforcement. L was moderating the panel and SiSi was connected via audio.

Slade began the conference. "We have been working on a theory and have some questions but I think we need to hear from agencies first. Mattey, please bring us up to date on what is happening in Canada."

Inspector Borge looked down at her laptop and then looked up at the camera. "We have been able to find at least one other site similar to the one that Alex found. It is storing ten ATVs and eight trailers. We have also determined that these vehicles are identical to ones that our Canadian contractor uses to service border fencing, sensors, and barriers. They are even the same color and make. The trailers were originally designed for forestry and timber harvesting. They can carry significant payloads. Our contractors use them to transport heavy supplies such as fencing and cable along with tools. They feel each trailer could easily carry three people on each side. Anyone seeing them from the Canadian side would not think twice about them. They are normally transported to the site by a flat-bed semi-tractor trailer. We have not traditionally stored them near the border. We have sent an agent out to speak with the principals for the construction contractor and the transportation contractor we work with. The construction company is located out of Ottawa and they normally use local labor with a foreman supplied by their company. According to the Sûreté du Québec, the agency that provides law enforcement in the area, where we located the storage facility, the transport company is owned by a man named Chao Wu. His company is located in Montreal but he lives in Quebec City. We will update you as soon as possible. We haven't discovered a third site on our side of the border. I see you have asked for particulars on the operation last year that moved women through the Great Lakes. I will have the records pulled and forwarded. I wasn't affiliated with that operation which was mostly conducted by our friends at ICE. By the time we were invited to the party, the victims were well within the United States. That is about all I have other than we are looking into the most recent request on Taurant and the multiple sightings. I am not going to rule out the fact that there may be more than one big mean French Canadian loose up here but I can attest to the times he has been seen by our agent and they are within a hundred kilometers of each other mostly along the Maine/Quebec border."

Oscar spoke next. "Mattey, we have been doing some thinking here. Are there any remote large abandoned locations near any of these sites that could house over a hundred people?"

Mattey stared into the camera surprised. "Did you say over a hundred? I will need to research it but my first response is yes. There used to be a thriving family lodge business, like upstate New York retreats in your country. There are several of the old buildings and facilities that were just left to decay into the environment. Many were stripped of any valuable building materials such as copper piping or furniture years ago. Some owners tried to stay in the business too long and many just locked the doors and disappeared leaving everything behind. I will do a cross reference to possible locations near the sites we have identified and get back to you. Don't you think managing a hundred unwilling victims would be a large endeavor?"

Slade answered. "No question but it is not out of the realm of possibility that it could be done with enough fear, intimidation, and drugs. We have also considered the possibility that not all of the cargo are unwilling participants."

That got the attention of Agent Cortez. "In the Midwest operation we recovered thirty-five women. We know at least twenty-five got through. Only a few of those intercepted cooperated with us. The rest refused to even speak to us. It is very possible some paid to be smuggled in. Some were transported by water and the others by transit vans through border stops. All of the land transport attempts were intercepted. Thirty women refused to cooperate and they were all sent back to their home countries. Five Asian women did cooperate. Two returned voluntarily to Asia and three were deported just as we were moving to trial. It was a case of one federal agency not knowing that another was making the effort to provide them status under the Continued Presence program. There was a breakdown in the timing. The prosecutions we got were all related to state laws. Two of the missing twenty-five were later found trying to sneak back into Canada. That would mean that approximately twenty of them were successfully smuggled into the United States. You raise an interesting point. I always thought that some of the women involved in that operation were a little too uncooperative. We had a devil of a time figuring out who they were and where they were from. In addition to the five Asians I mentioned, many of those recovered were from Central America. To answer the other question posed, we are still looking for the third site. Alex gave us great directions for the one she found. We have been searching in the area where we expect they will attempt a crossing and from our side, we have found the trail but no storage for these vehicles. We are actually having a bit of a problem with the definition of the border. We were surprised to find several areas where its not at all clear."

Inspector Borge interjected quickly. "What did you just say?"

Cortez answered. "We found two locations near that central location that had no fence. It doesn't even look like there was ever any fence."

Borge answered quickly. "I am looking at our GPS plot and I am showing fence along that section of the border. I am comparing it to your map and your map is showing fence along that border. Did you find this anywhere else?"

Alex was next to speak and there was no question she was a remote transmission. "Hi guys. Sorry to interrupt but I may be able to shed some real time intelligence on that question. After I found the storage facility, I began a zig-zag track toward the border to check sensors and place some of mine for personal security. I got about a mile before SiSi sent me a message to stop. I was working off the map ICE had loaded into my databank which was projected on my heads-up display. If you will indulge me, I am going to take a moment to put my helmet back on and show you something. I think it is more important you see it than looking at my gnarly face that hasn't seen as shower for three days. SiSi, you can take over while I shift here."

SiSi broke in over the audio feed. "Hi, everyone. The reason I stopped Alex was that according to my satellite plot of the border, Alex had crossed the border into Canada. Since I wasn't sure the Canadian authorities had given us that kind of authorization, I wanted her to confirm."

Alex broke in. "Thanks, SiSi, I'm all set." The panel on the video conference call then filled with a high-definition video feed of the forest. The camera caught the image of a telephone pole. Alex moved her head to pan the camera upward. There near the top of the pole was an electronic border scanner with a US seal on it. The sign below it contained a warning that you were entering Canadian land. Alex continued. "I hope all of you can read that sign. On the reverse side of it contains the same message but warns people that they are about to cross into the United States. The only problem with that is that I am standing about a half mile into Canada. This is a dead zone. Depending on whichever map you look at, this pole is not marking a border boundary between the United States and Canada. Someone has removed the fence that should be here as indicated on both official maps and installed this pole. I hate to make it worse but there is indication that this trail has been utilized for foot and small vehicle traffic for some time now. I wouldn't have looked for it here, but to be honest I just decided to not pay attention to the map and look for anything that might give us a clue as to what to expect. If I had stayed to the plot, I would have totally missed this section."

Agent Borges broke in. "That makes no sense Alex. That means that we would be alerted sooner if they were using that area."

Alex responded. "It would if that was a real sensor. I am guessing that sensor box you saw on the screen is deactivated or a mock transmitter. I will give you an example. Don't watch me, watch your alert screens on your computers. I am going to head back down this trail to where that storage facility is. See if I trigger anything."

Everyone watched the screens that L now projected on the conference.

After about three minutes, Alex broke in on the audio feed. "Did anyone get an alert?"

Slade answered for everyone. "Alex, neither system registered an alert."

"I thought as much. I am switching on my camera." She panned up to a more permanent looking iron post with a large sensor on the top and very official signs below the sensor. "As you can see from the video, there is no power to the sensor. I climbed up and confirmed that. It appears that the wire to the solar panel that powers the sensor was cut some time ago. This official sensor has not worked for a while by the look of the corrosion. This section of the border has been altered and is completely exposed. There are indications here of regular foot and motorized traffic as well. The path is clear but on both sides is overgrown. You would have to look to find it or you would have to know where it is."

There was silence. It seemed like it would never end. Slade broke the silence as tactfully as he could. "It would appear we have discovered a place on the border where alterations have been made that neither country was aware of. Someone went out of their way to misdirect the casual hiker or forestry or land use official. With your permission I will have SiSi fly our drones along the border and turn on their target mapping capabilities. Alex, get back to your base and stay there. Alex, please confirm that you have received that message.

Alex, please confirm. Alex,"

SiSi broke in. "Slade, she has turned off her transmitter. There are only two reasons she would do that. Either she shut it down to hide or someone else shut it down because she was discovered. My money is on the first option. I have scrambled Brad and the northwest recovery team to her location. Agent Borges, do we have permission to stray onto Canadian soil to approach from that direction as well?"

Mattey Borge answered immediately. "Of course, you do. I will activate one of our special operations teams to the area just north of where that fake sensor is. They will be alerted and in support of your activities. Let us know if we need to take the lead."

Oscar was up out of his chair and out the door in Maine and Slade closed the conference. "Agent Cortez do you have enough to do what you need to do?"

Cortez was ex-military. His answer was short and sweet. "Affirmative, we are on our way." The screen for the conference went blank.

Slade dialed L. "Get on the plane and meet us in Washington. We are going to need our resources close by. Please alert Aggie as to what has just happened. She needs to stay focused on finding Kip Patterson and we need to find Alex."

L responded as she walked to her room in Tampa and picked up her go-bag. I'm on my way. You sound so strange Slade. Are you alright?"

Slade didn't pause. "I am not alright. I am really, really pissed for the first time in a long time. See you soon and be careful getting here. We are stretched way too thin."

Slade had barely hung up when his phone alerted him to a call from SiSi. She spoke quickly. "I am sending you a video feed with audio from Alex's helmet. Stay on the line as you view it."

Slade pushed the secure feed alert and the video started to play. It showed a huge man picking up the helmet and looking at it as he turned it over in his hands. He spoke in French to someone off camera. He looked puzzled and then tossed the helmet into the nearby bushes. SiSi broke in on the phone. "He is speaking Québécois. Roughly translated he is saying that he thinks the helmet is some sort of toy and believes it's just from kids playing in the area. Facial recognition from our file of persons of interest has a confirmation on the face. It is Maurice Taurant."

Slade almost stammered. "What about Alex?"

SiSi responded quickly. Her track is showing her following along behind what the heat signature shows is a group of about five people. She is moving freely so she is not a captive. She is doing what Alex does best, watching and reporting. I have the track and am feeding it to the response team. I don't have the location of the Canadian team but they may be the close. Brad and our team are still ten minutes out."

Slade was quick to respond. "Slow them down. We want to allow Alex as much time as possible to find out as much as she can. Have the Canadian team stage close by."

SiSi broke in. "Crap. Sorry. The heat signatures just disappeared. That is strange. If they entered a vehicle, I would still be able to detect their presence. They just vanished. I have sent a message to Alex to stand by. Till I know where they are, I would prefer she not move into some sort of trap."

"Have everyone stage and send your last track and location for Alex to Brad. We may want to let Alex extract herself not to tip them off. She will know that. Keep me posted if anything changes."

SiSi broke in one more time. "Alex is safe. She just sent me a meme of a smiling cat. That is a joke between us. She is good. I will have everyone hold. My analytics tell me that the only way their heat signature disappeared like it did can only be attributed to one thing and that is going underground."

Oscar's number popped up on Slade's phone. "I'm going to field deploy and take over the secondary response team. I think Brad and his team should remain primary. I just got the notice from SiSi that Alex is safe but I need to confirm with her what she wants to do. I asked SiSi to link her to both of us as soon as she has full communication again. Can you think of anything else I need to be doing?"

Slade was quick to reply. "SiSi believes there may be a tunnel. She lost a heat signature for what appears to be Maurice Taurant and his cohorts. That would explain a good deal. The alteration of the border protection is really alarming but I am going to leave that one to the two countries to hash out. We need to develop a strategy to support our forces here on the US side. We are the target area for this. I have asked the FBI and ICE to step up their intelligence on the Americans that seem to be related to this."

Oscar answered almost immediately. "At the top of my list is Bobby Martel. He always seems to be the end agent in this stuff. Right up there with him is Horace Morton. Our teams have been studying their most recent photos and actions. I will get my thoughts on strategy back to you as soon as I speak with Alex. We need FBI and ICE data on where the most lucrative markets are for manual labor, the sex trade, and skilled sweatshop work like garments etc. That might give us a better handle on how to intervene all along the supply chain. There is no doubt in my mind we are going to miss some of these victims particularly if the border is more porous than we suspected."

Slade was listening intently. "Get with Alex and I will get with ICE and the FBI here. I think your idea about some increased agility all along the supply chain is a good one. Let's touch base as soon as you hear from Alex."

Oscar was already on his way to meet with Brad with six other team members. He was trying to decipher why the traffickers would be checking the border line. The only possible reason would be that they were getting ready to move their cargo.

Alex had followed the group until they disappeared into what looked like an old mine shaft. She worried they could have left someone to cover their retreat so she did not approach but she did paint the spot with her laser for SiSi to record on her map. She then took the long way back to the place where she had left her helmet. The big oaf had done exactly what she had hoped he would. He had picked it up, examined it and tossed it in the bushes. As sophisticated as it was, the model that Alex wore looked like a toy. He would not take it seriously and the camera built into the top front was invisible to someone that wasn't looking for it. There was no way he would know it was recording his voice and his image. She decided to move back to her base of operations and then move her whole operation forward closer to the actual border. First, she needed to get in touch with Oscar and bring him up to speed. She also wanted to suggest they put forward intelligence on the other two locations. She would discuss it with Oscar as soon as she felt safe enough to turn her full transmitter back on. She placed her helmet in an evidence bag that she would give to Brad. He was close enough she could almost feel him. She heard the sound of an approaching small ATV. She hid by the side of the trail until she was sure the approaching sound was made by someone on their side of this dance.

The ATV approached and Cari Freeport stopped almost opposite of where Alex was hidden. She had one of the Smithson dogs with her. The dog looked directly at Alex who emerged from the side of the trail. She walked up to Ruka and kissed her on the nose. Her tail wagged so hard she almost fell out of her carrier. They had worked together before and while Alex loved all the dogs, Ruka was her favorite. "Hi Cari. I'm surprised Brad sent you."

Cari nodded and scooted forward so Alex could get on the ATV behind her. "They thought I would create less of an alarm. I just look like some dumb blond on a four-wheeler with a dog. They don't know that Ruka is the most intelligent one on this thing next to that toy in your hand. Are you ready to get back to friendlier places and talk to the big guy who is now waiting with Brad?" Alex smiled as Ruka licked the back of her neck. Cari turned the ATV and headed back down the trail.

CHAPTER 20

Nothing stays static very long and when it begins to move,
it moves swiftly.

Lily was the first to get to the phone once they walked into the Smithson Evermore Headquarters in Burke, Virginia. They had received the FAA report Rufus had requested on tracking small plane activity around Virginia. She was surprised when she found Aggie in their operations center with FBI Special Agent Walt Haskell. Agent Wheeler was only moments behind her on the phone with Deputy Conner.

Aggie smiled and introduced Lily to Walt Haskell. Phelps joined them as he ended his call and shook hands with Haskell. "It's good to see you again, Walt."

Agent Haskell smiled at Phelps as he turned to greet Lily with a warm handshake. "Young lady, we have heard a good deal about you at the Bureau much of it coming from your new partner here. He says you have great skills and even better instincts. It is good to work with you. We have some new information that is cranking up our timetable a bit. I know you are aware that we have received a video along with the severed finger of Dr. Patterson which eventually led us to the identification of Horace Allen. Aggie and I are very uncomfortable with the way things are going. given that at least one of the original people involved in the kidnapping of Dr. Patterson has been found dead along with the ex-wife of another suspect we can't find in South America. Even though we have confirmation on the whereabouts of Aaron Frost, we are still at a loss as to the location of his wife, Lucy. The severing of Dr. Patterson's finger, the homicides in Virginia, and the situation surrounding Serena Moore in Atlanta give this case more urgency. The Senate hearing that seems to be at the basis of this whole drama is scheduled soon. As if that wasn't enough, the Senator feels she has seen Lucy Frost somewhere before. We have to get moving quickly for a good outcome on this."

Lily was the first to speak. "How is the Senator doing with all of this? Is she still committed to attending the committee meeting and voting?"

Aggie answered the question. "She is even more committed than she was before. For two people that are no-longer married, they seem to have an unusual sense of understanding about each other. She is convinced that Dr. Patterson's interjection of the word 'luxurious' is a clue. She is equally convinced that, upon hearing about Horace Allen, Patriot Green is somehow linked. That group is headed by Thomas Tandor. We have started passive surveillance at his home in Buckingham County, Virginia. We have agents out looking for Horace Allen but so far, the last we saw of him was leaving the Metro station at Vienna, Virginia. He just disappeared into the crowd."

Phelps interrupted the conversation. "That was Deputy Connor on the phone. He has been re-interviewing the people at Mountain Empire. It turns out that nobody actually knew much about Allen. He didn't hang around with many of the locals but one of the guys produced a photo of him taken at a birthday party for one of the airport director's kids at the local barbeque place. He is in the background with two people. One of them has been identified as Tim Sampson, the missing volunteer Ranger. The other is a much younger guy who nobody knows but one of the ground crew is sure was at the airport that day."

Aggie reached over and looked at the photo on Phelps' screen. "I have seen that face before. Let me take a look at the file. We are going to move L to Maine within the hour."

Lily looked shocked. "L is headed to Maine? That must be some operation up there to take the chief of our intelligence up there. Who do we have working for us on our case?"

Aggie smiled. "You have the person who started the intelligence file and passed it on to L. I hope I will be an apt replacement for you."

Lilly responded immediately. "I'm dumb. Just forget I said anything. I should have known that, but you are never away from either L or Slade."

Aggie smiled again. "Slade is in the other command center next door directing the Maine operation. I am in constant contact with Claymore Jenkins in Tampa who is handling all our necessary communications and research needs. We also have two full response teams standing by with FBI rotary transport and SWAT teams at the ready. I hope you feel comfortable with those resources because you will be running our part of the field operations for this in support of the FBI."

Lily looked shocked. "Where is Oscar? Never mind, he is in Maine, isn't he? I'm ready and Phelps and I have some ideas but we need to hear both of your takes on the timeline and next moves."

Aggie was busy sending the picture of Allen and the unknown man to Claymore's computer. She looked at Walt Haskell to continue the conversation.

"Based upon the tissue samples from Dr. Patterson's finger the people at the lab are convinced that it had been amputated no more than two hours before it was delivered. The digit had been cleaned up and the amputation had been done in such a way that Dr. Patterson will not be unduly impaired. He won't type quite as fast as he used to but other than that, he is not in any life-threatening situation for now. But all that could change the longer this goes on. Senator Patterson described her husband as someone who will endure whatever it takes for her to be unaffected by his abduction. He is described as someone who thinks before he speaks and believes in what he thinks. That is a great quality unless someone is threatening your life to say something you don't believe. The Senator is convinced he would rather die than be used as a pawn to compromise her position on anything. He passed out when they cut his finger off but didn't make a sound when they did it. It seems they even slowed the process down to get a reaction. It must have been excruciating. That is one tough cookie. She is going ahead with the hearing for him more than for herself and she is not going to support the bill. If she doesn't, it won't move out of committee so we need to find Dr. Patterson soon."

Lily looked at Aggie. "May we see the video?"

Aggie turned around and brought the video feed up on the wall screen behind her. There in high-definition video they watched as Kip Patterson read the statement then had his hand bound to a table and his finger cut off. Lily was making notes.

Once the film had run through for the fifth time, she held up her hand and spoke. "Here is what I saw. I believe there were at least five people in the room. The video shows a splice near the finger amputation which means they have good editing equipment. It is high-definition and they used a good professional high-quality camera on a tripod because it is stable. There are two people actually involved in the amputation. The first, the smaller one, begins and then stops. You can see the slight break in the video. It picks up after the edit with a larger person finishing it. I don't think they paused it to make it worse. I think the first person lost their nerve or there was a malfunction. I also think that compared to the others in the video, that person is smaller, maybe even a woman and not a young one."

Aggie sat back and smiled. She looked at Walt and Phelps. "Anyone got any doubts about why we selected Lily for our part of the operation?"

No one spoke until Phelps looked at Lily smiling. "Why do you think it is an older woman? I know you have a reason and I have learned over the past three days to trust your instincts better than my own in most instances."

Lily didn't even break a smile. "The smaller figure has a weak wrist. Using that tool requires hands and wrists. Since it is human flesh rather than metal that the cutter is designed for, it should have been easy. The person couldn't complete the cut. I think it was either a sprain or a more acute problem like arthritis or an inflammation like carpal tunnel syndrome."

Aggie smiled and hit keys on the computer that filled the screen with the image of Claymore in Tampa. "Claymore, any result on the picture?"

Claymore looked at the camera through at least three layers in his glasses. The youthful face and glasses hid the fact that Charles Claymore Jenkins was a decorated Army veteran who had left both his legs and most of his eyesight in Anwar Province in Afghanistan on his final tour. He smiled. "I have a confirmation. Hi, Lily." He was blushing.

Lily smiled back. "Claymore, have you worked your magic?"

"The young guy in the picture is Phillip Tandor. He owns a house in Middleburg, Virginia. His daddy Thomas has a house close by in Upperville, Virginia, not too far away. Utility reports show that senior isn't at the Upperville house very much. As you have heard, Thomas Tandor is the Director of Patriot Green. Also, I was listening to your discussion. I ran the body type profiling algorithm and I think Lily is right about the person in the film. One of them is definitely a woman. I can't comment on the age but she definitely has a bad right wrist. When you blow up the image on slow motion you can see it buckle just before the edit. It is definitely not the same person completing the amputation. Also, in case you missed it, the person holding the arm looks like they are moving into position to render aid. They move to the side and lift the arm slightly like they are trying to get something under the arm. It is the same movement we learned to slow bleeding. You can only see it in the last several frames of the video if you slow it down and look anywhere other than the finger. Someone moved too quick to stop the bleeding and got caught in the picture."

There was silence in the room. They were stunned. Aggie broke the silence. "Walt, this is your call and your operation. Tell us what we can do to support you?"

Walt looked at Phelps and Lily. "I would say it is time to stage on the three Tandor houses and get the warrant process started. I will get the office working on getting before a judge with these pictures. But you two said you had some ideas that you wanted to lay out. I would like to hear them."

Lily looked at Phelps and he began. "Based upon the information from the lab on Dr. Patterson's finger, we're confident Dr. Patterson is somewhere in northern Virginia. It would not be tough for a small plane to operate at any of the smaller airports. The FAA radar has a small plane leaving Blue Ridge Airport near Martinsville, Virginia, about three hours after the departure of Serena Moore from Mountain Empire. Martinsville is an easy drive from Marion. We believe Dr. Patterson was taken in a van from the airport and driven to Martinsville where he was loaded onto a plane and flown either to

Upperville, Virginia. Rufus believes that there would not be any record unless the pilot wanted one, particularly if the pilot is a frequent user of the airports. We checked the records. There is one pilot who owns his plane and provides services as a pilot to executives that need to commute between the DC area and their 'homes in the country'. His name is Sid Oldsmar. He is known as an upstanding but 'conservative' citizen who often flies businessmen. He has contributed to Patriot Green and supported their causes in the past but most feel he is not a kidnapper. I have asked an agent from the Roanoke office to find him and talk to him. I think he will tell the truth. Deputy Connor is trying to find out who else could have been involved in the accident with the two dead bodies. We think it was a joint deal to get rid of a bothersome ex-wife and a useless, jobless husband." He looked at Lily.

She continued. "We also think that it would be easier to convince someone that was not part of the conspiracy to fly Dr. Patterson who was probably drugged, if there was a woman involved. We think that woman may be Lucy Frost. I am going to have the agent with Serena Moore in Tampa get more information from her about Lucy. If she was a liability, we would have already found her by now. The two that were sent after Hank and Forrest Mack are being less than cooperative and Mexico has not taken that too kindly. We believe they were also involved with the homicides in Virginia. It is possible the two that went after Serena in Atlanta were as well. Someone sent them. We just don't know who. Phelps isn't as convinced as I am that Lucy was more of a player all along. I think something in the back of my mind registered during one of my early conversations with Serena. I haven't pinned it down yet but I'm close. We haven't talked about it because we just learned about Phil Tandor's presence at the airport, but it fits. I am confident we will find evidence about the Tandors at the houses but the point is to find Dr. Patterson. I think the key is to find out more about Lucy and the key to that is Serena. The fact that the Senator remembers her face makes me even more convinced."

Walt listened to what they had said. "I will put the teams on standby and have our legal staff ready with warrants for all three houses. I will stay in touch with Phelps and Aggie just to trim the communications links but we need to be ready to move as quickly as possible. Phelps you are our site commander on this one. Aggie, is it OK if we switch our command post to here to facilitate coordination?"

Aggie didn't even hesitate. "Of course. This room is yours. I will have staff set up the necessary electronics if you will get clearance from your agency. Lily will work with Phelps and we will provide you anything we can. At the moment we only have one rotary asset since we so committed along the northern border with this other operation, but as we narrow the target, we have more than enough air resources with our combined forces. Lily, we will make Pat Owens and Shelby Morris available to you as forward intel. They are ready to be inserted as soon as you decide where you want them. They will be equipped with the same gear that you and Alex have. They should give you very competent eyes and ears near two of these houses."

Phelps laughed. "If they are anywhere near as good as Lily, we might not need the SWAT teams."

Lily corrected him. "Yes, you will. We don't make arrests; we assist you guys in making arrests and right now you need to get to them before I do. Harmless people don't strap a person's hand down and cut off their finger to make a point. I am glad Aggie trusts me to be your primary on this one but I won't trust myself if I get anywhere near any of the people responsible for this." She looked at Aggie. "I know that it is huge for you to assign these resources to us right now. I promise we will return them within the next twenty-fur hours just in case we need to stage further back on Maine."

Aggie smiled. "See why we made her a field supervisor." She looked at Lily. "Get this cleaned up as quickly and as professionally as we can. No mistakes on our part. We want these court cases to. I will be here in the HQ room with Slade if you need me."

That concluded the meeting. Lily and Phelps moved toward the two command computers that had begun humming as Claymore confirmed the link between agencies. Walt Haskell left to get his part of the operation. Lily immediately dispatched Pat Owens to the house in Middleburg and Shelby Morris to the house in Buckingham County where Thomas Tandor had his main residence. Aggie went upstairs to the second command center where Slade was busy conferring with Alex and Brad in Maine.

Aggie smiled at Slade. "We are making good progress on finding Kip Patterson. Lily is coordinating our side of the operations with the FBI and she has adequate resources. Is there anything I can do for you?"

Slade smiled. "I can think of lots of things but not right now. This thing just seems to be getting bigger."

Aggie sat down. "Tell me about it and go slowly. Maybe a fresh pair of eyes and ears will help. You seem to be pulled in several different directions."

Slade began. "For a month we have known that they were going to attempt to cross with victims they have smuggled from Asia and Central America through Canada. Every sign has pointed to a connection between this effort and the one that smuggled victims into the Midwest last year through Toronto and the Great Lakes to Cleveland and Kansas City. The trafficking organization appears to have almost unlimited resources. They have been using those resources to confuse everyone about the border, alter the boundaries and sensors and have us chasing around after their principals. There is no question they are relying on the border's weakened exposure caused by shifting resources to the south with Mexico. It's just a mess."

Aggie thought. "Then I would suggest we focus. What is the last known contact we have that this is going to happen?"

Slade thought. "That would be Alex's discovery of the border irregularities and the close encounter with a group of the traffickers. SiSi determined that they must have a tunnel somewhere near the border because she lost the heat imprints on the infrared overhead from the drone. Alex turned in her helmet that was handled by one of the traffickers that everyone suspects is Maurice Taurant. We know this guy has had multiple sightings confirmed by Canadian authorities, some of them conflicting with each other. We know he can't be in two places at once. The close encounter with Alex makes Oscar and me believe he is doing one last check before they attempt something tonight or early tomorrow morning. Canada and our forces can't seem to focus on how to approach such a broad area. Even I can't give them my input because I really haven't decided what to do either."

Aggie smiled calmly. "Then my answer still stands. If it was confirmed that it was happening in an hour, where would you send our people?"

"I would send them to the location where Alex found evidence of transport vehicles and an unprotected border. She walked right across the border and didn't know she was in Canada until she confirmed her position with SiSi. I would set up our reception just inside what I know to be the border tonight and wait. I would lend just enough of our special resources to the US and Canadian Authorities to support them watching the other sites. I would ask for an agent to be with our team to make arrests and I would focus on the one site we have the most intelligence on."

Aggie thought. "Didn't the report say they found another storage facility at one of the other locations?"

Slade nodded his head in confirmation. "Alex is at the northern site. The middle site where there had been trail alterations had no storage. Brad and Chuck Freeport found a similar facility at the southern site."

Aggie replied. "We would never spread our resources that thin. I would suggest that we give specialized forward intelligence support to the federal agencies at the other two sites and move all our resources to the northern site with support from federal agents for arrest purposes. Sometimes too much collaboration weakens the field presence. It also can slow down the decision making. We can't save all of the victims from such a massive transport scheme but we can focus on hopefully saving the ones that will come across the locations we do have good intel on."

Slade was thinking as the phone rang. It was Bridgett Moss from the FBI. "I just got off the phone with Mattey Borge in Canada. We processed the prints your field lab lifted from the helmet. We had nothing on file. At the same time, we sent it to Mattey for Canadian processing. They had nothing either. However, they are linked to Scotland Yard's database and they got a hit from the United Kingdom. The prints belong to one Marcus Taurant. He has an English passport and birth certificate. He has the same birthdate as Maurice Taurant. Mattey is really pissed that they missed it. They are twins." There is no record of Marcus ever living in Canada. There is ample record that he grew up in England where he has a fairly hefty record. Mattey believes that explains the multiple sightings. Canada did not know there were two of them. Maurice has been in Canada with his mother since he was an infant. Marcus was raised by an aunt in England. There is no official record that he is in Canada. I don't know if that helps but at least it clears up some of the confusion about how Maurice Taurant could be seen in two places at once. It's easy, they look just alike."

Slade listened and was typing the notes onto the screen where Aggie could see them. She wrote on a piece of paper and slid it to him. It had one word. "Focus." Slade smiled. "Bridgett, while I have you on the phone, I want to suggest something to you. I think we should consider a different deployment approach. I would like to have you get together with the rest of the U.S. team members and consider that we divide up the response on our side of the border. I would like to focus our resources on the north site with a federal agent to make any necessary arrests. The Border Patrol, your agency and ICE response teams can take the other two sites. We have been chasing our tails to make sure we are all everywhere and that may not have served us well. The Canadians have been great about sharing their intelligence but we think we are hurting our operational capability by trying to be everywhere. If you could get ICE to concentrate on interception at the main transfer points and either you or Steve join us in the field with our team, we could probably stand a better chance of intervening and recovering more victims. The FBI could take one site and the Border Patrol the second. We would provide canine and forward intelligence support to help them."

There was silence on the other end of the line. "You know we have spent a long time trying to work together to integrate not just our agencies without too much help from above, but also in being able to work directly with you guys. Are you sure you want to take the risk? If we fail because we weren't all co-located, and recover just a few victims, then that will be used by those folks who would rather keep our agencies separate and confused and your agency out of the loop completely. Those of us who have worked together see the benefit. I'm not sure how the others will feel."

Aggie broke into the conversation. "Bridgett, this is Aggie. Sorry, this may have come out of my skull. As we were talking it occurred to me that if we rely so heavily on the 'group think' processing, we may be diluting our ability to rescue anyone. For all we know, they could have six other ways to get these victims in and we could all waste our time sitting on the locations we found. Just talk it over with your people. We are advisors here but we need to divide and conquer and each pick a mission. The victims may be mixed with individuals who are willing participants, maybe even helping control the unwilling ones, just to get across the border. Whoever they are, they are without much choice because of the people who are making their living from their suffering. Smithson will support you in any way but let's at least consider that for this one, we need to move where each agency has their strength."

Bridgett thought for a moment. "I will get in touch with everyone in my channel. Let's plan a strategy session for later today. We are running out of time so we will have to go with what is in place. But if each of us centers on what we are best at, we may be able to make this work. Just so you know, you have convinced me and I don't believe you will have a problem convincing Steve. He has always wanted to focus on getting these poor souls as they enter the country. ICE is more than willing to intervene once they are inside and will jump at the chance to focus on the transfer points. I just want the bad guys. Keep your phones on. I am going to run this through the task force and I will get back to you."

She hung up. Slade decided to make some decisions on his own for their resources. He had SiSi set up a conference with Smithson resources. In ten minutes, everyone was on the large screen. Slade began. "Oscar, I need you and Brad to relocate to Alex's position up north. Set Alex as forward so she can be secure to advise at our border. We have already pinpointed the location of the possible tunnel. Set Alex up on the U.S. side of that then provide her close backup. We are in the process of having federal agents with you for purposes of arrest and detention but your mission is to intervene and rescue. Have Chuck support the other locations but only on American soil and only for search and rescue. I want Chuck and his best dog with you and your team. It was too close with Alex the last time. I want our other intel people supported by drones assigned to coordinate with the FBI to intervene further back in the supply chain. We will miss some of the victims and I want you to give them support stopping them from transferring any victims for re-distribution. Let's have as few of those victims coming through that site getting to larger vehicles as possible. I will speak with the FBI to request local support from Maine State Police to help. I don't care if they have to stop every bus and truck on Interstate 95."

Oscar was first. "I was hoping we were going to concentrate our effort. I have one suggestion. I would like to increase satellite surveillance and send additional intelligence operatives to the central location where I am now. Having seen this area, I believe they are just going to cross with a vehicle that can carry people directly to distribution. It would be good to have our expertise there to help the Border Patrol and ICE. That is all I have."

Brad spoke next. "I concur. These guys are well financed but they are getting increasingly sloppy. Tossing Alex's helmet away as a toy shows a lack of sophistication. I think they have underestimated our readiness. A sane strategist would have taken the encounter with Alex to heart and shut that site down. If that appears to be the case, let's have our second team ready to deploy in the MH65 to support ICE with intervening further down the distribution chain. Also, I think we need to be patient. We move too quickly they can withdraw. We need to make sure Canada is ready for that. I like setting up where we know our soil begins."

Aggie cut in. "I think we need a Maine Forest Ranger with you. If anyone knows where those borders are, it would be them."

Slade finalized the conference. "Let's be in place within the hour. It may mean we are positioned early but I like being early to this kind of party. I will get on the horn with Maine and get you a ranger. As usual, that was a brilliant idea that we should have thought of."

Brad cut in. "Actually, SiSi thought of it. We have a ranger with us already but it might be a great idea for the other locations. It might not be a bad idea to put New Hampshire and Vermont on alert either. Sometimes a strategically parked State Trooper can make all the difference."

Slade answered. "All good ideas. Let's stay in close contact until we encounter movement. Oscar, you call the shots once you are all at the northern locations.

CHAPTER 21

All things, good or bad, eventually come to an end.

It was about an hour before sundown when it became apparent to Han and JinJing that things were changing rapidly. First, several vehicles arrived and parked outside of the lodge. All the women had been moved from the upper floors to the main one. These women did not seem to be under the same scrutiny as their group had been. They had more anticipation than fear in their eyes. It was the first time Han had confirmation that some of the people among them were there by choice not by capture. She managed to move close enough to JinJing to tell her not to speak or share any information with anyone but her. JinJing looked puzzled but agreed. Han also noticed that some of the captive women were being moved to another part of the lodge closer to the main doors.

Han moved as close as she could to the window to get a view without drawing attention to herself. She watched as some of the women were led to the back of the trucks. They loaded three captives, chained together at the wrists, with two unchained women. About forty women were loaded into the first truck accompanied by two of the original guards. A second truck pulled up and a group of 40 unchained women were loaded without guards. The truck pulled away. A third smaller truck pulled up and once again chained women were loaded with unchained participants. This truck held about thirty-five individuals. Han looked over her shoulder to see how much longer she could stand there and observe. She froze. Standing behind her was the man she had hunted. The monster who had dropped her daughter to a certain death pulled back his left hand and slammed it across her face. Senseless, she staggered back and fell semi-conscious at his feet. He screamed at her in French. "Was the look worth it you, nosey, useless bitch?"

JinJing saw Han fall from about ten feet away. She began to bolt to Han's aid and then she remembered her promise to stay close but no contact. She decided to create a diversion instead. She turned to a woman who she recognized as one who earlier had guarded her and lunged at her attacking her face with her hands and grabbing her hair and pulling her down to the ground. The woman was surprised with the attack as was the only other guard nearby. The huge man turned his attention away from Han just as he was getting ready to stomp her and screamed at the guard in English, "Get those two apart and chain the little one to this one. Let's keep the troublemakers together so if need be, I can dispose of them along the way. Neither one of them is worth much. They both have been fucked and I think the older bitch looks familiar. I know her from somewhere."

Just as he was finishing his tirade and the guards were chaining JinJing to Han who was beginning to recover slightly, he was joined by an equally large imposing, identical figure. Han had to blink the blood out of her eyes as she watched the two of them. She finally understood why she had not been recognized. There were two of them but only one had stared into her eyes as he dropped her daughter over the side of a boat. He was the one that had just beaten her. Her resolve solidified like steel beneath her obvious injuries. Neither of them would escape her. Maurice who had slapped her and had been her daughter's murderer, started toward her and yanked Han and JinJing to their feet. "These two travel with me. Bring another one over and we will make it a threesome. From somewhere behind the crowd, a woman partially limped forward into view. Maurice pointed at her. "Grab that one. She is about as useless as these two. No one will miss them. They go last with me. Chain them all together and put them in the van with a couple of the more reasonable ones."

Two guards came forward and chained Han to JinJing and then to the women they both recognized as the one who had been kicked so hard that her back was injured, Anna Lopez. Unwittingly they had collected the three women out of over a hundred who all held the same look in their eyes. Defiance is a beautiful thing even when it is surrounded by defeat. It's the stuff of legends and these three looked at each other for the first time and understood. Sometime before dawn, they would each become legendary.

They were the last to be loaded into a van waiting outside with two other women that were not chained. They could see everything that was going on. There were two larger transit vans that were full. Anna looked at the two women who were with them unchained and spoke to them in Spanish. They looked at her with distain. One of them spoke to Anna. "You are nothing but a pig. You have given yourself to these men and now you have forced us to have to travel with you. We are on our way to a new future. We don't need you holding us back." She pulled a knife from her pocket and threatened Anna with it. Just as everyone thought she was going to plunge it into her throat, a huge hand came from outside the truck and grabbed the woman and the knife. He pulled her into the center of where the trucks were parked and bellowed for all to look at him. All eyes were on him as he took the knife and slit the woman's throat and held her upright while her body shook as she bled out. The more she struggled the more she bled and it was over in several minutes. He dropped her at his feet, pulled out his pistol and shot her once in the forehead. Maurice then instructed two of his men to pour gasoline over her and burn the body. Everyone looked on in horror including the guards as the horrible smell of burning human flesh rose. Captive and collaborator alike looked on shocked by the example Maurice had selected to ensure that everyone complied.

One of the two large vans was secured and pulled out. There were two vehicles left including the van that now contained only four women. A black SUV pulled into the area. Dr. Terrance Concorde got out with two additional women. One was the Salvadorian woman that Anna had met at the clinic with Dr. Concorde who had introduced herself as Bettina Ocasio. Her face was still covered in bandages. The other was a young Chinese girl. JinJing recognized her friend, Lan Li. She didn't look damaged or hurt in anyway. Dr. Concorde looked at the burning body then looked at Maurice. He handed JinJing over first. "This one is worth more than all the rest. See to it she makes it to Detweiler and Morton. They already have a buyer in Virginia at a high price. This other woman has already been paid for in New York. I don't want to have to offer a refund. I see you still can't keep from killing our profits. Try to control yourself."

Maurice sneered. "She was about to kill your little muff of a spic you nursed back to health. We already had her money so who gives a shit. No one will miss her." He looked at the smoldering heap of what minutes ago had been a human being. "I will make sure not that much is left of her and your sweet little virgin chink will get delivered. I just want to be rid of all of these bitches. I thought you were going to keep this one until you could deliver her yourself."

Concorde laughed. "In our business things change. This woman is a friend of a friend. Make sure she gets the special safe treatment she deserves. If something happens to her, we will all pay dearly."

Taurant growled. "You rich, educated, assholes make me sick. We do all the dirty work and you get all the money and the pussy. One of these days, someone is going to figure out how to end your little game, you rich prick. I will laugh the day that happens. Don't call me anymore. This was too big and too disorganized. Find someone else to move your merchandise and fund your little shop of horrors. We are done."

Dr. Concorde just smiled and walked back to his SUV. A man, just as large as Taurant but much better dressed and heavily armed stepped around the side and held the door for him. Concorde spoke from inside the back seat. "You won't live long enough to see that Maurice. One of your own will slit your throat as easily as you apparently did to that poor girl." His man shut the door and without taking his eyes off Taurant or his finger off the trigger of the weapon he carried, and got in the front seat as the SUV pulled out slowly and undramatically as if to underscore how little Dr. Concorde worried about threats from an animal like Taurant.

Han was blinking and trying to clear the blood from her eyes. The woman who was not chained, reached over and used her sleeve to wipe her wounds. She smiled. She turned to Anna and spoke in Spanish. "I will never forget that scene. We had become friends on the journey. She had paid money to get to the United States. I'm sorry she threatened you. She was desperate for a new life and very tired. No one deserves to die like that. I don't think she would have hurt you. They told us we had to help control all of you because you had asked them to take you and then not payed. We were all offered a reduced payment if we helped. She has a husband and two children back in Honduras." The woman began to cry.

Anna then spoke to the crying woman in Spanish. "None of us will survive this unless we stick together." She pulled a handkerchief out of her pocket and leaned over to help clean Han's face. JinJing looked at Lan Li. She was clearly under the influence of something because she just sat there and smiled as her head tilted slightly to the right. Bettina Ocasio had been ushered into the front seat of the other van by Marcus Taurant.

Han nodded her head in thanks and took the handkerchief. Even half dazed she was watching the movements of every guard. One had gotten behind the wheel of the van they were in. Another came and chained the fourth woman and Jin Jing to them. It appeared that the ones who had been considered compliant were now being treated the same as the captives. Apparently, Maurice had decided that his little exhibition had probably not had such a positive effect on those that had paid him to protect them and deliver them to the promised land. Marcus got in the larger van next to Bettina and instructed the driver to move out. Maurice got into the van they were in and didn't even look back at his captives. He just smiled and told the driver to pull out. He had reverted back to French unaware that Han understood everything he was saying.

They drove for about thirty minutes until they came to a clearing. The larger van was already empty. Only the driver was waiting. Maurice and his driver got out. He told his driver to help him escort the women to the pick-up point and told the other driver to wait for them until they returned. He then ordered the women out of the van and led them into the woods. Han could see a light ahead. They reached an opening that descended down about twenty feet into a tunnel. They were led into the darkness. The narrowness of the passage forced them stay in single file as they made their way through the dark. Anna was determined not to let her injury hold her back. Han was in the lead and managed to keep contact with JinJing with her hand. All the women reached the far end of the narrow passage and emerged into more darkness. There was no moon but the stars gave enough illumination that they had to take a moment to let their eyes adjust. They were marched to a trailer where they were forced to jump up and sit on the edge. A frame ran down the center of each trailer. Their arms were forced behind them over the frame. A chain was run through the chains that held them together and secured to the center frame. If they slipped off the trailer or tried to get off, there was no question they would be drug under the trailer. Their trailer was attached to another trailer with at least six women, which was attached to a large ATV that carried more women. Once they were secured in place, Maurice came around and gagged each one of them. If anyone cried out, he could easily get to her and silence her. He was happy with himself. He had not reduced their profit at all this trip. He had been able to carry out his campaign of fear by killing two of his own and one of the ones that had already paid. He was ahead of his game. He climbed in and motioned for them to move out. He smiled when he discovered he could barely hear the sound of the muffled engines. Most ATVs could be heard from a mile away, but these had been modified. You could still hear them but you would have to be much closer. He looked around. He assured himself that there was no one around to hear them anyway. It would be thirty minutes and this last group would be off loaded and half the crew would be storing the vehicles and the rest returning the vans. His part of the job was about to be over. He looked around again just in case and tightened the grip on his weapon. He saw no one.

He saw no one because he didn't look up. From high atop a spruce, Alex was recording the whole operation with her helmet camera. A least twenty people were watching the entire process on both sides of the now corrected border. One of the people watching was Oscar Dorian who was waiting near the transfer point with a combined team composed of Smithson Evermore and the members of the ICE Anti-Trafficking Task Force that had been assigned to them. Back on the far side of the tunnel, a Canadian Customs Enforcement Team along with the Royal Canadian Mounted Police Force had already placed the driver waiting by the vans in custody. He had cooperated with a description of the lodge where the women had been kept. He had also already described the horrible scene that explained the still burning remains of the poor woman who had paid what little she had in the world to try to secure a better life in the United States. They would wait for the return of the Taurant brothers. Mattey Borges and Erick Brandhoff were positioned at the Canadian entrance to the tunnel. She had two full rapid response teams standing by ready to round up any of the traffickers and several agents specially trained in handling victims.

Similar operations were in place at the other locations.

The group moved out of Alex's range and she climbed down and stationed herself off the trail the vehicles had taken. She knew they had already returned some of the trailers to the shed and gone back across the border. She had been filming them since just before dark when she had observed the first of the traffickers arrive at the building to get the transport vehicles ready. She had watched as some of the vehicles were pulled out and set up with the center rails. She imagined that the center structures were designed originally to hold building supplies or logs secured on the flatbeds since they had a series of chains attached to them. She had watched as the first crew returned and stored the vehicles. Four people had moved at least thirty-two chained victims. It was well-rehearsed. Obviously, it was not the first time they had used this system. Once they had stored their vehicles, they moved back up the trail and into the mouth of what Alex now knew was a tunnel. Alex turned her attention to this trailer. This time she counted ten women chained on two trailers. She had received the message that the Canadians had closed off the far end of the tunnel and were waiting for the traffickers to return.

Alex looked behind her. She couldn't see them but she knew that Border Patrol Agent Steve Wiley and his team were hidden along the border in case the operation at the clearing missed someone. She had placed sensors along several other paths just to keep herself aware of her flanks. She didn't like surprises and she was now looking back down the trail where she knew the Canadian traffickers had come from. Her chest pack buzzed and her heads-up display began to dance. Someone was walking back up an adjacent path. SiSi advised that it looked like more than one person. She pushed her silent alert that triggered Brad and Steve who were her designated back up.

The ATVs had been moving according to plan when Maurice told the driver to stop. His brother Marcus was walking toward them on the trail. That was not the plan. Marcus looked a bit out of breath but he spoke. "Something wasn't right at the transfer site. Our American friends were there loading the vans but I had the feeling we were being watched. I waited and nothing happened. The cargo was loaded and I handed the woman off to Morton. It all went just as planned. It was probably my imagination but I sent the crew back anyway. I just thought I would look around. It's probably nothing."

Maurice looked at his brother and then looked at the driver. He spoke to the driver. "Give us a minute to off load some of these women." The driver nodded. He wasn't going to argue after what he had seen the past few days. Maurice got out of the ATV and moved back to the trailer. He unchained Han, JinJing, and Anna. "Looks like you girls are going to leave the trip early. I have my own plans for you." He then unchained Lan Li and had her stand alone.

Marcus looked at him. "What the fuck are you doing? We don't have time for this. What are you going to do with these four?"

Maurice laughed. "This old chink and I go way back. Remember last year when I caught all the shit for dropping the young virgin in the lake. This bitch was with her. She is probably an older sister or maybe even her mother. It is hard to tell with these Asians. But I am not about to let her go on. She obviously made her way back through the system which means she knows how it works. She has been way too chummy with this other younger one. I can find a use for her and the spic was a favorite of the good Doctor. He has finally pissed me off enough that I have plans for her as well. I wonder how he'll feel when parts of her show up on the doorstep of that mansion of his where he hides all nice and cozy with the wife and kids and his rich fucking doctor friends. Maybe I'll even leave part of her at his golf club. I got plans for all of them. You take this young one and deliver her to Detweiler yourself. You can ride in my place just keep a hand on her. Then head straight back home. I am taking these women back with me, at least two of them anyway. By the time anyone figures out they are gone, it will be too late anyway."

Marcus thought a moment. "Just in case this thing is screwed, give me five minutes to get to the transfer spot to make sure. I will then come back and pick you up."

Maurice hugged his brother. "You just head home. I will take care of these on my own. Get going." With that he turned and began walking back toward the Canadian side with the three women. Marcus got on the ATV with JinJing and the driver pulled out. Their progress was watched by SiSi on the scanner plot for the sensors. SiSi also had a clear idea of everyone on the trail from the drone that was operating above the entire site. There were three of them hovering above, the noise hidden by the night wind. It was SiSi that alerted Alex and Brad that the signature she was getting from the first sensor trigger indicated more than one person traveling back toward the border. Everyone went on standby until they could get eyes on. Alex was closer and moved to a good vantage point. She knew there were three or four traveling together from SiSi but didn't know who they were. It was time to be patient until more was known but just to be on the safe side, Alex drew her weapon.

Maurice continued to drag the three women up the trail until Han looked back and motioned for all three of them to drop. They all went down at one time which caught Maurice completely by surprise as they pulled him to the ground with them. Han immediately moved quickly and attempted to get the flush chain she had hidden around his neck. He was huge and she was small. The other two did what they could to give her enough mobility to stay with him but he stood up and pulled all three of them up with him. He bulged his neck out and easily snapped the chain. He faltered back to one knee but was able to get a hand on Han and pull her to the side. She fought him with everything she had. He managed to break her grip on his throat and grab hers as he lifted her off the ground. As she struggled, he back handed her almost knocking her out. He pulled his automatic pistol. Just as he raised the weapon, Han came to life once again and sprung as hard as she could toward him. As he leaned over to get a better hold on her, she plunged the toilet rod directly into his left eye moving it back and forth in an attempt to plunge it further into his brain. It was strong enough to penetrate but not stop him fully. He dropped her and grabbed the rod protruding from his left eye socket as he cried out in pain.

Alex was up out of her hiding place as Brad and Steve were racing toward the sounds and SiSi was correcting their movements. She had lowered the drone and turned on the camera. It clearly showed three women, injured and chained together fighting a giant. Anna had circled around behind him with the help of JinJing in an attempt to try to get him back on the ground. He could sense the move and flayed out with his right hand and was able to knock Anna to the ground. He turned back and tried to stomp Han but she had moved back just enough so that the huge foot just missed her head. His left hand was still holding the rod when Han attacked him again, this time trying to push the rod deeper into his brain. He anticipated that and reached up with both hands and caught her by the throat. He had her in a death grip and there was no question he was going to choke her to death or try to break her neck. He settled on the latter just as he realized that with both hands on her neck, he no longer had control of his weapon. He realized it too late. He heard the weapon go off just as he half turned to see the gun smoking in the hands of JinJing. He had been hit in the right side of his neck just below his jaw. He sank to his knees just as Alex arrived and secured the weapon from a shaking JinJing. Alex saw Anna and spoke to her in Spanish. "Help these two. Sit there together. No more fighting. We are here to help. She then repeated the instructions in English. Anna immediately dropped to the ground and motioned for JinJing and Han to do as well as all three sat down on the trail, their chests heaving from the struggle. Alex immediately pulled off her helmet and began first aid on Maurice. Brad and Agent Wiley arrived within a minute. Brad checked Han and began working on the chains that held the women while assuring them with just the tone of his voice that it would be OK. Wiley provided cover just in case more traffickers were in the area. Brad put a headset on Han and signaled SiSi to speak with her. SiSi first asked the question in Mandarin and then in Vietnamese. Han looked at JinJing and smiled and then requested Mandarin so that her young friend could understand. Brad put a headset on JinJing and then looked at Alex. "You will have to explain what is going on to the Hispanic woman. All I can do is smile." Steve moved up and took over the first aid as Maurice was no longer moving. Most of the far side of his head was gone.

Alex moved over next to Anna and spoke to her in Spanish while SiSi explained what was going on to the two Asian women. Brad stepped away and spoke into his mouthpiece. "Northern site is secure. We have one down in need of fast evac with gunshot wound and three tough-as-nails ladies who could use a great deal of care. We are clear for recovery services. He moved over next to Alex to work on the remainder of the chain that was now hanging from Anna's wrist. Brad freed her wrist from the chain. She looked at Alex and reached up with the same hand and touched Alex's face and began to cry. Alex wrapped her arms around her and let her bury her head into her shoulder as her body shuddered again and again with sobs. Han and JinJing were listening to what SiSi was saying to them over their headsets. Han finally looked over at JinJing and encircled her with her arms. She held JinJing while they both cried, Han for her lost daughter and JinJing for her lost innocence.

Alex suddenly straightened up. SiSi began speaking. Someone was moving rapidly back in the direction of Canada from the transfer clearing along an adjacent trail at motorized speed. They were in a perfect position to intercept whoever it was. SiSi alerted Mattey on the Canadian side to stage to intercept whoever it was. Alex and Brad were told to head to an adjacent trail to help. Then a second message came from the ICE intel monitor. One individual had left the transfer clearing on a single ATV and was moving southeast from the clearing. SiSi shifted two of the overhead drones as Alex and Brad moved off in a parallel direction. Steve remained with the three recovered women.

Steve was soon joined by the evacuation and evidence teams designated to help process the scene. The three women were going to be transported to Bangor to a church that had offered to provide them safe haven. JinJing was in the worst shape. She had never killed anything other than a chicken for dinner. She had no idea what to expect and so far, the only person who spoke her language was Han and the voice in the headphones. But she sensed that she was safe for the time being. They would be kept apart but travel together until all parties understood what transpired along the trail. For the first time in a long time, they were not captives or victims. At this point they were survivors and witnesses. Whether they understood it or not, they would be instrumental in whatever else happened as a result of that night.

Brad was on the phone to the Smithson Evermore Canine Team. Chuck had Ruka on his ATV and they were on a course to intersect with two ATV-mounted Border Patrol agents. They would be joined by Brad and Alex heading south on foot. Someone had recognized the trap and was now escaping on the ATV. Brad and Alex had the advantage of being able to move overland and not be hampered by trails. ATVs were great as long as they had a path to negotiate but they were not that great at trail blazing. Alex had been in the area for three days. She was familiar with the area since she had kept moving and noting her locations for SiSi to track. SiSi was giving them directions as they closed in from the northeast. One way or another they were not going to let this one get away.

Marcus had made sure that Bettina had been picked up by Morton and that both had safely made it to the main road. He went back to pick up Lan Li just as the cops were closing in on the vans at the transfer point. He grabbed her just in time to turn his ATV back towards Canada. But where was Canada? On the ATV, Marcus was thinking as fast as he could. Lan Li was crying from the rear seat of the ATV and bouncing from side to side. She wasn't totally aware of what was going on but even in a partial drug stupor, being thrown all over the inside of a bouncing ATV hurts. Marcus was looking at the GPS on his phone and didn't see the log that had fallen across the path. The ATV hit it going twenty miles an hour and catapulted the vehicle into the air as it turned over and crashed on its side in a thicket. Marcus came to his senses and reached back. Lan Li was conscious and crying with a cut on her head and a small gash on her leg. Marcus pulled himself off the ATV and then reached into the enclosed rear area and pulled Lan Li clear of the wreckage. He checked his GPS and headed straight up the trail dragging a stumbling Lan Li behind him.

Just before the accident, Lan Li had a moment of clarity. The effects of the drug she had been given were beginning to wear off. The accident had helped clear her head even more and she realized that this giant of a man that had her was beginning to panic. The look of survival came back into her eyes as he jerked her down the trail. He would make a mistake soon and she would be ready.

CHAPTER 22

*Deciding to focus on a solution sometimes takes more than
once to get results.*

Slade was looking at the preliminary summaries that were flowing in from the different locations where trafficking and smuggling had occurred. There were four attempts in all. An hour before the action started at the remote sites, a truck carrying forty individuals was intercepted as it tried to breach the checkpoint on US 27 near Arnold Pond. Border Patrol and Canadian Border Services had cooperated and bolstered personnel and it was ready for the breach. They were able to set up stop sticks on the Arnold Trail 100 yards before the lake and recover all the individuals in the back of the small truck and make arrests. It was a pure smuggling operation. That was the only area that had not been previously identified. At the southern location near Lake Penobscot which had been discovered early and had a similar storage facility to the one Alex had discovered, they were able to intercept 30 victims and make five arrests. The authorities had moved too quickly and were sure that at least some had gotten through and some were taken back across the border before they could close in. At the central spot north of Ravignon where they had found no storage facility, they later determined they had missed a large vehicle that had breached the border. Aerial video indicated that it had been much earlier in the day than the crossings attempted after dark. There was no way to estimate the number of transported individuals from that site. At the site where Alex and the team had staged near La Frontière, they had recovered thirty-five individuals and made ten arrests including four Americans that had been involved in the transfer of victims to a tractor trailer waiting near Depot Road.

Alex and Brad were still deployed following one or more individuals who it appeared were trying to get away by traveling southwest along the wooded area adjacent to the Canadian border. Chuck was on his way north to intercept with Ruka and a Border Patrol team. Oscar was headed with his team and an

FBI agent to back up Alex and Brad who were approaching from the north. At this site, they had waited until they felt that all the ATVs had turned back toward Canada before they moved in. The Canadian authorities were waiting for those returning to Canada. A team of Maine forestry agents had moved in to secure the ATV sites and had arrested five Canadians there. The storage facility was definitely on the American side of the border but just by several feet. It appeared that the one on the fleeing ATV had sensed that something was wrong and had sped away from the transfer point.

After the ATV flipped, Marcus was having a hard time catching his breath., He was sure he had broken a rib or two. It was almost impossible to make any headway with this drugged out girl falling and stumbling behind him. His thoughts began to turn to saving himself and letting this woman find her own way out of the woods. She was slowing everything down. He was close to a decision when Lan Li fell to the ground one more time. He released his grip and turned toward her just as she raised the limb and brought it squarely into contact with his face just at the nose level. He reeled and staggered backward as she turned and began to run as best, she could back the way they had come. She had broken his nose and damaged his right eye. He regained his senses and decided that his escape was more important no matter what his brother thought. He looked at his GPS and stumbled half blind toward the Canadian border. In ten minutes, he ran into Alex and Brad waiting patiently beside the trail. Brad was first to speak as he grabbed Marcus and forced him to the ground. "We thought you'd never get here." The Canadian team directed by SiSi was there in two minutes and took custody of Marcus who had been on Canadian soil five minutes after Lan Li had clubbed him senseless. Brad and Alex headed back down the trail to try to hook up with Chuck and the Border Patrol team.

They arrived at the ATV where Chuck and two of the Border Patrol agents were waiting. Alex spoke first. "Our big friend is in the hands of the Royal Canadian Mounted Police and the Canadian Border Services."

Chuck was looking worried. "I don't think he was alone. Ruka is making a racket to be let out of her locker. I think someone was with him and we need to find that person."

Brad answered. "Any idea who it could be?"

Alex answered for both of them. "I think it was at least one victim who got away from him. Maybe the injury to his face wasn't from the accident."

Chuck turned and retrieved Ruka from her transport cage. She was on her lead and ready to go in seconds. Ruka tracked back up the trail in the direction Alex and Brad had come from for about five minutes then stopped. She then reversed back down the trail and headed down an offshoot. Since it was dark, someone not familiar with the trail would not notice that the main trail went one way and the smaller trail led another. It would be easy to get disoriented. Chuck turned to Brad and Alex. "She's is acting like she is on a blood scent. Was the guy you took into custody injured?"

Brad answered quickly. "Oh yeah. His nose was beaten flat."

Chuck shook his head. "Then it's someone else. Ruka would have stayed on his track if he was the only one bleeding. There is someone else and they are injured. He keyed his microphone "SiSi, are you getting any heat signature moving away from us on the new-fangled droney thingy you have in the air?"

"Droney thingy? A multi-million-dollar piece of flying genius is not a 'thingy'! And, the answer to your question is maybe. Give me a second."

Alex laughed. "Thingy? Really Chuck, thingy? You have really pissed her off now. That is like someone calling Ruka a mutt."

Brad laughed. "Actually, Ruka is a mutt. She is a rescue that is only part blood hound. But point taken."

Chuck was too busy following Ruka down the path to pay any attention. SiSi came back on all their radios. "You are about seventy-five yards behind a very small heat signature. It looks more like a child or small animal than a person but it is stopped and from the terrain link, it looks like it is near a small stream. Ruka's tracking chip is registering and about to close in."

Ruka became more focused the fresher her trail seemed and the last twenty yards she would have been running at full speed had she not been on her tracking tether. Chuck didn't like letting his dogs loose until he knew what type of danger awaited. Ruka bounded over a small hill and they heard her hit water. They all crested the hill and turned their head lamps toward the splashing.

Ruka was all over Lan Li who had been partially submerged in the cold mountain creek trying to clear her head. She had stumbled into it in the dark. She was a mountain girl from China where similar creeks and rivers run. She looked up surprised and frightened when the lights hit her. She stood up not knowing what to do. Alex took off her helmet, shook out her hair and got into the creek with her smiling the entire time. Somehow Lan Li knew that she was no longer in danger. Ruka was busy licking her and wagging her tail totally happy that she had proven once again she was the 'Queen of the Kennel'. Chuck let her off the lead and they all sat down while one of the ICE agents radioed for assistance. Lan Li looked exhausted and she was obviously hurt enough to leave a blood trail. Once Alex helped her onto the bank, they could see the cut on her leg. Alex pulled out her kit and dressed it while they waited for the rest of the team to arrive. She put her headphones on Lan Li so that SiSi could reassure her in Mandarin that they were not going to hurt her and were there to help. It took about twenty minutes for an evac team to reach them.

An hour later Brad and Chuck were headed back to Bangor for a final briefing and Alex was riding with Lan Li and Oscar in a Maine Forestry helicopter accompanied by a female Border Patrol agent. None of them knew whether they were in the United States or Canada when they found her in the stream. They would sort that out later.

Slade was on the phone to SiSi. "You need to get to the staging area as quickly as you can. We are sending our chopper to get you. Brad and Chuck will finish up with the field operations and assisting folks at the site. You will be headed to us in northern Virginia. It has been a good night's work. We recovered over fifty people, and were able to get at least some of the bad guys. It looks like many of those recovered were trafficking victims. We need to debrief as soon as possible with all agencies. ICE and Border Patrol have indicated they are moving quickly with the non-governmental agency, the U.S. Attorney's office and local authorities to get many of trafficking survivors' status under the Continued Presence Program requirements. They have plenty of linguists in their pool so they should be able to handle the debriefing. Border agencies will be working for months to get the border re-established and try to figure out who else was involved."

SiSi answered in her usual professional legendary way. "Affirmative."

Slade sat down and looked at Aggie. "I'm not sure how many of them were recovered but I am sure some got through. I hope all this was worth it."

Aggie smiled. "Who was it that not ten hours ago looked at Oscar and told him that even if we just recovered one, it was worth it? By my count the effort recovered at least fifty people from two locations including the thirty-six at the northern site where we concentrated our efforts of support. Canada was able to take a whole group of traffickers into custody and it is too early yet to determine how high up the organization the arrests went but at least the Taurant brothers are out of action, one in custody and one in the morgue in Maine. That's not too shabby. Alex thinks that at least the four women she, Brad and Agent Wiley found in the woods will provide serious substantial assistance to the investigation and prosecution. The three gutsy women who took on that crazed giant creep were definitely not your normal victims. Let's hope cooler heads prevail when it comes to how they resolve the guy's death. Did that happen in Canada or the United States?"

Slade shook his head. "It doesn't matter. Alex caught the entire thing on her camera as did SiSi from the new drones. She would have killed him if the young Chinese girl hadn't pulled the trigger. He was killed with his gun and the video, as fast moving as it is, documents the whole sequence. I doubt either country would charge her. I can't believe Alex handled that so well. She braced herself and the camera hardly moves at all. And let's not forget that she had her weapon out ready to resolve the issue if need be. We were all almost too late in trying to be patient to catch as many of the bad guys as we could. We have done rescues but that one was too close for comfort with our people and the authorities spread so thin. And let's not forget that other Chinese girl who got away from the other Taurant and bashed his face in. I am constantly amazed by the courage of some of these survivors."

Aggie smiled. "On our other pressing matter, I need Alex to call me. I think there is more to be learned from Hank in Mexico that information will help us make some of the decisions we need to make in the next two hours to recover Dr. Patterson."

"Can't we give Alex some time to catch her breath? She has been going non-stop since we greeted her on the dock in the San Juan Islands. She hasn't been in a proper bed two nights in a row for the last month and most of that she has been sleeping in her sling high up in a tree."

Aggie laughed out loud. "OK, Dad. I have a suggestion. Why don't you ask Alex? I think that girl operates at 'non-stop' most of the time and my guess is she doesn't own a bed and sleeps in a hammock when she's home. I'm running out of time for Kip Patterson. It's no offense to Claymore but he's doing both L and SiSi's job right now and I'm about to wear him out with research requests."

Slade nodded and began typing into his computer. He looked up in three minutes. "SiSi is on her way here and L will be here in two hours. I think we should move Claymore to this location now that Maine is resolved. It will be good experience for him and we have plenty for both him and SiSi to do. That will put us back at full strength here. Alex is going to call you in five minutes. What can I do until they get here?"

Aggie looked at him. "I need a fresh pair of eyes to go over all the reports from both Lily and Alex about the kidnapping. We have several locations that Walt Haskell is looking at and we think we have a general idea of where they might be holding Dr. Patterson but we need to flesh it out some more. I also need someone to speak to Jorge in Puerto Vallarta to go over the regular video from the area where the guys were snatched. We need as much as we can get to help direct our attention."

Slade turned to his console and sent the request to Jorge. Then he began reviewing files. By the time SiSi and L arrived, he hoped they would be in the position to confirm information. Aggie turned to her console and typed in one name into the database and then uploaded a picture she had found in Lily's report from talking to Serena in Tampa. The name she typed in was 'Lucy Frost'.

The database was huge and related to almost seven hundred other databases all populated with legal public information and records. It also included several law enforcement databases that were available to Smithson Evermore through inter-agency agreements with each of the custodial agencies. It wasn't instantaneous like in the movies. Even with all the digitization of data elements, it still took time to process and cross-reference. But it wasn't long before Aggie had three new pieces of information that were important. First, she had a passport picture for Lucy Frost. It was current and it had been used three times to travel back and forth from Virginia to the Bahamas. That seemed odd to Aggie. For a woman so desperately close to financial ruin, three trips to the Bahamas seemed a bit excessive. Second, she found out Lucy's maiden name had been Smithers. She had grown up in Fairfax County Virginia and had graduated from George Mason University with a degree in political science. That was the same institution that Dr. Kip Patterson had graduated from a year earlier. She found that after she had graduated, Lucy had been employed at a think tank in northern Virginia before she abruptly left and went to work with Serena Moore at the insurance company. The third important find was the most important. Her passport records indicated that she had not ever been in Mexico. Either she used a different name to get to Mexico or she was never there. Aggie clicked on the passport picture and sent it straight to their facial recognition database. She suspected that Lucy had more than one passport and that she had more than one name. She also set up several inquiries to the database for L to work on. She wanted to know if Lucy was who she said she was and who she may have turned herself into. It was time to have Lily talk directly to Serena once again about their feelings concerning Lucy. Their policy was that once rapport had been established you maintained it. Victims that are confronted with too many questions from too many different people often concentrate more on adjusting to the new interrogator than they do to the answer. It was also time to ask the Senator if she had ever had contact with a woman named Lucy Smithers. Aggie hit the speed dial for Lily.

Lily answered in two rings. "Hey, what can I do for you?'

"I need you to have another conversation with Serena. I am making the arrangements to get her to a phone. She has been transferred to a safehouse the FBI operates in Sarasota. I am going to send you several questions but the gist of what I need revolves around her relationship with Lucy Frost nee Smithers. We need to know why and if Lucy would set Serena up. I also don't buy this 'totally devoted' nonsense either. I want to know if Serena traveled to Mexico with her own passport or if passports were provided. I can't find that in her debriefing. If Lucy had more to do with this than we think, we need to find out how much of that Serena can tell us."

Lily made it clear that she would standby for the call. While she was waiting, she was looking over the information supplied by the FAA on small plane transfers and the results of the FBI interview with Sid Oldsmar, the pilot in Martinsville, Virginia. There was no question that he flew three people to the Upperville Airport the morning after Dr. Patterson's last sighting in Marion, Virginia. It was two men and a woman. One of the men seemed to still be under the influence from a party the night before. The threesome seemed legitimate and the story seemed sincere. They paid up front in cash and the flight went without any problem. He dropped them off at the main terminal in Upperville, fueled up and returned to Martinsville. It was like many trips he flew for rich people wanting to get away from it all and then return home. He indicated that they were already waiting in an SUV when he arrived at the airport. The SUV pulled up to his plane. The couple helped their friend onto the plane and it was routine. The woman sat in the back with the inebriated man while her husband sat up front. Upperville is a private airport but the pilot had permission and all the necessary codes to use the facility. He was a regular there. The FBI showed him pictures of Dr. Patterson, Lucy Frost, Thomas Tandor and his son Phillip, Horace Allen, and Tim Sampson. He was unable to identify any of them as having been the passengers but he indicated that he didn't really make a point of noting their looks. He admitted that he really didn't get a good look at the drunken man at all.

Lily's phone buzzed with a message containing the number that Aggie had promised. She dialed and Serena answered. Before Lily could speak, Serena blurted out a question. "Have you found Lucy and Aaron yet. I'm really worried. The FBI is treating me much better than I expected given what I have done, but they won't tell me anything about Lucy or Aaron. I'm worried. Have you or Agent Wheeler discovered anything?"

Lily thought. It broke a conventional rule of interrogation that is never answer a question when you are the one asking them. She decided to modify the approach this time. "I have found out some things but how are you doing first?"

"I'm fine. I just want you to find Dr. Patterson before it is too late. I have been told that Forrest is still in Mexico and that he is cooperating. But he was never really even involved in the kidnap or the planning. He was just going to fly us back until they came back with the second loud guy."

Lily thought. "When you traveled to Mexico, did you travel together or did you arrive at different times and places?"

"I traveled separately from Lucy and Aaron. Forrest already lived there. I flew straight to Chihuahua and rented the house. Lucy and Aaron flew straight to Puerto Vallarta. I didn't see them until they had kidnapped Dr. Patterson and Mr. Kessler."

Lily thought again. "Did you travel with your passport or did you travel with one someone gave you?"

Serena laughed. "I was wondering when someone was going to ask me that. I was given a passport to use. It had my picture but it didn't have my name on it. The name I traveled under was Loretta Sampson. I don't know where they got that name."

"What about Lucy and Aaron? Did they travel on their own passports or were they given fake ones as well?"

"Lucy said they had received their passports in the mail. I never saw their passports. They had Dr. Patterson's passport as well. It had a picture of my dead husband on it with the name Tim Sampson."

"I didn't find those in your things you gave us."

"Once we had cleared customs, we put them all in a bag that Lucy carried. The plan was for her to dispose of them."

Lily paused to think. "I want you to think back about the beginning of all this trouble. Were the two of you dismissed from the insurance company at the same time?"

Serena thought but answered quickly. "No, that would have been too humane. They made me fire everyone else and then three months later, terminated me. Lucy was really hurt when that happened and didn't speak to me for months. I tried to call her and apologize but I was busy with a dying husband and on the verge of losing everything. After the funeral she called me. I was surprised but she had always been kind and protective of me. She maintained regular contact with me after that. I'm really worried about her."

Lily made the decision not to share the information that they suspected Lucy was part of the master plan. "Thanks. I want to make sure I understood what you said. Did you mean that you had no contact with Lucy after she fired you and that it was she who called you?"

Serena was quiet for a moment. "Yes. She called me to check on how I was doing after my husband died. I had tried to call her but she wouldn't respond. She apologized for not being there for me during his death but said she was working as hard as she could to keep her own house from being repossessed."

Lily was about to hang up but ask one more question. "Did you ever know what Lily's maiden name was before she married Aaron?"

Serena thought then answered. "Yes, she said it was Smithers. She even pointed her picture out to me in her high school yearbook. They had made a mistake with the spelling and it listed her as Lucille Smathers."

Lily thanked her an hung up. She called Aggie. "When L gets back, we need to find out who went to high school with Lucy Smithers and we need to find out if she was ever at risk of losing their home."

Aggie responded. "I've already been doing some research on Mrs. Frost. She went to Fairfax County High School. She graduated with honors from George Mason University and doesn't appear with Aaron Frost until ten years after she graduated. As a matter of fact, I am having a hard time finding out if they were actually legally married. That is on L's list to research. I will add the question concerning the mortgage to L's list. I have also checked the on-line site that tracks high school chums and discovered some interesting names in Lucille's graduating class. Thomas Tandor and Horace Allen had graduated from there during her sophomore year. That may just be a coincidence but I'm thinking it's not. The younger Tandor is too young to be an old associate but not daddy. Also, Kip Patterson was a year ahead of her at George Mason. Both were in the political science department. He went on to Georgetown. She went to a conservative think tank outside the belt line."

Lily also reported the information about the passport and the facts she had learned about the timing of Lucy and Serena's relationship following their dismissal.

Aggie thought out loud. "So, there was a breach of trust for several months where Lucy was out of contact and Serena just supposed she was angry at her over being fired."

Lily replied. "This is all starting to point to Lucy's involvement. Serena is really worried about her but my feelings are that Serena trusted her more than she should have. I think Lucy is up to her neck in this and there is one more thing. Serena said the name used on her fake passport was Loretta Sampson. That is the name of the dead woman in Virginia that was burned in the truck with Aaron Frost. That is more than a coincidence. Her ex-husband's name is

Tim Sampson. He is the ex-forest service volunteer who we feel is hiding out in Chile. Local authorities in Virginia think Tim Sampson had great motive to kill his ex-wife. Serena says that the last time she saw the passports, Lucy had them."

Aggie closed out the call. "I will get back with you as soon as L arrives and gets something to eat. I have Alex calling in on the other line. I need to get her to follow up on something. I will be in touch."

Aggie hung up and immediately connected to Alex. "Alex, how are you?"

An excited Alex on the other line answered quickly. "I'm super. Did you hear that we recovered a good number of the victims and helped with the arrests of a bunch of the traffickers?"

Aggie shook her head. 'Slow down Speedo, catch your breath. I need some advice. I'm trying to get a clearer picture of what happened that night in Puerto Vallarta. I have Jorge checking the video footage around the bar where Hank and Dr. Patterson were kidnapped. I need you to think if anyone there mentioned anyone else being around."

Alex thought for approximately 30 seconds which was a long time for her. "Jorge indicated that the taxi driver had been sprayed by a woman before she was put in the trunk. Also, some of the street folks talked about several folks hanging around so I can check that out with Jorge."

Aggie laughed. "I will check that out with Jorge. Can you think of anything else you can do to help us draw that picture better? We only have a couple of hours to make a decision if we are going to make any progress on saving Dr. Patterson before the hearing."

"Yeah, I can talk to Hank again or better yet have Lola talk with Hank. He sees everything that is going on around him although sometimes he doesn't quite recall it in the order that makes any sense to anyone other than Hank."

Aggie laughed. "Alex, that is a great idea. I will get Lola to talk to him in person. He will be waking up in about three hours."

Alex countered. "Well, it is almost six in the morning our time. That means it is three in the morning in Puerto Vallarta. Give it an hour or two and have them check on Hank. I bet they will find him on his veranda with coffee and a cigarette in his dressing gown."

Aggie laughed one final time. "That helps. You be safe. Slade wants you to get some sleep. Lily has got everything under control with the Patterson case so you may get to rest a bit before we decide whether you come here or head back west to your assignment."

"Lily gets to have all the fun. I am totally stoked right now and couldn't sleep. Do you have any need for another forward observer? I'm still tweaking the helmet which worked really well but I have some notes. The airport's not far. I'm sure I can be there in a matter of minutes."

"How about you relax for a while? You can help Brad and Chuck finish their duties. Call in when all that is done and we will make a decision then. As far as Lily having all the fun, you just started this conversation with how much we accomplished. I doubt any of that would have happened if you hadn't done such a good job and don't forget you did rescue Hank."

"Hank rescued himself, that doesn't count. Besides, who would harm Hank?"

"There is a giant in Canada that slashed the throat of a harmless woman who had paid him to smuggle her into the United States then set her body on fire in front of the other victims. He is no longer with us as you know. Remember why it is important for us to stay focused. You did a great job. Now get some rest and then wow them with your almost total recall, do you ….."

Alex stopped her mid-sentence. "Shit, I am such an idiot. Ask Lola to ask Hank for a description of the young guy?"

"What young guy?"

"The one that Hank saw when he came out of the club. I put it into the report but it didn't seem significant because we were working on a time frame. He said this one held his gaze and smiled. That means more to Hank than it does to me but it's worth checking out."

Aggie smiled to herself. "See, total recall. You're right. It needs to be checked out."

CHAPTER 23

*Astonishment and surprise are not the same reaction and the
difference is important.*

Alex had been correct. Lola was the perfect one to ask Hank about the young man and she did find Hank on his bedroom veranda in his dressing gown puffing on a cigar at 05:00.

She cleared her throat to avoid startling him. "Señor Hank, how are you feeling this morning?"

Hank started to speak but then decided to milk the situation just a bit. Lola was used to him doing that. "I tell you, Lola, it was horrible! Except for those wonderful people on that island that recognized my regal bearing, I was totally at the mercy of Forrest Mack. He didn't take me nearly as seriously as he should have. I've seen a lot with these eyes over the years. But thank you for asking. Is that more coffee?"

Lola smiled. "Yes, there is and it's special for you. I will get you some in a moment. Alex and Aggie wanted me to ask you a question about the night you and Señor Kip were kidnapped. Do you feel up to answering the question? It is very important for them finding Señor Kip."

Hank went indignantly silent for a moment. "Alex is always leaving me just when I have great plans for us on the beach and I haven't seen Agnus in at least two years. As far as Kip is concerned, do you realize he got me kidnapped?"

Lola reached over an touched his hand. "It was unfortunate you were taken but are you sure he was the target? It could be that he was just the unlucky one and you were the valued one who they really wanted. You put up such a courageous fuss you could have scared them. You charmed Mr. Mack into providing you shelter and sharing those wonderful and mysterious new friends you made. Don't forget it was you who turned on your phone so Alex and Pierce could find you. Anything you remember could make you a hero again."

Hank hadn't thought of that and decided to leave out the part about Forrest actually turning on the phone. He paused a moment then turned and faced Lola head on and smiled at her. "Lola, as usual, you are absolutely right. I need to take a moment out of my morning meditation to help find Kip. I can see how important it is. What is the question?"

Lola smiled and continued to hold Hank's hand. "You mentioned to Alex that when you came out of the bar, there was a young man nearby who you noticed. Tell me about him."

Hank smiled broadly. "Oh, he was very handsome and we made eye contact. He was across the street from the bar. If Kip hadn't been in such a hurry to get home and I didn't have to go back to the States so soon, we could have had a wonderful time."

Lola did not respond to the obvious inflection in Hank's voice. "Do you think you would recognize him if I showed you some pictures Jorge found on video?"

Hank laughed. "Sweet Lola, I could recognize that face in the dark. I'm sure he is too nice to be involved in this nasty business. I will look at your pictures but only because I know he will not be involved."

Lola spread out ten pictures on the table. There were high-definition stills taken from the local cartel's video surveillance system on the street. Hank looked at all of them very carefully. The young man that Manuel Guzman from the cartel had pointed out to Jorge from the video was in three of the pictures. Guzman had checked the cartel sources and determined that he had been in Puerto Vallarta for a week prior to the kidnapping but hadn't been seen since that night. Hank didn't take three minutes to tap his finger on all three pictures.

"See, I told you he was handsome."

Lola hugged Hank and stood up. "He is indeed. Thank you. Can I get you anything else?"

Hank thought. He always liked to take advantage of offers. "I can't think of anything right now but I would like my breakfast around 7:00. Just my normal toast and coffee con leche."

Lola stood up. "It will be my pleasure." On her way down the stairs, she texted Aggie the results. She thought to herself. Hank Kessler is a wonderful and peculiar man that is full of surprises and different nuances. His unpredictability was what she liked about him most. She hoped he would eventually decide to spend more time in the villa. When he had first arrived, he had a problem trying to direct the staff or her in how things should be done properly but gradually, Lola had convinced him to just relax and let the others do their job. She didn't know why he trusted her so much but she was glad he did.

***

In Virginia, Aggie took one look at the message Lola had sent and immediately sent out an intelligence update to all concerned. She walked into the command center where she found L at her console along with Slade watching video surveillance tape from their satellite feeds. At the far end of the control room in her normal seat sat SiSi with Claymore next to her at the master command module. She was bringing herself up to speed on the Patterson kidnapping, Claymore was calibrating the drones and completing the download of the information they had captured in Maine. Aggie noticed that SiSi looked really healthy. The time in Maine had given her some color. Normally, they had to force her to leave her command console. Aggie thought to herself that the time spent with Brad Freeport had been a very good thing for their little genius. Lily and Phelps Wheeler were sitting at the far end of the conference table going over their joint timeline.

Aggie spoke as she entered the room. "Hank has identified the individual in the picture I have just sent as being on the street at the same time that he and Dr. Patterson were kidnapped.

L spoke next. "Facial recognition has identified him as Phillip Tandor, the son of the head of the Patriot Green PAC, Thomas Tandor. He was in

Mexico across the street just before the kidnapping."

Lily sat quietly looking at the photo. A thought connected and then she blurted out her thought. "He was in the background of the pictures in Marion, Virginia, at the party with Horace Allan. His hair looks a bit different, but I will bet that is him. What if he is the man in the video from the airport that identified himself as Agent Peter Crescent, the fake FBI agent? That would put him squarely in the middle of all of this." She turned to Phelps, "Would that be enough for Walt to get a warrant?"

Phelps Wheeler shook his head. "Walt is playing this very carefully. We need to get more information but this is a very important link. All of these guys are well connected to people in Washington. We need to be sure before we go kicking in doors."

Lily thought a moment. "Someone needs to explain this immigration stuff to me a bit better. I have been looking at these businesses that are big supporters of Patriot Green. Many of them are in industries that are labor intensive like construction and manufacturing. There are some meat processing businesses and cleaning services as well as companies that deal with hand harvesting. Don't all of these people use lots of foreign labor. Why would they want to make it more difficult to allow people to come in and do this? Aren't the more restrictive criteria hurting their bottom lines?"

Phelps answered. "I think it is because they don't want workers who are seeking a better life. They want people that are slaves and easily managed. Slaves are made to feel helpless. People willing to go through the process of looking for a new life soon learn enough English and enough about our country to begin to press for better working conditions, pay, or support. When they are accepted and begin the citizenship process, they become eligible for benefits that many Americans resent. Cheap slave labor is easier to manage with fear. They become dependent upon their handlers and employers and are happy for any meager existence that is better than where they came from. Restricting the flow of legal immigrants boosts the number of people willing to escape their home countries into the United States illegally. We have prosecuted very wealthy and influential people who had an undocumented domestic servant working for nothing and totally dependent upon their employer. Slavery without chains is still slavery. That is not an official position, just one that occurs to me with your question. Our caseload is full of companies that regularly turn their head when illegals or a handler for illegals shows up with readily available obedient people to do jobs that many Americans wouldn't touch. Up until recently is was almost an accepted practice."

Lily thought a moment then continued. "Would this Patriot Green PAC be so infuriated with the conversation on immigration that they would go to the expense, risk, and trouble to kidnap Kendrick Patterson? We have two people kidnapped, four bad guys in custody, two dead people, and arson and a video showing them cutting off Dr. Patterson's finger. That is a ton of anger and risk just to get Senator Patterson to not attend a meeting. I'm still at a loss for motive. I don't think it is enough."

Aggie spoke up. "At this point we are not sure that the PAC is even involved. Any one of these board members is wealthy enough to fund something like this. Phelps is right. We have circumstantial evidence that there is a connection but nothing solid except for this Horace Allen person. We know he had Kip Patterson's finger and delivered it. We only have significant coincidences even if Lucy Frost, Horace Allen and Phillip Tandor have shown up at least twice. We know Lucy went to school with Tim Sampson and the senior Tandor and that Sampson's ex-wife is dead in a staged accident with Aaron Frost in the car with her. We have lots of suspicions but nothing linking all of it together enough to give us some direction. We know Thomas Tandor lives mainly in central Virginia. He also owns property in Upperville. The local records show that Phil, owns a house in Middleburg and that Lucy grew up in Fairfax with at least two of them. We suspect from the forensics on the finger that Kip Patterson is being held somewhere within hours of the Capital. But that could be in any direction. No judge is going to allow a warrant without something more."

Lily spoke next. "There has to be more. Did the Senator ever respond to the pictures of Lucy we sent?"

Phelps picked up his phone. "I will check."

At the far end of the room, SiSi leaned in and looked at her monitor She turned to Claymore and spoke. "Have we checked the satellite data on all of the houses that the Tandors are affiliated with in the Virginia locations?"

Claymore immediately checked his log. "We have some footage on the house in Upperville and the one in Middleburg. I haven't had a chance to review either of those. I just found out about the location in Buckingham County, so I will key it for the next pass in twenty minutes."

SiSi thought then spoke to the whole room. "I would like to launch two of the new drones from Maine immediately over the houses in northern Virginia. They are both within a two-hour drive to the Capital. Do we need a warrant for that?"

Phelps got on the phone to his superiors. He was off in five minutes. "They are going to get back to me on that but how different is that from just a normal surveillance as long as we are only monitoring who is coming and going. How long will it take to get them here?"

Claymore spoke up. "Marcus and I had them transferred on the plane with SiSi. They are already here. We thought it would be a good idea."

SiSi looked at him and smiled. "That is why I am so confident when you fill in for me." She turned to Aggie and Slade. "We can program the new drones with facial recognition for everyone you just mentioned in about 30 minutes. It won't be exact but it will get us close. We can also use some of the previous video and the photos we have to plot in body type and movement. If we can get any one of the people we know have had contact with Dr. Patterson in any location, we may be able to identify where he is."

"Lily broke into the conversation. I have Pat Owens standing by at the house in Middleburg and Shelby Moore is at the house in Buckingham County. I will get in touch with them for an update. They have not gone on property as yet."

Slade spoke next. "Do it. Phelps, please keep working to get official permission. Until we get that, let's just provide aerial reconnaissance enough to watch the comings and goings. That will also give us infrared data but set it just for the outside. Once we get a bit more legal guidance, we can reset it for structure penetration." He turned to L. "Do we have property plans for these buildings. FBI Hostage Rescue could make use of them if we get any indication where they might be holding him."

L responded. "I am requesting them from the individual counties and cities right now."

Claymore interjected as he looked at his screen. "I may be able to help narrow it down. I am looking at the utility data for the house in central Virginia. It is showing a use profile that indicates that the house has not been inhabited for several weeks. The meter is showing minimum use. Depending on what Shelby finds, we might want to have law enforcement just do a courtesy check to confirm that no one is there.

Lily had been silent looking at the photo collection. "I think we should get all of these pictures in front of Serena as quickly as possible. Let's see if she recognizes Thomas Tandor, Horace Allen, Phil or Tim Sampson.

Claymore responded. "That photo pack just went to the Tampa FBI office. Can I suggest something else? Can we send the pictures to the Senator? She might actually recognize one of them. She graduated from Georgetown. That's not that far away from northern Virginia and Dr. Patterson graduated from George Mason and Georgetown."

Slade responded. "Phelps can you make sure Walt gets the pictures to the Senator?"

L had been working quietly at her console during the entire conversation. She finally spoke. "I have been going through the video and blogs related to the PAC. I can't find any evidence that Thomas Tandor has been seen in public or commented on their discussion sites for at least three months. Up until that time he was all over every demonstration and post. One other interesting thing I discovered is that he was beginning to talk about perhaps working with the minority forces that Senator Patterson is involved with on a more middle-of-the-road approach. Some of his ideas seem to have been taken seriously by the working group. On the Patriot site he is criticized for 'caving in' to the liberals. But, for the last few months he has been missing in action."

They all looked around. Phelps spoke first as he dialed his phone. "I think we better speed up the check on the property in Buckingham County."

Kip Patterson had been counting footsteps since he recovered from the sedation after the amputation of his finger. He had counted his steps to the room they had taken him to. He had counted the footfalls he heard as the person come to check his wound, his medication, or leave his food. He was sure that person leaving the food was a woman. He knew he had not encountered stairs. He was sure he heard at least one vehicle and he had heard consistent air traffic overhead. He was being held somewhere within the approach pattern for a major airport. He had only heard one voice that was familiar to him and it was the same female voice he had heard in Puerto Vallarta. He was sure he knew the female voice. As he was finishing his thought, he heard more than one set of footsteps approaching.

The lock clicked, the door swung open and three people entered the room. He surmised they were all men just by their size. All were hooded and didn't speak. The first one in the room came in and covered his left arm in a plastic bag. The second one unchained his tether and they all guided him to his feet. They took several minutes to remove his clothes and then strapped him naked in a wheelchair. They placed a hood over his head and took him down the hall. They made a sharp left with him and then pushed him into what he felt was a bathroom. He was unstrapped from the wheelchair, and led into a shower where the water was already at a comfortable temperature. Between the three of them they scrubbed him all over. His hood was removed. He was in a well-appointed bathroom with a shower equipped with multiple shower heads. They washed his hair and scrubbed him again. It was a very thorough cleaning. Kip wondered if it was too thorough. When they were done, they dried him off, dried his hair and brushed it into place. He was put in a new set of scrubs and strapped back into the wheelchair. His hood was replaced and he was taken back up the hallway to the room where he had been kept. His tether was reattached and the plastic bag was removed from his wounded arm. A fourth person was waiting in the room. He was fairly certain this was a man as well. This person removed the bandages and examined his injured hand. The man cleaned and redressed his hand, and checked his vital signs. The man had significant medical skills. Kip was sure he was going to be sedated again but they all left. As he heard their footsteps retreating, he heard another set approaching. It became difficult to count. The door swung open again and his dinner was placed on the tray table and pushed up to his bed. The person then sat down in the chair near his bed. The hooded figure nodded for him to eat. He was certain the person in the hood was a woman. When Kip just sat there, the individual got up came over and using the knife and fork, cut off a piece of the chicken breast that was in the center of the plate, lifted the hood slightly, and ate it. Kip took this to mean that the food was not poisoned or laced with anything. The individual sat back down in the chair and waited. Kip sat up and ate most of what was on the plate. It took Kip about twenty minutes to finish his meal. He was trying to figure out how to retain the fork that the individual had used. That was not going to happen. The figure got up centered everything on the tray and removed it silently. Kip counted the steps as the person left. He had determined that the kitchen, or at least where the food came from, was exactly thirty steps further away than the room he had been taken to for the shower, but was closer than the room he had been taken to for the video. He was making a mental map. He had been left his iced tea and was about half way finished with it when he began to feel drowsy. "SHIT," Kip thought. Whoever his server was had tasted the dinner but hadn't touched the tea. That was where the sedative was. He began to drift off but more gently than he had before. This was not as strong a dose as he had been given before. He wasn't in pain. He wasn't hungry. He just wasn't free to leave. He also was sure he knew the person who had watched him eat.

Phelps Wheeler received permission to move forward to check the house owned by Thomas Tandor in central Virginia. With it also came authorization to proceed with adequate security and infrared data to be sure that the officers weren't putting themselves in jeopardy. That was a surprise to everyone. SiSi would provide them with the necessary aerial information to keep everyone safe. It would be Shelby's job to do and initial assessment of the property.

Lily spoke to her. "We need a preliminary assessment. You do not have drone support so be careful. Use your backup team for cover. We just need an idea of what to expect."

Shelby acknowledged the order and moved out. She inserted on the property from a mile down the road. It looked deserted. She checked the barn and other than a disturbed section of the dirt floor in the barn, it was clear. She returned to her truck and reported to Lily. "It looks like the place has not been lived in for some time. There are cars in the garage but no signs of life around the main house at all. There are signs that the barn has contained animals but there is nothing there now. I will stand by."

Lily reported Shelby's findings to the team in the command center. The decision was made to move forward on checking the property further.

The Buckingham County Sheriff's office would take the lead backed up by the Virginia State Police. Phelps was on his way to the airport and the short hop to State River Airpark near Buckingham. He would be there about the time everyone was ready and would stand by with the State Police. They repeated a thorough perimeter check including the out building and found nothing that seemed out of the ordinary just as Shelby had reported. Upon looking through the large windows on the first floor of the main house they confirmed the house seemed empty.

The deputies knocked on the door of the main house of the sprawling estate and got no answer. There was little to lead them to believe that anyone inside was in jeopardy. They had their central dispatch check for any record of a caretaker or housekeeper that could be contacted. While there was no legal reason to enter the house, they were unnerved by the fact so big a property would have no signs of life. People this rich didn't go away and leave their homes unattended. The dispatcher responded back with the number of a man who had been the local contact should the alarm go off. He called the commander of the squad back in five minutes. He told them that five weeks ago he had received a call from Phillip Tandor that he was no longer needed as an emergency contact. He had thought that unusual since on several other occasions per the request of Thomas Tandor, he had responded when there was an alarm. On two occasions he had been met by law enforcement and the fire department but it had just been an alarm problem. They were about to hang up when the man asked about the dogs. When the commander told him, they had no indication that dogs were present, he became agitated and insisted they check for the dogs. They were supposed to be fed, let out twice a day by the new caretaker. They were expensive professionally trained guard dogs.

The commander immediately had dispatch attempt to identify the caretaker and the moment his name came across the radio, Phelps Wheeler dialed his phone.

Walt Haskell answered on the third ring. "Phelps, what do you need?"

Phelps responded immediately. "We have a situation here. We don't have legal cause to enter the house belonging to Thomas Tandor. There are supposed to be two well-trained Dobermans here looked after by the caretaker. His name just happens to be Horace Allen, our delivery man."

Haskell took a long breath and said, "Stand by." He put Phelps on hold and dialed the U.S. Attorney's office in Richmond. He came back on the line in five minutes. "There is an authorization on its way to determine the welfare of all inhabitants of that address. The security service is on its way with a key and the code so you will not have to break the door in and they have been told to hold on making the call to the emergency contact in their records. I want to know immediately what you find when you gain access and then I want you back on that chopper headed this way."

Phelps relayed the message to the commander in charge of the Sheriff's team. The commander made a request from the State Troopers on scene to secure the access to the driveway. It wouldn't be long before a neighbor called a neighbor and soon the press would be waiting at the end of the long drive. He wanted to keep them there until he knew what they were dealing with.

Lily contacted Shelby and her team and told them to stand down. Law enforcement would take it from there. Shelby added some information. "I spoke with the man who lives across the road yesterday. I met him while he was walking his dog. He was curious about why I was there. I used our cover story of arbor research. He said he had not seen anyone at the estate for weeks. He struck me as the type of person who monitor the goings and comings of his neighbors. We will stand down."

Retired General Edmond Packer held Fetcher, his golden retriever firmly as the dog was reacting to the activity across the road from the entrance to his farm. State Police and Sheriff's Department vehicles were not a sign of anything positive but there didn't seem to be much activity other than them blocking the driveway. He laughed to himself. The pretty girl yesterday had fed him a line of bullshit the whole time. She worked for someone that probably had federal credentials. He bet old Tandor wouldn't like that one bit. He was always railing on about the broken machine in Washington and ranting about how hardworking men like him shouldn't have to stand in line for anything least of all the attention of the people in congress. Ed Packer thought Thomas Tandor hadn't worked a full day in his life on anything that could be counted as a real job. He had been handed everything just like that idiot son of his. He had long ago stopped paying attention to Tandor or the ravings of his ultra-conservative friends and as for the guy at the top of the government right now, Packer was sure he didn't pay any more serious attention to Tandor than Ed did. He just used him and his friends constantly to stir shit, and they were constantly stirring shit. That girl got the General thinking about when was the last time he had seen Thomas Tandor. He would have to check with Betty, his wife, but he felt it had been at least three months. He pulled on Fetcher's lead and turned and headed back toward the main house. Whatever was going on across the road on the Tandor Farm, it was none of his affair and he was glad not to be associated with the creep. As he walked up the driveway, he could see the Sheriff's Office entry team collected around the front door. He smiled at the thought of that machine Tandor hated so much kicking his front door in. He laughed and thought to himself. "Sometimes the machine works." Fetcher barked up ahead and brought him back to the present.

The senior trooper leaned his head left and acknowledged receipt of the radio transmission. He turned to his partner. "They entered the barn and found the remains of both dogs. We are to go silent on the radio and hold anyone for confirmation before they are allowed on property. The Sheriff's crime scene people are on their way as well as the alarm company. We are to allow them through but no one else gets in or out without authorization from the scene commander. They are sending Trooper 985 to cover the rear farm road entrance. Sounds like something is up and it's not good." The other trooper nodded and returned to back up his cruiser to block the road completely. Once in position, he opened his trunk and retrieved the form that would document anyone leaving or coming onto the farm. He made a note that just prior to them receiving the call, he had seen an elderly man and dog across the road on their driveway observing their position.

The Sheriff's team finished their search of the four outbuildings. On closer examination they found the remains of both dogs in that area of disturbed ground Shelby had reported. The were buried close to where they had been chained in the barn and both had been killed with what looked like a single bullet to the head. That was not something rich people did with valuable well-trained guard animals. The team had finished searching between the main house and the farm. They searched the garage connected to the main house and found four very expensive vehicles. The commander heard the announcement that the alarm company technician had arrived, was logged in and headed up the driveway.

They knocked four times then instructed the alarm technician to open the door and deactivate the alarm. He did so then stepped back outside as instructed to wait for further instructions. The team, just to be safe, made a tactical entry announcing themselves and covering for each other as they began the room-to-room search. It took fifteen minutes to secure the two floors above ground. They found nothing except a half empty bottle of expensive wine in the refrigerator. There was dirty laundry in the laundry room. That seemed strange. The commander posted two men on each floor and with the remainder of the team proceeded to the basement.

The basement level was like a separate apartment. It had four bedrooms, a kitchen, and a large living room as luxurious as the above ground floors. It had a separate stairway that led up to a private entrance at the rear of the house adjacent to the garage. At the far end of the main living area was a door that led to a very large utility room. The far end of the entire wall was covered with several side-by-side upright expensive freezers. They found Thomas Tandor in the one on the left.

CHAPTER 24

The end of one thing is always the beginning of something else.

Everyone in the command center sat looking at each other without a sound. It was SiSi who broke the silence by typing on her keyboard to enter a search parameter for addresses. Claymore shifted his attention to assisting her quietly anticipating what she would need next as L was scanning additional information now focusing on Phillip Tandor. Walt Haskell was on the phone to his legal representatives advising them of the discovery in Buckingham. Everyone was deep in thought as to what finding one of their primary persons of interest dead meant. All in the room were considering what it meant if Thomas Tandor had been dead before the kidnapping in Mexico. It was L that finally disrupted the silence looking up from her screen.

"I have received the floor plans for the houses in Middleburg and Upperville. They each sit on about five acres of land. The house in Upperville is a scaled down version of the one in Buckingham County. It has a connected garage but no barn. It does have a separate house adjacent to the swimming pool. Phil Tandor's house in Middleburg is as large as the Upperville house but is much more modern in design. The plans show a single story on top of a hill overlooking almost all of the property to the west. It could have a subterranean level by the way the layout looks, but the plan doesn't show it. The winding road that comprises the driveway is almost two miles long and is fully visible from the house. Young mister Tandor obviously wants to know when he has company and be able to see them approach."

Claymore spoke from the other end of the room. "The house in Upperville has an extra utility system completely separate from the main facilities that is documented but not operated by the power company. It seems to have a different account number and power source and is registered to a Tandor business holding. An extra meter is required and it is definitely on the property somewhere because it has a geocode that matches the rest of the house."

Slade who had been busy scratching notes since the announcement of Thomas Tandor's demise looked at Aggie. "What does that sound like to you?"

Aggie didn't take much time to answer. "It sounds like a separate function that is not on the plan. We have that type of arrangement at three of our facilities for our bunkered emergency recovery centers."

Lily looked puzzled.

Aggie continued. "Think of it as a separate stand-alone facility that you want to make extremely difficult to enter and even in some cases detect. It is the same setup that used to be developed for bomb shelters in the sixties and is used for more elaborate 'panic' rooms now. They have their own electrical systems with backup generators that are powered by natural gas or propane tanks nearby. Our facilities are built and designed to give us at least sixty days of operational capacity. Claymore, can you tell by the usage how often it is powered?"

Claymore concentrated on his monitor while his fingers flew over the keyboard. He wheeled himself back and looked at everyone in the room. "The main house and pool house power are on the public utility and their use pattern which is tracked by the power company shows what you would expect for a normal home. The extra system is independent and has been set up to not allow tracking. The meter for it registers near the pool house but the use on the pool house is on the public meter and it shows above normal for this time of year. If the geocode is correct, the extra meter has to be somewhere on the property. I would expect the shut off to be near the meter."

L who had been studying the plans sat back and turned to Slade. "There is nothing in the official plans that would indicate the need for an extra system and nothing on the plans that would show a secret room or facility."

Slade laughed. "If you looked at the plans for this facility, you would not see our emergency center which is located sixty feet below where we are sitting and is fully bunkered. Marcus has the system tested and reinforced on a monthly basis to make sure it is fully functional. We don't have one anywhere else in the U.S. We have one in the villa in Mexico and one at our facility in

Switzerland. They are expensive facilities to have but if you ever need them, you are happy to have them."

Lily who had been listening to the entire conversation interrupted the sequence. "It sounds to me like a perfect place to keep someone you don't want found. If it is not on the plan, it is probably not visible from the ground or the air. Even our drones can't penetrate concrete sixty feet down. But it also means that the people keeping Dr. Patterson either have to stay there with him or are coming and going. If any of the people we suspect might be involved show up, it could mean he is there and it could mean trouble. We need to know if there are people in that bunker."

From the far end of the room Claymore, almost under his breath, said, "You could cut the power off. That would kick it to auxiliary power. That would put out an identifiable heat signature that we could see and at least we would know more about it."

Everyone turned and looked at him. Lily spoke what everyone was thinking. "Say that again, Claymore."

He almost looked embarrassed. "If this thing is hidden and large enough to contain a number of people for a fair period of time, it is going to need a backup system that puts out significant power. It would be logical that it would be attached to the main house as well. Producing back up power produces heat. If you turn it off the main power to the house, the generator, no matter how it is fueled, or what it services is going to have to kick on. They are not quiet and they generate energy. I assume our system has backup power."

Slade nodded his head. "We have backup generators for both the above ground facility and the underground bunker and they kick on automatically if the main power has a significant interruption. We test them on a regular basis."

Claymore continued. "If we could find the meter, we could tell if it was running. It would not have that geocode if it were not on that property somewhere. We would also probably find a shut off switch somewhere either in the house or near the meter."

Aggie turned to Slade. "Claymore is right. Our backup systems run off of our solar supply which is completely off the grid in stored batteries. Even our system generators produce heat when the batteries transfer power during use. If we lose normal power, it automatically kicks on."

Claymore continued. "This thing would have to be drawing a ton of power throughout the day. If it is of any size and the space is occupied, it would draw at least as much as the house and that has been using power continuously. The air has to be cooled or warmed and it has to be kept moving."

Slade got on the phone to Walt Haskell who answered it just as he walked into their command center. He looked at Slade as he put his phone on the conference table. "Talk to me and please have some good news. We keep finding bodies and I don't want to find Dr. Patterson next."

Slade answered. "We are really stretching here but we think there may be some sort of hidden underground facility at the Tandor property in Upperville that would be suitable for hiding a kidnap victim. It doesn't show up on the plans nor is it visible from the air. The drone has been up over it for almost thirty minutes. Claymore has found evidence that there is a separate electric supply to it. The Upperville house's regular power use indicates it has been occupied for the last three weeks and using lots of power."

Walt interrupted. "What about before that?"

Claymore looked at the printout and answered. "It was running but not like it has been for the last three weeks. It is non-stop."

Walt continued. "That sounds to me like it fits the timeline for the kidnap. How would you find this other facility?"

Aggie continued. "Claymore suggested that we get the power company to shut off the power to the main house. That might help us track the backup supply kicking on with heat monitoring using our drone."

L interrupted. "I just checked with the gas companies in the area. Two weeks ago, a propane delivery was made to five underground storage tanks that are located in the woods behind the pool house. The company says they service the tanks and check their flow at least once a month. They have no idea what they are connected to but many of these large homes are equipped with this type of system to heat pools, provide auxiliary power or just power gas heating systems, stoves and ovens. They say this account is one of the largest they have. This last delivery was large and the bill is sent to a conglomerate owned by Tandor."

Walt thought for a moment. "We need a reason to get on the ground there and take a look around."

Lily spoke up. "We have people that can do that and not be seen."

Slade laughed. "Yes, we do, but they can't go on that property unless someone has given them permission to or they are backed by a warrant."

Walt thought and then almost shouted. "I think I can get us clear enough to put someone on the ground and maybe even closer. We just found the dead body of the owner of that house at another one of his homes under suspicious circumstances. He didn't put himself in the freezer. We have to consider that if we find young Mr. Tandor's to notify him, as next of kin, of the demise of his father we might panic the people holding Dr. Patterson. Let's put someone on the property to give us a closer pair of eyes. I certainly have enough for that."

Lily stood up. "If you give Agent Haskell one of our monitors, I can get him a live feed from my new equipment. It has been working beautifully for Alex. It's time I gave it a test. We can load the floor plan onto my data base for heads-up display and we can at least try to develop more information on that site. I already have Pat Owens one of our forward intel specialists at Phil Tandor's house. He last reported his is standing by just off property."

Slade looked at Walt Haskell. "How does that sound to you?"

Walt didn't hesitate. "I'm going to get Phelps and a hostage rescue team staged near that Upperville house. Just for caution's sake, I am going to set a second hostage rescue team near the Middleburg property where young Phil

Tandor lives. Maybe we will even catch him home when we go to tell him we found his dad."

SiSi broke in. "Unless you are there now, you will miss him. The drone indicates someone just left the house. He is headed west. It very well could be Phil. There is no other heat signature evidence coming from the house."

Lily picked up her gear and headed for the door just as Aggie stepped over to SiSi's module. "Use the satellite system to follow him and run the analytics. Keep the drone in place over the house. Claymore, stay on the Middleburg house and tell Pat he has authorization to set up on Phil's house in case he comes back. We need to set up for close ground support for both. We want all of this on the big screen in ten minutes."

Lilly was out the door and on her way to the staging area with Phelps. SiSi quickly programmed the satellite feed to alert on the analytics of the car headed west and both she and Claymore repositioned the drones. The two FBI Hostage rescue teams were deployed and standing by in locations close to each house along with State Police support if they needed to activate.

In Tampa, Special Agent Mary Close opened the door to Serena's room and walked in with her computer. "Serena, I know it's late but I need to show you some photographs to help us find Dr. Patterson."

Serena got up and put her robe on. "That is the least I can do. I can't sleep anyway. Show me the photographs."

Mary set up the lap top and turned it around for Serena to look at. "Take your time and tell me if you recognize any of these people. There are multiple photographs of each of them and some of them are better than others. Take your time. If they don't seem familiar it is fine but if they do, let me know."

Serena scrolled through the photographs. She looked up shocked. "The man I knew as FBI agent Peter Crescent is in the back of pictures 9, 14, 15. I didn't see him at any of the events but that is him. The man in photos 1, 7, and 8 is the man I knew as Patrick Henry the head of the event company I was working for. The other photos don't contain any one else that was related to this whole nightmare, but I recognize two other people in the group photos 2, 3, 4, and 5. They are shots from some of the events we planned and photo 2 is from the rally that Lucy and I went to the first time I was approached by Patrick Henry. This must be off the PAC website."

Mary finished making the notes on the first identifications and then came around the table to see who she was talking about. "Show me who you recognize."

Serena pointed to the first person. "This is Dr. Andrew Polk. He was my husband's physician during his sickness." Serena then scrolled to the other pictures and pointed out another man. "This man was the one that came to my house when they installed all the office equipment for Lucy and me. I never got his name. He was also the one that showed up to take it all back."

Agent Close then looked at the pictures. "You said Lucy was with you. Do you see her in any of these?"

Serena scrolled back and pointed with her finger. "Here in photos 2 and 4. She went with me to that first event as well. She even suggested it. That is her there just behind me. In picture 4, she is standing with a group of men. See, there is the guy that made the office deliveries and I don't know who the older guy is who has his arm around her."

Agent Close stood up and closed the computer. "Thanks Serena. That is very helpful. I am about to talk to Agent Wheeler. Is there anything else that you can think of?"

Serena shook her head no.

Mary decided to push. "Did Lucy know that guy with his arm around her?"

Serena shrugged. "I don't know, maybe. It was her idea to go to the rally. Maybe she knew him from being there before."

Agent Close smiled. "Thanks, get some sleep."

Serena laughed. "That's not something that comes easy to me these days. I know I am headed to prison and I know I did something horrible. I know Aaron is dead and I suspect Lucy is too. That is what I deal with when I close my eyes and if that is not enough, I picture Dr. Patterson who was resting peacefully the last time I saw him, dead in the trunk of some car someplace. I'm not about to be getting any sleep anytime soon."

Mary hesitated. "Serena, you did make some mistakes but don't discount the help you are giving us. That may turn out to be the one thing we need for a good outcome for Dr. Patterson. Just try to stay calm. I may have to wake you again but try to get some sleep."

Mary got up and left. Serena watched her go then got up from the couch and sat on the bed. She thought to herself about all that she had been through. Sleep was a necessary evil right now. She was dead tired. She got under the covers and cried herself into a semi-sleep with really bad dreams.

Mary Close was on the phone to Phelps Wheeler in ten minutes after checking and rechecking her notes and the photo pack. He answered immediately.

"Mary, I hope you have some news. We are really running out of time and we may have too many leads. What was Serena able to tell you."

Mary smiled. She loved working with Phelps. He was the classic old agent in a new form. "Serena was able to identify Phillip Tandor as the fake agent. She also identified the man she knew as Patrick Henry. That is such a bad fake name. He turns out to be Mr. Horace Allen. She identified a doctor that she didn't link with the group until she saw him. His name is Polk and he attended to her husband until shortly before her husband succumbed to his cancer. She identified Lucy Frost in a photo but the kicker is that Lucy is standing next to Thomas Tandor who has his arm around her in a very familiar way. I don't think it is just for the purposes of the photo. Serena didn't recognize him but she definitely recognized Lucy and also in that photo she identified the man who delivered and then repossessed her office furniture during the scam. That is none other than Tim Sampson our missing forest ranger. I think she is so traumatized that she is not connecting all of the dots yet. I also think that she is going to make a great witness once she gets past some of this. I hope that is helpful. I hear you found the senior Mr. Tandor in his freezer."

Phelps had been writing it all down. "We did and I'm just beginning to understand why. Thanks Mary, I owe you one. I'm glad everything is going OK there with Serena. I know she is stressed and scared to death, but I also think she is going to the key to the case. I have to go. I will keep you posted if we need anything else."

Mary answered quickly. "Be careful. I just got an update on the two in Atlanta. One of them is very near cracking and spilling his guts. We just don't know what to ask him."

Phelps responded before he hung up. "Ask him about the fake accident in Virginia. That ought to shake things up."

Phelps was on the phone with Walt Haskell in five minutes. "Walt, I'm on my way to the staging area in Upperville. The photos confirm that Horace Allen is the guy who approached and set up the kidnapping with Serena. She also identified Tim Sampson in the photos as the man who delivered and then took back the office furniture. There is also a picture of Lucy standing next to Thomas Tandor. He has his arm around her. Mary feels it was more than just a friendly gesture for the photo. What surprised Mary was that she identified Phil in the photo but that didn't seem to trigger anything in her head at the airport. That is the only thing that makes me think she is more involved than she is letting on."

Walt didn't even hesitate. "Have Mary go back in and ask her that question. She is on a very narrow path that might end up in disaster or redemption. She needs to grow some gumption and start connecting the dots. Do it now. I will talk to you at the staging area and it appears that Phil is on the move. SiSi is tracking him with her drone but we think he is headed to the Upperville house just by the turns he has made so far. Also, the Senator recognized the picture of Lucy Frost. It took her awhile to place her but she knew Lucy from debating her. Lucy was on the George Mason team and the Senator was on the Georgetown team. Now call Mary back and have her ask the question."

Mary knocked on the door and opened it. Serena sat up in bed. "Serena, we are troubled about something you told us. I need you to clarify it."

Serena didn't get up out of bed but she pulled herself up to a sitting position. "Go ahead and ask me."

"When I brought the pictures in showed you them. You identified the man as the fake FBI agent Peter Crescent. Since you obviously had seen him before why didn't you make the connection to him at the airport?"

"I never actually saw him at the event. I never spoke to him. Remember, I saw him in the background of those shots. There were hundreds of people at those events. I'm surprised he made it into the pictures."

Mary watched her carefully. "So, you didn't know he was Thomas Tandor's son?"

Serena looked at her curiously. "Who is Thomas Tandor?"

Mary thanked her and left her room. She called Walt Haskell when Phelps didn't answer on the third ring. She figured he was staging.

Walt answered. "Well, did she have an explanation?"

"She did and I have to say I believe her. She said she had no idea who Thomas Tandor was or that the fake agent was his son. All we had told her was that he was a fake. There is no evidence that she ever actually met either one of them before meeting Phil at the airport that afternoon. She maintains she never saw him at the gathering. I think that is possible."

Walt thought a moment. "I'm beginning to think that Phelps and Lily have been right all along. The only other common denominator is Lucy Frost or whatever the hell her name is. Thanks, I will make sure that Phelps gets the message. Good work, Mary, talk soon."

Mary smiled to herself and thought, "Wow, high praise from an old wolf. That works."

SiSi Holmes smiled to herself as well. "Gotcha!" She turned to the others in the room. "Facial recognition suggests the person in the car is Phil Tandor with an 80 percent certain by facial and body type. Unfortunately, he doesn't appear to be headed toward the Upperville house. He passed the entrance and continued to drive." She had been updating everyone with a message at the same time she was speaking.

Aggie spoke next. "We need to stage Lily's insertion. What does the computer tell us will be her best vantage point?"

SiSi spoke up. "She needs to be high on the hill behind the pool house. She will have a clear view of the structures and the drive and parking area. Once I'm authorized to reset for monitoring the inside of the house, she will be far enough away to be safe. FBI HRT-4 is staged a mile away. They have a five-minute response time."

Aggie looked at Slade and he nodded. It was that silent communication thing they had that sometimes weirded everyone out. "SiSi, you and L have command of our efforts. Keep Lily safe and get the FBI everything they need to make this happen."

Walt Haskell let everyone in the room know what they had found out in Tampa and also alerted them that they had been able to obtain permission for close surveillance and monitoring with a conditional search warrant if necessary. SiSi turned to Claymore. "Let's see what is going on in the house. I'm engaging the infrared. You stay on Middleburg."

L was on the communication link to Lily. Phelps and the HRT-4 leader could hear both SiSi and Lily. "Lily, you will need to approach on foot from the north to a location I am sending you on your screen. Hold there until further notice."

Lily laughed. "Check your screen. I am almost there. Who is on this property that I need to be aware of?"

Everyone who heard her laughed but none louder than Walt. "I bet she ran most of the way to beat them there. We will never know how she did that."

SiSi responded with her normal well expected response. "Affirmative. You are on station. Stand by we have a vehicle approaching."

Lily watched as a car came up the long driveway and rounded the main house headed for the parking area between the pool house and the main house. She watched as two men emerged from the car. She spoke softly into the communication pack microphone on her chest strap. "Two males just arrived. They are walking toward the pool house."

Claymore put his drone in hover mode, leaned over and confirmed that their heat signatures were registering. He saw them enter the back door of the pool house. He watched as they appeared to be waiting just inside the door. In thirty seconds, their heat signatures disappeared. He reported it immediately.

Slade stood up. "That was unexpected. Where did they come from and where did they go?"

Claymore answered the second question first. "They probably got into a shielded elevator."

SiSi spoke next. "Neither of them is Phil. He was headed in the other direction."

Walt Haskell came on the air. "Based on the body in Buckingham, we have been given the go ahead to detain Phil for questioning in the death of his father and to arrest Horace Allen on the evidence he delivered Dr. Patterson's finger. Both are now persons of interest in a federal kidnapping. I'm sending agents in the direction we last saw Phil. Just to be safe, let's wait until we have some idea of what we are dealing with. Since that house probably has very good video surveillance if not security personnel what do we know from the heat signatures in the house?"

SiSi answered almost immediately. "There are two in a small room near the kitchen. They are stationary as if they are doing what I am doing and looking at monitors. There are two in the kitchen but they are moving around like they are working. It's a bit late to be cooking but they are definitely in the kitchen busy with something. There are four people upstairs in two separate bedrooms. In the first larger room, the two appear to be in the same area like they are next to each other in bed. In the other bedroom, they are across the room from each other as if they are in separate beds. There is no movement. I suspect they are sleeping."

Walt communicated with the FBI Team Leader. "You have command. We will monitor."

SiSi raised the drone so the field of view got larger. They could clearly see the heat stamp from Lily above the house. Aggie spoke. "We need to work on better gear for our forwards that reduces their heat signature. If we can see her, with the right equipment so could they."

In twenty seconds, the rescue team began moving into position. HRT-4 members Skip Pointer and Amanda Phillips were in a single small delivery van as they approached from the road and stopped in front of the house. The two plain clothes team members walked up to the front door and rang the doorbell. A voice from the speaker next to the door asked who they were and what they wanted. They responded that they had a food delivery that had been delayed. One of the heat signatures from the kitchen began to move toward the rear of the house. The voice barked out orders to take the delivery to the rear door of the main house.

The two agents walked around the side of the house clearly covered by two snipers that had covered every door or window they passed and every window on the second floor that faced their approach. A man in a chef's coat opened the back door with a scowl and began yelling at them for being so late with a delivery. He opened the door wider and told them to set the two boxes down just inside the door. As he bent down to look in the box, he felt his left hand being twisted behind his back as a hand covered his mouth and pulled him outside. Agent Amanda Phillips took a tactical position just inside the door. Agent Skip Pointer used flex cuffs and a small gag to secure the 'chef' then returned to join Amanda. They picked up the boxes and moved toward the kitchen. Each had his service weapon pulled under the box. As they entered the kitchen, the other person there looked at them in surprise as one of the two security people stepped into the kitchen. Pointer leveled his weapon at the security guard as he put his fingers to his lips with the universal signal to keep still. These were no heavy hitters. Both of these people threw their hands up and complied. They were directed to the far side of the kitchen. The remaining security guard was watching the security monitors when he felt the muzzle of Phillips' Sig Sauer push gently against his right temple. He froze and just put his hands in the air. He was secured in the kitchen with the others. The two agents were now joined by three more in tactical gear with full night vision headsets who moved up the stairs silently to the unlit second floor. Everyone watched the monitors as they moved quickly to the first bedroom where the two were sleeping separately. These two were secured and gagged in the bedroom they were sleeping in. The team then moved on clearing each of the other four bedrooms before they got to the master at the end of the hall. No one else had been found. SiSi sent everyone a message they appeared to be just where they had been first discovered and still looked asleep. The team entered the room quietly just as one of the figures lunged for the night table. He only got a foot before Agent Andy Potter fired and stuck him with a taser. The other figure in the bed jumped up and away from his body as his convulsion stopped. The second figure was taken into custody immediately by the team leader Tripper Stanton, third man through the door. She was on the floor and cuffed in seconds. SiSi was reporting that there was no other movement in the house. The team reported no causalities and all in custody. They brought everyone down to the first floor. No one had stirred from the pool house and Lily remained watching from her observation post and sending video feed to the remainder of HRT-4 and Agent Tony Pace the operations commander.

All of those that had been secured in the house were removed from the property to a safe location for debriefing. The woman and man who had been jolted by the taser were allowed to get dressed. Neither was very combative. One of the team was busy in the security room with the video system. He had patched it through to the mobile command post. There was no way to know if the system was duplicated in the bunker they believed was under the pool house. They found an unlabeled power switch in the control room. The team leader had the main house secured and that team withdrew from the property leaving Skip Pointer and Amanda Phillips inside deployed near the back door. Sniper coverage continued for the safety of the team.

SiSi continued to monitor the entire property as did Lily. They had arrested eight people in the main house. An FBI team was busy debriefing them for additional information on the pool house. None of them was forthcoming with any useful information. The man who had been hit with the taser was identified as a member of Patriot Green who worked for one of the holding companies. The woman was his girlfriend. The chef turned out to be just that, a local chef who had been hired to cook exclusively for the Tandors. His assistant reported that they always prepared several meals and took them to the pool house where 'the others' ate. He hadn't seen either of the Tandors in over a week.

Of course, everyone with a badge knew that the surviving Tandor was headed in the opposite direction. They were more focused on Horace Allen and Tim Samson. Everyone remained in place while the commander and Walt Haskell were conferring. It was Walt's voice that came on the communications link. "We have decided to cut the power briefly to the entire property including the extra circuit we have discovered in the security room. Everyone stay alert and prepare for everything to go dark in five minutes."

Lily adjusted her shield and flipped her night vision eye piece down. She decided to set a sensor about 30 feet behind her and one the same distance on each side. She hadn't seen any other ways to get in and out of the place but she hadn't had time to survey the area properly. She set both sensors, alerted SiSi to their activation and shifted her focus to the pool house. She didn't have to wait long. A single figure emerged on the heat signature where the others had disappeared. Whoever it was walked straight out of the pool house and toward the main house. The figure was about halfway to the rear door when the lights went out.

CHAPTER 25

The end of one thing is always the beginning of

something else.

At the Smithson command center, they were all watching on the big screen. SiSi shifted the drone to cover Lily from the rear as one of the team members surrounding the pool house moved closer to the figure. At least two lasers painted the figure as it stopped just outside the rear door. Everyone was holding their breath.

The back door to the main house swung open. The figure slowly raised both of his hands into the air. The figure was instructed to enter by one of the agents in the house. He did as he was told.

Lily watched the whole episode and was about to report when she felt the ground vibrating. She was about to key her microphone and report the vibration when her rear sensor went off. She reversed her position and dropped silently to the ground. Through her night vision eyepiece, she saw a man walking briskly away from her. The sensor to her right vibrated and she saw SiSi message her that a second person's heat signature had emerged from the pool house just after the power was shut off. The track of the second person was headed on a course to go directly in front of her, or worse, over her. It was pitch black in the woods. She saw the glow of flashlight from the first man who had popped up behind her but not from the one headed toward her. That person's job was just like hers, to stay hidden. Lily remained motionless. Her screen indicated that at least one if not two of the hostage rescue team members were aware of her situation and were moving up. She prepared to protect herself when the figure stopped. A flashlight came on and painted the entire area between her position and the place where the man had emerged. The figure shifted course and crossed twelve feet away directly in front of her. As he walked away from her position, she saw two lasers painting his back. If he had turned, he would have never felt a thing. He kept walking down the hill away from her and then just seemed to disappear into the undergrowth.

Lily keyed her microphone and spoke in a low voice just in case. "There is another way in and out of that bunker. One person emerged from an opening behind me and I think the guy who came up on my left disappeared into the same opening. I am waiting for instructions but repeat, there is one figure moving north along the edge of the woods."

SiSi had picked up the image and was watching it from the drone with night vision as she filmed the entire thing. Claymore was already moving the drone to cover the road between the Upperville House and the Middleburg facility just in case. The hostage negotiation team was on hold in Upperville and the one in Middleburg was alerted to be on standby. The State Troopers on the road guarding the entrance had been pulled off the driveway to a secondary position between the two locations.

Further down the road, Horace Allen emerged from the woods and got into a pick-up truck that was always parked there just in case. He wasn't sure why the power had failed in the bunker but it would come back on. He heard the generators kick in. He had another task and didn't want to wait around. Allen answered his phone. "This is Andy. I didn't see anyone following you and Sid just phoned from the house and said it was just a power failure. I will pull your car into the garage. Looks like we were worried for nothing."

Allen sneered. "I never worry for nothing. That is how we have come this far. You just keep an eye out for anyone following me."

Allen hung up and dialed Phil's phone. Phil answered on the second ring. "Why are you calling me?"

"Everything looked good in the underground. The had a power failure but at least we know the generators worked for the underground and the elevator. I think we have waited long enough. I think it is time to make the final move tonight. Fuck that committee meeting. Tonight, we should use the good Doctor Kip Patterson to send a real message. Where are you?"

Phil answered quickly. "Carry on with the plan then. I agree we need to send the message now. I will call them at the house. You go and make sure they do the job correctly. I have another errand that needs tending to."

Allen didn't hesitate. "What fucking errand? I thought you would want to be there."

"Remember who you are talking to, you prick. What I do on my own time is none of your business. You just go make sure it is done."

Allen responded. "What do you want to do about Lucy and Tim?"

"Lucy was great in bed and she has balls of steel but I don't trust her worth a damn. And Sampson will have people all over his ass once they piece together that his wife was in that car he set on fire. At this point, either one of them would use us to make a deal. I don't need to be looking over my shoulder and neither do you. My guess is they will be finding my old man soon enough and that will give them probable cause to come have a very distressing conversation with me. I don't plan to be available for that. I'm leaving now. I just need to close one more deal before I'm out of here. I suggest you do the same. Your money has been transferred to your blind account. Don't even tell me where you're going and you don't need to know where I will be."

Allen thought a moment. "I will take care of it. Don't leave without making that transfer you little shit or even your inheritance won't be able to hide you well enough."

Phil hesitated one more time. "I will transfer more if you swing by my place and torch it. Do it so they can't find anything in the ashes."

Allen thought another moment. "One million or it stays just the way you left it trace evidence and all."

Phil answered immediately. "Done and make sure both levels get done."

Allen continued on his way to Middleburg. He would be there in ten minutes. Phil Tandor hung up. His car was stashed and the Tandor jet would be wheels up in five minutes bound for Boston.

Horace Allen was a naturally cautious man. He didn't trust anyone particularly the people he was conspiring with. He would have no problem killing everyone watching Dr. Patterson. He didn't want to be seen going into Phil's house. He parked a mile away and made his way to the back door silently along the east perimeter of the woods which ended near the entrance to the lower level. He had an uneasy feeling as he unlocked the door.

Pat Owens watched as he unlocked the door and reported. He did not get a good visual but Claymore moved the drone back to the Middleburg house.

Lily, accompanied by two members of HRT-4 team was exploring where she lost sight of the figure that had passed her. It took them about five minutes to find the metal manhole cover hidden in a thicket. The two team members covered the opening while Lily reported to everyone about their discovery.

Walt Haskell turned to Slade in the Smithson command room in Burke, Virginia. "Do you think they have Doctor Patterson in that bunker? The guy they took into custody in the main house is telling us that he is not there. He is coming apart at the seams but is too afraid to tell us where Patterson is other than to say he was doing well the last time he saw him. The man is shaking like a leaf. He claims he has no idea where he was taken but is sure he will be released once the Senator skips the committee meeting. It is going to take some time to get any credible information out of him. If we move on the bunker and Patterson is not being kept there, then we risk them alerting the others and I have a bad feeling about that. We have them contained and can pick them off just like we did this guy. So, do you think he is there?"

Slade thought then answered. "No, and I agree with you that if we raid the place now and find out he is being kept somewhere else, it will be a death sentence for Kip Patterson. We have the drone located overhead. Let's be patient. We still have time before the committee announcement."

Aggie spoke up. "I don't think we should plan on the committee's timetable.

SiSi looked up from her monitor. The man who left the Upperville house was in a pick-up truck that is parked about a mile from Phil's. Pat Owens has reported that someone has entered the garage there. She looked at Claymore. "Are we set up on Phil's house yet?"

Claymore reported. "The drone is overhead but minimal heat signature in the house."

Walt's phone buzzed. It was Phelps. "Lily and I are headed toward Middleburg along Route 50. We should be at Phil's house in about five minutes. I am going to stage with the HRT. Do we have authority to move on the house?"

Walt didn't hesitate. "I'm tired of chasing these people around. A warrant is on the way to the mobile command post in Middleburg. Take it with you when you set up and bring anyone in that house in for questioning."

Phelps responded. "Affirmative."

SiSi smiled at her desk when she heard her favorite response. She looked up from her monitor. "Both drones are in place and hovering."

L spoke. "From our conversation on powering secure sites, I ran a search on the satellite grid for anything resembling a small to medium solar farm. I narrowed the focus to any property owned by anyone involved with this case. I found one just outside of Upperville and guess what? It is entirely off the grid." L continued watching her monitor while typing on her keyboard. She sat back. "You won't believe this. That property is owned by Lucy Frost. So much for being indigent and homeless. There are no structures on it though so the battery storage is feeding another source. Claymore, is there anything irregular about the power structure at Phil's house?"

Claymore who was busy watching the drone and operating it with its joystick motioned toward his notes next to his keyboard. Aggie walked over and began to look through them. The house in Middleburg shows a normal electric usage but maybe there is something else on that property. We can have Pat check it out. My gut tells me we are running out of time."

Aggie looked at Slade and Walt. "They are getting ready to move Dr. Patterson or worse. L, how long would it take to find any other land owned by Lucy?"

L looked up. I sent the query as soon as I found the solar farm. There is nothing else in the county or the city that is registered to her. Her only other property is her house in Reston."

SiSi spoke to the entire room. "I have a heat signature that indicates a single individual is moving in Phil's house.

Walt stood a moment in thought and then called Phelps. "Where are you two?"

"We are just about to have the team execute. We are at the mobile command post."

"Ask Lily if she ever recorded where Lucy or Serena lived. Did I read that they lived near Reston, Virginia?"

Lily came on the phone. "She gave me the address. It is in the first report I took from her in Tampa. It will take L ten seconds to find it. You are brilliant. We are on our way to Reston. It should take us no longer that 30 minutes to get to Lucy's house this time of night. Tell your guys what to do."

Walt smiled and turned to the crowd as he picked up his radio to talk to the mobile command center. "She is a quick study isn't she." He contacted the HRT team leader in Upperville. "Tony, stand by to execute on that bunker. Take everyone into custody. I am sending a chopper to move HRT-3 to an address in Reston. Once the bunker is secure, turn the arrested over to the local interrogation team. Then relocate immediately to the Middleburg house to support a thorough search. Your warrant is in place. Seal that entire property. We need to find Phil Tandor."

L barked out the two addresses for everyone to hear. Walt was on the phone to his team leader in Upperville, Virginia. "Shut down all land line communication to that house and jam the cellular traffic. Shut off the propane source to the generators wherever they are. When I tell you, cut the power then shut that bunker down and arrest everyone in it and seal it. Don't move till I give the command."

Walt then got on the phone to HRT-3 Site Commander Mat Holcomb at the mobile command post for the Middleburg house. "Mat, your team is going to immediately relocate after that site is secure. We think there may be someone in the house. You will be supported by a warrants team from the Loudon County Sheriff's Office. Leave one of our agents with them. We are sending air support to pick up your team as we speak. Take any individual you find into custody then relocate to a staging area I'm sending you to in Reston, Virginia. Stand by there until I get better clarification on one of two addresses. You will be headed to one of them for a full rescue. I am confident Dr. Patterson is at one of those locations. I believe their entire communications system is located in the facility that HRT-4 is in the process of shutting down in Upperville. We will need to move quickly or Dr. Patterson is tomorrow's headline and not in a good way. Are we clear?" There was a pause while Walt waited. "Great. See you soon. Good luck."

He turned to the room. I can't believe I missed it. We all missed it. We have been following their false leads all the way."

Aggie was the first to figure it out after Lily just as Slade looked up and spoke. "They have been holding him at Lucy's or Serena's house. It's perfect. I'm betting they are at Serena's. She was supposed to be dead in Atlanta by now. For all they know she is. They are so compartmentalized they haven't figured out we have her. It's my guess Thomas Tandor has been dead the whole time. They never figured we would find him until later but he was supposed to be implicated as well. Jesus who thought up this crazy scheme."

Walt spoke first. "It has to be Phil. He has been at every step along the way."

L spoke next. "I'm sorry. I disagree. There is only one person that has been a part of every step along the way. She was the one who kidnapped them. She is probably the one in the video attempting to cut off Dr. Patterson's finger. Lucy Frost is the one who has engineered this whole thing. Little spoiled Phil is just along for the kicks. Horace Allen and Tim Sampson are along for the muscle. Forrest Mack was never supposed to get out of Mexico alive and if he had, they would have killed him too in Virginia. Serena was supposed to be killed in Atlanta. My money is on Lucy as the brains."

Walt spoke into his radio. "HRT-4, execute close down on the bunker." Ten minutes later they reported that all were safe, six subjects were in custody and that all were members of the Patriot Green organization. They did not find Dr. Patterson, Tandor, or any of the other principals. All of those taken into custody were local residents. None of them were cooperating but their communication system, which was extensive was off line permanently.

In Middleburg, the Sheriff's warrant team was moving into position to enter Phil's house. Members of HRT-3 were providing security. Pat Owens and Agent Andy Potter, one of the HRT team's snipers, were watching from a position behind the house that gave him a clear vantage point to provide security for any law enforcement officer threat from the rear of the house. As he scanned the area for movement, Pat smelled smoke. Andy Potter was above Pat on the hill. He smelled smoke as well. Potter realized that the smoke was coming from a vent pipe he was practically sitting on. He keyed his mike. "I have smoke coming from a concealed air shaft vent ten paces east from my position." He heard two other team members report the same. They heard the team leader from the Sheriff's office give the command to execute the warrant. The deputies approached the front door and hit it with a battering ram. The door flew off its very expensive hinges. They made entry and began to clear the house. It was two seconds before the radio reported a request for fire department support that there was smoke emanating from an interior doorway.

Agent Potter watched the rear of the house. Pat Owens pointed out a lone individual exit the rear garage door and head toward the woods at a fast pace. Two deputies were close behind him shouting commands for him to stop. Andy shifted his site to the figure. The man raised his weapon and fired four times before Andy very slowly pulled the trigger. The figure dropped like a stone.

All officers were told to hold their positions. Local fire and paramedics who were backing the local team entered the house as soon as they were given the all clear. The two deputies secured the weapon the man had pointed at them. Pat Owens bent over. him and compared the photo he had on his phone to the dead man. He reported to the command post. "The deceased individual is Horace Allen. The body was covered and Agent Potter secured his weapon as his commander joined him at his position and they started the "suspect down" protocol. Horace Allen received a complete triage examination that was over in two minutes. He had been dead within seconds after Andy fired. The fire team had been able to get to the subterranean floor and extinguish the fire before it spread to the remainder of the house. Part of the basement was destroyed but since there were no windows to allow more oxygen, it was more quickly suppressed. Everything in Middleburg was secure.

CHAPTER 26

*The key to focusing is knowing all the options and
considering them.*

SiSi held up her hand and put Lily on speaker. "We are approaching Lucy's old house. It has a For Sale sign in the front yard, Stand by."

Her voice came back on in five minutes. "This house is empty. There're no appliances in it and the electric meter is still. There is a real estate agent's lock box on the front door. This location is clear. We are headed to Serena's." With that she clicked off.

SiSi spoke to those in the room. "I had to land my drone for recharging when they executed on the bunker. Claymore has about thirty minutes more flying time than mine. He landed as the fire department arrived."

Slade was quick to respond. "Claymore, we are flying our helicopter in to pick up the drone. Can we charge it along the way?"

Claymore laughed. "Yes, I will get it to the HRT. They will have it down by the entrance to the Phil's property."

Slade was quick. "Claymore bring up Frank."

Claymore nodded and in two seconds they heard the voice of Frank Pierson. "Just tell me where, Slade."

Slade laughed. "I want you to put down right at the driveway entrance to the house. The State Police will block the road. Rufus has received clearance for you to fly straight to the southern tip of Dulles International where you will stand by to deliver the drone to the FBI HRT team members that will be arriving to pick it up shortly. They will relocate it to a launch area and Claymore will take it from there. It needs to go on the charger while you fly. What is your ETA?"

They heard Frank's voice come in loud and clear. "I can see the state troopers now. ETA to Dulles at this time of night is fifteen minutes tops. Have Oscar send me the clearance. This won't take long. I'll make it a load and launch."

Slade still thought the timing was tight. They were having to play catch up again. He also didn't like not knowing where Phil was. Slade couldn't get everything he needed where he needed it. Slade looked at Claymore. "Get me Marcus and get SiSi's drone on a charger." They heard Marcus respond from Tampa.

Slade continued as Aggie got Lily on her phone.

"Marcus, I need to know what surveillance resources, drones and such we have near here. I need to get something overhead at an address in Reston but our two birds are not where I need them fully charged. Do we have anything left here or nearby that is not in Maine or Mexico?"

Marcus laughed. "We have the prototype at the Burke office. It doesn't have quite the infrared capability the new models do, but we have rescued lots of people with that drone. It has to hover lower than the new models but it actually has better tracking and video and will be more suitable for that urban environment. The control module is on SiSi's master control board. Is that close enough? Also, as you know by Frank's availability, we have two of our helicopters returning from Bangor, Maine. Alex is going to be on the one headed to Tampa and Oscar is onboard with Frank. It looks like they just landed and picked up the drone in the middle of Route 50 just west of Upperville, Virginia. Do I need to divert the second one to support you?"

Slade interrupted. "No. We are good here. All of a sudden, I am drowning in resources. Thanks Marcus. Please stand by there, thanks."

SiSi turned in her seat with a big smile with a thumbs up which meant that her old drone, the one she called Bertha the Bat was charged and ready to take off from their landing zone on top of their building. She transferred control modules and 'the Bat' was airborne.

Aggie spoke quickly to Lily. "You will have drone support from 'the Bat' and we will feed communications directly to you and Phelps. He will have to be your cover with the HRT. Oscar is on the ground nearby. Are you good with that?"

Lily almost sounded delighted. "Old school. I love it. I am going to stick out like a sore thumb in my tactical uniform in this residential neighborhood. We are one block over from Serena's house. I have rigged my communications unit like a fanny pack and I am going to insert as a jogger. My camera is in my ballcap. No one will think twice about another obsessed jogger out at this time of night. I will be in touch when I am set up."

Aggie was adamant. "I am OK with that as long as you wait for the FBI backup before you get anywhere near that house. No heroics. We just diverted them from the drone pick-up to Serena's house and we have secured Fairfax Police Department's support. The HRT Team will have the warrant for Phelps to serve. You are eyes only at this point but take your weapon. I don't like any of these people. They have already stacked up too many bodies. Horace Allen is no longer a threat."

Lily didn't even respond but the video camera she had rigged to her baseball cap was already feeding a scene from the street as she jogged along the street. It was well lit and looked like a friendly neighborhood where an ex-insurance executive would live comfortably with her sick husband.

L split the screen to show the layout of the house that up until a couple of months earlier had been inhabited by Serena Moore. It was a two-story with a basement, a small yard and pool behind it. Walt was on the phone to Mary Close. "Wake up Serena, get her a headset and have her get comfortable. She is going to talk us through her house. I am having Smithson send you a floor plan she can go by."

Mary was off the phone and down the hall with an FBI communications pack and two headsets in five minutes. She woke Serena Moore for a third time from a fitful sleep. "Serena, we need you to get up and get dressed quickly. We are going to move down the hallway to a more comfortable room. I am going to show you a copy of the plans for your house. You will have this headset on.

You will answer questions about the layout of your house. I will explain all of this after we are finished. You have to trust me. We don't have time to tell you why at this point."

Serena didn't even blink. She was dressed in two minutes and following Agent Close down the hallway. They sat down and Close opened a laptop in front of Serena that had the plans L had just transferred. Mary motioned Serena to put on the headset. When she did, she heard Phelps Wheeler on the other end. "Serena, this is Agent Wheeler. We need your help. In a few minutes we are going to enter your house. You need to answer questions clearly as we ask them. Don't elaborate but answer to the best of your ability. Do you understand?"

Serena didn't bat and eye. She looked at the plans. "I'm ready. Give me a minute to orient myself to the layout I'm looking at."

She then heard another familiar voice. "Hi Serena, this is Lily. Do you have any type of video security on your house?"

Serena answered quickly. "When they installed all the office equipment, they put in an updated alarm system and it had some video cameras. I didn't understand why. The neighborhood is very safe and very quiet. They told me they disconnected the alarm system when they came and took everything away. They didn't take the cameras or the keypad. They never installed any recorders or monitors. I hope that helps."

Lily had stopped running and was walking like she was trying to catch her breath. She wasn't out of breath, but that is what a jogger would do. "Where were the cameras located at the house?"

Serena thought for a moment. "There was one on each of the front, back, and side doors. I believe there was also one on the back patio facing the pool. The side door leads to the garage. The back door leads into the basement level. Those are the only ones I was aware of. They told me they were being monitored by the alarm company."

Lily was bent over like she was catching her breath. She was really looking at the plans on her phone. She was watching L put a small circle in the area near each door. She had not marked the one on the patio.

They heard Serena break in. "I see you are marking the plan. The back-patio camera was next to the French doors but it was pointed to show the back yard and the pool area. That is where you should place the symbol. The others are placed correctly." L smiled as did Lily. Serena had caught on quickly.

Lily continued the questioning. "Serena, where was the room where they installed your office?"

Serena answered immediately. "It was on the basement level. You could get to it from upstairs inside or you could get to it from the back door I told you about."

"Describe that level to me as if I walked in that back door."

Serena thought a moment looking at the plan. "The plan we are looking at doesn't quite match the house. It shows that you enter at the end of the hallway and then walk a short way to the stairwell to get upstairs. Just past that stairwell was the original finished bedroom. The rest was really a large family room as shown here. We enclosed the stairwell and took part of the large room and built in a bathroom for my husband to use. He was in a wheelchair at the end so we made it ADA compliant. We also installed a full kitchen and another bedroom at the far end. He had a caregiver at the end to give me some time. It is like a small apartment now but both bedrooms are good sized. I was going to rent out the basement level since a renter could get to the garage by crossing the patio. I added a lock on the door at the top of the stairs that would give my renter privacy but I never got a chance to even advertise."

Aggie and Slade were listening to the whole conversation. Walt was standing next to them. He spoke what they were thinking. "That sounds like a great place to hide someone you don't want anyone to find."

Lily was making mental notes as she began to run again. "Serena, you talked about when they installed the security system. Did they put in any sensor lights?"

"You mean the kind that come one when someone walks past them?"

Lily smiled to herself. "Exactly."

Serena spoke. "Yes, but also in the backyard they had motion sensors that would trigger the alarm system inside. I know because the back-neighbor's cat, Hero, got into the back yard and set it off several times when I was working late. It scared me nearly to death because the alarm guy hadn't told me to expect that."

Lily narrowed in the conversation. "What did those sensors look like?"

Serena replied quickly. "They looked like the ones inside only in waterproof cases and they were larger. After it tripped that night, I asked them if they could adjust it. They told me they would but a week later they picked everything up but the cameras. It was all gone and the keypad had no power."

L spoke in the control room. "The communication line that is necessary for the alarm system was left in and it is active as we speak. The electric meter is running and has been registering use continuously for the past week."

Phelps heard through his earpiece. He broke into the line of questioning. "Serena, how long ago did you leave your house?"

Serena saw that the computer had a calendar on it. She looked up at Mary who nodded. She opened the calendar then spoke. "I locked the house up when I left for Mexico. That was twelve days ago. God, it seems like a lifetime now."

Lily broke in. "Did you give anyone else permission to use your house or look in on it while you were gone?"

"No. Lucy was the only one that had a set of keys and she was with me in Mexico. I wasn't even sure the house was still mine when we left."

Lily had completed the full circuit around the block and returned to Phelps. She spoke into her phone through the earpiece. "Serena, we are going to take a break. Please relax there and if you think of any other modifications that were made for anything in the house that is different from the plan we are looking at, let us know."

Serena broke in. "When we made my husband's treatment room there were two other modifications. We installed a separate air handler that had an up-graded filtering system on it to help with his immune system and we installed a separate cable system that had high-speed data transfer so that we could communicate his data directly to his oncologist. They were actually monitoring him as if he was in their facility. Until they made the decision to just go with palliative care, he was monitored on a 24-hour basis. Oh, I almost forgot, there was a closed-circuit video system to allow his nurse to check on him from the other room. I had a feed to my room upstairs as well. You could just plug a laptop into it and you could monitor his vitals, watch him and listen to him. That was still intact when they took everything else out. I was going to have it removed for privacy purposes if I got a renter but I never did. That is all I can think of that wouldn't be on the plans."

Lily spoke. "Serena, thank you so much."

Serena spoke one more time. "Lily, be careful if you go in there. The closet under the staircase was installed by the company. It was always locked but I know it was large. When I looked in there after they had taken everything else, there were a bunch of electronic hookups but nothing else. It used to give me the creeps when I went past it."

Phelps whispered to Lily. "She has figured it out what we are up to and is thinking ahead."

Lily smiled. "Remember that G-Man when you and your buddies go to throw the book at her." She jumped in the backseat and started to change into her tactical gear.

Phelps looked up. "Do you want me to go for a walk or something to give you some privacy?"

Lily laughed out loud. "A couple of days ago, I had to ask you for some privacy. Now you're worried that your little virgin eyes will see something they shouldn't?"

Phelps started to blush. "Three days ago, you were standing upright not turning yourself upside down in the backseat. It was a little different."

She laughed again. "I was naked with nothing but a towel around me trying to dry my hair without giving you a show. It is not that different and I am not upside down. Well, maybe a little upside down, but I'm back up now and you don't have to go for a walk. You have two girls. If they are anything like their mother, you better get used to sports bras."

He looked in the rearview mirror just as she pulled her shirt off and got ready to pull her pants up and put her vest back on. This time he did blush. He reached up and turned off the overhead light and got out of the car. Lily laughed as she straightened her ballistic vest and pulled on her black tactical shirt. She pulled the communications pack from her fanny pack and attached it to the front cross strap of her backpack. She pulled her Glock Model G23 out of the pack and slid it in the holster that she had attached to her waist and secured to her right thigh. She grabbed her helmet as she tucked her hair up under a black skull cap. She took a moment to apply some dark shade camouflage paint on her cheekbones and across her forehead and chin and she was ready.

They were parked in front of the house that was directly behind the Moore residence. A Fairfax County Police officer arrived and parked behind them and was greeted by Phelps. The officer walked with him up to the front door of the house as they rang the bell. Lily stayed in the car. The interior light went on in an upstairs bedroom, then in the stairwell and then in the foyer. The door opened and a sizeable man stood with a bathrobe and pajama bottoms on. He checked ID and then they both stepped inside. She saw a small face look out from behind the drape in the main living area. Then, as expected another Fairfax officer pulled up without their lights on. The lights in the house went out. The front door opened and Lily could see a tall man leading the little face that had appeared at the window, accompanied by his wife carrying an infant. They walked quietly to a second patrol car and all got in the back seat. Lily was glad the unit didn't have a prisoner cage in the back. The officer pulled out and was replaced by two more officers that went to the houses on either side. Fairfax Police were systematically and quietly evacuating people out of their homes and the line of potential fire. She emerged from the backseat of the car and put on her helmet as the car with the family pulled out. The little face belonged to a little boy in the back seat on his dad's lap. His eyes grew to twice their size when he saw her. All she could think of was that he might be thinking she was spaceman. She would look forward to meeting him later to explain that there were spacewomen too. Lily loved kids.

She walked up and entered the house. She engaged her night vision and walked through to the back yard being careful not to trip over toys. Once she was outside, she adjusted the clarity of her night vision scope over her left eye. It turned the left side of her face shield into a green world. When she got to the back fence, she took out a small tool and removed the screws holding a fence panel. She pulled it back just enough to thread her video feed snake through. She pushed two buttons and broadcast the entire backyard to Serena's house onto not only the monitor on her chest pack but the large screen at the Smithson command center and the Mobile Command Center for HRT-3. She was able to move the snake end remotely to first identify the cameras that Serena had described. They were all right where she said they were and all of them were active if you believed the red glow of their sensors.

L spoke into Lily's headset. "Let's take a look to your left."

Lily moved the joystick and the end of the video feed moved so that it looked directly down the fence line to her left. She found the sensor with its glowing eye halfway up the end post. Someone had reinstalled the yard sensors that Serena said had been taken when they repossessed the office equipment.

L continued. "Before we do the obvious and look right, let's take a moment and look down."

Lily panned the camera down. Almost directly below her on a metal stake in the foliage was a second sensor. She had been lucky that she had not pulled the fence plank back any further. She then panned to her right down the fence line and found two more sensors. She was trying to figure out how she was going to get closer with this setup, which was way beyond the security you would need for a home office, when Hero pushed against her leg. Lily looked down. Hero was a yellow Maine Coon cat that had to weigh at least 25 pounds. He was huge and he was friendly. She could hear him begin to purr through the helmet as he settled down on her left foot scratching his chin on her boot laces.

She heard L in her earpiece. "What on earth is that sound?"

Lily activated the camera on her helmet and bent down so everyone could get a look. Hero looked directly into the camera mesmerized by the small tiny blinking light, and purred on.

Lily was still for a moment as she thought how to deal with Hero without making too much noise. Slowly a plan formed in her mind and she reached down and picked Hero up. He was all cat not just fur. She quietly carried him back into the house.

Phelps looked at her with the giant cat in her hands and shrugged. "What else can happen on this case. Where did you find that beast?"

Lily stroked his head and answered quietly. "He found me and just in time."

Aggie was smiling at the whole scenario. Walt didn't think it was funny. "What the hell is she going to do with that thing. It needs to be out of there."

Aggie laughed. "Walt, if I know Lily, that little ball of fur is going to be her ticket into that backyard as soon as she figures out how to do it safely."

Walt snorted. "That doesn't look so little to me."

It took Lily two minutes to find Hero's cupboard where his food was kept. Actually, once she walked into the kitchen, he showed her. He would have pulled the cupboard open himself but the mother in the house had wisely attached a baby proof band over the knobs on the cupboards to keep her toddler out of them or to keep Hero honest. It was probably both. She pulled out a small can of cat food. She reached in the pocket on her cross strap and pulled out about thirty feet of 40-pound test fishing line. She then attached the line to the cat food can with a piece of tacking putty she normally would use to secure a video feed or power line. She headed toward the backyard. Hero was hot on her heels, half following her and half slapping at the fishing line that he thought was great fun. She took a small clip that looked like a fancy version of something you would put on a potato chip bag when you began to feel guilty. She used it to attached the can to the top of the fence above the left sensor. She threaded the line through the clip and then behind a tree that was just inside the yard. She opened the cat food and left the can on the top of the fence. She picked up Hero and walked back to where she knew she had a sensor on either side. She gave Hero one more scratch and then set him down.

Hero looked at her and then at the line. He was weighing his options. Lily was getting ready. She looked at the video feed one more time just as Hero decided the food had won. He pranced back toward the left side of the yard and in one leap hit the top of the fence. The can fell into the Moore's back yard. Hero, true to his name followed the can down. It dumped part of its contents and he stopped to feed. The lights in the house went on instantly on the main floor and the patio lights blazed and lit up the entire pool area. Lily waited until she saw a figure in the window and then yanked on the fishing line. The can clattered against the fence as it made its way back up with Hero in hot pursuit. Lily was over the fence just about the same time as she saw the figure looking to her left. As if he had followed the script. Hero stopped on top of the fence and looked toward the light. Lily saw the figure emerge from the French Door. He clearly had a gun in his hand. She also heard the woman's voice behind him. "Stop. It's just the neighbor's big fucking cat. Leave it and turn those sensors off. We don't need to draw any more attention than necessary. We have work to do."

The man cursed and went back in the house. The lights went out and Lily stared at the sensors on either side of her. She had probably activated them but she doubted anyone would notice. Almost as the thought passed through her mind, the small lights went out. The sensors were off. Lily looked at all of them and they were all dark. The cameras were still actively watching movement but she didn't need to get any further. She was in a position to be able to see everything except inside the basement level."

Inside the house Lucy's phone rang. She answered it. "Where are you and where is that idiot Allen? He should have been here by now."

Phil answered back. "The last I spoke with him he was on his way What is going on there?"

Lucy looked at Tim Sampson. "Patterson is sleeping. He has been no problem. He has no idea about what is about to happen. As soon as Horace gets here, we can get him ready to move."

Phil answered in a matter-of-fact way. "There has been a slight change in plans. I don't think we need to wait until the committee meeting. We need to be long gone by that time. The Senator will get the message and get in line, don't worry. Once the deed is done, you and Tim leave with Horace. The doctor is now expendable and should be left with Patterson."

Lucy didn't even bat an eye. "I'm good with that. He is soft and can't be trusted. He still believes Patterson is going to be returned. Have you heard from anyone else?"

Phil laughed to himself. "Who would that be?"

Lucy couldn't believe she had slept with this arrogant little shit. "Are we sure that Serena has been taken care of and the Mexico business is done?"

Phil didn't like her tone. "The house in Atlanta burned and the two dipshits Tim sent to do the work are probably drunk in some topless bar someplace waiting for the FBI to contact them. The two that went to Mexico will soon be dead if they aren't already. I told my Sinaloa contact they hated Hispanics. I even dropped some cash to sweeten the deal. They won't make it out of the country. Relax, we are on schedule. It's time for you to head south to the sunshine. If you are too soft on Patterson to pull the trigger then have Horace or Tim do it. Horace killed the dogs without a problem and he liked them. Tim can make believe it is that ex-wife of his. You knew Patterson had to go when we started this. You were all about hurting his wife. Now put Tim on the phone."

She handed the phone to Tim Samson as she began to put her blouse on. He took the phone.

Phelps' voice came over Lily's earpiece. "HRT-3 is here and we are all in position. The new drone is flying and we have heat signatures for three people. Two on the main floor and one stationary on the lower floor. The feed is going to the HRT who are setting up now. They are going to enter and neutralize on the basement level then proceed to the main floor. and the second floor after that. We believe the single figure is Dr. Patterson."

Lily was listening and watching her scanner and the back of the house at the same time. She could see the two on the main floor with her night vision. If she didn't know better, she would swear they were getting dressed but she didn't want to be distracted. She thought she detected another heat signature from her helmet sensor. She was doing the math. She knew Allen was dead. She did not know where Phil was but was sure he wasn't here. She heard the woman which she figured must be Lucy Frost. The guy with gun was probably the ex-forest ranger, Tim Sampson. The figure on the basement level was probably Dr. Patterson. That would account for the three heat signatures but two of them were standing so close that she was convinced the technology might read as one. Who was the other heat signature near the top of the basement stairs? She looked at the plot that had popped up on her screen from SiSi and the Bat. She could plainly see the two who were on the main floor begin to head upstairs. She saw another signature head down the stairs to the basement. She keyed her microphone. "There is someone else in the house. Repeat, there are four people in the house." She thought about the video with the finger amputation. They had all agreed that they had identified at least four different body types that had appeared on camera. Then it hit her. SiSi was sure Phil had been driving away. Horace Allen was dead. Who was the other person in the house? She heard Phelps' voice once more.

"Understood. We are on hold."

Lily heard the team leader give the order to stage for entry but hold for further intel. Lily saw the tell-tale lines of laser sights sweep the room where the man and the woman had just been. She then saw a small puff as the camera on the patio was decommissioned with a sub-sonic round that no one heard. She saw two team members set a charge on the entry to the side garage door and then retreat. She saw two more team members approach the door to the basement level and hold. She presumed that someone was already inside the garage.

Back at the Smithson command center everyone was studying video footage and reports. Who was the other person? They started with Forrest Mack. He was still at their place in Puerto Vallarta with Hank. The Mexican pilot had returned. It couldn't be him. L was the first to find two possible answers. "Who flew the plane from Houston the rest of the way and who provided the medical attention?" She keyed her Mike so that Lily and Phelps could hear her. "Guys, did we ever get any information on who flew the plane from Houston to Marion, Virginia? Lily responded first. Isn't it in the report?"

L responded. If it is, I can't find it."

Phelps was next. "It has to be in the follow-up we got from Deputy Conner."

L took a moment to do an advanced text scan. "I can't find any mention of it there."

Phelps was quick. He keyed his microphone and responded to everyone on scene and in the command center. We are going to need five minutes to get a better picture. We are one body too many inside. Stand by. We need to be sure we don't have another hostage."

He was off the radio and on the phone in less than a minute. The phone rang. "Deputy Conner, I'm sorry to bother you. We are about to make arrests but we apparently never figured out who flew the plane into Mountain Empire that day."

Deputy Conner didn't hesitate. "The only pilot we even identified was the guy who possibly flew the flight up to northern Virginia. Gimme a minute to check my flip pad." Phelps could hear him turning pages and wondered if he slept with his flip pad in the back pocket of his pajamas. He was back on in half a minute. "The only pilot identified was the cooperative guy based in Martinsville, Virginia. His name was Sid Oldsmar."

Phelps thought a moment. "I know he was questioned in Martinsville about the flight to Upperville but was he in Marion, Virginia, as well?"

Conner didn't hesitate. "I'm showing him as a person who came forward when we put out a request for information in Marion. We contacted Martinsville to do the interview with him. But his name is clearly on the list from Mountain Empire. You need anything else? I'm on a call."

Phelps apologized. "You should have told me you were working."

"Hey you're the one who said you were about to make arrests. That probably means you got all sorts of heavily armed guys with helmets, gas masks, and God knows what else that I wish we had here getting ready to knock the front off some bad guy's house. By the way, they arrested that ranger we talked to. It appears he had been letting Samson stay at his place the whole time we were talking to him. You can request a hold on him. He will probably be able to give you some additional information. He is in deep here as part of Loretta Sampson's death. I did a follow up report for you but you have probably been busy."

Phelps thanked him and ended the call. "Did everyone hear that?"

Lily acknowledged and L affirmed that the command center had received the message. Walt was on the phone to the HRT-4 commander still on the ground in Upperville. "Tony, take a quick look at your arrest log. Do we have anyone by the name of Oldsmar on the list. Tony Pace answered in three seconds. "Oldsmar, Sidney Thomas, male, fifty years old. He states he is a well-respected local pilot who is just exercising his right to protest the unreasonable takeover by criminals from Mexico. There is no question in our mind he knew about the kidnapping and may have assisted. Does that help?"

Walt continued. "Do you have anyone with any medical training that was in the bunker?"

Pace took a moment to speak with the FBI agent in charge of the debriefing. "Not that it is apparent but these people aren't talking much."

Walt thanked him and called the commander for HRT-3. Agent Mat Holcomb clicked his mike. "I am holding for further intelligence but started a five-minute countdown. Could this be Phil Tandor?"

L shook her head as Walt looked at her. "He wasn't headed toward Reston. Let me see if we can find his vehicle. It is a vintage Studebaker Avanti."

Lily broke in. "The two I saw have moved to the upstairs bedroom. The new figure I saw on my equipment is definitely a separate person. I can see all four images now. That figure appears to be waiting at the bottom of the steps. Wait, he is going up the stairs now. He has stopped half way up. What is he doing? It would be easier if we could hear them."

The HRT commander whispered a command and Lily saw the team near the back door place a small device high on the wall next to the French door. She heard static and then she heard amplified voices. Someone was shouting. It was the woman. She saw the fourth figure remain on the stairwell. She spoke quietly into her mouthpiece. "The fourth figure has free run of the house and is stopped halfway up the stairwell. That is not the behavior of a hostage." She could hear the electronic voice of the count down clock get to two. Then she heard the commander halt the entire sequence. All team members held their positions.

Lily watched as the figure started back down the stairs. He paused at the bottom. Then he moved toward the room where they suspected Dr. Patterson was. Lily spoke quietly into her microphone. "The extra image is in the same room with Dr. Patterson by the back door."

Agents Liz Sanders and Phil Brass were located just outside that door. Lily saw them attached another contact microphone just above where they were crouched. A second feed came through Lily's speaker.

"Dr. Patterson wake up. We have to get you out of here. Don't make a sound. It's OK. I am here to help."

Agent Allen Carsen of HRT-3 spoke next. "I have visual of two suspects moving from the second floor and headed to the main level."

Mat Holcomb the commander cut in. "All units hold until my command. All locations report.

All of the teams reported. "Front entry team ready."

"Side entry team is in position."

"Back entry team ready."

The commander was about to give the order when Carsen reported that the back door had opened and that two figures had exited the house. Sanders and Brass intercepted them quietly and moved them away from the structure leaving the back door open handing them off to other team members.

The HRT commander heard the report that they had Dr. Patterson secured. He also heard a report that one of the figures was running through the house toward the stairs. He then keyed his microphone so that everyone could hear. "Go."

Mat Holcomb and Steph Haslem were in the lead with two other team members entering from the inside garage entry. Allen Carsen, their covering officer, painted the room with laser. Brass and Sanders came through the basement and secured the lower floor. On the main level, Holcomb was the first up the stairs. He looked to his left in the darkened room and secured it as the team members went past. Steph Haslem secured the second door just as Holcomb had each shouting clear while the other team members announced they were law enforcement and for all occupants to show themselves. As they entered the first upstairs bedroom Tim Samson opened fire. He was hit twice once by Haslem and once by Tom Jarrett. He wasn't dead but he wasn't going to get up either. Steph secured his weapon and cuffed him as the team covered the door. Holcomb was on the radio. "We are missing one. Where is the woman?" Ten seconds later, the lights upstairs went on followed by the lights down stairs.

Lily quickly turned off her night vision eye piece as she felt a purr against her leg. Hero wasn't interested in anything going on in the house. He just plopped down next to Lily and began to purr. She reached down and stroked him as she watched the house. Then she remembered Serena's words. "The closet under the downstairs stairwell!"

Lily was up and moving with her weapon drawn. She made it inside the door as she called out to Agent Sanders who was just starting up the step. "Closet under the stairs!"

Liz Sanders reversed on the steps and made it to the bottom of the steps just as a muzzle flash erupted through the closet door. She was hit in the upper right chest and was thrown back against the wall. She still managed to fire a single shot as she bounced off the hallway floor. Brass swung over the slim banister and hit the door with both feet. There was another muzzle flash and the round pierced the door near the top just missing his head and lodged in the ceiling molding. The door had exploded in on Lucy Frost who was struggling and gasping with a wound just below her left nipple. Brass screamed into his microphone. "Officer down and one suspect down lower level. I need medical ASAP!"

Allen Carsen had moved to cover Lily while continuing to cover the entire house until he heard the stand down order. The house was filling up with law enforcement and medical personnel responding. The light in the downstairs hallway came on and two combat medics rushed into the entryway. One stopped with Lily who had begun rendering aid to Liz Sanders while his partner went to assist with Lucy. A second set of medics headed upstairs with a transport litter for Sampson.

Tim Sampson was alive and struggling to survive. He was secured and out of the house five minutes after the entry was made. The nine-millimeter round that had knocked Liz Sanders down had hit the upper panel of her ballistic vest. She was bruised and had the wind knocked out of her but she was fine. Brass kept Lucy covered while Terry Cole removed the door and took the EC9s Ruger from under Lucy's right arm. It was purple, small, and deadly with four rounds still available. She was bleeding from the wound to her left breast and trying to retrieve her weapon. When she caught a breath, she cursed at them. Cole moved the door and Brass pulled her out of the closet and secured her arms behind her. Even as the paramedic began to treat her, she struggled and cursed and spat. Cole assisted the medic who declared that they had to get her to the hospital quickly. She was placed on a gurney and sedated quickly. She was on her way seven minutes after she had fired the shot that hit Liz Sanders. Sanders and Lily watched from the rear of the ambulance she had been placed in. Sanders looked at Lily. "You saved my life, you know. If she had fired while I was on the stairs, I'd be dead. Thanks."

Lily didn't want to risk a hug but touched her on the arm and smiled. "You'd have done the same for me. I'm just glad I remembered that the closet was there. Your plans didn't show it and you guys were in so quickly I wasn't sure you had seen it." Lily heard Phelps give her a command to hold for further instructions. She saw lights come on in several houses not directly in any line of fire across the street and was able to see additional police vehicles that had completely encircled the entire neighborhood. She got out of the ambulance and waited.

SiSi came on the line. "Lily, we want you to exit the way you went in. Phelps is waiting for you in the front of the house in back with an evidence tech to take your video."

Lily smiled to herself. "Where have you been Dr. Holmes? No doubt you were hovering just above the whole thing."

Lily had to laugh again when she heard SiSi give her standard response. "Affirmative."

Lily returned to the back yard, reached up to the top of the fence. She pulled herself up and over the fence in one complete movement. Hero had been waiting for her in the back yard. It took him two leaps to get over. He landed at her feet and followed her up to the house. She walked directly through the house and, just past the front door, walked into a bevy of lights and Phelps standing with several federal crime scene technicians. The technicians had never seen a Smithson forward intelligence operative in the new gear. Phelps had not seen it up close either. She unplugged the communication cables, raised the shield and released the chin buckle. She pulled the helmet off and turned it around. From inside the back panel, she removed a small self-contained hard drive and dropped it in the evidence bag held open by one of the technicians and spoke. "The infrared is on channel one, the audio is on channel two, and the video is on three. I have a video snake camera still in place on the back fence with its own hard drive attached. All the files are protected by a single word password which is Tippit."

She then turned and walked back into the house and pulled another can of food out of the cupboard and fed Hero and gave him one more long stroke head to tail as he purred and ate. "Good job, Hero."

CHAPTER 27

*The problem doesn't make the decision about resolution, the
solver does.*

Everyone breathed a sigh of relief at the news that Kendrick Patterson
was groggy but alive. Other than missing a portion of his left little finger, he
was in good shape. He was on his way to a secure medical treatment facility
maintained by the FBI. Lucy Frost was on her way via air medivac to another
secure medical treatment facility in Maryland where she would be under federal
lockdown. Tim Sampson was headed first to a nearby hospital in Fairfax for
triage and then if able, on to a secure medical facility near FBI headquarters.
Senator Patterson had been advised by Walt Haskell that her ex-husband was
alive and recovering. Walt's mission was now containment of the story. No
one needed the political overtures the reporting of the case would create at a
sensitive time in the discussion on policy related to immigration. The chairman
of the committee cooperated with the Senator and tabled the discussion of
the policy for two weeks to give all a cooling off period. The idea was to keep
everything they knew out of the press until they had everyone involved in
custody. Phil Tandor had to be found.

Unaware of all of this, Phillip Tandor had parked his Avanti in the
hangar where the Tandor Jet was kept at Leesburg Executive Airport twenty
minutes after he had spoken to Horace Allen. He was already on his way when
he spoke to Lucy. By the time HRT-3 had made entry into Serena's house, he
was a third of the way to an airport just outside of Lawrence, Massachusetts.
From there he would complete his last remaining business transaction and
then he would be off to Belarus. His company had property and holdings there
that he believed would provide him with the insulation he needed. He was
still getting used to the fact that the company was all his now. He didn't have
to worry about 'daddy' any longer. Financially speaking, he would be set as
long as no direct links were discovered that would connect him to any of the
murders. That would result in the feds freezing accounts. He was traveling

under a completely new passport with a completely new identity. He was almost home free but first he had to pick up his traveling companion. He had found her on a business trip to San Salvador. She had been totally devoted to him until his daddy stepped in with more money. He had been forced to teach her a lesson. He admitted he had gotten a bit carried away but the doctor in Canada had assured him everything had been repaired. There had been some problem with her delivery but he had received a call from Morton that he had her and she was even more beautiful than ever. Phil considered himself lucky. He was now finally out from under daddy's thumb. He was about to be rid of the crazy fuckers that his dad had recruited and no one was going to be left alive to make it difficult for him. Too bad about the others but as his father used to say, "Some of us are just chosen." He had discovered as he was loading his luggage that his laptop was missing. No matter, there was nothing but legitimate business stuff on it.

In Maine, it had taken several hours to sort out the scene that had taken place along the border. All the survivors were in Bangor with authorities from both countries. As it turned out, the three women that had been taken by Maurice Taurant had been recovered in the United States but that he fell across the official border and died in Canada. Han Tu, a citizen of Vietnam, had entered legally through Vancouver, Canada, and still had a legitimate visa. She was considered by the Canadians to be in the country legally and the victim of a kidnapping and human trafficking group. The U.S. authorities took the position that she had been brought into the country against her will. JinJing Zhao was a citizen of China and by Canadian records had entered the country legally. Her visa had expired but she was granted special consideration as the victim of a fraudulent scheme. They were tracking her papers but had issued her a new visa and China had agreed to supply her with a new passport. She too was believed to have been brought into the country against her will. Upon viewing the video tape taken of the killing of Taurant, all authorities agreed for the prosecutor to not pursue charges. JinJing was placed under a protected witness status. Han voluntarily agreed to remain to provide testimony. Both would receive security as the case was building until the remainder of the network was in custody. Lan Li, JinJing's friend, had been recovered in the United States. Maria Montalba and Steve Wiley from Border Patrol along with Bridgett Moss from the FBI and Emilio Cortez from ICE made their case that all three were material to their human trafficking investigation and all were granted protective status. All were cooperating through interpreters and thus far had confirmed the involvement of both Taurant brothers, and a mysterious doctor who had treated all of them for their injuries. Bridgett Moss had taken on the task of following up on some of the people who they felt had made it through to the United States along with Emilio Cortez from ICE.

As Lily was finishing her report in the Virginia office, Phelps walked in to say goodbye and get one more piece of vital evidence. She looked up as he spoke. "I guess this is the end of the road for us with this little caper. It was good working with you."

Phelps stepped across the room. "Lily, you are way beyond any partner I have ever had the pleasure to work with. I don't suppose I could talk you into joining the FBI?" He extended his hand for a farewell shake.

Very uncharacteristically, Lily pushed his hand away and encircled him in her arms. She spoke into his shoulder as she hugged him. "No, there is no chance of that. There is just too much paperwork and not enough hiding in the bushes for me. You take care of yourself, Phelps. Be careful, not just for those sweet kids and your beautiful wife, but for me too. Thanks, so much for how you handled this. It works better for us if we have accepting partners with the agencies. You are an amazing agent and I look forward to working with you again and seeing you and your family back in Tampa. You said you needed something else.?" She released the hug. Phelps was blushing.

He gained control. "Yes, actually. Here is a list of loose end questions I would love for L to take a look at. There may be something in the final report that will help me track down Phil Tandor. Until we have him in custody it is still an open case in my book. Can you have her forward anything she finds to me?"

"Keep you phone on. Knowing L, she has already run an analysis for you. Take care." Phelps turned and walked out of her office.

At the same time Phelps and Lily were saying goodbye, Bridgett Moss and Agent Cortez were sitting in a comfortable room at the shelter in Bangor talking with Anna Lopez, the Honduran victim that had also been treated by the doctor. Both Moss and Cortez spoke Spanish.

Anna had just finished the description of what happened in the woods. It confirmed everything they had heard up to that point and had seen on the video. Anna was able to give a much more thorough statement about Maurice Taurant killing the woman. Bridgett spoke to her softly. "When you were rescued, you produced several plastic bags. Can you tell us about them?"

"I have been collecting these things since my sister and I were kidnapped in Mexico. I took the little plastic bags from the ship captain's room. He kept pills in them to sell to the crew. The first is from him. Every time he pleased himself with me, I would take his ejaculation and put as much as I could in the bag. The second and third bags belong to the doctor that treated me for my injuries. He treated my back and ribs and gave me painkillers. He was gentle but he also pleased himself with me numerous times. Beth looked at the bags with astonishment. "Is that a toothbrush head in the fourth bag?"

Anna nodded. "It was used by the doctor."

Agent Cortez looked at her tenderly. "How were you able to keep these? Weren't you searched like the others?"

Anna smiled. "I told you, the doctor was gentler and they don't think much about a woman's privates unless they want them. That is where I hid the bags. It was sometimes uncomfortable but they handled me differently. I think the doctor liked me. I think the rest of them believed all of us were too stupid or weak to think of these things. We were property to them, not women."

Bridgett showed her a business card and a piece of paper. Anna nodded. "I found the card in the doctor's office. I think it has his name on it. I think he kept me very close to where he practices medicine. Perhaps even in the same building but I never saw anyone other than him, his body guards and another woman he was treating. On the paper is the ship's name. I don't know what it means but I copied it."

Agent Moss looked at the card and turned to Emilio. "Dr. Terrance Concorde, Surgeon. St. Jean Chrysostome, Québec." She handed the piece of paper to Emilio as she said the name of the ship out loud. "Tandor Hannover."

Emilio took both pieces of evidence. "I will get on the phone to Mattey Borge and the Coast Guard." He left the room.

Bridgett Moss smiled at Anna. "You know that is a pretty incredible thing to think to do under the circumstances, Anna. That is a very important piece of information for our friends in Canada and for us. We know you were rescued with the two Asian women. Can you tell me about anyone else that you were held captive with?"

Anna thought for a moment. "There was the other young Chinese girl. I never knew her name and there was one more woman. She was Salvadorian. She said her name was Bettina Ocasio. I spoke of her just now. We were held in separate rooms but during the day we were able to talk. She was from San Salvador. I don't know how or when she arrived in Canada. She was there when I arrived. She had received several surgeries from the doctor. Her face had been badly damaged. She had either been beaten or had an accident. The doctor put her back together again. Except for the swelling, the last time had been very successful. When the swelling goes down, she will be beautiful. She received special treatment from the men holding us. The Chinese girl was treated differently because she was a virgin. The last time I saw her was when the giant man pulled the four of us off the wagon. She was put in front in the small vehicle pulling the trailer and taken down the trail with the others by the other large man. They were gemelos, twins."

Bridgett was writing her notes down even though the session was being recorded. "We are just about finished Anna. You have been so helpful. I just have one more question. How long has it been since you were taken in Mexico?"

Anna looked down. "I'm sorry, I don't know what month it is now but I was taken in January. We had been held at the northern border through the Christmas holidays but it was near the end of January when we got back to Matamoros. What month is it now?

Bridgett reached over and touched her hand. It was not uncommon for survivors of human trafficking to lose track of time while captive. "It is the middle of October. When did you leave Honduras?"

Anna's eyes welled up with tears. "We left San Pedro Sula in July of last year."

Bridgett stood up. "You have been so helpful but that is enough for now. We will be back in touch. Your paperwork is progressing through immigration. Once you have helped us, we will be making some decisions about your future."

Anna looked up. Is there any chance that I could remain in the United States? I have relatives here."

Bridgett stopped and looked at her. "I need to do some checking and you need to rest. Let's leave that an open question for now. You have been assigned an American caseworker. Let's see where this information leads us. I will keep you informed so check regularly with them. Have you started any language classes yet?"

Anna nodded her head. "Yes, it helps take my mind off what is left of my family. I don't even know where they are."

Bridgett smiled again and she turned to leave. "Anna, there are some people who helped rescue you that are working on that. We will keep you informed."

Bridgett left the shelter and headed back to their command center in Bangor. The chill in the air told her winter was coming on quickly. The justice department had not made the decision as to where they were going to prosecute the traffickers that had been apprehended in the U.S. She had pushed for the U.S. Attorney in Boston and the office had agreed to take on the case. She needed just one more link to make that happen. She was sure none of the smuggled individuals who had made it across the border were still in Maine. Massachusetts, and Boston in particular, was a different story. She was even checking sources in Rhode Island and Connecticut to see if a significant number of new faces had turned up on the scene. She got on the phone with Special Agent in Charge Elaine Miller who was serving as head of the anti-trafficking task force. Agent Miller answered in three rings.

"Are you freezing your hind end off yet?"

Moss laughed. "No but I don't think the winter is far away. How are things going with you?"

Elaine Miller had been an agent as long as Walt Haskell had. "I'm running Bill Paisley crazy looking for Morton and Martel. Detweiler is in jail up there with you guys. Nice work on that one. We know Morton was in Maine but he seems to have slipped through. Martel is hanging around Boston like he is waiting for something."

Bridgett smiled. "I think I know what he might be waiting for. I am going to go over the statements on what happened at the clearing where we took everyone in to custody. But if Marcus Taurant ran with a girl, it could be that Morton did as well. The Chinese girl that Taurant took was a 'special delivery'. There was apparently a Central American girl, that was considered special as well. We know that Morton was there and slipped through. He may have taken her with him. She may be traveling with bandages or a swollen face due to recent plastic surgery. That might help us. I will get more to you as this develops up here. My guess is that Morton has the girl and is headed to Martel to make a delivery. She is a link all the way to El Salvador."

Miller wasn't surprised. "I will get a team out on the street. Give me a better description when you get one and we will increase our surveillance on Martel. He is slippery but we have a good net over him. If he moves, we should be able to follow him. If we can stay on him, we might be able to catch them both with the girl."

Bridgett thought how she would finish the call. "Have you ever worked with Smithson Evermore on a case?"

Miller laughed. "No one that has been in the bureau as long as I have, has not worked a case with Slade and Aggie. Why, did they find something in Maine that could be helpful?"

It was Moss's turn to laugh. "They were amazing support but they have these drones that are incredible. They had a forward intelligence agent, Alex, who was unbelievable. They may be of assistance in tracking Martel and even Morton when and if we find him and the girl."

"I will make the request as soon as I hang up. I'm assuming that their child wizard SiSi Holmes is still the major player with their technology?"

Agent Moss confirmed. "SiSi is actually in the Washington area. Smithson just helped the Bureau with another issue there."

"Ah yes. The issue none of us are supposed to know about that involved two HRT teams. I will get a call into Smithson immediately. Thanks, and you be careful up there. My guess is you won't be there long. The word is you will be headed closer to us in the Boston area for prosecution. Talk soon."

After he said goodbye to Lily, Phelps Wheeler and several crime scene investigators were going through the evidence from the house in Middleburg, Virginia. About half of the downstairs space had been destroyed when Allen had set the fire. He obviously had heard the team outside and panicked without finishing the job. The other half of the lower level was a wealth of insight into young Mr. Tandor. There was enough private porn to fill a large library. It was all home video of Phil, several other males of like age, and several older men all with women of almost every nationality, size, and shape and age. Some of them were very young looking. On a flash drive packaged by itself, Phelps found research on Serena Moore and the doctor who had been taken into custody at Serena's house, Dr. Andrew Polk. He was the one that had helped Kip Patterson out of the backdoor right into the welcoming hands of HRT-3. They now knew he was the one who had provided all of the medical assistance and had dressed Kip Patterson's finger after the amputation. He was giving them detailed information on the time prior to, during, and leading up to Kip Patterson's kidnap and rescue. He had confirmed that Lucy Frost had been the brains behind the recruitment of Serena Moore. According to his testimony, Lucy had recruited Tim Samson and Horace Allen to help in the kidnapping. Polk had been pulled into the crime through massive gambling debts and blackmail. He had gone along with everything because he was convinced they were going to release Patterson. The night of the raid he overheard Frost and Samson arguing about who was going to kill Patterson. It occurred to him he would be killed as well. He decided to get Kip out the back door. He said none of them had any idea that the FBI was right outside but that Lucy was on her way down the stairs to kill both of them when she screamed that the back door was open. He offered the theory that when she heard the commotion from the HRT entry upstairs, she knew she couldn't go out the open door and couldn't get back up the stairs, so she hid in the closet.

Phelps was looking through the stacks of material. He closed those files and inserted the flash drive that had been found during the search. He opened the drive and a video menu popped up on the screen. Phelps scrolled through the files and found one entitled "Customs of Canada." He clicked on it and the screen came alive.

Phelps watched the screen as photo after photo of beautiful women flashed in sequence on the screen. Phelps suddenly stopped scrolling. The last ten pictures had been of the same woman. She was tall and absolutely stunning.

By accident he clicked on the picture and it sprang to life. What he had been looking at were not only pictures but thumbnails that activated video behind them.

Phelps called Fran Millsap, the FBI Crime Tech who had been the lead crime scene investigator at the scene. "Fran, Phelps here. I am looking at the copy of the flash drive of Tandor's files. Was this flash drive attached to a computer?"

The technician laughed. "It was inserted in an 85-inch high definition flat screen. Took up almost an entire wall with a series of smaller monitors below it. It looked like one of our command centers. By now you have probably discovered the thumbnails. There are more than a thousand videos, much of it porn but some of it just home shot video."

Phelps was looking at the video of the woman as he was speaking. "Did you notice that several of them were of the same woman?"

"We did and passed it on to intelligence. I got a short note back that they were processing her name through several databases. There are over a hundred of just her alone but none of them are pornographic. There are even about of a dozen of her with Phil Tandor's dad. They looked pretty cozy. She obviously meant something special to both of the Tandors."

Phelps continued. "Just one more question and I will let you go. Where did we find his computer?"

He knew she would take a moment to be sure. He could hear her fingers clicking on a screen. "We found the computer next to the driveway near the garage. It's possible that he just missed loading it. I have done that but only with my coffee in the morning. We are processing the contents as we speak. There is a ton of business records and lots of data on the Tandor foreign holdings. I will make sure to have intelligence get back with you quickly. But the flash drive was found and taken right out of the back of the big screen television. All he had to do was click the remote to watch. I haven't finished the analysis on the computer but I didn't find any of those files on it. The drive was like a private stash. One more note, the number assigned to his cell phone is routed through at least ten transfer stations. He doesn't want anyone be able to track him. Last evidence on possible location is where they found his car."

"You mean the airport in Virginia?"

The technician confirmed. "That's it. There just aren't a lot of those Avanti cars running around. It stood out like a sore thumb to the airport personnel. They appear to have known him well at that airfield and didn't like him very much. The word 'entitled' was thrown around a good bit. You should pull the records for the jet. It is based there but our agents didn't find it at that airport."

Phelps responded. "Thanks Fran. Let's stay in touch."

"One more thing, Phelps. Almost everyone else here at headquarters has been working with ICE, Border Patrol and their Canadian counterparts on a major trafficking case in Maine along the border with Canada. Bridgett Moss is lead in that case. You have worked with her before. Based upon that file you found, you may be able to make a connection between your case and that one. All those women on that drive had to come from somewhere and the collection of photographs and videos had us all thinking they were trafficked."

Phelps answered immediately. I will call Walt." He dialed the number as he returned to the evidence. "Walt, we have just found some very interesting evidence that may be linked to a human trafficking operation the Bureau has been involved with in Maine. Do you have a problem if I contact Bridgett Moss? I know we are keeping our case under wraps but the techs feel there might be a link."

Walt thought a moment. "I just saw a request from Elaine Miller who is in charge of that area for trafficking to link to Smithson. Do you think there is a good reason to take the additional risk of information leaks on our case?"

"If we are going to catch Phil Tandor, I think we need to expand our focus. Evidence at his house makes me think he is a customer for trafficked victims. Intelligence is trying to explore the vast Tandor business holdings. There are significant possibilities for refuge in Russia, Venezuela, and other places where our extradition treaty is difficult to negotiate. I would like to increase our chances of getting him before he is out of the country if possible."

Walt said two words into the phone then hung up. "Authorization granted."

SiSi Holmes received the request to provide drone support for Agent Elaine Miller about the same time she received the authorization to share the list of persons of interest in the Maine case with SAC Miller and Agent Bridgett Moss. She checked the inventory with Marcus and put in the order for two drones to be shifted to the Smithson Evermore office in Boston. She looked over at Claymore and spoke. "Claymore, how do you feel about going to Boston for a couple of days."

He laughed. "I haven't even unpacked here yet so I can be ready to go in thirty minutes. You sure you don't want to go. It is pretty close to Maine?"

SiSi scowled. "Do you want to go to Boston or do you want to go back to Tampa where you can practice not being obnoxious."

He replied meekly. "Boston sounds good." He unplugged his headset and turned his wheelchair toward the door.

Aggie walked in just as Claymore was rolling toward the door. "All of us are headed back to Tampa. We are no longer needed here."

SiSi spoke up as she handed her the requests for support from Agent Miller. Aggie looked at it and turned to Claymore who had paused in the door. "Claymore, get your gear and be ready to leave in ten minutes. You are headed to our Boston Office. We will move Lily that direction since Alex is headed home." She turned to SiSi. "You and L will be returning with us to Tampa. We need to get back on full watch. We will be supporting them from the headquarters. We leave on the jet in and hour with Rufus. Lily and Claymore will be with Frank Pierce and Oscar in the MH65E. SiSi, start the shutdown sequence for this control room and I will see you downstairs. Activate your mobile command system. We will be wheels-up within the hour."

Within that hour, the Smithson Evermore facility northwest of Boston near Lexington, Massachusetts, was manned and ready to go. Normally, Brad Freeport would be heading the operations out of this facility but he was still engaged in the final debriefings of the Maine operation. Oscar Dorian was taking over for him. L was providing intelligence coordination, SiSi was handling all interagency communication and technical support. Lily was on station to provide any field intelligence support that was necessary and Claymore was with her to fly the drone or operate other surveillance in support of the FBI mission. Slade, Aggie, SiSi, and L had just reached cruising altitude when L first made a possible connection. She turned to the others in the jet. "Our last satellite contact for Phil Tandor was at Leesburg Executive Airport. That is where the FBI found his car parked. He wouldn't leave his car there if he wasn't flying out. I have an idea. Can I check with aviation sites to see if we can determine the flight plans of any aircraft that might have left near the timeframe?"

Aggie was first to respond. "The FBI has put out a BOLO for him. All major airports, train stations, etc., will be covered. What do you think we can add to the search?"

L shrugged but answered strongly. "We know him better than your average officer with a flyer in his hand or a picture on his screen. We know he has no problem changing his name. He was in and out of Mexico and we had to put it together from our analysis of the information Serena provided. He has almost unlimited resources that include at least one airplane. We can focus, which is something you are always telling us to do. While I think Lucy was the shot caller in all of this fiasco, Phil was the money and the most careless of the bunch. If he has no idea we found his father, or that the others are in custody, we can start at the last place we knew he was, and focus our effort. I think we can find out his intentions and maybe his location or future destination. It just seems to me that we have more to offer than just waiting around."

Aggie thought a moment. "Do your research but let's focus for no longer than 24 hours on finding Phil. Our priority now is the request to help the FBI find two of the American traffickers from the Maine operation. The FBI believes they have one of the trafficked women with them. That comes first, but if you discover anything that will help the federal agencies find Tandor, let Slade and me know immediately."

L nodded her head and turned to her console. She made a request through channels for the flight plans and documentation of any aircraft that might have left Leesburg, Virginia, during the time frame in question and any aircraft owned by any of the sixteen Tandor business holdings in the United States. She also sent an email to Phelps Wheeler about what she was doing. She wanted him to be kept in the loop since he had been the main liaison on the ground. It would be his job to finish up trying to apprehend all of the individuals involved. She then settled back in her seat for the rest of the flight.

Claymore and Lily arrived and went immediately to the Smithson facility in Lexington. Just as they arrived, they received a message to contact Agent Miller. Lily made the call while Claymore checked the largest of the drones that had been transferred from Maine. He also attached a backup fully charged battery. He didn't know who the target was yet but wanted to make sure they had enough power to stay airborne for a long time.

Agent Miller didn't know Lily Michaels but she had heard plenty about her over the past few days. Phelps Wheeler was making it known that she was exceptional as a working law enforcement partner and Walt Haskell had called her twice to give her the parameters he felt would make the best use of the Smithson resources. He also gave her a detailed explanation of the equipment that Lily was using and her ability to give close undetected surveillance. Miller was not easily impressed but having those two colleagues sing the praises just strengthened the feelings she had developed years ago working with Earl Tippit, Slade, SiSi, and Aggie. Agent Moss had arrived at the Boston field office and was sitting next to her with her full briefing notes. Miller asked her to transfer a copy to L at Smithson so that everyone would be on the same page. SiSi was contacted for the secure transmission code and even though they were still thirty minutes from landing in Tampa, SiSi responded and set up the entire process. She knew L would need about fifteen minutes to get settled so she arranged a full secure video conference to take place once they landed and were in their Tampa headquarters.

CHAPTER 28

*Things don't happen without a cause. Sometimes it's nothing
and other times it's everything.*

As the video conference began, Lily was drawn to one small element that caught her eye. Anna Lopez had managed to write down the name of the ship that had taken her and her sister from Matamoros, Mexico to Halifax, Nova Scotia. Lily was probably the only one on the conference that had heard the name before. L was on the video conference busy collating the information from the different interviews so she hadn't taken notice. Lily wanted to confirm what she was hearing. She interrupted the conversation about fifteen minutes into Moss's summary. "Excuse me, Agent Moss. Would you please read the name of the ship that was identified?"

Bridgett looked back through her files and repeated the name. "Anna identified the ship as the Tandor Hanover. Why? Does that mean something to you?"

Lily texted L who immediately began a search of the ship's registry and owners. Lily answered for both. "I am fresh off another case that began in Mexico and ended in northern Virginia. Two of the principals in that case had the last name of Tandor. The older one, Thomas Tandor was found dead two days ago at one of his properties in central Virginia. His son, Philip Tandor, remains at large with a federal warrant for his arrest in connection with that case. That seems to be a strange coincidence."

Elaine Miller snorted. "I don't believe in coincidences, do you?"

"No Ma'am, I do not."

L brought up a screen for all of them to see. SiSi pushed the notify button to request Aggie and Slade join her in their central command center. L had projected the official registry of the Tandor Hannover. It was Dutch registry and listed as a medium grade container ship. It was older and had its own loading derricks but fit the Panamax classification. Its regular route was listed as the eastern and gulf coast of Mexico, the United States and Canada. At 950 feet long with a beam just over 100 feet, it was capable of passing under the Bridge of the Americas at the east end of the Panama Canal. Its last five trips had been solely along the east coast of the United States. L then switched the screen to the owner ship page. It was owned and operated by Tandor World Logistics with Phil Tandor as the Chairman of the Board. There were some interesting names on that Board of Directors that Bridgett Moss recognized from the victim interviews including Dr. Terrance Concorde of Quebec, and a Mr. Chao Wu of Quebec City.

Elaine Miller watched her reaction then asked Lily the question that was on everyone's tongue.

"I know we are not supposed to be talking about the kidnap operation that just concluded but obviously by Bridgett's reaction to what L just put up on the screen there is a connection. I know you have been tasked to be discreet and in our agency that means you keep the information you have secure from anyone without a need to know the particulars. But, if there is a link, I need you to tell me what it is. I will work out the rest with Agent Haskell and our bosses."

Before Lily could answer L patched Slade into the conversation. "Elaine, this is Slade. It's nice to see you again. The name Tandor has been taking up quite a bit of our time lately. I know most of the details about the Maine case. Lily wasn't assigned there. I think the better person to answer the question is Bridgett since I believe she has already made the link."

All eyes turned to Agent Moss. "One of our best witnesses, Anna Lopez has supplied us with the name of a Canadian doctor who treated her for injuries she received during her transport. He also repeatedly had sex with her while she was captive. His name is Terrance Concorde. Another of the trafficking victims was a Chinese girl named JinJing Zhao. She thought she was coming to Canada to work in an office in Vancouver. Instead, she was transported all the way from Vancouver to Quebec City and delivered as a purchased bride to a businessman there. His name is Chao Wu. He owns the largest trucking and transport concern in eastern Canada. The girl maintains that she was sold to the Taurant brothers because Mr. Wu found her 'too old'. She also testified that she was raped by Wu's nephew and that may have had an impact on his decision to not keep her."

Miller spoke up. "That is definitely not a coincidence. Are we keeping our Canadian counterparts informed?"

Moss answered almost immediately. We have shared everything with the agents who were assigned to the case. Anna Lopez also gave us information on another Hispanic woman that was part of the operation the night we interrupted it. She had met the woman who she identified as Bettina Ocasio from El Salvador. We have a picture of her, or at least what she looked like before she left El Salvador, that has been circulated."

Miller spoke up again. "Make sure that gets to our friends at Smithson and also send it to Agent Phelps Wheeler who is still on the case out of Virginia. If the connection between these cases is what I think it is, he needs to be in the loop."

Slade spoke next. "Elaine, we have two drones ready to go but they are not as effective in urban environments as they are out in the countryside where we have been using them. Lily is also standing by and we can transport her fairly quickly anywhere you feel you want someone to provide close up intelligence. We are ready to go. You just tell us when and where."

Elaine Miller laughed. "Slade if I knew that, I would have her there already. Thank you. As far as we know, Bobby Martel is sitting tight in his condo in downtown Boston. He hasn't moved in days. Our last sighting of Horace Morton was when we lost him in traffic on I-95 south just north of Haverhill, Massachusetts. If he has the girl he won't go near Martel. The good news is, no one has ever trusted him with money so it is doubtful he will make the transfer to the buyer and there is no reason why he would have a special delivery victim with him if they didn't already have a special buyer."

L broke in. "Excuse me folks. I think I just found Phil Tandor's jet. My FAA source just reported that it left Leesburg, Virginia, with no filed flight plan. It shows up next at Hanscom Field near Bedford, Massachusetts, where it had to request clearance to land because of air traffic. It has been there since. The jet is registered as part of the Tandor business group. It is normally kept in Bedford but was moved to Leesburg, Virginia, three weeks ago."

Oscar Dorian surprised everyone as he walked into the meeting. "Sorry to be late everyone. L what kind of aircraft is that?" Miller smiled recognition, Bridgett Moss smiled something else and Lily Michaels watched both of them.

L was quick to reply. "Glad you made it out of the Northwoods. The plane I am talking about is a Pilatus PC-024. The fleet registry shows they own three of them."

Oscar laughed. "That is a very new, very versatile aircraft. That would give the owners options to land in a variety of places. Can you give us the total picture on their whole fleet and where the planes are located now?"

Miller interjected. "As usual when I work with you guys, I sometimes need to catch up. This is one of those times. Why would we care?"

Lily looked at Oscar. He nodded and she answered the question. "Because as soon as Phil Tandor gets wind that his operation has collapsed around him, he is going to head for safe haven. Not every bad guy has a fleet of jets at his disposal. Those jets have ranges that differ. Some can make it a very long way without refueling; most would need to stop. We have a program that could narrow the possibilities down through comparative analysis." She looked at Oscar. "I'm guessing we are talking about target countries where we have no formal extradition treaty or those where the negotiation is difficult." Oscar nodded.

Miller laughed. "I knew I should ask but just to be sure, we are talking about a fleet of private jets?"

L interrupted again from the screen. "We are talking about a huge fleet of jets worldwide. They have two Bombardier Global models that are definitely capable of transoceanic flights and at least six more mid-size and smaller jet aircraft. This would make even Rufus jealous."

Miller questioned. "Rufus?"

Oscar answered. "Rufus Songbird is our chief pilot and in charge of the maintenance and flight operations of our fleet. It is large but this sounds bigger."

L continued. "There is one more interesting piece of news. One of those large jets is also at Bedford."

Agent Moss spoke up. "Phelps Wheeler is lead on trying to close out the Virginia case. I need to get him up to speed on this quickly. I think Morton is in the area with the Salvadorian woman to turn her over to Martel for delivery. I think it is highly likely that Phil Tandor is here to take delivery and use one of those planes to flee to sanctuary. I just don't have a great deal of information on what this girl looks like."

Agent Miller shrugged. "You talk like we can get Phelps here quickly. I don't have the travel budget to get him here and I doubt the FBI will be willing to flood his case with more resources."

Lily spoke up while SiSi, who had been monitoring, was contacting Phelps to patch him into the conference. "We don't know what she looks like but we have lots of photos of Phil and of her before. We know he has traveled on fake passports before. His weakness is arrogance and ego. He would change the name but not his appearance. We need to have close surveillance on the airport and we need to tighten the surveillance on Martel. If he is the only one, they would trust to transfer the woman, the two will have to meet."

SiSi's voice came over the intercom. "Phelps Wheeler will be joining the conference momentarily on his way here on one of our Citations at our expense. I am going to patch him through once he gets on board and we have secure communications. He just sent me a series of photos that should appear on your screen in about a minute. L is running diagnostics on them now for facial recognition and body type."

Miller laughed. "It has been too long since I worked with you people."

Slade interjected. "Elaine, this is what we do and why we do it. Phelps should be at your location soon. Oscar, do you have everything we need there to get Lily deployed?"

Oscar responded as he watched Lily nodding yes. "Yes. I can't believe his jet is at the same airport I just landed at. I want to put part of the team there as well and I would love to have Claymore operate ground scan and whatever aerial surveillance we can use. That would give us very good coverage there. I'm not so sure about monitoring Morton or Martel. Downtown Boston is a tough call unless we have an exact address like we did in Reston."

Miller broke in. "That is something I do have the resources for. We will double up on Martel. I agree with Lily, he is the guy we need to watch because he will be the guy at the transfer for the money unless they change their pattern."

The screen blinked on the wall in front of them and Phelps Wheeler joined the conference from the cabin of one of the Smithson jets. "Hello everyone. I hope you can see me. I can't see you all that clearly but I have sent the images of a woman that was the dominant subject in Phil Tandor's movie and photo collection. The technicians tell me they have identified her as Bettina Ocasio of San Salvador."

Agent Moss almost exploded. "Bingo. That is the woman who Anna Lopez named as the 'special delivery' who was being treated by Dr. Concorde in Canada. There is the link we need. I'm not sure how much help it will be. We don't know what she looks like now."

L interjected as she put images on the screen. "But we do know who the doctor is and we have plenty of video to help us map her body movement and physio type. The analysis program is working as we speak."

Miller spoke next. "Bridgett, get in touch with Mattey Borges and see if she can persuade the doctor in Quebec to provide us more information. I'm thinking she is going to have enough to have a serious conversation with him." Agent Moss was up and out the door to not interrupt the conference.

Miller continued. "Phelps, we have identified a couple of the Tandor jets housed at the airport where you are going to land. I would suggest you stay there and meet up with backup and support. Phil Tandor is your main concern and if L is correct, our best guess is he will be returning to that airport. I just had another thought. Does the Tandor business have any other assets in the area, houses, planes, anything that could aid in his escape?"

L answered. "I'm not showing anything any closer than upstate New York. I think he is going to leave from that airport."

Slade interjected. "Just in case, we are going to move part of our team in Maine to that location. Which airport is it L?"

"Floyd Bennet near Queensbury, New York. They have one light jet there. It has limited range and I am showing nothing large enough to leave the country even through Canada."

Slade continued. "Just the same, Oscar deploy whoever is not still committed from Brad's team to Floyd Bennet just in case. Elaine, can we have an agent as well if we need to make an arrest?"

Elaine thought a moment. "The best I can do is a local officer with the one of the U.S. Marshall fugitive squads. That should take care of it."

Lily looked at Oscar. "Do you think it's time I headed to the airfield?" Oscar nodded.

"I will be staged at Minute Man National Park. I'm worried about the drone in that airspace."

Claymore cut in from his control desk. "Good worry. That whole airspace is restricted for our little toy all the way back to Lexington. I would have to be so low the drone would be easily spotted. There is just too much air traffic. Reston was OK because it was nighttime and could get low. Remember all of them were inside the house. This is a totally different situation. We are not up over a sparsely populated area like an island off the coast of Mexico or the Maine Border. Ground based thermo scan is definitely a possibility. Lily, you'll need a full technical pack for this one."

Bridgett Moss rejoined the group just as it was breaking up. She spoke to Elaine Miller. "Mattey Borges and Agent Brandhoff are headed out to ruin the good doctor's day. It appears that the information and the evidence that Anna provided are enough to arrest him and charge him with a number of offenses. They are armed with a search warrant for his house, his office, and any other address associated with him. They also have sent agents to arrest Chao Wu. His trucking business keeps coming up on their radar including supplying vehicles for a contract company to maintain the Canadian side of the border. It also appears that the titles to at least two of the ATV vehicles confiscated in the Maine operation come back to one of his junior companies. It is no wonder that they were able to attempt such a large operation. If Tandor is officially linked to all of these others, this is a huge world-wide network that reaches all the way to the middle east, all across Europe into parts of the Balkan states and, you guessed it, Central America. Our people have already contacted Interpol and activated our International Operations group. Mattey believes that taking the Taurant brothers down along with this Dr. Concorde and Wu, will put a huge dent in their operations. Wu evidently has resources all the way across Canada including a transcontinental bus service from Vancouver to Halifax."

Elaine Miller raised her eyebrows. "I want you to join me here in Boston to coordinate with Smithson to find this girl, and get Tandor. Either way we are going to take Morton and Martel out of this game on this go around. I am tired of dealing with them as is Washington. I will use my time to go wider with our group and Interpol. We need to get as large a chunk of this as we can. If what your witnesses say is true, these people have been flooding our country with trafficked and smuggled people to a much greater degree than we have thought. We probably can't stop it but at least for these jokers, we can work together to make it much more difficult for them. Please have your team continue to work with the Canadians to get as much evidence as we can to identify people who may be here already. These are professional people. They are going to keep records and they are going to track their inventory at least to the border. What is happening with Marcus Taurant?"

Moss laughed. "He has shut his mouth completely."

Miller thought. "Let's up the stakes on him. His brother is dead. He is fairly familiar with the Canadian penal system, or at least he thinks he is. I think he probably also knows what would happen if we seek to prosecute him here. We definitely have him identified with one of our witnesses who he was trying to take back across the border. See if Mattey won't drop a not-so-subtle hint that we want to bring him back here for prosecution. See what effect that has on his tight-lipped stance."

Moss laughed again. "Do you really believe that will make him think twice?"

Miller finished her thought. "I don't think the overgrown dumbass thinks at all. I think his murderous dead brother did all the thinking and not too clearly. But these guys normally have a fear of our federal prison system. Let's see if he has watched enough TV that it has an impact."

Bridgett Moss nodded her head. "I will call Mattey and advise her of what we are doing and see what she thinks."

Miller had one more question. "If we can't fly that damn drone, what other tool do we have that we can use to stop this transfer?

Moss smiled. "We have Lily Michaels. If she has the same equipment that Alex Pellegrino had in Maine, we are going to have significant ability to observe and capture what is happening. Lily demonstrated those tools in Reston from what Phelps tells me. I saw what Alex was able to do first hand. They are decades ahead of us in their equipment and ability to capture intelligence. They developed their new headgear for use by our military and have made it available to us. We really didn't know what to expect in Maine. This time we know exactly who we are looking for and where they may meet. Once Lily is in place, we will have a significant advantage. We just need to not lose Martel once he gets going."

Phil Tandor was getting frustrated. He had called Allen twice and no one had picked up. He hadn't seen anything on the news about Patterson. He knew that the kidnapping had been a great diversion from their main event in the north. Lucy had been too adamant about the kidnapping. For her it was some ancient personal vendetta with the Senator but he also felt it matched perfectly to keep attention away from his northern operation which had been very profitable. Patterson's death should have at least made it to the second page. There was nothing. He was even more pissed that Allen wasn't answering his phone. He was supposed to have burned his place and taken care of everyone at the Moore house. He had heard nothing. He was beginning to get suspicious but Martel had contacted him and told him to sit tight. The package would be delivered tomorrow morning and within minutes they would be on their way to safety. He was getting cabin fever. He hadn't left the hangar where the plane was stored since they had towed it in. He looked up at the Bombardier Global 6500. He owned the only one he knew of outside of corporate jet share services. He would be out of the country and in his new home with her before anyone knew he had left. He just needed to be patient. It wasn't his strong suit.

L looked over at SiSi. "I have just been looking at the phone data that the FBI sent over for Bobby Martel's phone. Why would he order six three-course meals along with wine and have it delivered to another address?"

"Maybe he was sending someone a gift?"

L laughed. "Or, maybe he was sending someone dinner because they can't go out for dinner. There is enough food here to serve several people."

SiSi turned in her chair. "Send me the address for where the meal was sent. I will make sure Lily and Phelps as well as Agent Moss get the message."

"Add Agent Miller to that list. Remember, she hates to be the last to know."

SiSi responded. "Affirmative, I remember now. Three years ago, we assisted her. I liked her. She is no bullshit."

It was L who turned in her chair this time. "SiSi, did you just use the phase, 'no bullshit?' My how a couple of weeks in the north country can change a girl's speech pattern! I think Brad uses the same phrase a good bit."

SiSi didn't even look up. "Just give me the address, please." She smiled to herself.

The address was the maintenance office at the airfield where Lily and Phelps were located. Miller sent an agent to talk to the delivery man. He told the agent that he had delivered that meal and two others to the office of the jet service in hangar number five. He worked for a home delivery service He picked up the food from the source restaurant and delivered it to whoever was in the office. SiSi forward the information to Lily.

Lily contacted L. "Who owns and operates the jet executive service in Hangar 5?"

L took a moment to search her records then responded. "It looks like it belongs to a company registered in the United States. I don't see a direct connection to Tandor or anyone else on this list but big money buys silence."

Lily thanked her and turned to Phelps. "Someone has been sending large meals to Hangar 5 and leaving them in the office. Do you think Phil would lower himself to the point that he would not leave the plane?"

Phelps thought and responded. "He would if he was getting worried. Perhaps he is waiting for a call from someone before he feels it is safe to move. He also may be watching for confirmation that his little plot with Dr. Patterson was carried out."

"If that's the case, he is going to be getting antsy to get going. He has been in that hangar for at least 48 hours since he landed. We know he is not using the cell phone we have the number for. He must have switched. I am going to set up and focus on that hangar. We are lucky, the woods run right up behind it. Maybe I can get close enough to set a microphone or get a good scan with my helmet. Can we find out what is in that hangar? We suspect a Pilatus is there but what about the bigger jet?"

Phelps thought. "I am going to go poke around. A plane like that is new enough and unique enough that someone will not be able to keep quiet about it. Let's see what we can find out. Time for me to go undercover. You get in position and let Oscar know to provide you cover from behind."

Lily laughed and batted her eyes. "G-Man, it is so sweet of you to worry about my behind." Phelps got up and left without saying a word. Lily checked her equipment. She had plenty of cover to approach from the park as long as she didn't run into people on a walk. She stored her helmet in her backpack and waited until she was sure there would be less civilian traffic and moved out. The helmet alone would attract a crowd. It took her fifteen minutes to be less than fifty feet from the rear of Hangar 5. It stood by itself on the south side of the field. She could see most of the parking lot and the approach to the hangar. She put on the helmet and lowered her shield and began to watch. She laughed when she saw Phelps pull up in a vintage Mercedes convertible. He looked like the cover of Prep Man magazine if there was such a thing. He got out and walked out onto the tarmac. He was approached by what looked like three mechanics in overalls and a fourth guy in slacks and a dress shirt. This last guy was obviously a manager or sales guy. They all started talking and Phelps went inside another office not connected to the hangar she was watching. She saw another car pull up in the adjacent parking lot. She was fairly sure they were Phelps' cover team.

In about thirty minutes she saw Phelps come out with the guy in slacks and shook his hand. Phelps had what was obviously a packet of sales information under one arm. He got into the convertible and pulled out of the area and headed for the airport exit. The man in slacks watched him go. Lily hit her communication button. "SiSi, a call is about to be made from the location I am painting with my laser. Can you see where the call is going?"

SiSi responded. "Affirmative, stand by." She was gone about ninety seconds and returned. "That was strange. It pinged on the same tower and it looked like it was answered by another cell inside the building. I will try to identify the cell."

"Go ahead but it is going to come back to a pay-as-you go with no subscriber name. Let the others know that I believe that Phil is in that hangar. Phelps may have just stirred the pot up enough to get Phil really nervous."

Lily then moved the selector switch on her communications pack to her cell phone and dialed Phelps. It took a moment to connect since her signal was being scrambled. "The guy you just spoke to made a call as you were driving away. It was answered by a phone inside the hangar. By the way you make a great advertisement for a golf membership."

"It was all I could think of with short notice. The office I was in is located just across from the hangar door. It was closed. The small office in the hangar is not normally open unless they are there servicing the jets inside. Normally there are four small ones parked in and around that hangar. There are only two now. Everything else has been moved out."

Lily thought. "The guy in the slacks told you all of this?"

Phelps answered. "Of course not. He wanted to sell me a jet. The three mechanics were the ones that gave me most of the information. They don't know much about the planes in the hangar. They do not service them. That hangar has its own crew that is only there when the planes are being serviced, or prepared for either take off or storage. My three new friends say the activity has been weird for four days now. They normally are not restricted but their boss told them the airport received a request to remain clear of the hangar. That has only happened when movie stars or major millionaires have come into town."

"Did they know anything about the food delivery?"

Phelps answered. "They did not but said it is not uncommon for food service or catering companies to deliver food to the hangars to be loaded onto flights. They did say that is normally done last minute just before the plane heads to the runway. They said the only thing unusual was that they had seen none of the crew around there for two days. I think you are right. Phil is inside that hangar waiting. He is having food delivered once a day, probably in the evening, and just waiting until he hears something. I'm going to update Bridgett and Elaine to see if they have any ideas. Do you have any?"

Lily answered quickly. "We can wait but we need to be watchful. Phil has got to be going crazy in there. We also need to get a pair of eyes on the front of this building. I am going to set a microphone as soon as it gets darker. I am not picking up any sort of security other than the video surveillance on the fence. See if you can help me with that. I just need ten minutes and we really do need someone across from the front."

Phelps confirmed her requests by repeating them. "I will let you know when we shut down those cameras. Otherwise, be careful. If he has the sales guy watching for him, he may have others."

Lily asked. "Why would anyone help this little crackpot?"

Phelps answered quickly. "His daddy was the head of a major ultra-conservative political action committee with over four thousand small donors. Don't forget there are a large number of people out there that don't trust anyone and that PAC played to their fears and concerns. It is a great way to recruit helpers. You would not believe some of the stuff that is coming out of the people we arrested in the bunker. Stay alert. Consider this a dangerous situation and don't underestimate Phil. That last one is not from me. It is from Oscar."

"I love that you two are so concerned about me. This little space girl is just fine. I will be waiting for your signal to go over the fence."

CHAPTER 29

*You cannot hold your breath forever, but you can be careful
about knowing when to breathe.*

Oscar was sitting in the Smithson command vehicle watching the entire airfield from their satellite overheads. He saw where SiSi had located Lily on the map. He decided to take several of the team and move in closer. He didn't like the fact that Lily was in the middle of so much activity. The FBI team was staged on the far side of the airport near the public entrance. They were close enough to move quickly if they were going to arrest Phil and anyone else but not close enough to come to Lily's aid if she got into trouble. They had been lucky in Maine and even luckier in Reston but Oscar didn't believe in luck where his people were concerned. He had not been happy about how exposed Alex had been. He nodded at two of his team members and all three of them moved out of the van and into the woods on the side opposite from where Lily was preparing to go over the fence and set a microphone on the building where they believed Phil Tandor was hiding. They had just moved into position and watched as Lily was up and over the fence. She placed the microphone on the building and was back over the fence in less than three minutes. Oscar thought to himself how special his people were. He moved the backup about ten yards closer.

He heard Lily come on the talk around channel. "You get much closer and I will be distracted by your cologne."

Oscar laughed to himself then answered. "We don't wear cologne. We have you in sight. You can deactivate your sensors. We will pick them up. The park has cooperated and closed for the night. We have it to ourselves. Phelps has sent someone in undercover to the building fifty yards in front of the entrance to that hangar. We have wide angle surveillance on it. SiSi will patch it to me. You have enough to watch for."

Lily clicked her microphone to affirm she had received the message. She settled down and tuned in her listening device. She was getting a great deal of static. She messaged SiSi.

SiSi sent her a message back. "They have a jammer operating in that hangar. Let me see if I can neutralize some of the sound. These people are more sophisticated than we thought."

Lily settled in and began to scan the area visually. She watched for almost an hour before anything began to happen. She noticed a golf cart approaching from her left. It had a single occupant. It didn't go to the front. It went to the back door which was directly across from her. She concealed her position even more. The man in the cart stopped next to the door, looked up and saw the microphone housing. The door opened and a man in a pair of coveralls and a ball cap stepped out and greeted the guy on the cart. The man on the cart gave him a large bag insulated bag like a soft cooler. The guy in the baseball cap retreated with the bag back inside and shut the door. The delivery guy then returned to the cart and headed back in the direction he had come. The whole transaction had taken less than five minutes not including the time for the cart to disappear around the corner of the far building. She felt her communications pack vibrate. It was Phelps.

"What the hell was that? We couldn't see from our side."

Lily pushed a button to send him the video from her helmet. "I think that was his food arriving. I didn't pick up any conversation but the guy on the cart may have seen my microphone."

Phelps responded. "I just got confirmation he was not the same delivery person we talked to. He has more than one person for that task. If he spotted the mic we will know soon enough." He clicked off.

They continued to wait for another hour. Suddenly, Lily realized that the static on the microphone had cleared up a bit. She could hear someone moving about and talking in the hangar. Then she heard the sound of music playing very softly. She imagined that Phil was inside listening to music while he ate. She was straining to hear better when her display went live with a signal from SiSi that there was an incoming call to the cell phone they were monitoring.

Lily listened as hard as she could but could only catch every third word. Then everything went silent. To Lily that was not a good sign. She felt that the guy who had seen the microphone had probably phoned Phil to let him know. She remained very still. Then the silence was broken.

Someone inside was screaming at the top of his lungs and obviously upset. Lily saw the signal that SiSi was taping her feed. "You have exactly three hours to deliver her or I will deliver you to Boston Harbor, you smarmy fuck! People like you don't tell people like me what to do. I have already paid for her surgery. Deliver her to me. Use the same plan we agreed to. I don't ever want to hear from you or any of the other assholes you work with. We will no longer do business with you and you say one word to anyone and the Feds will receive a very nice little package of evidence about all of your stinking operations. You think I give a fuck about the Canucks? I am in charge of the operation now. You fill my requests not the other way around. Now figure out how to get her to me. I am out of here as soon as she arrives."

As soon as the shock had worn off, Phelps texted everyone on the secure system. "That sounded like he had just received some bad news and that Martel is going to stay put and we need to watch for Morton."

Lily texted next. "Unless he spotted the microphone and wanted to mislead us. Either way he doesn't feel as secure inside as he did five minutes ago."

SiSi interrupted everyone. "Stand by for short video feed with Agent Miller."

Everyone one set up to receive their instructions. Miller came on line in two minutes. "Martel just received two phone calls. The first we believe was from Morton. It was from what has to be the last pay phone in the Boston area. The second was the tirade we just heard. I am assuming that is Phil Tandor. I think Lily is right. We stay quiet and see what happens. I am going to move on Martel as soon as we take Phil into custody. Bridgett has advised me that she would like to wait until we have Phil, Morton, and the woman all together. Phelps, I am certain you are good with that but since you are lead agent on scene, you make the call based upon what goes on there. That is all I have. Everyone stay alert and stay safe."

During her briefing, it was Phelps and one of the surveillance team members that noticed it first. Phelps came on the talk around channel. "Someone just walked out of the front door of the hangar and lit up. Stay alert. He is probably going to walk around to the rear of the building. If he finds the microphone, he is liable to make a run for it."

Lily came on the channel. "He won't find the microphone. I replaced it five minutes ago with a sensor that is labeled to detect gas. Even if he sees it, he won't be able to figure out what it is. We may be able to get visual confirmation on him."

The figure was taking a long time with his smoke. It was a cheap cigar laced with a good bit of marijuana. The aroma carried across to the opposite hanger. He finished the cigar and began to walk around the building. He got near the corner of the building that was nearest the parking lot and the lamp clearly exposed his face. It was not Phil Tandor. He continued his walk and stopped by the back door and looked up at the sensor. He appeared to recognize it for what Lily had hoped he would and continued his walk. He got back to the front and walked back inside.

Phelps came on the talk around. "That was not Phil Tandor. Who in the hell was that?"

Oscar responded. "It doesn't matter. SiSi just did a voice recognition and the voice that we were able to capture on the feed from the microphone was Phil's. He is in that hangar. He's just not alone. That guy could be a bodyguard or a pilot or just another flunky to keep Phil company. Stay sharp. What we do know is that whatever is going to happen is going to do so in less than three hours.

Lily came on next. "By the smell that just drifted this way, he is bored enough to need a bit of recreational weed. Some bodyguard. Do you want me to replace the microphone?"

Oscar left it up to Phelps. He answered quickly. "I don't think you need to cross that fence again. They will be coming back. Let's hope they have more than just food this next time."

Everyone settled in again to wait. They waited another hour.

Elaine Miller's voice cut in on the talk around. "Two people just left Bobby Martel's condo. That is the first sign of life in three weeks. It looks like they are headed the opposite direction from the airport in a ride-share. The surveillance team is on the car and we are tracking it with a helicopter. Who could he have with him? We are trying to get cooperation from the ride-share company to determine where he is headed. Standby. If they aren't headed your way, my guess is no one else is and there will not be a delivery. Something has changed."

Everyone was focused on their positions when they heard Oscar on the talk-around channel. "I have a surprise for everyone. Claymore has been operating a scanner near the main entrance to the airport from a house that is located adjacent to Hanscom Drive just before the place where the road splits. There is a van that just turned onto the road that has at least four heat signatures in it. He is not going to be able to follow but everyone stay alert. This could be it."

It took the van five minutes to enter through a gate and pull into a hangar area some distance from Hangar 5. It stopped in front of a hangar which was closer to the end of the runway. Phelps moved the FBI team up closer to the position in an airport service van and asked the FBI agent monitoring the front of the hangar to remain in place while he repositioned so he could get a better view of the newly arrived van. He saw four people emerge and then the van pulled away and headed out of the airport property.

Lily had stayed focused on her position watching the area around Hangar 5. She was taking nothing for granted. Oscar had moved her cover team even closer. The FBI agent who had been watching the front of the hangar was the first to see the golf cart reappear from the direction of the main entrance. This time it had two individuals in it. It pulled to the front of the hangar and one person got off and went in the front door. The driver remained on board and returned back in the direction it had come from. Oscar came on Lily's monitor. "Stay focused. We know where he is. The rest of this is just diversion."

Miller heard this and moved up a second FBI warrant team closer to Lily's position. She wasn't about to lose these people now. She looked at the electronic situation map that Smithson was providing. SiSi was marking all the resources in real time. Elaine thought about how much she wished it was always like this. She saw a new image come on the map. "Anyone know who or what that is coming in the back gate?"

The FBI team leader that was close to the runway end reported. "It is another van. The logo says it is flight services. It is headed to another hangar on the far side."

Miller responded. "All units remain where you are until we see how this develops. I wouldn't be surprised to see a tour bus pull up. They are really doing a good job of giving us different things to look at. We now have a triangle at opposite ends of this thing. I'm open to ideas on where to focus next."

It was Lily that broke the silence with a request to SiSi. "SiSi, what is the wind direction?"

SiSi responded on the secure message device for all to see. "Wind out of the northeast. It followed with a runway designator."

Miller understood immediately. "All units stand by. I am checking with the Massport right now."

Lily was watching the rear of the building when she saw three people emerge. They moved silently toward the front of the building. She keyed her microphone. "I have three individuals at my location moving toward the front of Hangar 5. The FBI agent watching the front picked up the three and acknowledged.

Lily then heard Oscar. "We need to move closer. Phelps is headed this way. We are going to clear this building. Lily and the other Smithson agents were over the fence in two minutes and moving up to the rear of the building in a tactical formation. Lily took up the position nearest the door. Oscar motioned her to test the door. It was locked. They split into two teams and moved up opposite sides of the building. They were near the front entrance when they heard the large overhead door begin to raise. Lily immediately dropped her shield to screen what she knew was going to be a blast of light from inside the hangar. Just as it flipped down, she heard the engines begin to whine that high-pitched sound they all make. Lily looked up to see the Bombardier logo begin to move past her. The big jet was pulling out of the hangar and headed straight for the end of the runway that was designated for take-off that night. Lily remained where Oscar had told her to hold and turned her attention to the other aircraft that was still inside the hangar. The Smithson Team moved closer to the smaller aircraft. It was a Cessna Citation Longitude. It was similar to the new Smithson jet. It sat motionless and silent. Lily saw Oscar move over toward the door switch but stay hidden.

Her headset crackled with Phelps' voice. "We are on the way. Repeat. We are on the way."

Lily saw an FBI Swat Team member in full gear enter through the front door. She watched as Oscar lowered the door after the rest of them were in and turned on the lights to the hangar. They began a systematic search of the entire building. It was done in three minutes with all areas except the plane secured. One of the team went up and inserted the access key into the socket near the door and switched the power ramp to the on position. The door was secured from the inside. The team had trained in this situation many times for air piracy and terrorist situation. They attached an alternate power source to the control panel and took over access to the aircraft. They then moved back to take up secure position. They waited.

The large jet that had moved out of the hangar only moments before had been stopped by two large FBI swat vehicles at the end of the runway. The small glow of a laser sight had prompted the pilot to shut the aircraft down and open the cabin door. There were two pilots who worked for Tandor, two wealthy members of Patriot Green, and several women without documentation

Miller came on the communications channel. "We have the other team in place, repeat the other team is in place. Secure that aircraft and arrest the three who walked out the back of the building. Phelps came on the air. All three have been arrested. They are all illegal. We are about to move on the Citation."

Phelps moved up near the jet and used a bull horn. "You need to open the door or we will blow it. This is the FBI. You are under arrest. Please open the door and come out. Phil, it is time to give it up. She is not coming to meet you and you are not flying out of here. Open the door."

From inside the aircraft, they heard Phil's voice. "Fuck you, Agent. I do not recognize your authority. I am a sovereign citizen of the United States and I do not acknowledge your agency. You are on private property. I am warning you to leave this hangar or I will take lethal action."

Phelps motioned for the agent to activate the door with the relay. "Phil, I understand that you feel special, but your fantasy is over. Dr. Patterson is alive, Lucy, and Tim Sampson are in custody, Horace Allen is dead and we found your father's body. In a month or two this plane and all the others will belong the United State Government as will all your holdings and whatever cash you have stashed in your bank accounts. It may take us some time to track it all down but we will. Your friends in Canada are all in custody and in about five minutes Martel will be in custody. We know that someone is in there with you and we know Morton was with Bettina or whatever name she is going to go by. They won't be joining you. They have left you behind."

Just as Phelps was getting ready to give the signal to open the door, they heard the hum of the door mechanism as it cracked open and the steps began to descend. Out stepped Robert 'Bobby' Martel with his hands above his head. He was unnerved by the red dots that painted his chest as he stood there. "Don't shoot. Please don't shoot."

Phelps had him walk to the bottom of the steps where he was handcuffed. "Where is Phil hiding in the aircraft."

Martel looked down and laughed. "He has decided to make his last stand in the head."

Lily laughed out loud. "He's hiding in the bathroom?"

Phelps passed Martel off to another agent. He and two of the FBI team members walked up the steps. They carefully cleared the cockpit and forward cabin holds. Phelps spoke loudly. "Phil Tandor, you are under arrest for murder, kidnapping, and conspiracy to commit human trafficking. Open the door or we will come in and get you."

A weaker voice screamed from through the bathroom door. "You can't speak to me that way. You have no right to speak to me that way. I will have your job. I know people at the very highest level of government. You're done you stupid bastard. I'm calling my lawyers right now."

Phelps answered. "Let me know which ones answer so we can charge them as well. It would appear that once they heard of your father's death, they were very willing to withdraw their support. Any of them that will take your case now will be bottom feeders. Since we have frozen all of your assets, I doubt you will have much luck. You killed or participated in the killing of your dad, Phil. No one wants to do business with you. That is why Morton and your girlfriend are on their way separately. You shouldn't have trusted her Phil. That was not smart."

The door to the bathroom unlatched. Phil walked out wearing a pair of mechanics overalls and a baseball cap. He was doing his best to look regal. It wasn't working. He had started to grow a beard and had changed the color of his hair. With all that, he was still easily identified by his ego.

At the bottom of the jet stairway, Lily looked at Oscar who laughed and shook his head. She began to understand. "This Bettina isn't a victim, is she?" He shook his head. "How long have you known?"

Oscar smiled. "You were setting the microphone when L came on with the information that she had found another jet registered to a subsidiary of the Tandor business holdings operating out of San Salvador. She found it at the Amelia Earhart General Aviation Authority terminal at Logan. It is a Brazilian made Embraer Praetor 500 with more than enough range to reach anywhere they needed to go. Thomas Tandor transferred the jet to that holding along with other assets before his untimely death. Bettina Ocasio, or should I say, Bettina Tandor is not a trafficking victim. She is the CEO of the new corporation that Thomas Tandor, her late husband set up. Morton had orders that if anything happened to Thomas, he was to take Bettina to safety. She wasn't trafficked in the Maine victims' group; she was moved separately. The girl in the bandages that appeared the night of the operation is one of the illegals that we arrested across the airfield. She was always meant to be a decoy. Bettina came across the border with her new face and totally new legal documentation. She was already headed to her new life before we ever set up."

Lily looked up to see Phelps leading Phillip Tandor down the steps of the jet. Phil couldn't seem to get his crying under control. Lily looked at Phelps. "You could have told me, Phelps."

Phelps handed Phil off to another agent. "What did you want me to tell you? You were focused on the hangar and doing an excellent job of it. You were invaluable in this operation. There he goes right there. We have recovered the woman with the bandages and while she turned out not to be the one, we were looking for, she is a trafficking victim. She will be a really good witness for both us and Canada. She hasn't been here with Phil the entire time. She was on the last cart. By the time we discovered what was going on we still needed to stay in place. I'm sorry it's not as cool as rescuing a kidnap victim but it is pretty cool that our work has now discovered the entire superstructure of the network that kidnapped, traded, and moved hundreds of people across the border. If they get Morton and the real Bettina, we will have everything we need to move on the others involved in the operation from shipping captains to pilots and bus drivers." He stopped and looked at her.

Lily looked at Oscar who started to laugh at her. She redirected her wrath. "You, you are as bad as he is." She walked over and hit Oscar as hard as she could in the arm. When he didn't even flinch, she was about to hit him again.

He grimaced and said softly, "Ow." All three of them burst into laughter.

SiSi was providing coverage for the FBI operation at Amelia Earhart. Agent Miller and Agent Moss were waiting inside the aircraft that was sitting on the runway. In the cockpit were two heavily armed SWAT members and the airplane was completely under the control of the FBI, Boston Police and the Airport Police. The FBI helicopter had watched as Bettina and Morton had gotten out of the ride-share at the main entrance and then hailed a regular taxi cab to take them to the General Aviation airside. There they had the desk clerk, who was really an FBI agent, accept Bettina's documents as the owner of the aircraft and told her the crew was already on board. Bettina had smiled broadly and remarked about how she hoped there was enough champagne on board for the flight. The desk agent had smiled. "Everything is ready for you Mrs. Tandor."

Bettina and Horace Morton walked up the steps and entered the jet. They were surprised to see the two female agents sitting there. Morton reached behind him and was quickly intercepted by a SWAT team member who relieved him of his gun.

Elaine looked up at Morton. "We've been expecting you, Horace. Bobby is in custody. You are under arrest for so many things I am going to let the other agents read them off to you. Get him out of here."

Bridgett Moss then looked at Bettina. "I am glad to find you looking so well. The good doctor did a great job. It is true. You are even more beautiful than you were before. According to the passport you just provided to our agent at check in, you are traveling on your Salvadorian passport which has a visa for both Canada and the United States. However, you will be detained because you were in the company of a known international felon and human trafficker. You were married to someone that we suspect died in a suspicious way, and we are not going to allow you to leave just yet. Until we clear this up, I will take your passport and please consider this airplane impounded. Until we can prove that you were not a part of this conspiracy, you will be staying with us. We will try to make you as comfortable as possible."

Bettina sneered at her. "I am not afraid of your American jails. I have survived much worse in my own country."

Agent Moss answered without fluster. "I am sure that is the case but we will be more than willing to give you the opportunity to compare them until we clear this up." An agent stepped up, handcuffed Bettina, and led her down the jet's steps and away to the federal holding facility.

Everyone in Tampa sat back in their chairs. Aggie looked at Slade. "Well this has been an interesting couple of weeks. I feel like I need another vacation."

SiSi spoke up. "Oscar is on the line for us."

Oscar appeared on the screen along with Lily. "We are finished up here. Lily and I have turned over our materials to Phelps. We are about to pick up Claymore and our equipment and head back south. Anything else you need here?"

Slade answered. "Great job all the way around. Just get back here safe. When we saw things beginning to finish up, we got the jet ready. It is waiting for you at our hanger. Lily, you look distressed. Is there anything wrong?"

Lily looked surprised. "I'm fine Slade. I guess I'm more tired than I thought and I acted like an ass when I found out the whole story. I'm sorry."

Aggie spoke up. "It would have pissed me off too but the timing was last minute like it gets sometimes and the mission we assigned you was very successful. I had to force Alex to take a break. Am I going to have to do that with you?"

Lily smiled and looked at Oscar. "No, I'm ready. I have some notes on the equipment that I want to go over with Alex and I can use some downtime. I'm ready for a Cuban sandwich and a couple of days at the beach."

Lily saw Phelps walk up to them. "I understand that your jet is ready. We will give you a ride. Claymore is already on board. I guess this really is goodbye. I don't think we have any bad guys left to chase together on this one."

Lily went over and hugged him again. "G-Man. There will be plenty of others for us to work on. I'm sorry I got mad at you. I can be an ass sometimes."

Phelps smiled and held her more tightly. "Yes, you can." He hung on so she couldn't get her arms free to punch him.

Slade's personal phone rang. "Slade, this is Kip Patterson. I just wanted to take a moment to thank you for all you did to bring me safely back. According to Henrietta and Walt Haskell your people were outstanding. I also understand that you were able to rescue Hank Kessler. I would like to hear your version of that story sometime but let's wait until he gives me his version. I'm sure it will be very different and that difference, I know, well be entertaining."

Slade laughed. "Dr. Patterson, I am really glad to hear your voice. We were very worried for a good part of the time that we weren't going to be as successful as we were. It was actually a bit of information from Hank that helped focus our efforts. It had to do with a young man that caught his eye. It helped us identify one of the people involved."

Patterson laughed out loud. "That is my Hank. Can't remember what time it is or which pills to take but he could pick out a handsome young man out of a lineup ten years from now and tell you everything about the situation when he first saw him. Is Hank alright?"

Aggie came on the line. "Hey Kip, it's Aggie. He's fine. As a matter of fact, I think I am going to send two of our folks down to Puerto Vallarta for a few days to get some beach time in and help settle him down. I hope you are recovering from your ordeal. How is the missing digit going?

Kip answered immediately. "It is going as expected. I'm sure once I get used to it, it will be just a source of interest. I can't say that was enjoyable but thanks to you people it wasn't worse. If one of those people is Alex Pellegrino, that will quiet Hank right down. Between Alex and Lola, they will be able to get him focused again if that is even possible. Thank you both again so much. As it turns out I finally remembered who one of my kidnappers was, Lucy

Smithers. She had a 'thing' for me back in college. The last time I saw her she had just lost a debate to Henrietta." He hung up.

Two minutes later the phone rang again. "Slade, this is Henrietta Patterson. I can't believe Kip hung up before I could speak to you. Let me just add my thanks. I think everyone did a superlative job but the impact of your efforts I know were appreciated by not just us but the federal agencies as well. I have been advised that you also had an operation in Maine. Thank you so much for staying with our efforts to recover Kip. It must have been a very busy time for you. I will let you go and please thank all your people that were involved. Walt can't stop talking about them."

Slade had always been charmed by the Senator. "Henrietta, thanks for the personal call. But most of the praise goes to the FBI. They stayed on the case and really worked hard to get everyone involved."

"I know. It was above and beyond, which is unusual these days. I am still dumbfounded by Lucy Smithers. I think I may have spoken to her five times twenty-five years ago."

Slade was direct. "Sometimes that is all it takes. We never know who we're helping or who we're pissing off." Slade hung up. "Let's get our dynamic duo headed to Puerto Vallarta tomorrow for a week of beach time. It feels like we didn't get to finish our vacation. I don't know about you but I'm exhausted."

Aggie smiled at him. "Too many time zones in too short a time all going the wrong way. I have had dinner prepared for us upstairs. Security is set for the night. L and SiSi are meeting friends in Ybor. Let's just enjoy each other's company. I'm sure I can think of something that will relax both of us." She took his hand and led him to the private stairwell.

The next morning Alex and Lily were headed off to Puerto Vallarta and ten days of downtime. Claymore was given a week off for covering for SiSi and being so valuable during the operation. SiSi was pressing to have him assigned to the headquarters team on a regular basis. She made a good case with the increasing use of their technology. Brad Freeport was back in Maine for a couple of days with his family then he would be off to his base of operations in

Lexington, Massachusetts, where they had all just finished up. He managed to find time to talk with SiSi at least twice a day. Perhaps there was more than just technology that was moving SiSi to ask for Claymore's reassignment. It didn't matter. Slade and Aggie made it happen and Claymore was now a vital part of the central operations team.

CHAPTER 30

*Most processes don't end, they morph into other actions that
lead to new challenges.*

Three weeks later on the outskirts of Baltimore Maryland, Phelps Wheeler sat next to the bed Lucy Frost was handcuffed to. True to her nature she had agreed to provide information on her co-conspirators in exchange for consideration of a lighter sentence. The bullet that wounded her during the rescue had missed her heart by less than half an inch. That was the last element of good luck that Lucy could look forward to.

Phelps was in the final stages of his last interview with her. Walt Haskell was watching from a chair across the room and a technician was video taping the interview. Both had been amazed at the ability of the woman to maintain a constant smirk that only occasionally morphed into sneer. It was amazing to watch the contempt spread.

Phelps began. "Tell me about Serena Moore."

Lucy laughed for the first time which unsettled her attorney sitting next to her. "She is nothing."

Phelps answered. "Nothing? What about her role in the kidnapping in Mexico?"

"I needed a pilot in Mexico, she knew one. I needed a house to stash Patterson, she had one. If the two assholes that Tim sent to kill her had done their job in Atlanta, we wouldn't be sitting here. She was weak before her husband died and weaker afterwards. She would never have made it as far as she did at Kenderson Park Insurance if I hadn't bolstered her up. She was nothing then and is nothing now."

Phelps didn't hesitate. "Speaking of the Tandors..."

Lucy interrupted. "Which one? They are both idiots. Thomas will set a new record for stupid in hell. As for little Phil, word here is you found him hiding in a toilet. A fitting end to a turd I would say, wouldn't you?"

"If you hated them, why do business with them?"

Lucy smirked more than she had. "Come on Agent. I sense you are smarter than the average dick. They had more money than you can imagine and none of it was earned. They lost more of the family money than they added. Pussy hounds are all alike. They make a million, then they give their latest female obsession two million. All men are alike that way, easily manipulated, easily disposed of. I needed their financial support. I had a score to settle with Henrietta Patterson and their PAC was good cover."

Phelps settled back in his chair. "What score could you possibly have with Senator Patterson? Please don't tell me because of the politics. You are much too smart a woman for that."

"Nice try Phelps. You hit a nerve. The situation was the perfect match for a diversion for their more important foray into 'International Importing'. The Tandors knew little or nothing about the politics of immigration and even less about the economics of it. But they liked money and they had a ton of it and were making more every day. They had the business organization with subsidiaries that were international. Hell, have you seen the fleet of planes they own? Most trafficking operations would die to have that kind of funding and worldwide connections. But I wanted to hurt Henrietta."

Phelps waited a moment then asked. "So, Kip Patterson's kidnapping was a diversion to draw attention away from the operation and to settle some beef you had with the Senator. Lucy, what could make you hate the Senator so much that you would kill her ex-husband?"

Lucy returned to the smirk. "Henrietta Patterson is never going to change her mind about immigration. The fact she happens to be right is not an accident. The fact she is having such a hard time getting her point across goes back to my original observation about men. She is surrounded by a sea of idiots that people like the Tandors help elect with their political action committees, their money and their endless army of disaffected and forgotten fools. At Georgetown, she was the golden girl. She never lost a debate or an argument, including the one she had with me during her final year. I won the debate but she still prevailed. I have hated her since. She wouldn't remember me, little mousey Lucille Smithers. I've changed. I've had to. With idiots like Serena around, it suited me better to be the power behind the throne. No one ever noticed. I have to hand it to Henrietta. Kip Patterson was a good match for her. I was even interested in him. He is so smart. They would still be married if he preferred women to men. I was going to hate killing him but I was sure he would be able to bring us all down if he lived. The whole point about human trafficking is to keep your business out of the newspapers. With the death of the ex-husband of one of the leading opposition senators, a smuggling operation across the border into Maine wasn't going to make any news at all."

Walt interjected from across the room. "So, you were involved in the trafficking as well."

Lucy smirked. "You don't think the Tandors could have done it on their own, do you? They needed someone with logistical skills. That was me. It was easy to get the job. I just slept with both of them. Once our plan was hatched, I didn't need either one of them any longer and old Tandor already had the hots for the Central American whore they imported. Problem was that Phil had the hots for her too. It was really interesting to watch their pissing match. When Tim told me Thomas was dead, I knew we needed to speed things up. I had to leave some things to the others. That was my mistake. Trusting dipshit men to get things done right. That is why Aaron was so perfect. He did everything I told him to. The most dangerous people in the world are those that will do everything they are told without question. They can't think for themselves. That was Aaron but he was getting too bold. He had to go. If I had asked him to inject himself, he would have. "

Phelps leaned back. "I have to hand it to you, Lucy. You may be one of the most cold-hearted criminals I have ever dealt with."

Lucy leaned back and looked at her lawyer and then at Phelps. "I will take that as compliment, Agent. You can't have a warm heart and sell human beings into slavery. But you are young. I'm sure someone will come along that will make me look like a saint."

Lucy's lawyer shook his head and uttered just one word as he gathered his papers up. "Doubtful."

At almost the same time, Agent Bridgett Moss and Detective Tom Warren from Buckingham County Virginia Sheriff's office were sitting across from Phil Tandor and his attorney in an interrogation room at the federal holding facility in Boston. Bridgett took the lead on the questioning. "Phil, what happened to your father?"

Phil looked at his attorney "He trusted Lucy Frost too much and she killed him."

"The postmortem examination of your father's remains tells us that at the time of his death, Lucy wasn't in Virginia, Phil."

"Well don't look at me. I was in Mexico. Stop calling me by my first name. My name is Mr. Tandor to you."

Tom Warren laughed.

Phil spit out the next sentenced. "What are you laughing at, you weak-assed shit? You let a woman do your talking? What kind of a man are you to let this bitch do your work? Oh, that's right. She's a fed and you're just a country-bumpkin cop from the middle of Virginia. What do you know about anything?"

The detective didn't take the bait. He remained calm. "Here is what I know. Phil. I know that on the date your father was killed he was celebrating his marriage to Bettina. I know that you became enraged that he had married her. She was supposed to be for you. You were mad at her because she went along with it. That is how she received the injuries to her face. You see Phil, she wasn't ever interested in you or your father. She was interested in the money and the business. She and Morton have testified that it was you that cut your father's throat after he fell asleep in a drunken stupor in the downstairs apartment. Morton picked up Bettina after you beat her and sent her in the small jet to Canada so the good doctor could put her face back together from your handiwork. They are cooperating, Phil. Neither one of them likes you very much. Bettina was looking forward to never having to work again, particularly in the sex trade. That is where you found her, Phil. She worked in a brothel in San Salvador. She learned her skills well. Morton was never very far away from her even while the doctor was putting her face back together. He stayed close so that she didn't become a casualty to Maurice Taurant. She was never trafficked. She was an American citizen through marriage. She and Morton crossed legally back into the country and headed straight for Morton's apartment. She worked her magic on Morton just as she had on your father but she did tell us, she had to do hardly anything to get you to do anything she wanted. By the way, since you felt it was beneath you to clean up after your father's death, Mr. Morton took the murder weapon with your fingerprints and DNA all over it and placed it in the freezer with your dad's remains as insurance. That is what this country bumpkin cop knows, Phil. Excuse me, Mr. Tandor, but I think we are done here." They were. The detective and Agent Moss stood up and left the room. All Phil's lawyer could do was shake his head.

Over the following months the case in Maine went forward. With the testimony of Han Tu, the Canadian and American authorities pursued and were successful in getting convictions on thirty-five individuals involved in the Taurant trafficking network. She was not only able to provide testimony for the current case but provided additional information which led to more arrests in the first operation where her daughter was killed. Han had decided to return to Vietnam where she worked with her government to develop stricter policies for reducing human trafficking. She would visit Canada and the United States often to tell her story and raise awareness to the trafficking of Asian women to North America.

JinJing Zhao provided detailed testimony that was instrumental in the conviction of Chao Wu, and ten individuals in Vancouver that had participated in her trafficking case. Wu was also convicted and sentenced along with two others for the murder of his nephew. JinJing was also instrumental in the conviction of the Taurant brothers. With the help of testimony from Alex Pellegrino and the Smithson video, she was never charged for killing Maurice Taurant. Lan Li, JinJing's friend also provided testimony for the prosecution of Dr. Terrance Concorde as well as testimony related to the organization in Vancouver. Her testimony was essential in clarifying what had happened at the transfer clearing. She saw the bandaged girl moved but was able to clearly identify another trafficker other than Morton. After the dust settled, it was determined Morton had never been at the clearing. She asked to return to Canada and join JinJing. The Canadian resettlement program granted them status as trafficking victims and found them both legitimate jobs in Vancouver. The relationship between Han and JinJing would continue to prosper during the prosecutions. As it would turn out, they would be life-long friends.

Anna Lopez became the star witness in Canada and in the American trafficking prosecution as well. She was granted status under the federal guidelines to remain in the U.S. and with the help of Smithson Evermore and social services was reunited with her family who were allowed to enter the United States under special dispensation. She would continue to testify for almost four years during different phases of several prosecutions as the federal government dismantled the vast Tandor business empire.

Kip Patterson fully recovered from the ordeal and even spoke two weeks after his rescue to the previously scheduled conference on collaborative immigration policy. His ex-wife Henrietta Patterson continued to push in the Senate for a more reasonable approach but the original bill was withdrawn. The once powerful political action committee known as Patriot Green quietly slipped into non-existence with many of its followers trying to jumpstart other groups. Without the financial support of the original group of wealthy backers, sustaining the group became impossible. The facts of the actual kidnapping of Dr. Patterson were never revealed.

Hank Kessler loved the undivided attention of Alex and Lily he had for ten days and complained loudly when they left to go back to work. Lola was able to quiet him down after they left. He invited some of his new friends from Tiburon Island, but they never accepted his invitation. He explored the concept of building a house in Punta Chueca across the channel from the island but found it to be cost prohibitive for security reasons. Several people had to explain to him that all cartels are not created equal. Jorge and Lola finally were able to get through to him that he needed to remain in Puerto Vallarta where he was indeed considered special and he had other Gringos he could be with.

Forrest Mack was never charged by anyone. In Mexico, it was determined he was a hero for rescuing Hank Kessler. Slade had flown to Puerto Vallarta to satisfy himself and the Mexican authorities that nothing more had to happen with Mack. Slade and Aggie were impressed with Mack. He was offered a job if he would relocate to the States. He turned it down. He wasn't fond of the politics that had fostered something that would even consider kidnapping. Slade then made a counter offer to base him in Puerto Vallarta. He turned it down stating that he was very comfortable with the simple life he had created in western Sinaloa. Slade made a third offer which included a new helicopter, service to his airplane, and a large grant to the Seri people. Forrest accepted the third offer with the caveat that it not be a new helicopter. He didn't want to become too commercial. He agreed that he would fly for Smithson on any mission they needed with proper training, but he would remain on Tiburon. Uneasy about the role the Hermosillo police had played in cooperating with the two who had been sent to kill him, he relocated to a permanent home on Tiburon as its only permanent non-native resident. He did so with the blessing of the Seri. He never saw or communicated with Serena Moore again.

Ironically, it was Lucy Frost's testimony that clearly indicated Serena Moore was not the leader of the kidnap plot. Serena pled guilty to a greatly reduced probationary sentence under substantial assistance and was given a new identity and start by the Federal Witness Protection Program. Her testimony was essential in the successful prosecution of Lucy Frost, Tim Sampson and Phil Tandor. All received life sentences in the federal system. Dr. Andrew Polk was convicted of kidnapping. In exchange for his role in rescuing Kip Patterson, he was given a reduced sentence of twenty-five-years in a federal facility where he used his medical training to assist the prison health services. Tim Sampson was also prosecuted by Virginia and received the death penalty for the murder of his wife. He is still on death row.

Several of the business partners who had been part of the Tandor empire and board of directors were prosecuted for various crimes related to their involvement in the trafficking of humans. It was proven that they readily provided a customer base for men, women, and children who were trafficked to the United States from Mexico, Central American, Canada and the Caribbean Islands. The domestic service and agricultural sectors were prolific with people who had voluntarily been smuggled to the United States but were then pushed into involuntary servitude with almost no wages through the threat of discovery or violence. But the most severe sanctions were reserved for those fine upstanding business leaders who readily participated in the slavery of women in the sex trade. There were five escort services that were brought down in the process of each defendant trying to sweeten their own deal at the cost of their fellow co-conspirators. The entire network extended as far south as Brazil, as far east as Belarus, and as far west as the hills of rural China.

The two men who had traveled to Atlanta were held and then charged under the federal statue for kidnapping and murder. Phil had implicated them to get a life sentence in the federal system for kidnapping. The two that Phil sent to Mexico didn't fair as well. Their total ignorance of the state of affairs in Mexico led them to think that claiming they were deputized by the FBI would give them protection. Once that was disproven by the consulate, they clearly fell under Mexican law. Since the Mexican authorities didn't want to have to house them, they were charged with illegal possession of a firearm. That carried almost no sanction and they were released onto the street. One was found the morning after their release hanging outside the police station from a lamppost. It took some time before all of the other one was identified. Parts of him were found with parts of another poor soul who had crossed the cartel.

As a result of the prosecutions, the federal government was able to seize or freeze assets worth well over several billion dollars. Similar results happened in Canada except for Mr. Wu. He remained silent. He remained silent while he lost his transportation empire. He kept still while his house was seized. He kept to himself in prison. He had only one visitor, his former housekeeper.

Aggie, Slade, Lily, SiSi, L and Alex were standing on the veranda on the top floor of their building in the Channel District in Tampa looking out at the construction of their new headquarters that was half finished. It was Aggie that broke the silence. "OK folks, it's time for the hero hour. It is a long and somewhat silly tradition but we need to carry it on. I see everyone has a drink. Alex, you go first."

Alex thought a moment. "OK, this is going to sound strange but my hero is Hank." Everyone groaned but she continued. "Hank's keen eye was what led us to make the connection to Phil which helped Lily focus. But I have a second hero."

Lily protested. "You only get one hero."

Alex ignored her and pulled out her phone. She had made the picture of the smiling Seri tribesman holding a large snake as her phone's wallpaper. "Every time I look at my phone now, I will be reminded that I am not nearly as good as I think I am. He is my hero as well." They raised their glasses in a toast.

Slade smiled. "L, you are next. Do you have a hero in all of this?"

L thought for a moment. "I do. It is our own Charles Jenkins."

SiSi laughed. "You pick Claymore?"

L smiled. "I do. For a time, he was covering for both you and me. He has great instincts and seemed to be just one step ahead of us. I know SiSi has asked that he be made part of the team. I would suggest he train in intelligence analysis and resources as well. He was amazing on this case and gave both SiSi and me time to breathe."

Aggie smiled. "That is a good choice and a great idea. They raised their glasses. Aggie continued. "OK, Lily, who is your hero in this case?"

Lily smiled. "That is easy. My hero is Hero the cat who lives in the house behind Serena's in Reston, Virginia. He is the new man of my dreams."

L laughed. "Those dreams are getting a bit crowded, Lily. Phelps isn't a bad hero either."

Lily glared at her. "Hero, the cat isn't married with two kids and an amazing wife. He's easier and he listens better."

Slade laughed. "I've never heard of a cat that listens to a human."

Lily retorted. "That is why Hero the cat is my hero. He did everything I needed him to do."

SiSi interjected. "Sounds like someone has a control issue."

Aggie interrupted again before Lily could vocalize the glare, she was giving SiSi. "To Hero. SiSi, who was your hero in this case?"

SiSi didn't hesitate. "I have four. Hear me out. The first is one of the most courageous women I have ever heard of, Han Tu, of Hue, the Socialists Republic of Vietnam. The next two are Chinese women from the mountain provinces who endured so much and were able to provide even more, JinJing Zhao and Lan Li of the People's Republic of China. And, my final hero is Anna Lopez. She was kidnapped, loaded on a ship, raped repeatedly, beaten and still had the presence of mine to collect evidence. That is more courage than I think I could have mustered and way more courage than anyone other than Han that I have ever seen. I really admire Anna Lopez. Here's to all of them. Those women are the real heroes here. I will never forget them and I never even met them."

Alex spoke. "I had the pleasure. You are right. They are all amazing."

There was silence for a moment then Slade raised his glass which prompted the others. "To our law enforcement partners this time who get paid way less than we do and are the reason we do what we do. To Walt Haskell,

Special Agent FBI, Bridgett Moss, Special Agent, FBI, Elaine Miller, Special Agent in Charge, FBI Human Trafficking Task Force." They all repeated and drank.

Aggie spoke next. "Please raise your glasses to Agents Maria Montalba and Steve Wiley of U.S. Border Patrol, and Agent Emilio Cortez, Agent, U.S. Immigration and Customs Enforcement, and finally Inspectors Matilda Borge of the RCMP and Inspector Erick Brandhoff of the Canadian Border Services." They all raised their glasses.

Lily finished. "Please raise your glasses to Special Agent Phelps Wheeler, FBI and Deputy Donald Conner of Wyeth County Sheriff's Office, two real officers of the law who respect their jobs and know how to work together." They all raised their glasses.

Slade made one more announcement. "Since we have made the decision to add Claymore to the central team, there is one other adjustment I would like to announce. As you know our research and development laboratory is located outside of Boston. I have decided to expand our capabilities to provide additional advanced tools to our law enforcement and military partners over the next three years. To do that, I will need someone with field experience and the technical skills to make sure we are successful." He turned to SiSi. "The job of Director of Research and Development at Smithson Labs is yours for the asking is you would like it."

SiSi was stunned. "What about my duties here?"

Slade was quick to respond. 'We can always add you if needed from Boston but there are new challenges we need to meet and as you have pointed out, Claymore is really good at the job here. You have confidence in him as we do. If he needs help, you will only be a click away and we need new tools and cutting-edge advancement that is based on knowledge gained from actually working our cases. No one else has that combination. Of course, you don't have to accept."

SiSi blinked. "Boston area?"

L chimed in. "You could look at it as Brad's area."

SiSi glared at her but answered. "I would be honored to take on that responsibility. When do I start?"

Slade smiled. "Whenever you are ready, SiSi. Whenever you are ready."

The others left the veranda to go down and eat. Aggie and Slade would be dining on their own again. It was happening more and more. She looked at him. "This was difficult. It stretched us and particularly you, to the limit. We are not getting any younger. We need to either focus our efforts more or expand our resources. Moving SiSi is brilliant but we can't continue to be all things to all people. Have you thought about who could replace us?"

Slade thought a moment as he took her in his arms. "I have to keep reminding myself that we got into the kidnapping because of Hank. We would never have been involved otherwise."

She pulled back slightly and looked into his eyes. "As we have worked over the years, we have made friends all over the planet. Are you trying to tell me that if one of Earl Tippet's daughters were kidnapped, we wouldn't spring into action? Or how about something happens to Bailey or Lydia or any of the other survivors we have rescued? Slade Smithson, are you trying to tell me you would not move heaven and earth to help this family we have created? I don't believe it for a second. You are going to have to decide about our roles and who will take them over. We are not getting any younger."

He held her close and kissed her. "We have to develop more sophisticated equipment like Lily and Alex used and more comprehensive intelligence gathering tools like the drones SiSi is so proud of. We have to continue to attract new talent at least as special as the people we already have. I also have had this idea about doing something more for the survivors of this. They need support and new ways of helping them recover and regain their lives." He held her close and kissed her.

She kissed him back. "Now, that isn't quite the role I was talking about but the kiss will do for a start." She took his hand and they made it to the doorway before the alarm sounded and speaker delivered a message that was coming in all-too-frequently. "We have received a new request. "All members of the HQ response team, please report to the Command Center for initial briefing."

About the Author

Vance Arnett lived with his wife Jane in the Channel District of Tampa, Florida. He worked for over three decades as an applied anthropologist in the justice system. In 2021 they relocated to Greenville, South Carolina where he continues to write.He is the author of two other books and is currently working on the third book in the Smithson Evermore series which will be out in Summer of 2025. Vance enjoys the great outdoors as an avid fly fisherman and hiking in the Great Smoky Mountains the upstate area of South Carolina. He also writes on creative thinking and intentional living which can be found at authorvancearnett.com and on entries on Substack.